Rio Grande Fall

RIO GRANDE FALL

RUDOLFO ANAYA

WARNER BOOKS

A Time Warner Company

Warner Books, Inc., 1271 Avenue of the Americas, New York, NY 10020

w A Time Warner Company

Printed in the United States of America
First Printing: September 1996
10 9 8 7 6 5 4 3 2 1

Library of Congress Cataloging-in-Publication Data
Anaya, Rudolfo A.
    Rio Grande fall / Rudolfo Anaya.
        p.   cm.
    ISBN 0-446-51844-1
    1. Private investigators—New Mexico—Albuquerque—Fiction.
    2. Mexican Americans—New Mexico—Albuquerque—Fiction.
    3. Albuquerque (N.M.)—Fiction.   I. Title.
    PS3551.N27R56   1996
    813'.54—dc20   96-1394
                                                        CIP

Book design by Giorgetta Bell McRee

There are many ways to fly, the old people taught us. So I say to you: I fly in dreams, I fly in love, I fly in the morning when the light of the Señores y Señoras de la Luz fills my soul with clarity. I fly in beauty, the beauty of the land I love, the people, the sounds, sights, and smells of all that I am. I am beginning to find my power.

To all those people who have helped me along on my path, I dedicate this book.

RIO GRANDE FALL

Sonny felt the soft pressure of the eagle feather across his chest. The soft voice of the healer was calling him back from his vision. He smelled the sweet aroma of the burning copal in the room, and he struggled to rise out of the dark shadows where he had been running with a family of coyotes.

Thin wisps of copal smoke floated over the altar and curled upward. The traditional healers of the Río Grande burned sage or romero, common herbs growing in the New Mexican countryside, but Lorenza was burning copal, the incense of the Aztecs.

Praying to the saints, burning copal and instructing Sonny on how to find the coyotes, his guardian spirits, were all part of the cleansing ceremony she had just performed on Sonny. The limpieza was to rid him of the ghost that had plagued him all summer.

"You have susto," Rita had told Sonny all along. "Your soul has been inhabited by Gloria's ghost. That's what causes the fright. Go to Lorenza. She's a curandera; she can help you get rid of Gloria's ghost."

Sonny had felt the shock of Gloria's spirit when he entered her bedroom and Frank Dominic had pulled back the sheet that covered her body. She had been murdered that June night, and her body had been drained of its blood. Rita believed that Gloria's spirit, still lingering in the room, had entered and taken possession of Sonny.

Her spirit had attached to his, and its needs had sapped his energy. All summer he had felt depressed and distracted. Even nights with Rita suffered. He needed to be cleansed.

So Rita had finally persuaded him to see Lorenza Villa, her good friend. A very nice-looking curandera, Sonny thought. Lorenza was about thirty-five, her body rounded but firm. Her clear, brown skin was the color of Mexican milk chocolate, and her black hair fell around her shoulders, dark and luxuriant. But it was her bright brown eyes that held those who dared look into them.

When he first met her, he thought she was cross-eyed, as each eye seemed to look at him from just a slightly different angle. Then he remembered that the face of a shaman has a pronounced right and left side, and so, he figured, a right and left eye. The right seemed to smile; the left looked deeper into his thoughts. Perhaps there were two women in her, two souls.

Which eye gazed at the lover when she was making love? Sonny wondered.

Yes, sensuous, with a smile that was reassuring and seductive at the same time. She moved with grace, self-contained, every ounce of energy a fluid movement. When she touched him, a tingle of arousal ran through him.

She clapped her hands to awaken him, and the drumming had stopped. When she began the ceremony, she had put a tape in the player, and the sound of the drum helped transport him to a place where he could finally rid himself of Gloria's spirit.

He opened his eyes and looked at her. She smiled, her full lips the color of the bright prickly pear fruit of late summer. Her long, dark hair cascaded down either side of her face, creating a black shawl that fell over her full breasts.

She moved to the small altar in a corner of the room. A statue of the Virgen de Guadalupe stood surrounded by flowers, herbs, and votive candles. The statues of other saints filled the lower tier of the altar: the Santo Niño de Atocha, St. Anne, and the black San Martín de Porres.

Also arranged on the altar were milagros, small ex-votos probably brought to her by other clients, a pearl rosary with gold crucifix, a photograph of a man on crutches, a child's scapular, a pocketknife, a book of fairy tales.

A shaman who prays to the saints, Sonny thought. His mother believed in the saints, prayed to the saints, trusted in their power. He thought for a moment of his mother lying in her hospital bed, recovering from the heart bypass operation. He had stayed with her for three days. Her recovery had been excellent. Still, he told himself that tonight he would drop in and see her.

There was a santo for every need. For don Eliseo the saints were Lords and Ladies of the Light, men and women whose souls were filled with clarity.

Lorenza rose and placed the votive candle Sonny had brought at the feet of the virgin. She lit it, bowed in prayer for a moment, then turned to him.

"Concentrate on the smoke," she said.

"Gloria's gone."

"Yes."

"Someone fell from the sky."

"Death," she whispered.

The last thing he had seen in his vision was a body falling from the sky. Why did Lorenza say it was an image of death?

"Are we finished?" he asked, still feeling groggy. Was he back from the river world of the coyotes? Back from the vision?

"For today," she said, then she went out and closed the door behind her.

Yeah, Sonny nodded. What a trip. With her help he had gone to a place he had never dreamed of. Now as he looked at the dark smoke rising from the candle, he saw it take the shape of the head of a coyote.

There it was again, his nagual. His guardian spirit in the animal world. He stared at the smoke as the figures of coyotes took shape and rose in the curling wisps. The same coyotes he had met during the cleansing ceremony.

Then he closed his eyes. Maybe he was imagining the coyote in the smoke, just as he had imagined them during the trance. Lord, he had smoked marijuana before, but the mota only made him groggy and sleepy, so he never became an aficionado. Grass brought no visions.

A year ago he had done the peyote ceremony with don Eliseo and a handful of his Indian neighbors up in the Sandias. A beautiful vision quest. The forest had come alive, the trees danced to music, tiny animals scurried along the forest floor, a king bear appeared, spoke to Sonny. But not even that extrasensory perception induced by the peyote compared to the vision today.

He opened his eyes. The curling smoke of the candle had turned white, wisps rising around the statue of the virgin, the smoke cleansing away Gloria's ghost.

The images of his journey to the world of spirits returned, and one in particular didn't make sense—at least it didn't relate to the coyotes. He had seen someone falling from the sky.

"Death," Lorenza had whispered.

He rose, took the gold Zia medallion from where he had hung it on the altar, and put it around his neck. It was the gold chain and medallion he had taken from Raven only months ago.

He thought for a moment of Tamara Dubronsky's words: "Now you are the new Raven."

He shook his head, put on his shirt, and went out of the room and into the kitchen. Rita and Lorenza sat sipping tea on the ledge of a small beehive fireplace. The adobe walls were soft, feminine, tranquil. For centuries the Indians and Mexicanos of the valley had been building the earth houses, using clay to make the mud bricks. There was something about an adobe home that made one feel connected to the earth.

Rita rose, took Sonny's hands, and looked into his eyes. She saw that for the first time in months there was a spark in his eyes, a smile on his lips.

"How are you, amor?"

"Bien," he answered, and looked at Lorenza. "I feel like I've been in another world."

"I told you Lorenza could work magic," Rita said.

She had tried to doctor him with herbal teas all summer, but she knew the source of his illness was deeper than her herbs could reach. She knew Gloria's spirit had invaded Sonny's soul.

"I believe you now," he said as he took the cup of tea Lorenza offered. "Gracias."

"De nada," Lorenza replied.

He looked at the two women, both daughters of the Alburquerque Río Grande valley. Daughters of the old Hispanos, Mexicanos, and Indians of the valley, a blend of genes that over the centuries had produced what Sonny thought were the most beautiful women on earth. The full-bodied, brown-skinned Nueva Mexicana woman, a mestiza with the beauty of the earth and sky in her soul.

Rita's hair, black like Lorenza's, curled around her shoulders and glistened in the morning sunlight pouring through the window. Her brown eyes sparkled.

He saw how alike they were. Hermanas. They could be sisters. Rita was his age, Lorenza maybe five years older. A ripe age. Sonny wondered if men came to have their souls cleansed just to be near her, to smell the sweetness of her body and to watch the way she moved as she worked.

He smiled. Both women smiled back, for the moment allowing themselves to bathe in his obvious admiration.

Rita glanced at Lorenza. She knew Sonny admired women, liked the way they moved, danced, and talked. He admired their physical beauty, but he also respected and trusted the unique instincts of las mujeres. That is why he could learn from them, as he had learned today from Lorenza.

Rita knew Sonny had led a dissolute life after his divorce a few years ago. He was young and trying to understand why his marriage to Angie failed, and so many a weekend had been full of drinking and dancing along the Fourth Street bars, especially at the Fiesta Lounge.

That's where they met, danced, and fell in love. He began to show up at her restaurant, they dated, and for two years they had been happy. They fitted each other, kindred lovers who plumbed each other's sensuality, kindred souls who shared their most intimate secrets.

She had proposed marriage, he was the first man who ever came up to her expectations, she liked to be with him, and she had fallen for him. Besides, he was thirty and he had sown enough of his wild oats. Now he needed a home, she thought, a family, a place to work, a garden. He needed children. He needed a wife, and she intended to be that woman.

At first he joked about getting married, but the more he was with Rita, the more he realized she was the right woman for him. It was time for him to settle down. Then came the Zia summer with its evil, and Sonny took a slide into lethargy. Gloria's spirit haunted him, and the thought of Raven wouldn't let him rest.

"What did you see?" Rita asked.

"I saw Gloria," he said. "Or her ghost. Then I saw four coyotes. They were at a place near the river, a place I had forgotten. It was my abuelo's farm near Socorro. My parents used to send Armando and me there when we were kids."

"It was a beginning," Lorenza said, glancing at Rita. "Most people don't usually meet their guardian spirits during the first limpieza. But our compañero is gifted."

She looked at Sonny and he returned her smile. "Hey, all I did was follow your instructions."

"The coyote spirits came to you, so that is one way to the world of spirits. You can go deeper."

"Another session?" Sonny asked.

"If you want to *truly* learn to use the power in your vision," Lorenza replied.

During the cleansing ceremony Sonny had entered the underworld, what Lorenza called the world of spirits. There he found the coyotes by the river, and running with the coyotes did bring a sense of power, but what did it all mean?

Lorenza sensed his questioning. "We're losing the spiritual knowledge of the old people," she said. "I studied with curanderas in Río Arriba, learned their prayers and ceremonies. I also listened to their cuentos, the stories they told about men and women who could turn into animals. Some could turn into owls and fly at night. Those brujos, some good and some evil, knew the world of the nagual."

"The nagual," Sonny repeated. The animal spirit of a person. An Aztec word, like *copal,* which she burned. In the old folk tales brujos or sorcerers were said to use these supernatural animals. A brujo could actually turn into his nagual. Rita had told him Lorenza had studied with brujos in Mexico, and in this case brujo didn't mean just witch. It meant something more powerful; it meant men and women who could enter the world of spirits.

"Our cuentos are full of stories that taught us about people who could take the form of animals," Lorenza said. "The stories are full of brujas and the spiritual tricks they played. That world exists. It is the world of spirits, what the New Age people call energy."

"And there's a way to enter that world, like I did. To get rid of Gloria's spirit."

"It has always been so," Lorenza answered. "But most of our people are losing touch with that world."

"Why?" Sonny asked.

"The young no longer pay attention to the spiritual values of our ancestors."

"Too busy watching TV or listening to rap," Sonny suggested. "Maybe that's one reason why I quit teaching. The kids are into the pop world, videos, whatever." He shook his head.

"What will happen to us if we let our spiritual traditions die?" Rita wondered.

"We can't," Lorenza said. "To lose them now would be to give in to evil. So we pay attention to the messages of the ancestors."

She glanced at Sonny.

"Learn to fight Raven," he said.

She nodded. "Even in the smallest ways. Like the artists who are going to burn the Kookoóee this week. Federico Armijo and his friends. They resurrected el Coco, the bogeyman our parents warned us would get us if we were bad boys and girls, and they gave him life again. They're getting our kids interested in their folklore. So it's up to us to keep the way of our ancestors alive."

"El Coco is from the world of spirits," Sonny said.

"We all move back and forth from that world to this." Lorenza smiled. She knew Sonny was open to learning. He had gone on his first vision quest and come back stronger.

Sonny thought of don Eliseo. The old man had said that when he died, the old culture of the Nuevo Mexicanos of the Río Grande valley would disappear. The young people just weren't keeping up the traditions. Don Eliseo, a man in his eighties who knew the old ways, was a link to history, as was Lorenza Villa, who lived and practiced the old ways of curing the soul.

Sonny sipped the tea, a mixture of herbs with a hint of mint. The aroma was soothing and pleasant. The ripeness of autumn was in the air. In the stillness of the morning he heard a gas saw. Someone was cutting wood for winter, and far away the whinny of a horse. Here in Corrales a lot of people kept horses.

Down the road the Wagner Farms fruit stalls were full of homegrown apples, and ristras of red chile hung drying in the warm October sun. In the fields huge orange pumpkins were ripening for Halloween. Autumn was his favorite time. It was also the season of his birth. In late October he would turn thirty-one.

"Qué piensas?" Rita asked.

"How good all this is," he answered.

Another sound interrupted them. The blast of a burner, a whooshing sound, then another.

Lorenza glanced out the kitchen window. "The balloons are coming over the river. Want to watch?"

"Yes," Rita said, and Lorenza led them out onto the small patio extending from the kitchen.

As they stepped out, they were greeted by the sight of hundreds of brightly colored hot-air balloons floating in the clear air. It was the first week of October and the first day of the Alburquerque balloon fiesta. The morning's mass ascension filled the air with the bright globes. They had been launched from a large field near Journal Center on Alameda Boulevard, and those that caught the easterly breeze were floating across the river, colorful blossoms in the quiet morning air, brilliant in the morning sun.

The balloons moved across their view, punctuating the morning stillness with the occasional blasts of fire from the propane burners.

Around them the towering cottonwoods of the valley were touched with the first hint of autumn gold. Across the valley, the Sandia Mountains—blue, granite-faced peaks born of a fault in the earth long ago—rose as a backdrop for the balloon show. On many a summer evening the mountain blushed, the color of a ripe watermelon.

"Qué maravilla," Rita said, enraptured by the sight of balloons as they floated peacefully overhead.

"Quite a sight," Lorenza said.

"Bucks for the city," Sonny mused.

The Hot Air Balloon Fiesta of Albuquerque, as it was billed, had grown into an international event, drawing people from all over the world and bringing millions of dollars into the city's coffers. It had become the biggest moneymaker for the city, surpassing even the state fair in September.

But the people floating in the balloons know nothing of the traditional world of Lorenza, Sonny thought as he looked up.

"I've always wanted to take a ride," Rita said.

"Hey, why don't the three of us go up?" Sonny asked.

Sonny loved to fly. He had spent a year learning to hang-glide off the ten thousand–foot–high Sandia Crest, and he had taken helicopter lessons. Flying was part of the release he had sought, perhaps part of the danger, when he was going through his divorce.

Lorenza laughed. "No, gracias, I'm too bound to the earth to get in one of those things."

Nearby, the neighbor's dogs set up a howl as the balloons floated over, and his horses raced across the field, raising clouds of dust and whinnying nervously.

Susto, Sonny thought. Animals also fear the unknown.

He turned to Lorenza. "I haven't felt this good in months. Your medicine works. We should celebrate."

"We will," she said, nodding, "when the time is right."

Her reticence told Sonny there was something left to be done. Something was still affecting Sonny, and finding the coyotes in his vision was only a first step.

The phone rang and Lorenza went in to answer it. "Howard Powdrell," she said to Sonny when she returned.

Sonny glanced at Rita and went in. Why would Howard call?

"Howard?"

"Hey, compadre, hate to bother you, but I thought you'd want to know." Howard's voice was subdued.

"What's up?"

"Veronica Worthy's dead. Just now."

"How?"

"She fell from a balloon. I'm here now, Montaño and Coors, near the river."

"Fell out of a balloon?" Sonny questioned. "Accident?"

"No. Can you come?"

"I'm on my way."

Veronica was the state's witness against Tamara Dubronsky. Sonny knew Veronica had murdered Gloria, but she could also implicate Tamara Dubronsky. Now she was dead.

Raven, he thought immediately. Raven's back! With Veronica dead, there would be no case against Tamara, and that meant she was free!

Sonny hurried out to the patio. "Sorry, but we gotta go," he said to Rita.

"Qué pasa?"

"That was Howard. Veronica, the witness in the Dubronsky case, has just been killed."

"Oh, no," Rita cried. "How?"

"Fell from a balloon," Sonny repeated what Howard had told him and looked at Lorenza Villa. His vision: someone falling from the sky.

"You don't have to—" Rita said, and stopped short.

No, he didn't have to go. It was a city police case, not his, but she knew Sonny had been troubled all summer not only by Gloria's spirit but by the disappearance of Raven.

"Raven," she whispered. His body had never been found.

Sonny nodded. "She was the prime witness in the Dubronsky trial. Without her Tamara goes free. Maybe it's better if you stay."

"No," Rita said, and turned to hug Lorenza. "Thanks, Lorenza, thanks for everything. I only hope . . ." She didn't finish.

"Gracias," Sonny said to Lorenza, embracing her.

"Cuidado," she whispered.

"I will," he said, and took Rita's arm. Lorenza walked them to the front door and watched them drive off. A body falling from the sky could mean many things, she thought as Sonny's truck roared up the dirt road. A man being born. A man dying. Icarus flying to the sun, then falling from the sky. Sonny.

Brujos, the old men and women of power, could fly. The stories of the Indians and the Mexicanos were full of incidents that revealed this power.

Raven could fly.

Sonny knows this, she thought as she turned to look at the thick river bosque that lay beyond her home. There in the shadows she spotted a movement: a pair of coyotes. They stopped, looked in her direction. The coyotes of his vision, his nagual, she thought. They've been watching.

The coyotes moved into the brush and disappeared, and Lorenza hurried back into her house. I should have realized the falling body meant an actual death, she chided herself. How much more danger lies in store for Sonny?

She hurried into the consultation room. She gasped when she saw the candle wasn't burning. Quickly she took a match and lit it. Perhaps it wasn't too late. Black smoke rose to form an ominous cloud, a dark mushroom cloud, no, the shape of a black balloon. There was death in the sky.

Rita, too, felt the same disquietude as she and Sonny drove

out of Corrales and south on Coors. She looked at Sonny, sensed his concern.

Above them, many of the balloons floated west toward Petroglyph Park on the volcanic escarpment of the West Mesa. They would land in the empty spaces of the mesa, coming to soft and safe landings in the wild grass and sage. But for Sonny and Rita the peace and beauty of the flight had been shattered.

"I saw a body falling in my vision," he said, "then a few minutes later Howard calls."

"You saw Veronica's death during the limpieza," she said. "Do you think Raven would return to kill her?"

"Yes. Now I know why Lorenza said to keep my feet on the ground."

And, he thought, so did don Eliseo. "Keep your feet on la tierra," the old man had said. "Leave the flying to the astronauts. They are flying up there because they want to escape from our madre tierra. We must stay and take care of her. There is no other mother."

Ahead of them he saw the flashing lights of the police cars. Traffic on Coors had slowed to a crawl, and the dirt road to the river bosque was blocked off. Sonny turned into it and stopped at the roadblock. One of the cops there recognized Sonny.

Jerry Candelaria usually worked narcotics at the airport and the train depot, but today, in plainclothes, he was standing next to the uniformed officer diverting the television vans and other reporters off to the side.

"Hey, Sonny, out for a drive?" Jerry asked, looking into Sonny's truck, also greeting Rita.

"Que tal," Sonny replied. "What happened?"

"We have a very dead woman. I haven't seen the body, but I heard it's gruesome."

What the hell was a plainclothes narc doing at the scene of an accident? Sonny wondered. "You smell drugs?" he asked.

"Nah, I was just driving by. I live nearby," Jerry replied. "Just thought I'd help out."

"Qué pasó?" Sonny asked. He wasn't in the mood for chatter,

but he knew cops. One needed to go around, not straight to the point, to get anything from them.

"The DA's witness fell from a balloon. She's dead, and Schwartz is pissed. That's all I know. Were you invited?"

"Howard called me," Sonny said, nodding. Jerry looked at the cop in uniform, who stepped aside.

"Take care, bro," Jerry said, then stepped back and waved them through.

Police cars were parked along the shoulder of the dirt road. Sonny pulled over near the tree line, and he and Rita followed the sandy path into the bosque. The path continued under a canopy of trees, then opened up into a large, clear area. A brush fire had burned this area clear a few years ago, and the trees hadn't yet reclaimed it. The place where the body of Veronica Worthy lay was cordoned off.

Sam Garcia, the chief of police, stood nearby with a couple of plainclothes cops. He was talking to Ben Chávez, the writer, who lived on the West Mesa. Chávez seemed to be taking notes.

Every time I've run into that man he's taking notes, Sonny thought. Writing stories. Had he seen Veronica fall, or was he always just on the fringe of things when they happened? There was no doubt Benjamín Chávez knew just about everyone in the city, anyone who was anyone, and that sooner or later he would write them into his novels.

Garcia glanced up, spotted Sonny, frowned, and returned to his conversation with Chávez. Right now Garcia wouldn't talk to the press, but he trusted the writer.

Howard, who had been standing by the tarp-covered body, waved and came over to them. Sonny thought he recognized the DEA officer who had been talking to Howard and now moved away.

"How's it going?" Howard asked, as he shook hands with Sonny. "Hi, Rita." He took her hand. "How are you? You look as beautiful as ever."

"Gracias," Rita replied.

"Who's the DEA guy?" Sonny asked.

"Joe Flannery. They've been buzzing around all week. Anyway, I thought you'd like to know about Veronica."

"You sure it's Veronica?"

"Affirmative," Howard answered. "I've viewed the body. You want to?"

Sonny hesitated. No, he didn't want to see her. It wasn't his case. He had no interest in getting mixed up in it. He glanced at the area that had been cordoned off around an old cottonwood stump split long ago by lightning. The white slivers of the huge trunk rose up from the blackened roots. The tarp covering the body lay curled around the jagged, bony fingers of stump that rose skyward. Veronica had landed in a place cursed by lightning.

But if I don't see her for myself, I'll never be sure, Sonny thought. Ah, what the hell is one more dead body. She's dead, and she means nothing to me. Veronica had killed Gloria; now a swift justice had been served.

"Any witnesses?" Sonny asked, angry at himself that he was buying time. Tamara Dubronsky would never be implicated in the murder of Gloria Dominic, and as far as Sonny was concerned, he didn't give a damn. Let Garcia and the DA handle it!

"There was an anonymous call," Howard answered. "Someone reported seeing a body fall. Otherwise, she could have been here days before being found. The strange thing is there haven't been any calls from the balloonists. The phone call came from someone on the ground."

Sonny looked around. There were no houses along this part of the river bosque. The shopping center lay to the north, and the Christian Children's home just behind it. Someday the Montaño bridge would cross the river near here, but for now the area was deserted.

"Was she flying alone?" Sonny asked.

"Don't think so," Howard replied.

Sonny wiped a thin veil of sweat from his forehead. Murder, Howard was saying murder. He had known it all along. Now he had to see the body; he had to make sure the woman lying under the tarp was Veronica, the fat wife of Raven, the woman who, as far as he was concerned, had led Raven's cult to kill Gloria Dominic.

"You're thinking what I'm thinking," Sonny said.

"Yeah," Howard said, "and there are four black feathers on the body."

"Damn," Sonny groaned. Raven's calling card!

Raven had returned, Howard knew. The feathers were Raven's signature. He had taken Veronica up and pushed her out of the hot-air balloon's gondola.

"Okay," Sonny whispered. "Let's see the body."

Rita held his hand for a moment, then let go, and he walked with Howard toward the tree where Veronica's body lay. The cop standing near the tarp stepped aside.

Howard pulled back the tarp and Sonny winced. The lifeless body of the woman was impaled on one of the slivers of the cottonwood stump. She had landed faceup on a sharp spear of the old tree. Her mouth was wide open, frozen in a scream of terror; her large fish eyes stared up at Sonny. The spear she was lodged on was so white it looked like the rib of a whale. Her chest was ripped open. Blood covered the bare stump, soaking her clothes, soaking the sand around her.

A large green fly buzzed lazily around the body and lighted on the pale forehead of the dead woman.

"Chingao," Sonny cursed, and turned away. It was an ugly sight.

"Maybe there is justice in the universe," Howard whispered. "She was going to die from the fall, but hitting the sand around here might not have killed her quickly. This is ugly, but merciful. And, perhaps, fitting," he added.

Veronica was one of Raven's four wives, the women of the Sun cult. Raven, probably with Tamara's help, had brainwashed them into taking new identities, new names. He gave them a sense of power in their lives by creating a family, the Zia cult, a perverted way of life with an unbalanced, antinuclear agenda. The women gave their bodies and souls over to Raven, who promised to deliver them into a new life, a new covenant whose goal was to clean the earth of nuclear material.

"Yeah," Sonny said, nodding. He knew what Howard must be thinking. Stabbed right through the heart, like they did in the old Dracula movies to kill the vampire.

A second fly, glowing green-iridescent in the morning sunlight, appeared and buzzed around the tarp, attracted by the blood that stained the area.

"Where's Tamara?" Sonny asked.

"Far as I know she's still in that psychiatric hospital in Santa Fe," Howard said. "Excuse me, it's called an 'equilibrium retreat.' She's probably teamed up with that quack who, for a hundred bucks, drives her to a spiritual vortex."

"Ecstasy on the mesa," Sonny said.

"Yeah. Tamara's attorney convinced a judge she needed R and R from the stress the cops put her through, so she's been relaxing at the spa. But now that Veronica's dead, she's probably packing."

Yes, Sonny nodded. The DA's witness was dead, and there would be no trial for Tamara.

"Tracks?" Sonny asked and looked at the ground around the tarp-covered body.

"Tough to make out in this sand," Howard replied. Beads of perspiration popped on his wide, dark forehead. "When I got here, they were already blurred by the medics who got here first, but there are a few tracks here—" He pointed to tracks that disappeared down a path into the thick river brush.

Sonny looked into the bosque. A shadow moved. He walked slowly toward the thick forest of cottonwoods, Russian olives, river willows. He followed the depressions in the sand, smelling for spoor, like a river coyote would smell the area of a recent kill, checking details, checking for danger. The tracks led into the river bosque.

Were they Raven's tracks? Had he come out of the bosque, checked to make sure Veronica was dead? Had he left the four feathers for Sonny? Raven always left clues.

Sonny looked up, sniffing the air. The morning was already warm. The temperature would climb into the seventies, then drop into the forties at night. The most perfect, and most enchanting, time to be in New Mexico. And now this.

He could see the sluggish waters of the river through an opening in the trees. The water level was low in the Río Grande this time of the year. Peaceful and mellow as the season. The brilliant green leaves of the river alamos shimmered in the breeze; their rustle carried the distinctive sound of fall. A few cottonwoods were tinged yellow, the first sign of fall.

He looked closely at a foot trail that led into the river bosque. Shadows moved, then disappeared. The hair bristled along Sonny's neck. There were coyotes along the river, maybe that's what he had seen. They hunted at night. People who lived along the river heard their yelps piercing the night. Even along the acequias of the North Valley, one sometimes caught sight of a coyote or a fox on the hunt.

Veronica was dead, a stake driven through her heart. Raven wasn't done with Sonny yet.

Veronica would have told the court that Tamara Dubronsky had been the Zia queen, the power behind the Zia cult, and she had ordered the murder of Gloria Dominic. She would also have implicated Raven, and maybe tell what they did with the half-million they took from Gloria. Now she had been silenced, and there was no case.

"What now?" Howard asked as they walked back to Rita.

"Let Garcia handle it," Sonny answered. "Why the hell should I get mixed up in this?"

Howard shrugged. Both knew why.

Rita took Sonny's hand and looked closely at him, trying to gauge the effect of the sight of the dead woman. He didn't need another lost soul clinging to his.

"Ah, two of my favorite people," Sam Garcia interrupted. He was irritated because as far as he was concerned private detectives were a pain in the ass. Insurance case grovelers. Missing husband hounds. But when it came to murder, leave it to the cops! That's what they were paid for.

But he respected Sonny. He had to: Sonny had broken the Zia cult case.

"What brings you out, Sonny?" the police chief said. "Hello, Rita."

"Looks like you lost your witness, Sam," Sonny replied.

"She was out on bond! What the hell am I supposed to do, baby-sit everyone who can make bond?" Garcia shot back.

"What do you have?" Sonny asked.

"Not a damn thing!" the chief answered, glancing at Howard. He paused and looked at the television cameras that waited just beyond the ropes. He hated talking to the press.

"Any record on the balloon?" Sonny asked.

The chief shook his head. "I talked to Madge Swenson at balloon fiesta headquarters. Veronica Worthy was not registered to fly with the fiesta. She's definitely not one of theirs."

"Where's the balloon she was in?"

"Found it over by Cottonwood Mall. Propane tank must have exploded. The thing burned to a cinder."

Howard shook his head and glanced at Sonny. They both knew the chief was only wishing that Veronica had gone up alone.

"Just bonded out and she rents a balloon and she goes up alone to enjoy her freedom," Sonny scoffed. "Pués, buena suerte." He took Rita's hand. "Vamos. Nothing for us to do here. Say hello to Marie, Howard. So long, Chief."

"Humpf!" the chief coughed. The woman was dead. Saved the state a trial. Case was closed as far as he was concerned.

"So long, compadre," Howard called, and watched Sonny and Rita plod through the sand.

"What do you think?" Garcia asked his forensics man.

"Raven," Howard replied.

"I don't believe it," Garcia groaned. Howard was the best forensics man in the region, but just then he didn't want to believe him. "I should've gone fishing up in the Jemez," he muttered. "Merhege called, said the trout are biting. Instead I get this!"

Howard wiped the sweat from his forehead. Sonny was playing it cool, but Howard knew he was worried. Raven had returned for revenge, and Sonny was the target. It didn't look good for his friend.

Francine Hunter, followed by a young man carrying a TV 7 television camera, was waiting for Sonny at the yellow ribbon.

"Hello, Mr. Baca, Francine Hunter, TV Seven. I'd like to ask you a few questions."

"I thought you were with channel four," Sonny replied.

"I quit. Besides, I really like working with Nelson Martínez."

The handsome Nelson Martínez and very respected Dick Knipfing were the top honchos on TV 7. A good team, Sonny thought. So Francine had joined them. It had done nothing to improve her hairdo, which flopped over her forehead into her eyes.

"Talk to the chief," Sonny said. "I don't know anything."

"Come on, Sonny, the chief won't say a thing." She kept shoving in front of the other reporters. "He'll talk to Conroy Chino, not to me. Was it an accident or not?" She pushed the mike in front of Sonny and motioned for her cameraman to roll.

"Don't know," Sonny replied.

"Nobody flies alone. Did she fall or did someone push her?" She kept shoving the mike into Sonny's face.

"Talk to Garcia. I'm not on the case."

"But you've lost your prime suspect in the Gloria Dominic murder case!" Francine exclaimed.

"The DA lost his prime witness! I haven't lost anything!" Sonny shot back, and pulled Rita away. "Talk to Garcia! Or the DA!"

Just then, the mustachioed DA pulled up in his Ford Bronco. He glanced at Sonny and frowned, just like Garcia, except his frown was darker. He hurried past the mob of reporters to the scene.

"Mr. Schwartz!" Francine Hunter called, and hurried after him.

Sonny and Rita got into the truck and drove in silence across the Paseo del Norte bridge. The tranquillity of the Saturday morning was gone. Rita sensed the change in Sonny.

Sonny exited on Second Street, then drove over to Fourth, where he stopped in front of Rita's Cocina, one of the most popular Mexican food restaurants in the North Valley.

"Want some coffee?" she offered. She knew he needed to talk about the limpieza, but it was nearly noon and the restaurant was packed. He preferred the quiet of the truck.

"It was Raven," Rita said.

"Yup."

"He's alive, that's why his body was never found. And he's crazy," Rita said. "He killed Veronica to keep Tamara from going to trial. Garcia knows."

"But he acts like he doesn't. What I'd like to know is who they sent to bond her out."

"One of Raven's wives."

"Probably. Raven's crazy, but he sure as hell wouldn't show up at city hall."

He looked at Rita. She knew what he was thinking. Raven would come after him next.

The hell with the whole thing," he said, trying to change the subject and the mood. "I'm not going to get involved. Let Garcia handle it. I've got more important things to do. Like getting rid of the ghosts." He smiled. "I get to feeling better and I might carry out my threat to marry you."

She smiled. "You're a tough man to corral, Sonny."

He leaned and kissed her. "I'm ready. Been thinking a lot since summer. Today, Lorenza really helped to open my eyes. I think a few more sessions with her and I'll be as good a brujo as anyone."

He laughed, for he didn't quite believe what he had just said, but he was beginning to appreciate Lorenza's powers.

"Hija, the trip she took me on this morning was incredible. You ever been in one of those limpiezas with her?"

"Yes."

"I found the coyotes, and you?"

"Hummingbirds."

"Hummingbirds?"

"The hummingbird is not just a nectar and pollen gatherer. The war god of the Aztecs was called the lefthanded humming-bird."

"Ay," he said, and pecked at her lips. "That's because you are a flower. A rosa de Castillo."

She returned his kiss.

"I want to be the only hummingbird at your sweet lips," he said, looking deep into her eyes.

She was a lovely woman, a complex woman, and there were times when he didn't understand Rita, times when her soul was deep within the petals of the flower, her beauty. Of one thing he was sure: he loved her.

"Sometimes you're so romantic," she whispered. "I like that."

"It's in your power," he replied. "And speaking of power, where did Lorenza learn so much?"

"Here, and in Mexico," Rita replied. "It wasn't easy. She had to endure a lot. The secrets of the curanderas were not easy to learn, and Lorenza went into the world of the brujos."

"What do you mean, the world of brujos?"

"It's a long story. She started with a nursing degree from UNM, and she was good at her work, but something kept telling her that modern medicine, for all its wonders, was not serving the older Hispanos who came to the hospital. They got their shots, got their operations, then went back home to doc-tor themselves with the remedies of their ancestors. In other words, the doctors weren't taking care of their spiritual health."

"And the priests?" Sonny asked.

"The religion along the Río Grande is complex. Sure, the priests know about brujería. They know the people believe in the effects of witchcraft, but they don't mess with it."

"Afraid of the devil," Sonny suggested.

"You might say that. To believe that a witch can cast a spell leads to them having to know exorcism, and few do. They really don't know about it. So the padrecitos scoff and call it paganism."

"The Church doesn't want anything to do with that. Using eagle and owl feathers, and burning incense? They shudder. The first Spanish priests in México ravaged the altars of the Aztecs to get rid of paganism, a religion they couldn't understand. The Franciscans did the same to the Pueblos here in New Mexico. But the beliefs persisted, and the work of the curanderas persisted. Lorenza knew this. She really wanted to help the people, especially the old folks, so she began visiting the old curanderas in northern New Mexico. The healers there had been passing down remedies for centuries. Those women know how to care for the soul. They know how one soul can affect another, which means they know the world of brujería."

"But not all of them were into evil?"

"Oh, no. The hechiceras, those with evil in their hearts, did evil. Lord, there's been evil in the world ever since the first ear of corn was found infected with signs of witchcraft. The good curanderas know this, and they know how to cure evil curses. They know how to go in search of lost souls, troubled souls, wandering spirits, enchanted souls."

"That's what I am, an enchanted soul," Sonny joked.

"Sí, amor, you are my enchanted spirit." Rita smiled and fondled his dark, curly hair.

"Anda, go on. Tell me more."

"Lorenza visited the Hispano villages and the Indian pueblos, on her own quest long before she fully knew what she was looking for. First, learning the herbal remedies, then massage, the work of las sobadoras, who straightened out bad backs long before chiropractors came to this territory. These women knew instinctively that in sore muscles and nerves resided the dark properties of anger, envy, jealousy. Vientos, evil winds that twisted nerve and muscle. The humors, hot and cold, and the balance that needs to exist. These old practices were a way of looking at the world. She learned the healing ways of the Nuevo Mexicanos who live along the Río Grande. She also learned some of the medicine of the Pueblos from the medicine men and women. But she needed to go deeper."

"Deeper?"

"The curanderas were reluctant to talk about witchcraft."

"Por qué?"

"What they knew they only shared with each other. In other words, those beliefs and teachings had gone underground. The old people were afraid outsiders would find out and some reporter would come poking around and write half-baked stories. In the pueblos the Indians stop them at the gate. Anthropologists and reporters have written terrible things about the subject. Crazy articles. Some wrote books. They knew nothing of curanderismo, but publishers were paying for their junk."

"So they went underground," Sonny said.

"Yes. One of the curanderas, I think her name was doña Agapita, advised Lorenza to go to México. She went to Tlaxcala, and that's where—"

She paused.

"Go on."

"She found the brujos, men who could fly."

Sonny's eyebrows knit. "You believe it?"

"Yes."

"So she learned to—"

"Yes. They recognized her power. I guess you're born with the power of the witch or not. They knew she had it, so they took her into their confidence. She lived in the village at the foot of the mountain with rainmakers, conjurers who can affect the weather, weathermakers who could bring rain or stop hailstorms, men who prayed to and believed in la Malintzi—"

"La Malinche?" Sonny interrupted. "The consort of Cortés?"

"No, not Malinche. Malintzi, the spirit of the mountain. Lorenza learned from hechiceros, the powerful brujos who worked white and black sorcery, those born with the gift of inner vision. They could cast spells; they could kill."

Raven casting spells, Sonny thought, the body falling from the sky. He had seen it. Lorenza had led him to see what Raven was up to. How could he doubt?

"She learned from the people who could transform themselves into animals," Rita finished.

Was that Lorenza's magic? She'd taken him into the world of the naguales.

"Transform into animals? You sure that's what she said?"

"Yes. Those sorcerers are the most powerful people in the world of brujería. They're dangerous, because in their animal form they acquire tremendous power."

"She found her animal spirit."

"It nearly killed her," Rita said. "I saw her when she returned from México. She was nearly dead, a bag of bones, thin and brown as a salt cedar. Her eyes were glazed. She had looked into another world. She touched me and I felt the electricity, and even as near death as she was, she felt my stomach, pinched hard, and drew something out. I hadn't told her I had been having real bad stomach pains, and my doctor said he needed to operate, but whatever it was, she pulled it out, just like that. Like you would pick a rock from a stream, dripping wet. But I was cured. Then she fell into a deep sleep. It took months for her to come back."

"Back from where?" Sonny asked.

"That other world. The world of the nagual. . . ." Her words were barely perceptible.

"Sounds like that guy, Don Juan. Yaquí magic," he chuckled.

"Don't laugh," Rita replied. "Lorenza's for real. And we don't have to go to the desert of Sonora for our beliefs. They're right here in the valley, all around us."

Sonny looked at her and a slight shiver went down his back. He knew when Rita was serious. And much of what she said about the place were things don Eliseo told him. The Río Grande valley was a sacred place, full of ancient spirits. Full of knowledge.

"Yes, here," he mused.

"You know the stories people used to tell. About witches who took the form of owls or coyotes. Witches transformed into large balls of fire and seen dancing in evil places."

"Yeah," Sonny nodded. "I heard plenty of cuentos from my abuelos, and from my parents."

He thought of a story his father used to tell. Two men were

on their way home from selling their cattle. Late at night they found themselves on a deserted llano, and then they came to a lighted hut. The hut belonged to two old women, so the men asked permission to spend the night. The men were suspicious of the two women, so they pretended to sleep. Late in the night they watched as the two women put unguents on their bodies, danced, sang, washed themselves in a tub. They turned themselves into owls and flew up the chimney. The two men wanted to know if what they saw was witchcraft or a dream, so they rose, covered themselves with the witches' unguents, repeated the dance they had seen, and turned into owls. They flew up the chimney to the rooftop. From there they saw a gathering of owls in the dark night, presumably a gathering of witches.

A large, black cat suddenly appeared and attacked the owls, snarling and scratching. The two men watched, and realizing they might be attacked by the cat, they flew back down the chimney and washed away the unguents in the large tub of water. They turned back to their human form. Just as they got in bed, the two women returned, blood covering their feathers. They, too, bathed in the tub. The two men watched, terrified, as the two women returned to their human forms and likewise went to bed.

As a boy, Sonny was awed by this story. He thought his father told the story to entertain him and his brother, Armando, but as he grew older, he thought more and more about it. Did his father tell the story to Sonny and his brother to teach them something?

Sonny remembered his father lowering his voice when he finished the story. "In the morning when the two women invited the men to stay for breakfast, their hands and faces bore the fresh scratch marks of a cat."

Was the story a warning about women? Puberty had come, and like the other boys, Sonny and Armando were looking at girlie magazines some of their friends sneaked from their older brothers, and wondering about the mysterious world of sex.

"Always wear your scapular," he remembered his mother adding at the end of the story. "It will keep you safe."

He had made his first holy communion when he was seven. The scapular became frayed, worn, and dark with body sweat.

Finally, he lost it, one summer day when he went swimming in the river. He and the gang of friends had stripped and thrown their clothes on the river willows. Sonny had hung the scapular with care on the limb of an old dead cottonwood tree branch. The tree was white, like bone, its bark long ago peeled away. Perhaps it had been hit by lightning, and now it lay on the sandy bank of the river. When they came out of the water, the scapular was gone. Sonny and his friends searched, but it was gone.

Now as Sonny remembered losing the scapular, he felt chilled. He had believed that the scapular protected him, and without it he was vulnerable. The protection of the church and its saints was gone. But he had shrugged it off. What the hell, it was only a piece of string with the image of St. Christopher on one side, the Virgen de Guadalupe on the other. He had worn it a year, longer than most of the other kids in his gang, and then it was gone. So what?

"The two men?" Sonny had asked his father. "Did they have protection?"

"A pistol," his father answered. That was the night he told Sonny that when he died Sonny would inherit the .45-caliber Colt of the Bisabuelo, Elfego Baca, their great-grandfather and one of the most famous lawmen of the turn of the century in wild New Mexico.

He showed the pistol to Sonny and Armando. "This will keep you safe," he said.

"Why Sonny?" Armando asked, jealous.

"He's the oldest," the father replied.

"But we're twins," Armando insisted.

"He was born first," his father said.

Firstborn, inheritor of the pistol of Elfego Baca!

Sonny's jaw dropped. It was a moment of magic—to touch the pistol of Elfego Baca, his great-grandfather, the man known in stories as el Bisabuelo. The pistol had been in the family for years, and now their father said it would be passed down to Sonny.

"Having a gun in the house is dangerous," Sonny's mother protested.

"All power is dangerous," his father answered. "This is how

my grandfather kept law and order. This is how he kept the abusive Tejanos from mistreating the Mexicanos."

His mother shook her head. "I don't like it."

"The world is violent," his father said to Sonny and Armando. "You have to protect yourselves. But never, never aim the pistol unless you are going to use it. We are not here to take anyone's life. But you have to protect yourselves."

"A bullet cannot stop evil," his mother said resolutely.

"It can if it has a cross scratched on it," his father had responded.

Why am I remembering these stories? Sonny thought. Did it have something to do with the limpieza? In spite of viewing Veronica's body, he felt incredibly light and free of the dark thoughts that had been oppressing him. The thoughts of that scene with his father rose so clear, like a vivid dream.

Today, when Lorenza first ran the eagle feather across his stomach, he felt the same sensation as he had in June when Veronica cut a Zia sign around his navel. The cut, even though it was just skin deep, had left a scar. The round sun and the four radiating lines of the scar remained a constant irritant.

For Rita the scar was an outward sign of the ghost within. Raven and his cult had cursed him. That's why he had finally agreed to see Lorenza.

She had put the eagle feather aside and pressed at his navel. Sonny felt an urge. He groaned, "Ahhh."

"There is a dark bird pecking at your soul—"

A dark bird? Raven, he thought. Sonofabitching Raven was still hanging around with his hocus-pocus.

"You need to go on a journey," she whispered.

Where? He wondered, then said, "Vamos."

He had loved Gloria. She was more than his cousin, she was the first woman he had ever made love to. Did her spirit cling to Sonny because she wanted revenge for her murder? Or was Raven capable of manipulating Gloria's ghost to harm Sonny?

"Tell me what you see," Lorenza said.

Two persons in the curandera. Lorenza and someone else. Was that other entity he sensed the nagual Rita alluded to? He saw the eye of a bird. An owl from the Nile of Egypt. Which eye will heal me? Sonny wondered.

He told Lorenza his story. It happened one early June morning. He remembered the date clearly. The Dukes were playing that night, and he had planned to go to the baseball game. It was the same day don Eliseo, his octogenarian neighbor, had picked to cut down the old cottonwood in his front yard. Then the phone call came that Gloria Dominic had been murdered. Gloria's mother, his tía Delfina, had called and he had driven her to Gloria's house.

Everyone was there: Gloria's husband, Frank Dominic, who was running for mayor, intent on being *the* political power in the city, in the state; Police Chief Garcia, an old friend of Dominic's and a constant thorn in the side of the private investigators in town; Howard Powdrell, número uno forensics man with the city police crime lab, and Sonny's compadre. Without Howard's help Sonny couldn't have solved the crime.

"Find my daughter's murderer," tía Delfina had cried, stuffing a few crumpled dollar bills into Sonny's hands.

But he didn't solve the murder just for his aunt, he solved it for himself. Gloria was his cousin, a beautiful and talented woman, and once, only once, she had given herself to him.

That was it, but the memory lingered. Years later she married Frank Dominic, and together they set out to rule the city. She didn't love Frank, but there they were, on the surface the perfect couple, wealthy, planning the great downtown renewal that would bring a canal water system to the area, making the city a Venice on the Río Grande.

But Gloria wasn't happy, and she wasn't well. She fell under the spell of Tamara Dubronsky, a forty-year-old widow of enticing charm, a cosmopolitan beauty who intrigued the natives. The mystical Tamara was psychic. She told people their fortunes, raised money for the city symphony, and as Sonny found out, she was the sun queen, leader of the Zia cult, the group that murdered Gloria.

Qué piensas?" Rita asked, drawing Sonny from his thoughts.

"Raven."

"He's dangerous." She shivered.

Raven had been Tamara's lover. Had he come to rescue her? The FBI was still looking for him for trying to bomb a truck carrying high-level plutonium waste from Los Alamos Labs to the Waste Isolation Pilot Plant site in Carlsbad. The WIPP mines were huge caverns dug into the salt beds of the area, a billion-dollar industry for the region.

Small towns without any industry to support the economy were turning their land over to the feds to store radioactive waste, and now even the Mescalero Indians were plotting a private dump for the poison. Storing nuclear waste had become big business.

"Do you think Tamara's still with him?" Rita asked.

"I don't think so. Tamara's too smart to have anything to do with anyone in trouble with the law. Raven used her to get the money to buy explosives and equipment. When they found out Gloria was carrying half a million she had extorted from Akira Morino, they killed her."

But who gave the orders to kill Gloria? Raven or Tamara?

Sonny figured Tamara wouldn't dirty her hands in blood, so Veronica killed Gloria. They drained her blood, mixed it with earth in a vase, and offered it to the sun so Raven would succeed in blowing up the WIPP truck.

Sonny had stopped him. On the small bridge that crossed the rain-swollen Arroyo del Sol on the east side of the Sandia Mountains, Sonny, Rita, and José Escobar had come upon Raven in time to stop the dynamiting of the WIPP truck.

In the struggle that ensued, Raven fell into the arroyo. The flood carried his body away. Buried in the tons of sand somewhere, the state cops theorized after their search didn't come up with a body.

Now Sonny knew better. Raven had survived. Somehow he had survived the flood and was alive. He was out there now. Maybe it was Raven's dark powers Lorenza had to cleanse away. That's why he needed to go deeper, to get past Gloria's spirit and get to Raven.

Sonny remembered visiting Raven's compound on the east side of the Sandia Mountains near La Cueva. Raven's women were four enslaved souls who constituted the Zia cult. And how did the handsome and quite charismatic Raven keep the four women to do his bidding? He offered them sex. Sex with the sun king, Raven, keeper of the medallion of the sun, the same Zia medallion Sonny had ripped from his neck before Raven fell into the arroyo.

Tamara had joined Raven's crazy plan because she feared a nuclear holocaust; she feared the cold winter that would envelop the earth after a nuclear war. Unfounded fears? The cold war *was* over. Not for a woman like Tamara who had lived through cruel deprivations as a child. She had once told Sonny her Gypsy mother had to sell her body to keep the young Tamara alive.

The DA made a deal for Veronica to turn state's evidence. The DA wanted to bust Tamara Dubronsky. Veronica was a small-fry, and Tamara a shark, and implicating her in the murder meant good press coverage, headlines that helped political careers down the line. If Tamara Dubronsky went up on murder one charges, the trial could turn into one of the most spectacular the state had ever witnessed.

"Tell me about Gloria," Lorenza Villa had asked.

He told her what he had seen. The pale, naked body of Gloria Dominic on the bed. When he saw it, he felt something in the room.

"Something cold," he said. He didn't know how to explain it.

"Were you afraid?" Lorenza asked.

Sonny hated to admit it, but he nodded. Yes, he had been afraid.

"You felt the soul of the dead woman," Lorenza said.

Sonny didn't believe in ghosts. He had seen Lorenza in June, a short visit, and that's what she said then, but his cynicism, something he felt he had acquired during his university education, kept him from going through the cleansing ceremony she had proposed then.

But three months of bad dreams and disorientation had persuaded him to try the cure, to try the old way of dealing with the dark energies eating away at him.

"It's susto," Lorenza said. "You were shocked by her death."

"Yeah, but I've seen dead people before," Sonny said.

"But you were very close to Gloria."

Sonny nodded.

"She had just died," Lorenza said. "Her soul was in the room. This is the way it happens. The body dies but the soul lingers. It has unfinished business. A powerful woman possesses a powerful soul."

And Sonny, she knew, for all his bravado and machismo, was a sensitive soul. He was a man who drew souls to him. Gloria's spirit had invaded his, and it was still drawing on his energy.

"Why so deep in thought?" Rita asked.

"Sorry, I was just thinking. Lorenza asked me if I was psychic."

"You are," Rita said.

"No, I'm not. She asked if I had had a past-life experience or caught a glimpse of the future."

Rita waited.

"I told her maybe. Maybe when I was a kid."

"Go on," Rita encouraged him softly.

"I used to hear voices. Or I thought I heard voices when I was a kid. My parents used to take me and Armando to visit my abuelos down in Socorro. Armando went off to smoke cigarettes at the pool hall. I wandered alone into the river bosque. I thought it was a scary place to be, but something pulled me down there. I would walk, sit, listen to the trees, the river, the animals. . . ."

"What animals?" she asked.

"Coyotes," he replied. "The river coyotes."

"Did the coyotes run from you?"

"No. That was strange. My abuelo said the coyote doesn't trust anyone. He's been hunted too long, so he doesn't trust man. They had a den there by the river. There was a spring flowing into the river, a grassy open area, and a huge, fallen cottonwood tree. Under the alamo they had their den. When I found the place, I thought they would run, but they didn't. I would spend hours watching them play with their young. I told my abuelo about the coyotes, and he looked at me kind of strange and said I was blessed. I guess he meant the animals trusted me."

Rita nodded.

"I remember, once, I was about twelve, and we were playing baseball. Me and the kids I ran around with. Suddenly I felt I wasn't in my body. I was flying overhead, and the game became clear to me. I could see the kids in their exact place, and I knew ahead of time if the batter would get a hit. I knew who would win the game. It was a strange feeling, but it was real."

He looked at Rita. "It's nothing." He shrugged.

"It's important," Rita said.

Maybe he could sense things, but when he told his friends

about the things he saw, they said he was weird, so he began to shut out the visions when they occurred. Even now it felt strange to talk about those moments when he felt he was flying, but the clarity of his visions had grown since he came into possession of Raven's medallion.

"Go on," Rita said.

"Once there was an accident. We had played late, it grew dark. We left the park and were walking home. I had a vision. I saw the accident before it happened. I knew Robert Martínez was going to get hit by a car. The scene was clear in my mind. I looked up and saw Robert and Nick Pino horsing around as they walked. Before I could say anything, Robert stepped out into the street, and a car came out of nowhere and hit him. It ran over his leg and broke it. There was nothing I could do. I couldn't shout or move. But I knew it was going to happen."

Sonny was recalling many images, times when the power of vision had come upon him.

"During the limpieza, Lorenza instructed me to go back to the room and see Gloria's dead body. I saw her as clear as if she was right in front of me, now. So white and pale. I felt like reaching out and touching her."

"Did you?"

"No."

"Why?"

"I don't know."

"She was dead."

"Yes. But in the back of my mind, deep inside, I thought I could bring her back to life. Crazy, huh?"

Rita shook her head. "Not crazy."

"You two think alike." Sonny smiled. "Don Eliseo told me the story of el hombre dorado. The man who came seeking the fountain of youth. Some bad people got hold of him and took his soul, and they painted him with gold. Now he can live forever, but he has no soul."

"But you have a very sensitive soul," Rita said. "By not touching Gloria you opened your soul to fear. That shock is what we call susto. Gloria's spirit attached itself to yours."

"That's what Lorenza said."

He thought of Tamara Dubronsky. He had faced her the following morning, told her Raven was dead, and she replied that Raven couldn't die. Raven's soul was born again in Sonny, she said, with a perturbing smile that told Sonny she believed what she said. So it was fitting that Sonny wear the Zia medallion, Raven's symbol for the Zia cult.

"Maybe Raven's also in me," he whispered.

Rita sighed. Yes, he would have to go deeper into the world of spirits. This is what Lorenza was preparing him for.

"Shock affects the soul," Rita said softly. "Any shock can create susto in the nervous system, but the really bad susto is when another soul frightens you, enters you. It can lead to depression. The other soul is taking your energy."

"Like this summer," Sonny said. He had felt so low and distracted he couldn't even make love to Rita. Some nights when he lay beside Rita, he didn't feel the urge. The worry compounded itself.

"I loved Gloria," he admitted. "Once, when I was in high school, I felt I was the only guy on the high school team that wasn't messing around. The other guys bragged all the time about the girls they were screwing. I was supposed to remain pure, you know all that Catholic stuff. I could talk to Gloria about it. She understood. She was—what?—ten years older, she knew about life. I used to go by her place, visit, and even then I guess I sensed she was as lonely as me. The week I graduated, she let me make love to her."

He paused, thinking back to the evening she had been waiting for him, the presents she had bought him, the wine and candlelight. She made the move, and suddenly the years of friendship, the years of desire kept in check, all dissolved into a night of intense passion. It was his initiation.

"So when I saw her dead . . . I don't know. It did something to me. Anger, grief, I wanted revenge. Maybe I did let her soul in." He laughed.

"Maybe," Rita said. "But now her spirit has to move on, release the living. That's the rule of life and death."

He looked at her. Her brown eyes smiled. She understood him. Lord, she seemed to know what swirled in his thoughts.

"How do I get involved in these things?"

"Somebody has to fight Raven."

"And I'm elected. I told Lorenza about the Zia sign that Veronica cut around my navel. When she had me hung up like a goat, ready to kill me. Before you and don Eliseo rescued me."

"The Pueblo people use the Zia as a symbol for the sun," Rita said, "but Raven and his pack have taken it as their symbol. We have to take it back. The Zia sun is good and life-giving, not negative."

Yeah, Sonny thought. Take back the good power. Take it back from the bad brujos, the sorcerers who do evil.

"Lorenza believes Raven has the power of a brujo. He lives in the world of spirits. That's why he's so strong. I had to find the coyotes, my guardian spirits. For now, it's the only way to fight him.

"The first part of the cleansing was the burning of incense, the sweeping away with eagle and owl feathers, the bird of day and the bird of night. She was preparing me for my journey. She played a tape. A soft and distant drum. I closed my eyes. The drumming was like the beating of my heart . . . 'imagine a lake,' she said, 'or a cave, a spring. A hole that goes into the earth. It must be a place you know.' And she told me to sing a song. Make one up. So I began to sing to the beat of the drum."

He paused and looked at Rita. "The words just came to me: 'To Grandfather Sun I send my prayers. To Tata Díos y los santos I pray. To the four directions I send my prayers. I pray to the kachina spirits of the mountains. May the power of my ancestors fill my soul. Guide me on the path of the sun. Fill me with clarity and goodness.' "

"A beautiful song," Rita whispered.

"Something happened as I sang. I lost consciousness. I was drifting. . . ."

He was a cloud, a shadow, flying over the llano of eastern New Mexico, and he saw Santa Rosa, a town he had visited as a child with his parents. He hovered over a lake, Hidden Lake, a hidden jewel of a lake on the wide expanse of llano.

In the vision his father was on one side, his mother on the other, Armando played nearby. His father wanted them to know the state, so often he took Sonny and Armando on trips—fishing up in the Taos mountains; to see the maples turn red in October in the Manzanos; driving up to the Jemez to lie in the hot mineral springs that bubbled up from the depths of the ancient volcano; exploring the Bosque del Apache, to see the arrival of the snow geese and the whooping cranes in the fall; watching the Navajo fair and rodeo in Gallup in August.

"I want you to know your land," his father had said. It was part of their education.

One summer evening they found themselves in Santa Rosa. They stood by the edge of a lake with Ron Chávez, a friend of his father's, and as the sun set on the small, blue lake surrounded by ocher sandstone cliffs, Sonny looked upon what he thought must be the most enchanting place he had ever seen. Hidden Lake. He remembered it clearly, and when Lorenza instructed him to find a lake or a pond, he thought of the jewel of a lake in the red sunset he had seen long ago.

"A lake," he whispered to Rita. "I was to enter the lake. Begin the journey to the underworld, that place where I would find my troubled soul. I had to meet the animals. 'Dive in,' she said. 'It is a passageway. Don't be afraid. Dive in. Dive to the bottom. Don't touch anything along the way.'"

He stopped. What had happened after that was weird. He looked at Rita.

"Damn." He shook his head. "Just as I was about to dive, the image of the lake faded, and I saw Gloria!"

"Gloria became the passage," Rita said.

He nodded.

"What did Lorenza say?" Rita asked.

"Entering Gloria was a journey into Mother Earth, the world of spirits, a place so deep in my mind I'd never been there. Gloria haunted me, she also wanted to help me. I entered her, fell, saw growths like poisoned mushrooms. Those, Lorenza explained afterward, are signs of the sexual abuse she suffered in life. Some who fall through a spring or lake describe similar growths. Anyway, now I have some power to fight Raven."

"You found the coyotes."

"The coyote is my nagual. They came to give me power."

Sonny shook his head. He felt strong, stronger than he had felt all summer. Finding the coyotes, the run with them, it had all filled him with energy.

Lorenza had passed the eagle feather over his body, brushing away the dark energies. In its place he felt a lightness, like the Señores y Señoras de la Luz that filled don Eliseo's universe. They came over his body, filling him with light from head to feet.

He had resisted when Rita first proposed they visit the healer, but now he sensed the power of the woman. She was driving away the susto in his soul and replacing it with the power of the coyotes. Okay, the trip he had just been through was making a believer out of him.

She prayed and chanted over him, in Spanish and in the old Nahuatl language of the Aztecs. She burned more copal and prayed to the Virgen de Guadalupe, the sacred mother of the Americas.

When the ritual was concluded, she passed the candle Sonny had brought over his body, then she lit it. The images of the coyotes he had seen in his vision appeared in the smoke.

"The coyote is the loner, like me," he said to Rita. "He runs across the range and snips a sheep here or there, feeds his family. He's shot at and hunted by the ranchers, but he survives. He's a survivor."

"The Indian legends say Coyote is a trickster," Rita reminded him. "Always getting in trouble, but teaching the people through his antics."

"You know, Lorenza could've helped Gloria."

"Yes. She died a horrible death, with all that pain inside. She turned to the wrong persons for help. Raven used her, took her money, then had her killed."

She looked at Sonny. "You feel good about the limpieza."

"Yeah. Lots of energy. I even feel like—" He winked.

Rita smiled. "You want to come by tonight?"

"Sure. I feel better. I feel great!"

She kissed him and stepped out of the truck.

"Cuidao, amor," she said, and walked into the restaurant.

5

Sonny drove to his house in Ranchitos. A few of the old adobe houses of the once-farming community still belonged to the old Mexicanos of the valley; the rest of the area had been subdivided by developers. Pockets of the once-traditional, Hispanic North Valley were dotted with the expensive adobe homes of those with enough money to buy the subdivided land and build large customized homes. The old settlements of the valley had been razed and the fields plowed under and covered with homes built for professionals who worked in the city.

Gentrification, the local press called the process. Displacement, the Chicanos countered. Real estate taxes went up and up, and the old Hispanos of the valley had to sell. As more of the displaced families sold and moved away, the original ambience that once drew the moneyed folks to the North Valley was lost. A few realized they had cracked the golden egg that drew them to the area in the first place.

Don Eliseo and his two friends were busy in the front yard when Sonny drove up. He and doña Concha and don Toto were roasting a basketful of green chile that don Eliseo grew in his field by the house. Don Eliseo slowly and methodically placed the shapely, green peppers on the grill, turned each one with care, and when the thin skin was brown and roasted, he picked up the chile and tossed it in a pan.

Don Toto's job was to make sure the just-roasted chiles were kept covered with a wet towel and steaming, thus making the skin easier to peel off. He also kept the wineglasses full of his own vintage, a North Valley wine that came from vines his family had cultivated since the seventeenth century. He now had no more than a dozen plants, but he bottled enough to keep him and his friends in wine all winter.

Doña Concha, dressed in jeans and a white blouse, with circles of rouge heavy on her cheeks and her thin lips etched with deep purple lipstick, kept pushing up on her ever-sagging bra as she peeled the skins off the toasted chiles. She wrapped eight or ten of the home-grown hot peppers in a plastic bag, and they were ready to be placed in the freezer for winter use.

They were roasting the last of the green chile. The ones that had ripened red had already been strung up in ristras. Three long, fat ristras of red chile peppers hung on the front wall of the house, drying in the warm southern exposure.

"Elfego, cómo 'stás?" don Eliseo called. "Come have a sip of wine."

Sonny walked across the dirt road to sit under the shade of the tree with them. He felt at ease with the old people, and they liked to joke with him as much as he liked the banter.

"Hi, honey." La Concha smiled. "If I didn't have my hands full of chile, I'd give you a hug. No quiero enchilarte."

"Concha querida, you can enchilarme anytime." Sonny kissed her cheek, then took the cup of wine don Toto offered him.

"Híjola!" Concha smiled wider. "Did you hear that, boys! He's feeling like a hot chile!"

"Maybe the curandera helped," don Eliseo said with a wink.

Concha nudged Sonny. "Did she roast your chile?" She burst out in a fit of laughter.

"Atta boy, Sonny!" Don Toto slapped him on the back. "That Lorenza is a honey."

"She's too young for you." Concha grinned at Toto.

"At forty they're ripe," he countered. "At your age, you got ganas but no juice." He chortled.

Concha glared at him. "See this?" She picked up a roasted chile from the grill, wilted and cooked. "Toto's!" She laughed anew.

"Pués, más sabor when it's cooked," don Toto said, smiling. "Put a little salt on it and wrap it in your tortilla!" He smacked his lips.

"A hot chile wrapped in a tortilla." Concha winked at Sonny. "Ain't that sexy!"

"Muy sexy," Sonny agreed, and sat in the old lounge chair don Eliseo kept beneath the giant cottonwood. The day had grown warm enough to work outside in shirtsleeves.

"But you don' sound too happy," don Eliseo said. "How was la curandera?"

"She was all right," Sonny answered.

"Only all right?" don Eliseo asked. The old man knew when something was bothering Sonny. Two years the young man had lived in the small adobe across the street, and during that time Sonny had become like a son to don Eliseo.

"Maybe Sonny needs someone with experience," Concha said. "Like me."

"She's right," don Toto agreed, refilling their cups. "Concha used to know all the curanderas in the valley. And she could cure el mal ojo."

"Take an egg and place it on the person's forehead," Concha said. "Rub their body with it, especially the stomach. Then break it open in a glass of water. You will see el mal. Most of the time it's just someone who looked at the baby too long," she continued. "You know, like when the baby is so cute and you adore it. When one adores the soul of another person, you pull it out. A baby's soul is young and innocent, so it's easy for an older soul to draw it out. It makes the baby sick. The spirit is strong, sabes. So you can draw the soul out, like when you fall in love, ese!" She kidded Sonny. "I bet Rita's got your soul wrapped up!"

"Hot tortilla!" Don Toto laughed and drank.

Sonny smiled.

"So you get out of harmony, como dicen los indios," Concha continued. "The person who puts the mal ojo has to spit on the baby's forehead. A lot of people think it's the spit that makes the baby well, but no, don't you see, honey, it's the breath. The breath is the soul, the breath gives back the soul to the baby. Makes it well. Ah, we used to have curanderas all over the valley who knew how to cure everything. Mujeres fuertes. They cured everyone, delivered babies, and—"

Here she paused and her bright, greenish eyes stared into Sonny's. "They fought el demonio. They were the only ones who knew how to fight the diablo. La gente doesn't realize it, but when the last curandera died, there was no one left to fight the brujas del diablo. Oh, there's a few here and there, young women who want to learn, like Lorenza. Pero qué saben? They don't know how strong evil is. Look around you, look at what's happening to la gente. The kids are crazy, and so are their parents. Dope, booze, violence. The diablo is loose, and there's no one to fight his brujas."

Don Eliseo and don Toto nodded.

"Oh, there's the medicine men in the pueblos," la Concha concluded. "But the people don't go there anymore. They go to the shopping malls, to the movies, but not to the right medicine."

"The old ways are dying," don Eliseo said.

The three old friends—Snap, Crackle and Pop, they called themselves—had helped Sonny track Veronica in June. They had led Sonny right to her house. When Veronica hung Sonny like a goat and was ready to kill him, it was don Eliseo and Rita who rescued him from becoming one more sacrificial victim of the Zia cult. They believed Veronica was an evil sorcerer, a bruja, in the worst sense of the word.

Sonny told them about Veronica's death.

"Válgame Dios," la Concha said, and made the sign of the cross when Sonny told them how Veronica died.

"A bad death," don Toto said philosophically. "She did evil, and that's how she died."

"She killed Gloria," Sonny said. "Raven gave the commands, but Veronica carried them out."

He looked at the withered field of corn and saw again Gloria Dominic's body as he had seen her the morning of her death. The perfectly sculptured body lay on the white satin sheets, frozen in the grip of death, the blood drained from her body. It was the same image that off and on had appeared to him all summer because, as Lorenza and Rita said, Gloria's spirit had come to live in his. Her revenge was not yet complete. She wanted those who killed her punished.

The souls of those who died a violent death could not rest. They became wandering spirits, roaming the river, the acequias, the cemeteries, the dark roads at night.

La Llorona was such a spirit. A woman who had committed the worst of sins: killing her children. She was doomed to search the river where she had thrown the bodies. La Llorona, the wailing woman, a story that made children shiver. Was the story a warning to children that even in parents lay the awful possibility of infanticide? All the stories and cuentos carried a message, and maybe that's what the story of la Llorona taught.

"The limpieza will help," Sonny whispered.

"A limpieza takes the bad spirits out." Concha nodded.

Don Eliseo studied Sonny. Sonny was respectful, he took time to talk and listen to the old stories, not like his real sons and daughters who were spread out all over the city and were too busy to visit.

"So, la Tamara Dubronsky will go free," don Eliseo said. "And somebody murdered la Veronica?"

"Yes." Sonny nodded and looked at the wrinkled face of the old man. Don Eliseo's eyes were crystal brown, as bright as the morning sun he worshiped. The light of eighty years had filled don Eliseo, filled his spirit, and it shone on his face and in his eyes.

Sonny finished his wine and got up.

"Raven," the old man said.

"He's back."

"Póngate la cruz," Concha whispered, and again made the sign of the cross.

"Come to claim what's his," don Eliseo said.

The old man knew Sonny was wearing Raven's Zia medallion. Raven's cult and the Dubronsky woman still had a claim on Sonny, and it was not yet resolved.

"Yup," Sonny replied. "I have to get him before he gets me."

"You can do it, Sonny," don Toto said.

"Pero con cuidao," la Concha cried out. "That Raven is a brujo, he can fly. Those brujos have a lot of power."

"And I don't," Sonny said.

Concha glanced at don Eliseo.

"Did the curandera speak of the coyote?" don Eliseo asked.

Sonny smiled. Ah, the old man knew. He had told Sonny he had the coyote spirit within.

"Sí." Sonny nodded.

"Pués, ten fé. Trust her," don Eliseo said. "She's young and strong—"

"Not like us gastados," Concha said.

"You have to trust her, Sonny," don Eliseo repeated, "but it's not gonna be easy. Raven is a brujo. He can fly."

"You never know if he is a man or a raven," Concha said.

"Some fly through the air like balls of fire," don Toto whispered, and took a swig of wine.

They believed. They had heard many stories of men followed by balls of fire out in the llano or in the forest. Men who swore they had seen the leaping fireballs following them.

Yeah, Sonny thought, they knew.

"Bueno, I better get some rest."

"Stay and eat lunch with us. I'm cooking chile con carne," Concha said.

"The best in the West," don Toto said, smiling.

"Gracias," Sonny answered, "but I have a few things to do. Adiós."

"Adiós," they called, and Sonny walked across the dirt road to his place. He entered the warm house and turned on the swamp cooler. Even in October, the warm sunlight pouring through the kitchen window had heated the small house. On the way to the kitchen he paused in front of the credenza and looked into the mirror. He pulled the medallion from beneath his shirt and let it hang free.

Raven had returned to free Tamara Dubronsky, and to do that, he had to kill Veronica, but Tamara was too damn smart to tie up with him again. Raven had returned to get Sonny.

Or maybe Tamara had hired a mafioso, or someone local, to get rid of Veronica, and then had the raven feathers planted just to throw Sonny off guard.

In the fall large flocks of crows returned to eat at the city dump during the winter and to roost in the cottonwoods of the river at night. All winter the huge flocks rose in the morning to scavenge, and returned at dusk to sleep in the bare trees of the river. They did not hunt prey; they ate roadkill and trash. What if the four feathers were simply dropped by one of the river crows?

No, he knew better. The feathers were a message for him. Raven took Veronica up in the balloon and pushed her. He knew that, and Howard knew that, and even Chief Garcia knew that, but there wasn't a shred of evidence—unless Raven had shown up with the bail money, using Gloria's money to get Veronica out of jail.

No, for crying out loud! He was too smart for that. He would show himself when he wanted to, not before.

But the murder would certainly disrupt the balloon fiesta. There were thousands of people in town for the event, seven hundred pilots registered, and the gruesome death would not be good publicity. First day and someone had fallen out of a balloon. It would be on the six o'clock news and in tomorrow's paper it would be plastered on the front page.

He had read in one of Ben Chávez's novels that in the old days witches were buried in caskets woven from pliant cottonwood branches, so their bodies would rot quickly into the earth. They were not buried in the campo santo, the sacred ground of the church cemetery, but along the river bottom, in the wet clay.

Standing in front of the mirror, Sonny remembered stories he had heard as a child, stories his grandparents told when he went to visit them in Socorro.

Witches had to be killed with a bullet marked with a cross, bullets blessed with holy water by a priest. His father had told the story of the man who was haunted by an owl. He tried to kill the owl, but nothing worked. For months the man could not sleep, he could not rest. He was near death when he finally scratched a cross on the bullet and had the priest bless it with holy water. With that bullet he shot the owl when it came at night.

In the morning he found blood at the foot of the tree where the owl had perched, but no owl. He hurried to his compadre's home, and he and his compadre followed the trail of blood to the house of an old woman who was known to be a witch. She had put curses on many of the people of the valley. The man had exposed her, and she had turned her wrath on him. They found her dead, killed by a bullet marked with a cross.

"Stories," Sonny said to himself, "just stories."

He touched the medallion around his neck. Wearing it had become an obsession. He had kept telling himself that he would turn it over to the DA. After all, it *was* state's evidence.

He remembered what Tamara said the morning they arrested her. She told him to keep the medallion and wear it, because he was the new Raven.

"Raven cannot die. He will return, and your only hope is the medallion."

What the devil did she mean? That the medallion gave him power over Raven? If so, Raven had returned for it.

How in the hell did I get mixed up in the world of haunted souls? he wondered.

Perhaps he had always been involved in it. The stories of people changing into animal forms, flying, the brujos—even the simple warning not to awaken someone asleep too abruptly, because the soul was not in the body but flying about. The soul could fly and bring back what was known as dream. It needed to return quickly to the sleeping body.

"Go wake your father," his mother said, "but walk softly and whisper to him." And he would enter the bedroom and call softly "Papá, papá . . ." until his father stirred.

"La vida es un sueño," don Eliseo had quoted Calderón de la Barca, "so we are always dreaming, and our soul is the greatest dreamer. It loves to fly about to gain the knowledge of the world. Did you ever go to a place you thought you had seen before?"

"Déjà vu," Sonny answered.

"Qué?"

"It's French. To explain the feeling we have been there before."

"Sí, de-je-voo. I like that word. The franceses have a way with words. Imagine, even their babies can speak French!" Don Eliseo slapped his thigh and laughed. "You get it? The French babies are so smart they can speak French."

"I get it, I get it."

Sonny studied his image in the mirror. Damn, he was thirty, face it, thirty-one at the end of the month. When the kids came calling "Trick or treat" at night, he would be celebrating the passage of one more year. So what, what's one year, he thought. I'm still número uno stud, in perfect health.

You handsome cabrón. He grinned, and flashed his white, even teeth. Lean and muscular, with dark curly hair; women liked him. His eyes were dark brown, sometimes dark as coffee beans, depending on his mood. So he hadn't been feeling well. Lorenza's cure would fix that. He wanted to believe.

He remembered Raven's dark features, the long, sleek hair drawn back in a ponytail, the hawk nose. Sonny's nose was similar, his chin strong, jutting, with a dimple. He did bear a resemblance to Raven, perhaps looked more like Raven than he did his own twin brother, Armando. In the barrios of the South Valley, where Sonny grew up, he and Raven could pass for brothers.

Sonny fingered the medallion. He'll come for it. He needs the power of the Zia sun.

The phone rang and startled him. It was Madge Swenson, the director of the balloon fiesta. "Have you heard?" she asked, and Sonny told her he had been at the scene. "I want to talk to you," she said.

"About the murder?"

"Not over the phone. I need to talk to you."

"Why?"

"I, I need help. Can you come by? I'm at fiesta headquarters."

"Do you have a list of balloonists who went up this morning?" Sonny asked.

"Of course we do—" She stopped abruptly. "Are you working for someone?" she asked.

"Only myself."

"How soon can you come?"

"I'm on my way."

He hung up the phone. So the very tough and very attractive Madge Swenson was calling. A murder on the first day of the fiesta could spoil a lot of plans.

Sonny took a quick shower and put on a fresh shirt. He knew the balloon in which Veronica went up wouldn't be listed, but there were other troubling thoughts that began to bubble around the fiesta. He needed to know who was in town, who was flying.

On the way to the balloon fiesta grounds, he called Howard on his cellular.

"Howie, anything new?"

"Checked into the bailing," Howard replied. "Veronica had agreed with the DA to testify against Tamara if the DA would let her out of jail. She was going insane inside, she claimed. The DA agreed, and late yesterday a woman showed up with a quarter-million in cash."

The night she was murdered Gloria Dominic had received a lot of money from Akira Morino. No doubt part of that bankroll had just been used to bail out Veronica.

"So Veronica had one night of freedom," Sonny said. "Who was the woman?"

Howard chuckled. "Sister Hawk."

"One of Raven's women," Sonny said.

"Sure. The name, address, everything is phony. The DA, of course, is very embarrassed."

"Yeah, I bet." Sonny smiled.

"The chief is having our artist do a composite now, but yeah, it will probably turn out to be one of the women in his group. Or an anonymous that Raven hired off the street. It's no crime to bail out a person, even if that person gets killed a few hours later."

"So Veronica spent the night with Raven, enough time for him to induce her into the morning flight. She went with him, trusting him . . . There's something else, Howie, something else."

"Qué?"

"I don't know, just something bothering me. Any good witnesses?"

"Nope. Garcia's boys have talked to a lot of people on the West Mesa, but nobody actually saw the fall."

"Except the anonymous tip."

"Right, but whoever called hasn't stepped forward, so we're at zero."

"Madge Swenson just called. She wants to see me."

"It's bad publicity for the fiesta."

"Yeah."

There was a pause.

"You going?" Howard asked.

"I'm on my way."

"Ah, the plot thickens, Watson. Why is it all the nice-looking women in Alboo-kirk call you? Didn't you go to school with her?"

"No, she was up at El Dorado. We met when we were seniors, a student exchange, you know, the counselors dreamed up this program for the home boys from the South Valley to go see how the other half lives. We were supposed to go up and live with a family in the Heights for a week, and some of their kids came down to live in the barrio."

"And you wound up with Madge's family?"

"Yup."

"God loves you."

"Yeah. It turned out eighteen-year-old Madge was interested in more than homework."

"Glory be!" Howard exclaimed. "Lots of sex?"

"No—"

"Whaddayamean, 'No'!"

"She was a *nice* girl."

"Ah, say no, please say no."

"We had fun. I met up with her again a few years ago. I was a security guard at the balloon fiesta two years ago. They needed someone who could fly their chopper—"

"Then you got some?"

"No."

"Hey, I'm going to start worrying about you, bro!"

"I had just met Rita."

"I see. So now?"

"So now I'm curious."

"Bueno. Cuidado with the hot stuff. I've seen her on TV, and she is a *bad*-looking woman."

"Ten-four," Sonny replied, and hung up the phone.

The cab of his truck was hot. A fly buzzed against the window, reminding him of the murder scene.

He wasn't stopped by entrance guards as he drove into the balloon field. He could see a row of tents resembling a carnival midway lining the road. Apparently the death of Veronica Worthy had done little to dampen the enthusiasm of the crowd. People thronged the tents, eating and shopping for souvenirs.

At Fiesta Control, in a large building east of the launch field, the atmosphere was more subdued. Shocked balloon pilots stood in line, waiting to enter the building. The police had called in everyone who had been up that morning, and now the last of the very concerned pilots waited to be questioned by the cops.

Garcia's methodical procedure at work, Sonny thought. Would it turn up a clue? Probably not. Those who had witnessed the murder would have come forward by now. Or were afraid to. The press swarmed like buzzards, eager to get a lead on the story for the evening news.

Madge's secretary was waiting for Sonny. She ushered him past the crowd and into Madge's office.

"I'm glad you came." Madge rose from her desk and greeted him with a firm handshake, a smile, then a soft kiss to the cheek. "It's been a while."

"I haven't been around a balloon launch since I worked for you," Sonny said.

"You look good," she said.

"You, too." He smiled.

"Thanks for the compliment," she said. "I've been on a roll, till this morning." She pointed to a chair for him. "Coffee?"

"I'm fine," Sonny replied.

"I've got the jitters," she said, taking her cup of coffee from the desk and sipping. "God, things are screwed."

Sonny studied her. He had enjoyed working with her when he was a security guard for the fiesta. She was a very attractive woman, and she quickly let Sonny know she was interested. Madge was a sexy-looking blonde, toned to perfection, long legs, and the ensuing years had added charm and poise. But today she was troubled; a shadow weighed heavy in her eyes.

"I'm divorced," she had told him one afternoon while they had drinks at a Heights sports bar after work. She loved to fly, and she had been taking Sonny up in her balloon and teaching him to fly it.

"I just met someone," Sonny replied, thinking of Rita. "I'm kind of a one-woman man nowadays." That's the moment he realized he truly loved Rita, because an offer from a woman like Madge came around only once in about a million years.

"I should feel insulted," she replied, "but don't you know, that only makes you more of a challenge. Maybe one of these days you'll be free." She smiled. She hated to be turned down, but she understood.

But they hadn't kept in touch after the fiesta, and now two years had come and gone, but a lustful chemistry still sizzled between them.

The secretary came in with a tray of fresh coffee and cookies, placed it on the table, and left.

"Here's the list of our registered pilots," Madge said, served him coffee, and nodded at the list on the coffee table. She sat across from him.

Sonny picked it up and glanced at it. There were over seven hundred registered balloonists, so the list would take time to check.

"It was a tragic accident," Madge said, "but the news media's trying to make a big deal out of it."

Sonny looked into her bright blue eyes. Lovely eyes, he thought, but he remembered the old rule Manuel López had taught him: everyone is capable of murder, given the right circumstances, the right motive.

"A big deal?" Sonny mumbled through the cookie he had bitten into. Chocolate chip, his favorite.

"It's not murder!" Madge replied with irritation. "And the woman who died wasn't one of our entries! She didn't go up in a registered balloon. But every year a few mavericks go up on their own. They're the ones who get in trouble. That's what happened this morning. It was an accident!"

Ah, Sonny thought, Madge is trying to disassociate the fiesta from the murder. Makes sense. Her job is to run the fiesta, and she's been doing it so well she's one of the most powerful women in the city. She can call the mayor's office direct, and the governor, and she's got the Chamber of Commerce eating from her hand. But today she's also got an *accident*.

"The press doesn't give a damn if Veronica was registered or not," Sonny said. "They're going to play it up as 'death at the fiesta!'"

"Yes," Madge said, "and that's the rub. But she went up alone, not from our field. The woman went up alone, ran into problems, and panicked. She fell."

"You've got the whole story, don't you."

"That's our statement to the press."

Protecting the fiesta, protecting the tourist dollar. Sooner or later it came around to money. It was the fiesta's first day, and *if* the balloonists and the thousands of tourists stayed away, or left early, the 20 or 30 million bucks they brought to the city went with them.

Sure accidents happen. A few years ago two men had been killed on the first day of the week-long festival. Their balloon hit power lines, but the next day the program continued. But that *was* an accident. If Veronica's death was murder, the board would be forced to close down the fiesta. And if the pilots and their families felt there was a murderer stalking the fiesta, they'd pack up and go home.

"It's going to cost us," Madge repeated. "I talked to the mayor. We're trying to smooth things out."

Sonny was studying her carefully. He knew that after high school Madge Swenson had married a California entrepreneur who was interested in New Mexican artists. The Santa Fé style was the rage in California, and there were buckets of money to be made. Madge and her husband, Bud Swenson, opened an art gallery in Santa Fé; they prospered, acquired an international clientele, and moved higher and higher. Those who came to their opening receptions began to expect lines of coke, as well as the usual champagne and caviar.

Even the "Californicated" upper crust of Santa Fé raised eyebrows when Bud Swenson threw one of his openings. They knew the coke flowed, the afternoons grew wild, and in the evenings all kinds of sexual combinations were available. And it was well known that Madge orchestrated the parties.

Then one day, so she told Sonny that afternoon at the Heights bar, she had stepped outside her million-dollar home in Santa Fé to enjoy the autumn morning. She was drinking coffee and trying to awaken in the primal light of the dawn when a red hawk landed on the adobe wall.

The epiphany of sunlight and a hawk told her the darker side of the Santa Fé lifestyle had gotten out of hand. She left Bud Swenson and landed a job directing the balloon fiesta.

She had learned to fly a hot-air balloon when she was running the Santa Fé gallery. She became enthralled by flying; it became part of the relaxation they offered the rich clients who came to stroll the Santa Fé plaza and buy art. But drinking champagne and screwing dumb, rich bozos a quarter-mile high lost its glamour. More and more she wanted to be alone in the silence of space; ballooning became her meditation.

That morning she drove downtown, filed for divorce, and walked away from Bud, the gallery, and everything it had come to represent.

She had already met and become acquainted with some of the early New Mexican balloonists, the Abruzos and Andersons of world fame, so during the last two years she had traveled to the major balloon events in the world. She and a few others had turned the Alburquerque fiesta from a local event into a multimillion-dollar business. She had created a power niche that she loved.

"You lost something, too," she said, "the Dubronsky case is washed, isn't it?"

Sonny nodded.

"Sorry," she said.

"El destino," Sonny said.

"Destiny?"

"Yeah," Sonny acknowledged. "This morning Veronica Worthy ran into someone who had a different idea about her fate."

"It wasn't murder," Madge said, arching an eyebrow and crossing her long legs. She leaned toward Sonny. A very seductive perfume touched Sonny's nostrils. Her blue eyes bore into him.

"It was," Sonny answered.

"By whom? Tamara Dubronsky? From that spa they've got her locked up in?"

Sonny shrugged. "Everything's possible."

"That's crazy," she said. "The woman is too smart."

"Yes," Sonny agreed.

"I need your help," she said, and took his hands in hers.

Here comes the hook, Sonny thought, feeling the soft coolness of her fingers, inhaling the sweet cologne.

"The fiesta can't afford this kind of publicity. Believe me, the press is going to milk it. The prime witness of the most interesting murder case in thirty years falls from a balloon. But the press will call it murder. It could ruin the fiesta, and it could plague us in the future. Work with me, Sonny. Clear this up. Discreetly."

Discreetly? Sonny thought. How in the hell do you "clear up" a murder discreetly? And what is there to "clear up" about an accident?

"There's nothing discreet about murder."

"It wasn't murder!" she said, pulling away. "It was an accident as far as the balloon fiesta board is concerned."

"I'm sure," Sonny said, noting the sarcasm in his voice. He had no good feelings for Veronica—she had tried to kill him—but she was human and she had been murdered. Now Madge Swenson and her people wanted to sweep the murder under the rug.

"Sonny, we're the biggest tourist moneymaker in the city. In ten days the fiesta drops thirty million in the city. We're known worldwide. A murder could spoil things."

"You can't cover up a murder," Sonny said, and got up.

She, too, rose. "I'm not asking you to cover up a murder. The community knows you. What you did in the Dubronsky case made you a hero. A Chicano detective, fighting for law and order, that's something. If you said this morning's tragedy was an accident, people would listen."

"Lie?" Sonny retorted. "You're asking me to lie?"

"Not lie!" Madge shouted back. "It's not proven it's murder! I talked to Garcia, he has no clues! I've talked to the mayor. Marisa doesn't want to ask you personally to help, but she understands our position!"

"Holy tamales." Sonny sighed. "Where else is the pressure coming from?"

"My board is meeting right now. Everyone wants an answer.

The major networks are going to splash it all over the evening news. CNN is already here. I get interviewed next."

She was in hot water, and she was asking for help. But it wasn't the kind of help Sonny could deliver.

"My board is prepared to pay very well."

"For me to say it was an accident?" Sonny shook his head. "Let the cops take care of it."

"And let the chips fall where they will." Madge frowned.

"That's the way it is with murder." Sonny nodded. "Thanks for the list. I'm sorry, I can't help."

"Can't blame a woman for asking. If you change your mind, call me. Call me anytime. You know where I live," she added, then briskly turned back to her desk.

She had tried to buy him, Sonny thought as he walked out to his truck. Damn the woman! He wanted to be angry, but no, he understood where she was coming from. The whole fucking city profited from the fiesta! You just didn't throw a money-maker like that away, not without turning every card you could find.

So Madge turned Sonny's card, and he was a wild deuce. He wouldn't make a statement for money. Madge was an aggressive woman. Now murder had clouded her empire, might even tumble it down. She was going to fight, fight with everything she had, including the see-me-anytime offer.

He drove home and sat in his kitchen and pored over the list of balloonists. It was a who's who of hot-air ballooning. Many countries were represented. There were balloon bums as well as royalty on the list. Tough competitors, first-year entrants, and the wannabes who thought that by mixing with the pros, some of the magic would rub off. There were people from the movies and high finance. And there were the middle-class pi-lots who mortgaged homes and cars and wives just to buy a balloon to fly in the early morning, because flying had gotten into their blood, because it became their religion, because they got their jollies floating up to greet the morning sun.

Sonny scrutinized the list, circling, making notes, marking

names. Three names he recognized from newspaper articles were the focus of Sonny's attention.

Mario Secco was from Italy. According to the last account Sonny had read, Secco distributed South American cocaine in Europe. Heroin from the Cali cartel flowed through his network into Libya, into Sicily, then into small ports along the Adriatic. During the recent bust of Cali directors, Secco had also been arrested, but in Italy the mafia had protected him. Secco was acquitted.

Secco took time off and went around the world flying hot-air balloon competitions, accompanied by an entourage of beautiful Italian women. Just yesterday the newspaper had reported that Mario and his friends had taken over an entire floor of La Posada downtown.

The second name that drew Sonny's attention was John Gilroy. He had an Alburquerque address, and Sonny immediately recognized the name. Gilroy was an ex-CIA agent who, using the alias Juan Libertad, had flown money and supplies to the Nicaraguan Contras. He had been shot down and captured by the Sandinistas, exposed to the world, then freed. He was contrite while in captivity, but once free, he told the press he and his right-wing gang at the CIA, code-named Libertad, were flying into Nicaragua to rid Latin America of communism, to help the freedom fighters.

He had received a medal from the Reagan White House and became a lecturer in ultraconservative, far-right circles. But he got too carried away. Iran-Contra was plaguing President Reagan, and "Juan Libertad" received a stern warning from his superiors. Get out of the limelight and keep quiet, or else. The publicity he was receiving had gone to his head, and he came close to admitting that the CIA was flying in arms and bringing out dope, which was either sold to buy more arms or to line the pockets of the agents.

Inside the CIA Libertad's job was to make sure the Contras beat the Sandinistas, if one believed the Washington rumor mill. And that revolution was to be only one in a long line that had begun with the fall of Allende in Chile. Libertad's directive from within the CIA was to foment revolution against any government perceived to be left-leaning in Latin America.

Their most recent activity was reported to be advising the Mexican commander of the federal troops going in to put down the Chiapas peasants. Commandante Marcos had immediately been branded a communist.

But Gilroy talked too much, and he was drummed out of the CIA. He retired to Alburquerque and took up ballooning. It was a nice hobby, but Sonny suspected his real purpose in life remained to expose the evils of communism in Latin America.

Dope, Sonny thought. On the way back from Central America, those who knew the Cali cartel network and everybody else involved in supplying the Contras stopped by Noriega's Panama and filled their planes with high-quality stuff. Fortunes were made, laundered through Swiss banks, and the junk piled high on the streets of this country. A finely tuned organization with enough money to buy government bureaucrats along the pipeline delivered the dope to America's doorstep. And the cops kept blaming the pusher on the street corner.

And finally, Sonny studied the name of Alisandra Bustamante-Smith, a journalist from Bogotá who had received worldwide attention when her husband was murdered by the cartel. Bustamante had written an exposé on the Cali cartel, believing the Colombian government when it said it was getting tough with the kings of the drug empire. The government had promised her and her family protection, but the day before she was to hand her story over to her editor, her husband was shot and killed as he was leaving for work.

The Colombian government not only couldn't protect her, but she had been fingered from the inside. She fled north with her young son. Staying in Colombia meant danger or death to her and her child. She wound up in a small college in Texas, teaching journalism. She swore she would never write again.

She became a kind of a cult figure, but she wanted nothing to do with the publicity. She remarried, a journalism professor who was into ballooning. She traveled with him but kept a low profile. She obviously wanted to forget the world that had taken so much from her.

There were others, Sonny noted. A lot of very interesting people had come to Alburquerque for the balloon fiesta.

Was Garcia running these names through his computer? Was Matt Paiz over at the FBI? There could be a battle taking shape in the skies over Alburquerque, and Veronica Worthy was just the first casualty.

Around six he took a break and turned on the evening news in time to catch the interview with Madge. She sounded confident, Sonny thought, as he watched Conroy Chino holding the mike in front of her.

". . . I'm at Fiesta Control with Madge Swenson, the director of the balloon fiesta. There's a big break in the investigation of the accident this morning. Miss Swenson, is it true you've found a witness?"

"Yes, a couple actually saw the accident," Madge responded, and Sonny leaped forward and turned up the volume. "Mr. and Mrs. Arthur Fiora from Corpus Cristi saw the woman fall. She was flying alone, and apparently reached for a loose drag line."

"Liar!" Sonny cursed.

The camera shifted to a nervous Arthur Fiora standing between Madge and his wife. "Yes," he stuttered. "Me and my wife saw the woman fall. She reached for a rope and fell. Just fell. It was an accident. I told the police everything."

His stolid wife nodded in agreement. "She just fell."

The phone rang. "Sonny, are you listening to the news?" It was Rita.

"I can't believe it!"

The phone signaled a call waiting. "Hold on," Sonny said, and pressed a button.

"Cover-up," Howard said.

Sonny groaned. "Do they think they can make it stick?"

"Sure they can." Howard sounded cynical.

Conroy Chino was wrapping up his scoop. "Was there anyone else in the balloon?" he asked.

"No, she was alone. My wife and I saw everything." Here he tugged at the stocky, tearful woman who stood beside him.

"It was an accident," she said, and wiped at her pink eyes.

Conroy turned to face the camera and wrap up the newscast. He had beaten Francine Hunter to the interview and had scored a big story, and he smiled. Behind him Madge Swenson also smiled and led the shaken Mr. and Mrs. Fiora away.

"I can't believe Madge would—"

"Cover it up?" Howard said. "She lives in the real world. There was a big meeting at city hall this afternoon. Apparently they cut a deal."

"They can't afford to lose the fiesta," Sonny added. Madge Swenson's very words.

"By the way, Tamara's back home. Anything I can do?"

"Keep your eyes open, compa."

"Don't take it personal, bro. That's the way the wheel is greased. When you're Black, you learn that early. Adiós."

"Yeah," Sonny said, and Howard's phone clicked dead.

"Rita, sorry, that was Howard on the other line."

"I can't believe they would cover up. What can you do?"

"Go hunting."

"Qué?"

"I'll explain later. Buenas noches, amor."

Sonny hung up the phone. He grabbed a light jacket on his way out. The October air was cool. Don Eliseo and his friends had put on sweaters. They had finished roasting the basket of green chile. In the warm afternoon they had been enjoying Toto's wine. Now Concha rose, stretched, and walked into the house, on her way to check the chile con carne she was cooking. The old friends would eat like kings—two kings and a queen.

Meanwhile, in the dark of the river bosque, shadows were moving. Coyotes hunting. Or humans.

Creatures of the night, Sonny thought as he drove down the dirt road that dead-ended at the edge of the bosque. The Montaño bridge would rise somewhere to the south of him, one more link bonding the West Mesa to the east side of the city. This dirt path led into the bosque. Ahead was the murder site.

Sonny fished a flashlight out of the glove compartment and thought briefly of taking the .45-caliber Colt that was his great-grandfather's pistol, but decided not to. With only the light in hand, he started down the sandy trail.

When he came to the site, he aimed his flashlight at the tree stump. The hair on the back of his neck bristled, and a sudden shot of adrenaline made his heart jump. There on the cottonwood spear lay the impaled body of Veronica. Sonny gasped. He pulled back with a start, then cursed himself. He flashed his light again and the body disappeared. Shadows playing tricks. He breathed a sigh of relief.

"I don't need another ghost," he whispered.

And yet he would have sworn he *had* seen Veronica's pierced body, her lifeless eyes staring at him, the cottonwood sliver stained with blood. He thought of the coroner's crew who must have lifted the heavy body from its impalement. Those men and women had to go home to families. They had to sit down to supper and eat. How could they erase the image from their minds?

He heard a sound and turned. Sonny ducked as an owl swooped overhead, flapping its large wings as it skimmed just over his head, then disappeared into the dark.

As he turned he saw, in his peripheral vision, a shadow moving where the trail entered the river forest. "Hey!" he called, and the shadow disappeared.

He entered the bosque, pursuing the shadow he had seen, wondering if he was following human or creature. When he paused to point the flashlight into the river forest, he was alone. He listened. The huge cottonwoods hung over him, a dark canopy. Surrounding the narrow path were Russian olives, river willows, and clumps of salt cedars. This was the haunted forest wherein la Llorona and el Coco lived, creatures from scary childhood stories.

A bird cried, and far away an owl responded. A cold breeze rustled through the trees, like skirts brushing a floor. The presence of la Llorona looking for her baby.

The breeze subsided and the weight of the dark silence made Sonny shiver.

"Damn, I'm a grown man," he said aloud, "not a kid."

As a child, he and his friends played along the sandbars of the river in the summer. Sometimes they played late into the evening, and darkness caught them far from home, far from the lights of the barrio. Then someone would cry "La Llorona!" and they would run, their fear a rush in the blood.

Sonny cocked his ear and sniffed the air to catch the scents of the dark bosque. Decay was in the air. A few gold and brown leaves had already fallen to the ground. In the next few weeks the cold nights and shorter days would turn the entire bosque yellow.

Wait! There was another scent in the air. Food. Somewhere a pot of beans was simmering. He smelled fresh coffee. Yes, he had been right.

He stood still, heard someone breathing, out there, just beyond the beam of the flashlight. His flesh crawled with goose bumps. The shadow ran and Sonny stumbled after it, entering a narrow path overhung with trees.

Branches whipped at his face, cut at his arms, and still he pursued the sound ahead of him. How strange, he thought, that he should be pursuing the creature in the dark instead of the other way around. If the shadow was the legendary Llorona, she should be chasing him.

The weak beam of his flashlight didn't reveal the trip wire on the path, and when Sonny hit it, a giant creature came swinging at him from a tree branch, knocking him over. Sonny cried out and struck back at the huge shape. The grotesque face of the creature that dangled from the tree groaned, then swung back. The long thin arms of the creature whipped at Sonny, flopping crazily.

Sonny leaped to his feet, his heart pounding. "Pinche mono," he cursed.

He leaned against a tree and pointed the light at the figure swinging from the tree. The misshapen head was white, its eyes a bright orange, its hair the bark of withered branches. It swung back and forth, toward Sonny then away.

Sonny pointed his light at the hanging effigy. Someone had placed the trip wire to release the large puppet guarding the path. Someone didn't want visitors, he thought as he wiped sweat from his forehead.

It had almost worked. When the dangling puppet jumped out at him, he had been thinking of la Llorona, and for a moment she had come alive. Whoever had planted the swinging figure had done a good job. The expression "scared shitless" came to mind.

"Admit it, Baca, you almost ran." He smiled. He poked the face of the giant puppet with his light. "Buenas noches, don

Coco. What are you doing out so late at night? You're ugly enough to terrorize the weakhearted."

He wondered if he should forge ahead. Maybe the next trap would be a swinging sword, something to lop off the head of those who didn't pay attention to Mr. Coco. He wasn't welcome; no one was welcome in this dark part of the bosque.

The silence was eerie.

He heard a rustle behind him, turned, and flashed the light at the shadow he had been chasing.

"Come out," Sonny said. "I'm not a cop."

There was a wait, then a voice said, "Go back, hermano. You're not welcome here."

"I want to talk, " Sonny answered, aiming the light slowly from tree to tree.

"There's nothing to talk about," the voice replied, this time farther to the right. Sonny turned but could see nothing.

"A woman was killed near here today, that's something to talk about," Sonny insisted.

There was a silence, and then the voice again. "What difference does it make?"

Yeah, Sonny thought, what difference does it make? Veronica was a murderer, and justice had been served.

"It matters," Sonny answered.

Another long silence, then the voice said, "Turn off the light."

Sonny turned off his flashlight. The dark under the cottonwood branches was almost complete. Somewhere down the path, in the darkness, he thought he saw the glow of a fire. He waited. Whoever it was moved, circling Sonny, moving closer, until he stood before Sonny.

"Why does it matter?" the man asked.

Sonny peered into the dark. He realized the man he was talking to must be one of the homeless people who lived along the river bottom. Up and down the river bosque, they constructed huts of old boards, tin scraps, and cardboard. They went into the city only for food, returning to live all summer in the brush, away from the society that shunned them. It was October, and most had already moved to the shelters downtown. Some had begun to move to Arizona and southern California for the winter. A few stayed put, making the cottonwood forest their home even through the winter.

"Anyone dies, we should care," Sonny answered.

"The poor die every day, hermano, and no one cares," the man replied.

He was right. More and more homeless were pushed to the edges of society, stripped of their dignity, made refugees. They became shadows in the streets of the city, the living dead everyone pretended not to see. The homeless died every day, and nobody gave a damn.

"Who are you?" Sonny asked, anxious to turn on the light and see the face of the man, but knowing that would spook him.

"Diego," the man answered. "Y tú?"

"Sonny Baca," Sonny answered, and held out his hand in the darkness. He felt Diego take his hand. His eyes were getting accustomed to the darkness; he could see the man.

"Sonny Baca," Diego pondered. "Not the vato who was in the news?"

"I'm a private investigator," Sonny answered.

"Chingao. I should have known, carnal. Only someone like you would come in here."

There was a pause. Sonny felt the man's uneasiness. They didn't want to be found out, and he had found them.

"Bueno," he finally said. "Come meet my familia."

Sonny followed him down the winding path of the bosque until they came to a clearing where a small, protected campfire glowed. They didn't want it spotted by the cops; they didn't want to be harassed. Around the campfire the figures of three men and one woman waited.

"We heard you shout," one of the men said, and stepped forward.

"I found a man not afraid of el Coco," Diego replied as they walked into the light of the fire.

The men looked searchingly at Sonny. Someone coming this late into the camp usually meant no good.

"This is Sonny Baca," Diego said. "The detective who was in

the paper this summer." Diego introduced him. "We keep up with the news, hermano. This is my wife, Marta. Our daughter Cristina is sleeping in the tent."

Marta shyly held out her hand. "We have coffee," she said.

Sonny shook her hand and thanked her.

"Here's the other compas," Diego said. "Peewee. He used to be big in computers in the Silicon Valley. He's a Reagan trickle-down statistic. Got laid off and found it's hard to get a new job at fifty. He didn't have any CDs to cash in, so to make a long story short, he's homeless."

"Sonny Baca, gee, it's a pleasure to meet you. Diego read the news stories on the case you were involved in this summer. Wouldn't let us rest until he read every last news item," Peewee greeted Sonny. "And I *do* have a home," he corrected Diego.

Diego slapped him on the back and said, "Yes. This is home. This is Busboy," Diego introduced the young man of the group. "High school dropout, no skills, so he washes dishes when he can."

Busboy smiled and shook Sonny's hand.

"And this is Peter," Diego said of the older, dignified man who stood by the fire. "He's a news addict. Listens to the evening news, then tells us what's going on in the world. We have to listen, we're his disciples."

Peter took Sonny's hand warmly. "Any friend of Diego's is a friend of ours. Sit, please. We have only an old box to offer you, but among friends it is a chair fit for a king. And Marta's coffee is fit for the gods."

He drew a box for Sonny, and Marta handed him the cup she had poured from the coffeepot on the coals.

"What brings you to our humble abode?" Peter asked.

"He wants to know about the woman," Diego said, and the others looked at each other nervously.

"How did you know about us?" Peter asked.

"I followed a hunch," Sonny replied, not explaining he had sensed them in the bosque. He knew the homeless had camps along the bosque, and when he saw the shadows in the brush, he guessed one of the groups had reported Veronica's death.

"We don't want anything to do with the cops," Diego said. "They find out and they'll come down and kick us out. Then we have no place to go. We're settled here; we just don't want anything to do with the cops."

The others nodded.

"I know," Sonny said, "but there's been a murder. If you saw it, you are involved."

He sat and told them about the woman who had been killed that morning and about her role in Gloria Dominic's murder.

"We're sorry about that," Peter spoke when Sonny was done, "but we just don't want to be involved. We were once. I worked in television in southern California. I had a good career. But—" He paused. "Let's just say that those with power over me didn't like what I was digging into. I planned a show on the murder of Rubén Salazar."

"The Chicano reporter killed at the Silver Dollar Café twenty-five years ago," Diego said. "During the Vietnam Moratorium march in East Los. They murdered him."

Peter nodded. "It appears so. He was covering the Chicano movimiento for the *LA Times*. Anyway, those in power don't want Chicanos to realize they have muscle in numbers. Salazar was being followed by LA County sheriff's deputies. They *knew* he was in the Silver Dollar. He was fingered by a Cuban agent. Or a Colombian."

"Drugs involved?" Sonny asked. He knew the Salazar story, how the murder had been swept under. He had a friend, Ricardo, in LA who had produced a play around the tragic events of Salazar's death. He had dug up a lot of dirt, and for that the county sheriff had made life tough on him.

"From Colombia to LA, a direct line. Salazar was about to crack the story. They killed him. I was about to expose what I had learned when I got fired and blacklisted."

He paused. All grew silent.

Sonny sighed and sipped his coffee. That's how it was. The organizations dealing in dope could silence anyone.

He looked at the group huddled around the fire. *Anyone* could be silenced, and he didn't want to bring danger into their lives.

He also knew whatever he said wouldn't make the reality of their lives vanish. Living in the cardboard boxes, scrounging food, working odd jobs, and like Diego and Marta, raising a child to whom they could promise no future—it wasn't easy.

"You don't have to tell the cops, tell me," Sonny said.

"And you won't tell the cops?" Diego asked. He stared at Sonny across the bright glow of the campfire.

Sonny shook his head. "I can't promise." He knew that somewhere along the line he might have to tell Garcia.

"Pués, hay 'stá," Diego slapped his knee. "What we say tonight can be in the papers tomorrow." He looked at Busboy. "What do you say, hijo?"

Busboy squirmed. A young man of nineteen or twenty, he scratched the stubble on his cheek and spoke.

"I don't know. I wish I had never seen the black balloon. I knew it wasn't good. But I got in trouble with gangs at school for saying what I knew was true. The worse thing to be is a snitch."

"What school did you attend?" Sonny asked.

"Río Grande."

"I graduated from Río," Sonny said.

"Yeah?" Busboy said. He was impressed. Here was someone who did something exciting for a living, and they had gone to the same school. "I dropped out," he said sadly. "Had to help my family, and I never was good at reading. I could get jobs in fast-food places, but I could never work my way out of those."

Yeah, Sonny knew.

"But we know the truth shall make us free," Peter said, and stood. "There are some events we don't create in life. They come to us and force us to confront ourselves." He looked around at his friends. "I think we have to tell Sonny what we know."

Diego turned to his wife. She had remained silent. Perhaps of the group, she suffered most. She was a woman who could not offer her child the security of a real home. She could not buy her dolls, or a piece of candy, or a notebook and crayons on the first day of school. The men struggled against the world, and she against the future and the deep pain within. It weighed on her every breathing moment.

She looked at her husband. "Always you tell me, Diego, that we must not be afraid. We are free people. We have so little, but we are free. Others may be afraid of losing what they have, but we have only our dignity to lose. We must not be afraid."

Diego smiled at her. He looked at his friends and nodded. "Okay, Sonny, we'll tell you what we know." He looked at the others and they nodded.

Diego poured himself a cup of coffee and sat on a crate across from Sonny. The light from the glowing embers cast serious shadows on his face.

"We were on our way to the Christian home near the church. Going for winter coats. We saw the balloons on the other side of the river and stopped to watch. But one black balloon came directly over the trees on this side. It seemed to come up from the river. It was low enough for us to see the man and woman in it. When it cleared the trees, we saw the man strike the woman. Then he pushed her over."

"It was murder, plain and cold," Peter added.

"The woman fell and we ran to her. She was dead. You saw how she died."

Sonny nodded. "Did you get a look at the man?"

"He looked over the edge of the gondola, so we got a good look. He was young, maybe your age. Dark hair."

"Long hair, like in a ponytail," Busboy said.

"One side of his face looked like it was burned," Diego said.

"Burned?"

"Yeah, like one side was deformed."

"Did he see you?" Sonny asked.

"That's why we're afraid," Peter said. "He saw us run toward the woman."

Yes, Sonny thought, they had reason to be afraid. They were witnesses, and Raven didn't like to leave witnesses. The effigy figure with which they blocked the path would not keep him away.

When Sonny returned home, it was after midnight. He had told his new friends Raven's story. They had to know what they might be getting into. Raven had murdered Veronica, and Diego's family had witnessed it. Sonny realized they were in danger.

But why would Raven try to save Tamara from her day in court? Didn't he realize Tamara wouldn't touch him with a ten-foot pole after the aborted WIPP fiasco in June? She was a survivor, and she would do anything to save herself. Maybe Tamara had Gloria's money. Raven needed the money to get out of the country, or maybe, just maybe, he was crazy enough to plan a second attack on WIPP.

Had Tamara arranged for Raven to bail out Veronica and waste her? Ah, Sonny thought, as much as I dread it, sooner or later I have to talk to her.

As he opened the door to his house, Sonny felt the strain of the day's tension in his shoulders. The ceremony with Lorenza Villa had created an inner peace he had not felt in a long time. The journey through Gloria's body, the tunnel to the underworld, had been frightening, but the meadow and the coyotes had been uplifting, filling him with energy. But all that had dissipated.

Maybe in a world of violence it was impossible to retain an inner harmony. He learned from don Eliseo and Rita, and now from Lorenza, that keeping the soul in harmony was a constant struggle. The soul was fragile, it could be fragmented, any trauma or shock could weaken it. Other souls could invade or cling to it, as Gloria's soul had invaded his.

The curandera cleansed away those spirits or energies that became attached to the soul; the shaman could fly in search of the lost soul.

"Damn, how did I get mixed up in this again?" Sonny mumbled, then hesitated as he put his key to the doorknob. He slowly drew back. His sixth sense warned him someone was in the house or had just been here.

Don Eliseo, he thought. The old man came to check on me. No, it was someone else. Sonny thought back to the night in June when he and Rita arrived at her home to find the goat's testicles nailed to Rita's porch. It was the first warning from the Zia cult. Now a sensation along the back of his neck felt as it had that night.

He turned, checked the dirt road for strange vehicles, but no, only the neighbors' cars and trucks rested under the cold October moonlight. All was quiet on La Paz Lane. Across the street even don Eliseo's house was dark. The old man was already asleep.

Sonny shivered in the cool night air, then whistling softly "Hey, Baby, Qué Pasó," he returned to his truck and took his pistol from the glove compartment. The old single-action Colt. Tonight he was going to be armed.

He entered the front room slowly and flipped on the lights. Everything was in place, but he was sure he felt someone's presence. He walked into the kitchen, turned on the light, and again found everything in place, but he still felt the tingling sensation that danger was near.

He thought of checking his bedroom, then shrugged. "Chingao, I'm getting paranoid. Too much talk about ghosts."

He placed the pistol on the kitchen counter and reached into the cabinet where he kept a bottle. As he poured himself a shot of bourbon, he felt the gold medallion beneath his shirt. He felt a strange power from it, a feeling of invincibility. As long as he wore the medallion, he felt safe. He had worn it all summer.

It was a valuable and unique piece of gold, he rationalized, and he had to keep it safe. Besides, it really wasn't his. It was state's evidence—or it used to be state's evidence. Now there would be no trial. Maybe, as Tamara had said, it really did belong to him.

"Pués, here's to Raven." He chuckled, and downed the drink. He winced at the burning, coughed, remembered the afternoon Tamara invited him to her bedroom, the sanctuary of the goddess of love, the Zia cult queen. She served wine spiked with peyote buttons so the journey into her past lives would be heightened. Señor Peyote, that brujo who lived in the plant, would help transport her into her past lives. So would sex. The orgasm, she had told Sonny, was her channel into past lives, and therefore a twisted sort of immortality.

But Sonny said no. He got as far as the door to her bedroom and turned back.

"You are so old-fashioned," she teased him. "Keep your woman, I don't mind. Come and see me when you want. We are old souls, darling, we belong together. You do not understand how deep my love is for you. Go for now, darling. We will meet again. Our love cannot be denied. I am always near you."

After all the years, she still affected a foreign accent. Russian, Polish, Gypsy—no one knew. She could turn it on, like she could turn on the charm and get people with big bucks to contribute to the city symphony, her pet project as an Albuquerque socialite.

She had raised money for Raven to carry on his crazy plans to stop the WIPP project, but why?

You and Raven are old souls, she had said. Two old souls she was destined to love in the cycles of time. Her karma.

Yes. Sonny smiled and poured himself a second shot. She really did love him, and her soul hovered over him, watching, waiting.

What if Raven was right? The disarming of the nuclear weapons from the Cold War was producing piles of plutonium cores, and the DOE wanted to bury them at the WIPP site at Carlsbad. Or store it at Kirtland Air Force Base. That's why the base had been spared from closure, because the cores from Pantex were going to be stored in the Manzano Mountains. Ten miles from downtown 'Burque! The city was to become the dump for all the nuclear waste in the world.

"Qué chinga!" Sonny cursed and stiffened as he looked at the reflection in the kitchen window.

For a moment the image of Veronica Worthy appeared on the window. He rubbed his eyes, the image shifted. He saw Tamara Dubronsky, a beckoning Tamara, whispering his name, calling to him.

"Come to me," she said seductively. "You are the new Raven."

Then the image of a man in black appeared, momentarily reflected in the window. Sonny jumped aside, and the bat the assailant swung crashed down on the kitchen cabinet. As he went down, Sonny reached for his pistol, hit the floor, and spun. The man in black struck again. The bat smashed on the floor, barely missing Sonny's head. Sonny raised the pistol but a kick sent it flying, and the assailant came down on him.

The man was strong, hooded in black so Sonny couldn't see his face. They rolled on the floor of the small kitchen, grunting and thrashing, until Sonny was able to land a solid punch and reach again for the pistol.

Then a second person appeared, and a boot clamped over Sonny's hand.

"Raven!" Sonny gasped, at the same time he felt the hooded

man hit him hard on the face, then the undulating waves of darkness. The man held him while Raven loomed over him.

"Where's the medallion?" Raven's voice was harsh. "Where is it?"

He had picked up the pistol and now held it to Sonny's forehead.

Through the grogginess from the blow, Sonny heard the words. The fragrance of vanilla touched his nostrils. He groaned, tried to rise, and felt the cold muzzle of the pistol on his forehead.

"Don't know—"

Raven cursed. "Game's over!"

Sonny heard the sharp click of the hammer, the cold metal of the nuzzle vibrated against his forehead, and he felt his bladder go weak.

But the explosion that should have come after the click didn't follow; his brains weren't blown from his head. As his father had taught him, Sonny had put the hammer on an empty chamber, a safety position on the pistol, and just then the old rule of the West had saved his life.

Sonny felt everything winding down to slow motion as he looked up into Raven's face. The entire left side was pink and scarred, a raw slash that had healed by itself, without the attention of a doctor. When Raven fell in the arroyo, the water must have scraped his face along the gravel bottom, against stones and debris, cutting chunks of flesh away. A large scar ran from his forehead down his left eye, making the eye droop, disfiguring the entire side of his face.

Raven cursed and cocked the pistol, but before he could fire again a roar filled the small kitchen, like thunder during a summer rainstorm, and plaster came crashing down around Raven and his partner.

Sonny felt his body relax and fall away into darkness; he was dying. He was rising in a gold balloon, the basket in the shape of an ojo de Dios, like the God's eye at Tamara's. Below him he could see people waving good-bye. Rita, his mother, Madge Swenson, don Eliseo and his friends.

He heard a thunderous voice in the void. It was the ghost of his great-grandfather, el Bisabuelo, Elfego Baca himself, the famed lawman from Socorro County now gazing down at Sonny and scowling. "You fucked up again, Sonny," the old man said.

Then he shouted: "Drop it!"

The pistol clattered to the floor.

Sonny groaned, saw the shadows of Raven and his friend disappearing. El Bisabuelo had come from cowboy purgatory to rescue his wayward grandson.

"Thanks, Grandpa," Sonny groaned, looking up at the figure of the famed lawman standing with his shotgun cradled in one arm. Plaster sprinkled down from the ceiling and covered him with white chalk and pieces of debris.

"I'm not your grandpa," don Eliseo said, and knelt beside him. "You okay?" He raised Sonny's head.

"Okay." Sonny smiled. "Ears ringing . . . ."

"Sonny," don Eliseo repeated. "Count my fingers." He held up five earth-worn stumps.

"Can't count. I'm dead," Sonny moaned.

"No, hijo," don Eliseo's strong voice replied. "Not dead."

Sonny's eyes fluttered. "Not dead?"

"No."

"Qué pasó?" he asked, opening his eyes.

"Those two tried to kill you. I took a shot at them."

Don Eliseo had arrived in time, with his vintage shotgun. There was a round hole in the ceiling above him. That was the blast he heard.

"Where do you live?" Don Eliseo asked.

" 'Burque."

"What state?"

"Nuevo México."

"You're going to be all right," the old man said.

"That was close," Sonny said.

"Very close," don Eliseo agreed.

"Gracias."

"De nada. What are neighbors for?"

He helped Sonny to his feet, propped him in a chair, wrapped ice in a towel and put it on his chin where he had taken the blow. He fixed some strong coffee and Sonny drank. When the waves of vertigo passed away, they talked.

"Wanna go to the hospital?"

Sonny shook his head.

"A doctor should see that. Maybe you got broken bones."

"No, I'm okay," Sonny groaned, and rubbed the cold ice pack on his neck.

"Okay," don Eliseo replied, "but let me feel the bumps while they're warm."

He felt softly and surely along the edge of the bruises, his rough farmer's hands like the hands of a healer as they searched for broken bones. Sonny winced but sat still. The old man knew what he was doing. He always did.

"No cracks. You have a hard head," the old man said.

"I get it from the Bacas," Sonny replied.

"And from your mamá?"

"My good looks." Sonny smiled, holding the ice pack to his neck, feeling the pain of the blow.

"The brain is a wonder," don Eliseo said as he worked, "like the soul. A light burns inside."

"Life," Sonny whispered.

They hadn't cracked his skull. There where the occipital and the temporal bones of the skull came together was the fontanelle. The mollera, his mother called it in Spanish; the most fragile of spots.

When you were a baby, before I put you in the tub to bathe you, I splashed water on your mollera. When you go swimming, first wet the top of your head, she had told him.

Why? Sonny asked.

It's just a custom, she replied.

For don Eliseo, there at the top of the head, the light streamed in, like a tree receiving light and passing it down the trunk back to the earth. Touching the water to the head before diving in was to equalize the temperature, so the soul would not be shocked. It all made sense. Each little particle of folk wisdom made sense.

When the old man finished his examination and pronounced there were no broken bones, Sonny spoke: "Remember the story you told me this summer? About el hombre dorado? The man who came looking for the fountain of youth in the Río Grande valley?"

"Yes," don Eliseo said. "The evil brujos stole his soul. Then they covered him with a coat of gold. The hombre dorado is a man without a soul."

"Why the fountain of youth?"

"To live forever," the old man answered. "To be like God. Those who have sought the fountain of youth think they can fill up their canteens and take it home. Look at it this way, Sonny. Suppose I got here too late. Those two were going to kill you. But if you have that water from the fountain of youth, death cannot touch you."

"Raven plays games," Sonny groaned.

"Yes. Always remember that. He plays games. You two have been playing games for a long time. . . ." His voice trailed.

Sonny didn't ask don Eliseo what he meant. Right now he was just glad he was alive.

"Alive for the next game," Sonny whispered. Then to the old man, "Gracias, don Eliseo. You saved my life. Again." He was grateful for his old friend. No need to call Rita and worry her now; he would tell her in the morning.

"Ah, it's nothing," the old man replied, snapped open his shotgun and took out the spent shell.

"You only had one shell?" Sonny asked.

The old man smiled. "They didn't know that."

"Chingao." Sonny grinned in surprise. The old man had huevos. He had threatened Raven and his murdering friend with a second shot when he had no second bullet.

"And you?" don Eliseo asked, and handed Sonny his pistol.

Sonny popped the chamber out. Five bullets. The second shot would have killed him. Best carry it empty, he thought, and removed the five cartridges and set them on the table.

"Close," don Eliseo said.

"I know." Sonny nodded, looking down at his pants to see if he had wet them. "How did you—"

"I know the sound of your truck, hijo. I didn't hear them, but when I looked out the window and saw you going in the house with your pistol—'Pues, that's not good,' I said to myself. So I took down my old shotgun and came real quiet."

He looked at Sonny. The brujo Raven had returned for his revenge. This they both knew.

"Got here just in time."

"For sure."

"Ah, that brujo Raven is playing tricks. He knows he can't kill you."

Sonny was puzzled. "What do you mean?"

"He can't kill you with a pistol. No, what he wants to kill is your soul, your alma. That's why he wants the sign of the sun on the medal you carry. To use its power against you. Bueno, get some rest. See you mañana." He patted Sonny's shoulder, walked out, saying, "I'll get some plaster tomorrow, and me and Toto will patch your ceiling. Buenas noches."

"Buenas noches," Sonny called as the figure of the old man disappeared in the dark.

Sonny grabbed the bourbon bottle, crept into the front room where he fell into the well-worn easy chair and drank.

Lordy, Lordy, he had almost bought the rancho. But what the hell did don Eliseo mean when he said Raven couldn't kill him with a pistol. You could kill anyone with a well-placed bullet. Except a brujo.

"Me?" Sonny thought. He smiled. Yeah, if I keep running with the coyotes. He had learned something today—no, not just the goof he had made in not checking the house carefully. He knew that snafu could have cost him his life. He had learned something about the world of spirits, that world of the soul where Lorenza had taken him.

He tried to sleep, but he dozed in fits. Disturbing visions floated around him.

The figure of Death, la Muerte, the skeleton that the penitentes of northern New Mexico kept in the moradas, the old woman with bow and arrow who came in a creaking cart. Her carreta was pulled by the souls of Nuevo Mexicanos who had died. A lot of weary souls pulling the cart of death around the back roads of adobe villages, onto the new interstate highways, everywhere.

In the cart sat doña Sebastiana, la Huesuda as she was called by the village pícaros whose custom it was to poke fun at death, not fear it. She was a skeletal, grinning old lady, drawing her bow and aiming the arrows of death.

She aimed at Sonny, and the arrow struck him in the chest, where it would split the sternum so the cavity opened. But the arrow drew no soul. Doña Sebastiana gritted her teeth, squinted. I missed! I never miss!

She strung a second arrow.

During all the centuries doña Sebastiana had been claiming the souls of the Nuevo Mexicanos, she had never missed.

She placed a second arrow on her bow, aimed and let it fly. This time she was sure she pierced Sonny's heart, but he did not fall. She cursed again, her bones rattled and ached. Maybe she was getting old. She was hungry for the soul of this man.

Cabrón! she cursed. You cannot defy me!

She fired again, and again he did not die. She drew close and looked. The gold medallion had kept her arrows from penetrating.

Un brujo! she gasped, and drew back. Un brujo poderoso!

She had met the man who could not die. Quickly she turned her cart away, cracking her whip over the heads of those souls who pulled the creaking carreta, moving away in fury.

Sonny awakened with a start. Outside he could hear the creaking of doña Sebastiana's cart. He listened. No, it was the sound of branches scratching the wall. An October wind had risen in the night, sweeping cold air down from the north.

Where is my soul? Sonny groaned.

"Tamara!" he cursed, and sat up straight. He pulled the medallion from under his shirt and looked at it. For this he had almost lost his life! And she had put it on him, persuaded him to wear it! Called him the new Raven!

What if he had given it to Raven? Would that have satisfied him?

You are the new Raven, Tamara's seductive voice crooned. So clear he felt she was in the room.

Come to me, her voice beckoned.

Doña Sebastiana, Tamara, la Llorona! Seductive voices calling in the October night!

He grabbed the phone and dialed Tamara's number. Howard had said she had returned to her home on Río Grande Boulevard. She no longer needed to hang out in the expensive convalescent spa in the Santa Fé hills, cooling her heels while she waited for the trial. Or plotted so there would be no trial.

Sonny glanced at his watch: 2:00 A.M.

"Sonny," she answered before he could say hello, pronouncing his name Sun-neee. "Darling, I was just thinking of you," she said. "I just heard the news. It is terrible. Terrible. I know you want to see me. Come. Please come."

9

He washed his bruised and tender face, put on a clean sweatshirt and his warm leather jacket, poured himself a cup of cold coffee, and drove across Ranchitos Road to Río Grande Boulevard.

When she answered his call, he had stifled the impulse to ask her how in the hell she knew it was him calling at that ungodly hour. That was her style, to put one on the defensive, to keep one guessing.

He had said, "Raven's back," and listened to her soft laughter.

"But of course, darling. We knew he would return, didn't we? Chief Garcia called me about Veronica. It was a tragic accident. But all is forgiven."

Forgiven? Sonny thought. She's forgiving people! She was free, the DA had no case, so maybe she was in the mood for forgiving.

"Sonny. Please come. It would be so good to see you. I cannot sleep, the tragic news has upset me. I must see you."

He had last seen Tamara early in the morning of June 22, when he went to tell her Raven had been swept away in the arroyo.

Now Tamara is once again a free woman, Sonny thought as he drove up the driveway to park in front of the huge, rambling mansion set against the river bosque, away from the street.

The place was spooky. There were a few old Art Deco buildings in the city, but most of the North Valley residents preferred the ranch homes or the new adobes. But Tamara had inherited a real mansion, and Sonny thought it qualified as gothic—especially in the October night with a cold breeze whispering through the huge elms and cottonwoods that surrounded the place.

An owl called from the bosque, and the yelp of a coyote followed, mixing with the autumn rustle of the wind in the trees.

Yup, Sonny thought, it's definitely the season of la Llorona.

Sonny rang and Tamara opened the door.

"Sonny, I'm delighted to see you. Come in." She took his hand and drew him into the large foyer. Old Navajo blankets hung on the walls, a large Chimayo rug gave warmth to the brick floor. She closed the door and looked at Sonny. Her green eyes sparkled, a smile played on her lips.

She hadn't changed. She wore the same purple polish on her long nails, the same hint of lilac fragrance on her body. She was dressed in a gold satin gown that clung to the curves of her lithe body.

Holding both his hands, she allowed him to kiss both cheeks, a European protocol everyone followed with Tamara.

"I am happy to see you," she whispered. "I just today returned from Santa Fe, and I was sitting here thinking you would call. What a pleasant coincidence."

She led him into the large living area. A fire danced brightly in the huge fireplace, candles glowed around the room, no lights.

"Please sit." She pointed at the large divan. "Make yourself comfortable. There is so much to talk about. I was having wine. Join me."

She poured and offered him the goblet and lightly touched her drink to his.

"To us." She smiled, then sat next to him.

"You knew I'd call."

"Of course. You are a wayfarer cast into the night, and I am your Llorona. You are the man I seek."

Sonny put his glass aside. "They say la Llorona kills the boys she finds in the night."

"Darling, don't believe those bad things that men say about the crying woman. Men will tell you they've seen her, and she chases them. It is their guilt that forces them to see la Llorona on a dark night."

"Guilt?"

"Of course. Our lovely wailing woman is not interested in guilt-ridden men. She is a goddess of love, and she is interested in young men, young souls."

"I haven't heard this version," Sonny said.

"Well, doesn't everyone have a version of this woman of the night, woman of the river? I think she takes the boys she finds home with her. To her lair in the dark bosque."

Sonny raised an eyebrow.

"Of course. All goddesses need acolytes, votaries who become the priests of their religion."

"And what is their religion?"

"The goddess has but one religion, and that is one of procreation. But before the messy job of giving birth to men, there is the pleasure of sex. La Llorona takes boys to her grotto to initiate them into the art of love. You see, when it comes to the art of love, men are brutes. Oh, not men like you." She reached to touch his hand. "Most men. You are one of the few la Llorona would choose to initiate."

"Why?" Sonny asked, playing along.

"You are special," she replied. "You are the kind of man la Llorona takes to her love bower. You enjoy the pleasure of sex, you enjoy women. Most important, you respect the power in women. And what is that power? It's the energy of passion, the lust that is the energy of creation. To enter the woman is to know this."

Sonny smiled. He thought of Rita, the woman he loved and the immense satisfaction he received from her love. He thought of the power and secrets of Lorenza, the curandera who had guided him into the world of spirits. Of his mother, who after his father died had become strong and raised him and his brother. Women warriors.

"Yes, you admire and understand women," Tamara continued. "You know we are the mystery, the key to the universe. You seek that in women, and they respond. They are willing to share their secrets with you. I am willing to share my secrets."

She sipped her wine and looked at Sonny, her green eyes glittering with the soft light of the fireplace.

She had offered herself once before. Got him as far as the bedroom door. In the middle of the room sat the large round bed covered with silk sheets. A white-veiled canopy over it. It was the tent of a desert princess, a woman who knew the art of seduction. Soft sheepskins rich with lanolin, and the furry skins of white goats, lay on the floor, sensual and soft to the touch of bare feet.

A kiva fireplace decorated one corner. Tonight that fireplace probably had a fire in it, cedar logs burning, popping, emitting their sweet fragrance.

From the round bed radiated the four lines of gold tiles. The Zia sun symbol. One path led to the fireplace; the opposite tiles led to the altar, a dry piñon tree with polished branches reaching up to the high ceiling supported by old, weathered pine vigas. The branches of the piñon were decorated with small ojos de Dios, simple adornments of colored wool in diamond shapes.

Next to the piñon lay thin cottonwood branches for making the cross. At the center of the ojo de Dios was the cross. The wool threads were wrapped around the cross.

"A good way to enter visions," Tamara had explained. "These

decorations the natives call the eye of God are really the eye of Ra, the sun god. As I weave, I chant and enter the eye of Ra. I enter the realm of the sun, and the visions come. You, too, can journey into the ancient realms of the sun king. Let me take you on a journey."

Sonny had hesitated. The journey meant going to bed with Tamara.

The eye of God saw everything, or so he had been taught by his mother. His mother had tried to make a good Catholic out of him. The diagonal design of the ojo was a mandala, a labyrinth that led to the center, the eye of God. For Tamara the sun god was the Egyptian Ra.

"I take pleasure in you, and you in me, and in those moments of ecstasy, we enter the past lives of our youth."

She promised him a vision of eternity, eternal youth wrapped up in the orgasms of her flesh. That's why she sought a view into her past lives. Did the desire for illumination, like the hombre dorado's desire for eternal youth, lead one into a Faustian deal, selling one's soul in order to live forever?

The third line from Tamara's bed of love radiated to a stained-glass window on the south wall. During the winter solstice when the southern sun was low in the horizon, the window would be alive with color. The thick, stained pieces of glass created another mandala, another variation of the ojo de Dios, or the Zia sun. In the center of the four-leafed design nestled the round, golden sun.

The fourth line led through an open door to the large sunken tub where, Sonny guessed, the preparations for the lovemaking began.

She drew closer to Sonny. "Why so deep in thought?"

"I was thinking of your interpretation of la Llorona."

"It makes sense, doesn't it?"

"Yes." He had to agree that it did. Why couldn't la Llorona be a facet of the Earth Goddess, and her need be one of procreation? For that she needed the males she sought along dark alleys, along country acequias, under bridges spanning arroyos and muddy streams.

"Raven came to see me," he said, to change the subject.

"I should have warned you," she said, and reached out and touched the bruise on his forehead. "But you must have known he would return."

"To get me?"

"You must understand that the Raven who has returned is not the Raven we knew."

"What do you mean?"

"He's hurt. Not just physically, but his soul is not well. He is mad with revenge."

"He tried to kill me."

"Raven cannot harm you. As long as you wear the Zia medallion, he cannot harm you," she said. She drew closer and kissed him softly. The warmth and pressure of her body aroused him. He pulled back.

"I told you many times, you are one of us. You are an old soul who has lived many lives," she whispered, touching his cheek, her fingers like fire. "You have as much power as Raven, if only you could see within."

Sonny took the medallion from around his neck and handed it to her. "I don't need it to take care of Raven."

"Oh, but you do," she said tersely, pushing the offered medallion away from her. "Don't you understand? You stand in Raven's way."

"What do you mean?" Sonny asked. "The cops are looking for him, I'm not."

"He's not afraid of the police. They can't stop him—" She stopped short and wrung her hands. "Raven is extremely dangerous. When you interrupted his plot on the summer solstice, you ruined a cycle of time. He recognized you as an old enemy."

"Old enemy?" Sonny asked.

"Oh, Sonny, if you could only see, only believe that we are old souls, struggling through the cycles of time, caught in an eternal battle from which there is no rest. If you understood this, you would understand my love. I will do anything for you."

Her voice rang with emotion, and with what, Sonny understood, was a true expression of her love.

"I love you," she said. "I really do. And I will do anything in
my power to keep you safe. But I cannot enter Raven's world."

"The world of spirits," Sonny said.

She nodded. "But you will. In the meantime the medallion is
your only protection."

She took the medal and placed it around his neck. Sonny
knew something had gone wrong between her and Raven. He
was out to get her, too.

"He threatened you?"

"He called. You see, I, too, stand in his way."

Sonny didn't know whether to believe her or not. This summer they had been cohorts, now Raven was a threatening madman.

"If you know where he is, tell me."

She hesitated. "I don't know. He moves around, calls from
different places. Sometimes he mocks me. I am afraid of him."

Sonny raised an eyebrow. The Zia queen afraid of Raven?

"You find it hard to believe, I know. I'm supposed to be the
psychic, the strange woman who reads the past and the future,
and you think I had something to do with Gloria's death. Ah,
well, what matters now is that I want to help you."

She leaned to kiss him.

"I want you," she whispered in his ear, her voice soft, com-
pelling, her aroma sweet.

The energy he had felt from Lorenza's cure was gone. His
head throbbed. Raven had nearly killed him, and Raven would
strike again. He could cure his illness by stepping into the bath
for the tired warrior, by letting Tamara minister to his lethargy.
He could return to the arms of la Llorona, that childhood creature that often haunted his path when he ran home late at
night. He could be the new Raven.

Why not? he thought. Perhaps Tamara *was* the answer, a way
to get his juices flowing again, to find the energy that had left
him the day he saw Gloria's dead body stretched on the bed.

"It would be so easy," he said.

"Yes." Tamara nodded, fingering the medallion on his chest. "I understand the man you are and what you need."

Sonny pulled himself away.

"Why?" she questioned.

"Maybe I'm old-fashioned." He shrugged.

"Or afraid," she suggested, rising.

He smiled. She really knew what he was thinking. Yes, he had admitted to himself, perhaps he was afraid. If he entered the tent of the desert love goddess, he might not want to leave. Tamara was a siren, a lovely woman who no doubt knew how to please men. He would become an acolyte of la Llorona, answering her cry for love whenever she called.

"Do the boys la Llorona takes to her home by the river ever return home?" he asked.

She smiled. "Once you give your soul to the goddess of love there is no need to return. The men she calls to her are completely satisfied. You would be satisfied here. I promise you that. I truly care for you."

"And I have some people I have to take care of," Sonny said. "Thanks for the wine."

"This is the second time you've said no, Sonny. If I doubted myself, I would wonder what I'm doing wrong. But I know you too well. The time isn't right for us. So I will wait." She smiled her enigmatic smile, took his arm, and walked him to the door.

"Remember, wear the medallion. It protects you from Raven. He is extremely dangerous."

"I know that," Sonny replied. "But I don't think he's got much of a chance. Sooner or later the cops will find him. Where can he hide?"

Tamara shook her head sadly. "He is not of this world," she whispered, and Sonny wondered if he had heard her correctly as the night breeze whirled through the trees, and the leaves moaned to the caress.

"Buenas noches," she said. "Return when you're ready. My door is always open to you."

Sonny walked to his truck. In the east Sunbringer shone. Venus. The star of love, the planet of the ancient goddess.

Tamara sat up late at night and sipped wine, and her meditation on Venus had called Sonny to her.

He thought he heard someone call his name. A rustle in the wind. La Llorona. His grandmother had told him it was her husband who had murdered her children to drive her mad.

For Tamara, la Llorona was a love goddess, a Circe calling wanderers to her island.

He could have stayed, explored the possibilities, surely found some release from the weight of Gloria's ghost. But no, he had things to do. Promises to keep. And he had Rita.

Sonny, I'm proud of you, he said to himself, smiling, as he got into his truck and drove home.

10

Sonny awoke very late the following day. His head hurt and his face was bruised, but not as badly as he had anticipated. His stomach growled; he was hungry. He got up, put the coffee on, and looked across the way to don Eliseo's place. Sunday afternoon and the October sun shone bright and warm.

The old man sat in his chair. Concha and don Toto sat nearby. On the grill sat the coffeepot. Even from here Sonny could smell the fragrant aroma. They were frying eggs with potatoes and chorizo, warming the red chile con carne, cooking tortillas on the comal.

Don Eliseo was probably telling them how he had saved Sonny's life last night. His old shotgun was propped against the cottonwood tree. The two compas listened attentively. They were good friends, and he would never forgive himself if one of them got hurt because of him. Yet don Eliseo had faced Raven and his crony with only one barrel loaded. Damn!

Sonny sipped the hot coffee and felt better. He swallowed a couple of aspirin and leaned back to let the pain clear. He pushed the button on his message machine. Rita's voice reminded him he had promised to take her to the South Valley Autumn Festival that afternoon. She wanted to go, and she wanted to know where he was last night. His mother was also on the tape. Max had driven her home from the hospital. Not to worry; she was feeling great.

Finally Howard's message. He was taking his daughter to the balloon fiesta and later to the Museum of Natural History in Old Town. Did Sonny and Rita want to join them? Nothing new on the Veronica murder. The police were as anxious as anyone to believe the Fiora story, he added.

Sonny dialed his mother. "Hi, Mom, I'm sorry I didn't get there last—"

"Sonny, mi hijo, how are you? Don't apologize. You knew Max was coming for me."

"Yes, but—"

"No buts. I know you're busy. The woman's murder, I heard. I hope you don't get mixed up."

"Pues, you know—"

"I was afraid of that. Ay, Dios, since you were little, I could feel something pulling you into danger. Why? Is it the Baca blood? Like your bisabuelo? Maybe if you married, settled down—"

"Maybe."

"No maybes. You're thirty, almost thirty-one. Hijo, I want to plan a party."

"Yeah, that would be great. Have you heard from Mando?"

"He came to see me. Dios mío, but he has no sense. Now it's a new girlfriend. His 'lady' he called her. Bunny. She used to work at one of those clubs I won't mention. And she paints herself up like a—well, you know. But nice. What can I say, your brother likes flashy women. And he's got a new car lot."

"I heard," Sonny said.

"But he tries, and I love him. I love you both."

"Listen, I promised Rita to take her to the fiesta. Do you want to come? Can you?"

"No, thank you, hijo. I have to stay quiet for a few days. Max is coming over, and we're going to string a ristra. He found some wonderful red chile in Belén. I think that's enough excitement."

She laughed. She was feeling well, she liked Max, and the two would spend a quiet day together. Sonny, too, smiled, but he felt a loss. He wanted to do more for his mother, visit her more often, but the life he led got in the way.

"Listen, jefa, if there's anything I can do . . ."

"Just take care of yourself," she replied. "These people you follow can be dangerous. I worry about you."

"I'll be careful. You, too."

"Que Dios te bendiga."

"Gracias," he replied.

"Bye. Take care. Bring Rita over when you can."

"I will. Bye."

Sonny finished his fourth cup of coffee and headed for the shower. He stopped at the mirror. The dark around his eye sockets surprised him. He looked older, worried.

How quickly the worm turns, he thought. Or as Shakespeare would say, swift-footed Time carries an empty wallet.

He shivered, stepped into the shower, and turned the water on as hot as he could stand it, and he stood for a long time, thinking about Raven, knowing he had come to kill. After the very hot shower he rinsed in cold water, trying to reclaim his body from the aches.

While he dressed, Sonny thought of the little girl sleeping peacefully in Diego and Marta's tent. Cristina. He hadn't met her, but she haunted his thoughts. What kind of chance did a kid like that have? On this Sunday morning, all over the city, parents had gotten up to take their kids to church, or the balloon fiesta, or to soccer practice, or a football game, or just for a drive to buy red chile ristras and apples in the valley. Autumn was the most pleasant season in the Río Grande valley, the most mellow and bewitching in New Mexico.

But what did Cristina awaken to? A tent in the river bosque as home, and another day spent at the river camp. Perhaps a walk to a shelter where they received meager supplies of food and clothes.

It wasn't right, he thought, as he stepped outside. Too many kids like Cristina needed help. The first thing he had to do was get Diego's family out of the river bottom. Hide them. Raven knew they had witnessed the murder. Even if they moved their camp, they could still be in danger.

"Sonny, mi amor!" Concha called. "Come and eat with us."

"Can't," Sonny replied. "I slept late and I promised to take Rita to the South Valley fiesta. Want to go?"

"We have our own fiesta here," don Eliseo answered. "But come by later and have some coffee."

"You still need workers to clean your place?" Sonny asked. "I've got some friends that need a place to stay."

"Bring them," don Eliseo said. "I've plenty of room."

"Gracias." Sonny waved and got into his truck.

He had taken Diego aside last night and told him he thought they should leave the river camp.

"But where do we go?" Diego had asked.

The words were still ringing in Sonny's mind when he drove up to Rita's home. The last bloom of roses was luxuriant on the bushes around her porch. The trees were still green, but a few began to show a tinge of soft gold.

A magnificent row of marigolds lined one wall, thick and luxurious, a commotion of tall cosmos lined the other. There had been no hard frost yet, so the plants thrived in their last burst of energy.

"Poetry," Sonny thought, "flowers are poetry." Like the words he sometimes desired to utter when he made love to Rita. He wanted to tell her how much he loved her, to speak like a poet, but the words escaped him.

In the backyard Rita's small garden was loaded with the last produce of summer. The herbal garden was ready to be picked and dried. Rita worked hard at her restaurant, but she always had time for gardening.

"The earth mother prepares for sleep," she told Sonny. "Time of harvest."

"Time to eat piñon and tell stories," don Eliseo would say.

Sonny paused to enjoy the brilliance of the flowers. I'm a lucky man, he thought. To have Rita's love. She was very sure of her inner strength, and when Sonny came to her, she shared that inner resource with him. She accepted, took him in, opened her arms, and he entered to be renewed.

I gotta marry her, he thought, and wondered if the contract of marriage would affect the love between them. A lot of people his age lived a few years together before tying the knot. But nowadays marriages didn't seem to last.

Children. He knew he wanted children, and so did Rita. Children would make a familia. His seed coming to fruition in the Río Grande valley.

"The seed comes to the earth when the time is right," Rita had said. A gardener's words; a woman of the valley. She knew the ways of the earth. No wonder she got along so well with don Eliseo and his friends, and with Lorenza Villa.

Rita called hello from the door, appeared dressed in a white blouse and a colorful Mexican skirt. Sonny kissed her bare shoulder. "You look beautiful, morenita."

"Thank you, señor." She smiled; then her smile changed to concern. "Your face! Qué pasó?" She reached out and touched his bruise.

They sat on the porch in the sunlight, and he told her about Raven's attack and about finding Diego's family.

"Anyway, I'm okay now. But what do I do about Diego and his familia?" he said at the end.

"Do you still feel like going to the fiesta?" she asked.

"I'd like to, but I keep thinking of Diego and his family."

"Let's take them with us," Rita suggested. "It sounds like they might enjoy the burning of the Kookoóee."

Ben Chávez had initiated the building of a giant effigy of el Coco, and now Federico Armijo and a group of artists built it every autumn. El Coco was the bogeyman of many cuentos. Parents warned their children to behave or the Coco might get them. When the kids went out to play, they were told to get home on time or the Coco Man, the Cucúi, might get them.

Like la Llorona, Sonny thought. If Tamara's interpretation of la Llorona holds any water, does the Coco seek little girls? Is he the male spirit of the bosque? Llorona/female, Coco/male, two projections of mythic forces that live in the heart.

Today the giant effigy would be burned at sunset during the South Valley Festival del Otoño, and as it burned, the fears and worries the Kookoóee represented went up in smoke. El Coco was the communal scapegoat. When it burned, the ill luck of the past disappeared, and a new season began.

"The little girl will enjoy it. There are games for the kids, plenty of food, music."

"Why didn't I think of it?"

"That's why you have me." Rita winked.

They drove to the river, and Sonny walked to Diego's camp. When he emerged with the family, they were all dressed in their Sunday-best clothes. Sonny introduced them to Rita; then they piled in the back of the truck and drove south. Cristina sat in front with Sonny and Rita. She was shy, but she had taken an instant liking to them. She sat quietly, dressed in a faded pair of jeans and blue blouse. She wore her dark hair in two braids. Her face shone bright.

"I have to get them out of there," Sonny said.

Rita understood. "I can use Busboy in the restaurant," she offered. "And I have enough room to keep Marta and Cristina."

"I can't ask you to—"

"You're not asking, I'm volunteering." She put her arm around Cristina.

"Gracias, amor. That's a start. Maybe I can get Peter a job at one of the TV stations. Get Diego and Peewee to help don Eliseo. It's going to work out."

The South Valley fiesta was in full swing when they arrived. The day was clear and warm, and hundreds of people swarmed the park. People came from all over the city and from distant parts of the state to enjoy the fiesta. Some came to sell their wares. Students from the South Valley schools showed off their artwork, and in the nearby library they read their stories. At the bandstand PA system, the governor was droning on about how much he had done for the South Valley.

Families had come to enjoy the autumn harvest fiesta. Valley farmers had set up trucks to sell produce. Old friends met. The Festival del Otoño was organized by volunteers, South Valley residents who were proud of their neighborhoods.

Sonny parked and led his newly acquired familia from booth to booth, buying food and drinks for all. He had fallen in love with Cristina, and his happiness made him splurge. While they ate, Sonny told Diego and Marta about Rita's offer. All agreed it wasn't safe to go back to the river camp.

When dusk came, they headed for the baseball field where the effigy of the Kookoóee sat. Sonny stopped cold when he saw the giant figure. Its face resembled the face of a raven! The long arms seemed to be two dark wings flapping as they moved back and forth.

Rita sensed Sonny's hesitation. "Raven," she whispered.

Sonny nodded. Every year the figure of el Kookoóee was different, constructed by whatever artists happened to show up to help. This year the intimation of a black raven was clear.

Ben Chávez stood by the artists who had built the awesome effigy.

Ben Chávez greeted Sonny. "Cómo 'stás."

"Time off from writing?" Sonny asked.

"Oh, no, this is part of writing," Chávez replied. "Everything is part of writing!"

The artists around him nodded and laughed. Yeah, everything got thrown into the pot, flavored with creative juices, stirred, and allowed to simmer until the traditions came alive in new form.

"El Coco looks like a raven," Sonny said.

"Maybe," Chávez replied. "Could just be an old buzzard." He laughed.

"No, a raven," Sonny insisted. Anger rose in him. What the hell was Chávez trying to hide?

Rita heard the tone in his voice and squeezed his hand. She couldn't figure out why Sonny had suddenly tensed.

"So it's a raven," Chávez said, his face growing dark in the dusk. "Don't you know you need all the help you can get! Watch out for Raven. He's here tonight!"

Before Sonny could ask him what he meant, the artists pulled Chávez away, like gnomes or imps pulling away Pan, or a brujo. It was time to play, time to announce the burning of the Kookoóee, time to torch the monster. The magic of the evening now centered around the giant effigy, its head turning in the dusk, its arms swinging back and forth.

Chávez brought el Coco to life, Sonny thought, like he brings his characters to life. The writer *was* a brujo.

Sonny felt a tingling along the back of his neck. What did Chávez mean, Raven was here tonight? He looked at the huge crowd gathered around the effigy. Families with children, all smiling, all ready to enjoy the torching of el Coco. He turned and looked at the effigy. Did Chávez mean the evil spirit *really* resided in the figure? Is that why its look was so fierce and ominous?

Cristina tugged at Sonny.

"My father told me stories about the Kookoóee," she said. "When my father was little, they called Kookoóee el Coco. He scared the naughty kids. Now the Coco is the police. If they find us, they make us leave our home. Sometimes they tear down our home. Once they arrested my father."

"Why?" Sonny asked.

"He stole some food for us," she whispered. "Then my father made a Kookoóee, like that one." She pointed at the effigy which rose in the dusk, head turning, jaws with big teeth opening and closing, long arms swaying. "But he wasn't as big. He put it in the path that leads to our home."

"I saw it," Sonny said.

"I'm not afraid of it," Cristina said. "It's supposed to keep out the people who don't like us. I guess you weren't afraid," she said to Sonny.

"No, I wasn't afraid," Sonny said. "I knew I was going to meet you, and we were going to be good friends."

"Yes," she said, and for the first time she drew close to Sonny and Rita.

At the bandstand someone was singing, "Todos me dicen Llorona, Llorona. . . ."

Then Ben Chávez interrupted; the burning was about to begin. The children were asked to write their worries on pieces of paper, and the papers were gathered and placed in the Kookoóee's bag to be burned. Rita held the paper and Cristina wrote: My big fear is not to be with my family.

"So let's burn that fear," Rita said, and they tossed the note in the bag.

"Señores y señoras!" Ben Chávez called. "Time to burn el Coco! Time to burn the Kookoóee!"

An exuberant cheer went up from the crowd.

"Look!" Cristina cried, pointing to el Coco.

A young man with flowing black hair climbed up a ladder and struck the flares in the effigy's eyes. The Kookoóee seemed to come alive. Flares were started in the Kookoóee's fingers, so when he swung his arms, the red glow startled the crowd.

The other artists placed matches to a bundle of grass at the foot of the monster, and the flames rose quickly. The Kookoóee's head kept turning back and forth, and a voice boomed, "No me quemen! No me quemen!"

The children shouted with laughter, the parents smiled and remembered all the times their parents had warned them to be good or the Coco would get them.

The arms of the tall effigy moved back and forth, as if he was trying to escape the fire, and his head turned frantically, but the flames were already licking at his fancy costume. The bogey-man of the Mexicanos of the valley went up in flames while the crowd roared its approval. The wood popped as it burned, and a shower of sparks rose into the evening sky. The burning flares lent the Kookoóee a wild appearance. He swung his arms as if in agony. The crowd cheered.

"Burn, Coco! Burn!"

Bad news and poverty could be put aside for the moment. It

was a time of communal joy. The fears in the bag of the Kookoóee also went up in flames.

The burning lasted no more than half an hour, but in that time a cleansing took place. Joy spread throughout the crowd. And when the last of the Kookoóee fell into the hot embers, a cheer went up. Families headed home, the young stayed to enjoy an evening dance.

Sonny drove his newly acquired family back to don Eliseo's.

"Entren, entren," don Eliseo welcomed them. "Just in time for coffee." He smiled.

"Y pasteles de manzana," Concha said.

"She makes the best pasteles in the West," don Toto announced, beaming.

"Toto, you say the nicest things. If you weren't my best friend, I'd marry you and bake you a pie every day."

"For your hot pastelito, I'd marry you tomorrow," don Toto teased.

Sonny introduced his new friends, and they were warmly welcomed by the old trio. Concha fussed over Cristina. Everyone received a generous portion of pie topped with slices of cheese. Diego and his family slowly relaxed. It had been a long time since they had been welcomed in a home. They felt safe with Sonny, and now they felt at ease with Sonny's friends.

As they sat around don Eliseo's kitchen table, Cristina told them about the burning of the Coco. The storytelling began, and don Toto told the story of a witch who fell in love with a butcher. In the end she was turned into sausage when one day she disguised herself as a pig.

"It's the season of la Llorona," Concha said. "The kids call it Halloween, but it's really her season. Now that the earth is resting, it's time for telling stories."

"I remember one my grandfather told me," Sonny said.

"Tell it to us," Cristina begged.

"My abuelo was Lorenzo Baca," Sonny began. "This happened to him and his compadre when they were young men. They had been sent to the Rancho de San Martín to look for stray steers the roundup had left behind. The rancho was a deserted place at the foot of La Mesa de los Ladrones. My abuelo Lorenzo and his compadre came upon a gathering of brujos. They were in the form of giant fireballs, jumping and dancing in a circle."

"That's true," Concha said. "That's the way they used to gather."

"The men turned their horses and rode away, but they were pursued by one of the fireballs. It came leaping across the llano. They rode their sweating, lathered horses as fast as they could. They thought the fireball was the devil. They were grown men, tough vaqueros who had worked on the range all their lives. They had seen death, but till that day they had not known fear. Miles ahead of them lay the village of Socorro, and the church. They knew that was the only place on earth safe for them. They rode the poor tired horses forward, whipping the reins across the horses' flanks. The sky grew dark, and the fireball stayed right by them."

"Madre de Dios!" Concha made the sign of the cross.

"They couldn't outride the fireball. It came bounding across the llano until it was alongside the two vaqueros. My abuelo said the sight made his blood turn cold. He glanced at his compadre. His eyes bulged with fear. They knew they couldn't outrun the evil that had taken the form of the fireball. My abuelo's horse, exhausted from the run, finally fell, throwing him. He was bruised, but unhurt. His compadre reined up his horse and called for him to mount. It was no use. Two men on a tired horse would not get far."

"You can't outrace the devil," don Toto said wisely.

"He had a pistol, and when the fireball jumped in front of him, he took it from his holster and fired."

Concha cringed. As a child she had heard similar stories.

"The bullet hit the fireball. He fired again. Five times he fired."

"Were the bullets blessed at the church?" Concha asked.

"Quiet, Concha. Let him finish the story," don Toto whispered.

"The sun had set, the llano was dark. My grandfather could see the ball of fire plainly. He knew his bullets had struck dead center. The fireball seemed to breathe, to moan, and then it jumped away, leaving the two men alone. The pistol fell from my grand-father's hand. He was trembling. His body was wet with sweat. He turned to his compadre who held out a hand and helped him mount behind him. Together they continued to Socorro."

Sonny paused. He looked at Cristina. "Scared?"

"No," she answered. "My dad tells me stories like that all the time."

Diego smiled. "I was born in Belén. We grew up with all those stories."

"We have a lot of time for storytelling at our home on the river," his wife added.

"I'm never afraid," Cristina said. "My mom and I walk along the river to find firewood. Even at night. As long as we're to-gether, we're not afraid." She held her mother's hand.

"Well, storytelling time is done, and it's time to get you to bed." Sonny picked her up. "How would you like to spend the night with tía Rita?"

Cristina looked at her mother and father.

"Your mom can go with you. Your dad is staying here, be-cause in the morning he's going to help don Eliseo clean up his garden. Okay?"

"Okay." She nodded. She gave Sonny a hug. "Thank you for taking us to the fiesta, to see the Kookoóee, and for that scary story. You know what I would have done if I was your grand-father?"

"What?"

"I would have said a prayer. That gets rid of the evil."

"Yes." Sonny smiled, lifting her and handing her to her mother. "That would have done it."

Early Monday morning the sun came over the Sandias, illuminating the valley and the ascending balloons. A few wispy clouds drifted across the mountain, but they would soon disappear. The morning air was brisk but calm; it was a perfect day for ballooning. In fact, weatherman Morgan had predicted the whole week would be excellent.

The balloon games were starting. Today the competition involved piloting a balloon down close enough to grab a key tied to a tall post. It was a key to a new car, and the pilot who grabbed the key won the car.

Sonny called Francine Hunter who said, yes, she could use a part-time cameraman. Buoyed by the news, Sonny stepped out his front door and shook his head. Madge was crazy to have accepted the story on Veronica's murder, but what the hell, it was no skin off his nose. He ambled over to don

Eliseo's, where the men were having breakfast. They all greeted him warmly.

"Siéntate, siéntate," don Eliseo invited Sonny. "Have some café and almuerzo."

He served Sonny coffee and a generous portion of eggs, doña Concha's chile con carne, and hot tortillas.

"Diego was telling us about his familia. He's from the Padillas de Belén. I knew his abuelo, don Cipriano. Cipi, they used to call him. That family was originally from Los Padillas. Used to have a big huerta. Sold chile and maíz from there to Santo Domingo. But during the depression he lost everything. He, and a lot like him, went north, to Colorado to work in the betabel, or in the mines. He died in a train accident, near Raton. Those poor men used to catch a free ride on the freight trains. Cipi lost a leg, and by the time they got him to a doctor, he had bled to death."

Diego nodded. That's the story he remembered about his grandfather. Don Eliseo knew his family, and his knowledge of Diego's people helped, for the moment, to restore his sense of belonging. After being homeless the past few years, he had lost contact with old friends.

Don Eliseo also remembered Diego's father. He had served in World War II and lived through the Bataan March with the New Mexico National Guard.

Diego's father never fully recovered from the hardship of the march. He never had more than a small house in Belén, and when he died, his sons and daughters sold the family place. When Diego returned from Vietnam, there was no home to return to. He found his roots severed, and his wandering began.

"It's hard for la gente," don Eliseo acknowledged. "The políticos get the gravy, y la gente gets the bones. I survive because I farm, but even that is coming to an end. Look around you. The developers are buying all the land. Five centuries we have lived here, since de Vargas returned in 1693. But it's very difficult now. I used to be able to do all the work on my ranchito, pero este arthritis me tiene bien fregado. Oh, my boys come by once in a while, pero no saben nada. They got an education, and now they work with the pluma, not la pala. I don't blame them. Working a rancho is hard. I'm proud of them, but I can't do it by myself. I sure would be glad to have some help. Clean up the place before it gets cold. Maybe put in some firewood for the stove."

"We're ready to work," Diego said eagerly. "Aren't we, Pee-wee?"

"You bet, pardner. The weather's perfect, and I don't have a date."

They laughed. The new situation had made them all enthusiastic. Peter was to go to the TV station, where Sonny had landed him a part-time job. Busboy was to work in Rita's Cocina. And Rita planned to take Marta and Cristina shopping. She was already thinking of school for the little girl.

"A big change for my familia," Diego said when they finished eating.

"Yes," Sonny agreed.

"We appreciate what you're doing, compa," Diego said. "We've tried it before, but—"

Sonny understood. "Hey, we'll try again. The río isn't safe." He clasped Diego in an abrazo of friendship; then he and Peter drove away.

Diego had told him they had tried coming out of the river camps before, doing odd jobs around town, sleeping for a week in the shelters downtown, trying desperately to get back on their feet. But lack of education, no home address, lack of references, all made it difficult to break out of the cycle of poverty. He worked construction for a while; then he broke a leg and had to quit. Businesses just weren't hiring unskilled workers. The streets became a way of life, and each day more and more were caught in their web.

Sonny delivered Peter to Francine Hunter. Her cameraman had just quit, so she could use Peter for a couple of weeks, and Peter accepted the assignment gladly.

"I'll play dumb," he whispered to Sonny as they parted, "but it's going to feel like heaven to have a camera in my hands."

"You'll do fine," Sonny said as he dropped him off. He was glad all of Diego's familia was placed, and safe for the moment.

Now there was work to do, and he headed for the library downtown. He needed to leave the list of names Madge had given him with his old high school friend Ruth Jamison, the librarian. She greeted him warmly.

"Research?" she asked.

"Got a puzzle," Sonny said, handing her the list. He had circled those he needed researched. "Need to know all I can about these folks."

"Yes, sir." Ruth smiled.

She had helped Sonny with his research the past few years, not only because it was part of her work, but because she had admired him from the time they were in high school. Sonny also brought her more interesting requests than the usual term paper questions.

"The balloon fiesta murder," she whispered when she glanced at the names.

"Yes."

"Someone else has already called in a request for information on this man. John Gilroy. He's ex-CIA."

"Who wants to know about him?"

"Police Chief Garcia."

Good, Sonny thought. He's on to Gilroy. "Thanks for the tip."

"Anytime." Ruth winked.

Sonny promised to check with her later, then he walked down to Lindy's for coffee.

He needed to know a lot of things. Like where Raven got the balloon. He would check out the suppliers, but hell, Garcia would also do that. And Raven would either use a false name anyway or send one of his followers. Someone like Sweatband or Scarface. Sonny had fought them in an Estancia bar and beaten them. But Scarface died at the Arroyo del Sol bridge. That left Sweatband, the more sadistic of the two.

Sonny was convinced the key lay in the strange array of characters who had shown up at the Alburquerque balloon fiesta. The Fioras' story was a cover-up, and they were probably paid to be out of town by now.

Raven needed transportation, and he was probably buying guns. He was up to something new. He needed new allies. Who? Beneath the question lay the nagging question that the game was bigger, more complicated than the murder of Veronica Worthy.

Tamara was frightened, Sonny thought as he finished his coffee and drove to the North Valley, something he didn't expect from the woman. He peered up into the clear sky. A perfect day for ballooning.

The cool morning breeze that washed down from the Sandia Mountains usually blew from north to south. If conditions were optimum, the balloons took off and stayed low, floating south; then they sought higher altitudes for the wind that would return them to the vicinity of the balloon park. Their flight pattern formed a big rectangle—the "Alburquerque box." In this kind of setting, an experienced pilot could actually choose a course for the balloon.

But today the easterly breeze was pushing the balloons toward the river.

Sonny was listening to Selena on KABQ when the announcer, Gomez, cut in. Sonny tensed as he listened to the report.

"We're at the scene, confirming reports of shots fired at balloonists during the flight this morning. One balloon is confirmed down. I've just talked to an officer here at Fiesta Control. No one knows exactly what has happened, but witnesses have confirmed a shooting. A man in a black balloon was reported shooting at other balloons. The balloon of Mario Secco, an Italian, is confirmed down. Mario Secco has been rushed to University Hospital. He is reported in critical condition. Fiesta Control officers have issued an emergency call. All balloons associated with the fiesta are ordered down. I'm trying to talk to the director of the fiesta. . . ."

"Ah, damn," Sonny groaned. Unbelievable! Raven wasn't the type to go up in a balloon and start shooting at people. Had the man gone bananas? Killing Veronica was one thing, but to go up and fire randomly on people? What the hell was going on?

Sonny's phone rang and he lowered the volume of the radio.

"Sonny, I've been trying to get hold of you," Howard said.

"Tell me it's not real," Sonny answered. Howard had access to the police channels; he would know.

"It's real. The sonofabitch went after Secco!"

"Do you have confirmation?"

"Yeah. Secco died before he got to the hospital. A woman in his balloon is slightly wounded, in shock. She brought the balloon down. Dozens of witnesses saw the black balloon. It's Raven all right."

"Why? Why?"

"Who the hell knows. All I know is it's a mess!"

"I'm headed over there now," Sonny said as he roared up a freeway ramp. "Keep in touch."

"Ten-four."

Sonny switched on his police radio scanner. Harsh voices broke through the airwaves, shouting commands. The black balloon had been spotted drifting over the river. All units in the northwest quadrant were alerted. The alleged gunman piloting a black balloon was reported armed and dangerous. Approach with extreme caution.

Lots of luck, Sonny thought. The breeze was still holding, still pushing the balloons across the river. Raven could quickly disappear into the river bosque whenever he brought the balloon down.

But no, Sonny cautioned himself. Think straight. A balloon is slow, cumbersome. Why would Raven go up, take a chance of the prevailing winds to get him away from the cops after the shooting? Something wasn't jibing.

Sonny's phone rang again. "Sonny, I need to talk to you," a shaken Madge Swenson said. "Have you heard?"

"I'm on my way to your place now," Sonny answered.

"Hurry," she replied, pleading.

Fiesta Control was in an uproar when Sonny drove onto the dusty field. Since the Fiora news conference, Veronica's death had been confirmed as an accident, and that had tempered the initial fear. But now someone had opened fire with a rifle, and a few balloonists in the air had actually seen the shooting.

Sam Garcia was coming out of Madge's office when Sonny arrived.

"You again," the chief said brusquely.

"I was invited." Sonny shrugged.

"Sure, invited." Garcia scowled. "Just don't get in the way. Whoever in the hell is doing this is a looney. Bien loco."

"I knew that Saturday, chief. But you bought the Fiora story."

"I had nothing to do with Fiora!" Garcia exploded. "Don't you even suggest I had anything to do with Fiora!"

He gritted his teeth. Both knew the Fiora story had been concocted, and those who helped construct it were going to have to answer some tough questions now that a second murder had taken place.

Sonny didn't back down. "You knew he was lying," he repeated.

"There was no cover-up, Sonny," Garcia growled. "My department doesn't deal that way!"

"You knew Raven wouldn't stop," Sonny replied.

"I'll get that sonofabitch sooner than he thinks!" the chief snarled. "What's your interest?"

"Homeless people," Sonny answered.

The chief arched an eyebrow. "Homeless people," he grumbled. "Just stay out of our way, Sonny" was his parting shot. "And you better stay out of their way." He nodded toward the two FBI agents surveying the crowd.

Sonny watched the angry chief hurry away. Then he turned to greet the two FBI agents who were walking toward him. Mike Stevens, also known as Gorilla for his strong-arm tactics, and Eddie Martínez, one of the few Chicanos in the agency. Sonny's mouth went sour. He tried to stay away from the agency boys. They didn't like private investigators, and they were just too much hassle to deal with.

They worked for Matt Paiz, the regional director of the FBI, with offices downtown. Sonny looked for Paiz, but he was not around. He was letting Stevens and Martínez do their thing.

"Hi, Sonny." Mike put out his hand, acting friendly.

They were both dressed for ballooning, bright nylon pants and parkas. They had been mixing with the frightened crowd, sniffing around. Garcia had set up a desk and several officers to question the pilots who had gone up that morning, but Mike and Eddie were undercover.

"Didn't know you guys flew," Sonny said, and shook hands. He tried to be friendly.

"We don't. Heard you do," Martínez shot back.

"Hey, I'm not a pilot. Just here because Madge invited me." Sonny smiled, acting innocent.

"You gonna chase the guy who killed Secco?" Stevens asked.

"If they hire me," Sonny replied. They, too, were acting coy. They had to know Raven was involved.

"So what do you know?" Martínez asked.

"Only what I read in the paper. And you?"

Stevens drew close, his eyes narrowed as he whispered. His breath was sour. "Secco was a foreign citizen, Baca. That's why we're here."

"Secco also ran dope," Sonny reminded the agents.

"So you think he was running dope? Is that what you're saying?" Stevens asked.

"I told you, I read the papers."

"You walk a thin line, Baca," Stevens said. "I know the fiesta board is going to ask you to help. I don't mind you earning a living, just don't go fucking around with something you can't handle."

"I know the rules," Sonny replied. "But if I get a job here, I might take it. Times are tough."

"We just wouldn't want them to get too tough," Martínez said, and Sonny detected a threat in his voice. "Stay cool."

"Yeah, you too," Sonny replied.

He watched them walk away, disappearing into the line that stretched out of the lobby into the parking lot.

By now all the pilots had brought down their balloons and were returning to Fiesta Control for questioning.

Sonny shrugged and headed for Madge's office. Okay, Raven had now taken to the air, in a hot-air balloon, brazenly sporting his emblem, daring Garcia and the local agency boys to get him. But why attack Mario Secco?

"Sonny," Madge Swenson called and pressed through the crowd in the lobby. She took his hand. "I'm glad you came."

She was visibly shaken. The confident, assured blonde who never had a hair out of place was upset. She was a woman with a big problem.

"Your face?"

"I bumped into a door," Sonny replied, touching the bruise.

She shrugged. "Come in here," she said, taking Sonny's hand. "I want you to meet with my board."

Sonny thought a moment. What did he have to lose? He, too, needed to find Raven, and if he got help from the fiesta board, so much the better.

"Lead the way."

Madge smiled. "Thanks, Sonny. I won't forget this."

She led him into a conference room filled with twelve solemn-faced board members.

Sad disciples, Sonny thought, recognizing most. Local business people, hot-air balloon enthusiasts, all wealthy and powerful players in city politics and economics.

A tall, energetic man rose to meet Sonny. Dr. Stammer, Sonny thought. He didn't know the heart surgeon was into hot-air ballooning.

"Sonny, I'm glad you could come." He shook Sonny's hand.

"Dr. Stammer," Sonny replied.

"Jerry, please."

"You two know each other?" Madge asked.

"Through his mother," Stammer replied. "Dr. Branch operated on her. I just happened to go by one morning. Found the dutiful son sleeping. You'd been there all night."

Sonny nodded. "She's home now. Doing great."

"A wonderful woman, a wonderful woman," Stammer repeated.

Sonny remembered Stammer had come in with Dr. Branch. Stammer seemed to be hounding Branch, demanding something. Finally Branch had harshly told Stammer that they couldn't talk in the room of a patient, to see him in his office. Stammer stormed out.

"You fly?" Sonny asked.

"I let Madge talk me into it last year. Once I went up the first time, I was hooked. I love it, and I help on the board. Sit down, please. We'd like to talk to you."

Dr. Jerry Stammer, it turned out, more than helped out. He was the president of the board.

Sonny read the city newspapers to keep track of things. He had not made the connection a few days ago when Stammer stepped into his mother's hospital room, but now the articles on Dr. Stammer came filtering from his memory file.

When he first came to Alburquerque, Stammer had made a big splash at the Presbyterian Hospital, a hospital well-known for its pioneer work in open heart surgery. Stammer was not only a surgeon; he did research, and he had convinced a lot of people that the next step in heart transplants was putting baboon hearts in people.

There simply weren't enough human hearts to fill the need, so Stammer had set up a laboratory to raise baboons.

"I'm going to put Albuquerque on the map," he was quoted. "We're extremely close to finding the agent that will stop the body's rejection of a foreign heart. In fact, we have isolated the agents. I'm ready to go."

But the hospital board didn't see it his way. Baboon heart transplants were experimental at best, and there was no way they would approve Stammer's project. Stammer had invested millions in a laboratory to raise baboons, but his peers wouldn't let him go through with his scheme. Too dangerous.

Stammer struck back with fury, accusing the hospital board of medieval practices. For that he was ostracized, and he was on the verge of losing his business and his right to practice in the hospital.

Stammer introduced Sonny. "Ladies and gentlemen, this is Sonny Baca. You know him as the private investigator who was responsible for stopping the planned explosion of a WIPP truck this summer. He saved this state from a catastrophe."

Solemn faces smiled and nodded. Anyone who kept up with the news knew how Sonny had averted the disaster.

"I want to thank you for coming. You may not know everyone here, but I think it's safe to say we know you." Stammer leaned across the table and stared at Sonny. "You know the mess we're in."

"Yes," Sonny replied, looking into the intense blue eyes of the man.

Stammer was tall and muscular, about fifty, his graying hair in a crew cut. He looked athletic in his flying outfit, but as intense as the time Sonny had seen him in his mother's room.

"I'll come to the point," he said, and glanced at Madge. "We need help. We made a mistake when we believed the Fioras. Now one of our official entrants is dead. We need professional advice."

"The police are investigating," Sonny interrupted. "Mario Secco was an Italian citizen. The FBI is also investigating—"

"We know, we know," Stammer interrupted. "But we don't have the kind of time those investigations might take!" His eyes bore into Sonny. "We like to think of our fiesta as a safe place where balloonists can come to fly. They can bring their families. Ballooning is a family sport. It's nice, clean fun. But today we have a lot of scared people out there. Half the entrants are getting ready to pull out. We face financial collapse. We need to catch this murderer now! Today! My board is prepared to pay whatever fee you set, plus your expenses."

"Any fee?" Sonny asked.

"Within reason," Stammer responded.

"Can you build a home for a homeless family?"

Stammer frowned. "We're not a construction company. This is serious."

"I'm serious, too," Sonny responded, and stood. "You want to catch a murderer, I want a home for a family of six. Your balloons fly over the bosque, and up there the world is bright and clean and beautiful! But down in the bosque people are living in cardboard shacks."

He paused, realizing he had gotten carried away. He looked at the faces of the people on the board. Their blank expressions told him they didn't know what he was talking about. As Stammer said, they weren't into building homes.

"A hundred thou," Sonny whispered. With that he could build a home for Diego's family. Habitat for Humanity built homes quickly and on the spot. He could have Diego and his family in a home by Christmas.

The members of the board stiffened. They leaned to whisper to each other.

Stammer looked at his colleagues, and in a rough voice he cut through the hushed whispers. "We have no choice," he said, glaring at them. "We must cancel all flights until we can *guarantee* the skies are safe. People are leaving right and left. This is a disaster, folks, a goddamned disaster!" He turned to Madge.

"What do you think?"

"He's worth every penny," she replied. "As you say, we have no choice. It's not just canceling all future flights and losing the entries this year, it's our reputation which is at stake. If this isn't cleared up quickly, we could be dead next year. People don't come to a balloon fiesta where there's danger."

She turned to Sonny. "The city police and the FBI are looking for the person who shot Mr. Secco. If they find him first, we don't pay." Here she looked at the board members. "If Mr. Baca finds the man who shot Mario Secco and clears this up before the police, we pay."

"That sounds fair." Stammer nodded, looked around the table, and the others nodded in acquiescence. The fiesta lasted ten days, and each day it was canceled meant millions of dollars lost. They had no choice.

"What do you say, Sonny?" Stammer said. "We expect immediate results. We can't wait."

"It's a deal."

"What makes you think you can find the man in the black balloon before the police?" one of the board members asked. The man ran one of the biggest sporting goods stores in town.

"Intuition," Sonny replied, and turned to Madge. "What do you say we go flying tomorrow?"

"Fly?" she whispered.

"We've canceled tomorrow's flight." Stammer shook his head. "There's a madman out there—" He paused and looked at Sonny, then at Madge.

"Weatherman Morgan says there's going to be good flying weather. Hate to waste it," Sonny said.

"I'm game," Madge answered, smiling, knowing what Sonny was suggesting. Go up and draw the man in the black balloon out. Why not? The cops wouldn't do that, but Sonny would.

"I see." Stammer nodded. "But it's too risky."

"It's the only way I know," Sonny said, his eyes fixed on Madge.

She returned his stare. Sonny had proposed danger, and the excitement washed over her and rose in her voice.

"Let's do it!" She nodded.

"We can't be responsible," Stammer muttered, looking around the table, then at Sonny.

"Take out a one-day life insurance policy on us," Sonny suggested.

Stammer looked puzzled, then grinned. "Not a bad idea." He chuckled. "Thank you for your time, Sonny. Madge will see to it that you get whatever you need."

Madge stood and Sonny followed her out of the room.

"I haven't been up in a balloon since I did security here," Sonny said in the hallway. "I need someone with me who can fly, or I'd take my chances myself."

"Will it work?" she asked. "Will whoever murdered Mr. Secco be crazy enough to come after us?"

"I think so. Have your men place a half-inch sheet of steel on the floor of the basket. An inch sheet if you think the balloon can carry it and still fly."

"Only on the floor of the basket?"

"Yes."

"Anything else?" she answered.

"Put out a press release. You and I are going to fly, but absolutely no one else. Announce the time, location, everything."

"Done."

"It could be dangerous." Sonny's brow knitted. "I know who killed Mario Secco. He wants me, so he's going to take a chance and come after us. You have to be sure you want to—"

"I am," she assured him; then she leaned forward and kissed his cheek. "See you in the morning. What time do we fly?" she asked.

"Sunrise. I'll pick you up at five-thirty."

"No, I'll pick you up." She winked.

Hasta mañana," Sonny said, and walked out.

Sure he was fishing, but he knew Raven would take the bait. Time and again Raven played games, drawing Sonny out, positioning him. Well, it was time to play games back.

Sonny walked through the crowd outside to get to his truck. He tried Rita on his cellular, but there was no answer. They were still out shopping. He had to see Lorenza Villa, he thought. He called her, and yes, she was free. He drove across the new Alameda bridge to Corrales.

The balloon fiesta board wants to save the festival, and I want to catch Raven, Sonny thought, but the whole thing was a bigger game. The FBI knew about Raven, but agent Mike and his sidekick Eddie weren't talking. And what would Raven have against Mario Secco?

Lorenza opened the door and greeted Sonny. "Buenos días, Elfego. Come in."

"Buenos," he answered, and entered. "Thanks for taking the time."

"Rita told me everything," she said as she led him to the kitchen. "The fiesta has turned tragic."

She was barefooted. A cotton huipil molded to the soft contours of her body. She motioned to a chair. "Would you like some coffee? Or tea?"

"Café, gracias," he replied, and as she served him coffee, he told her about going to see Veronica's body. "There's no doubt. She was murdered."

"By Raven."

"Yes. Why did I see the body falling? As if I knew that she had been killed?"

"Your vision told you Raven had returned."

"And the coyotes?"

"Your nagual."

My nagual, he thought. I find the coyotes, I run with them. Is she saying I am *of* them?

Coyotes? He had seen them as a kid, and once in a while on the range. One summer he had worked a ranch with a friend near Cabezon, and he ran into one. His rancher friend took a shot at the coyote, but it got away.

Ranchers hated coyotes. Poisoned them, shot at them. Still, they survived.

"What does it mean?" he asked.

"The coyote is your guardian animal," she replied.

He stood and walked to the window that faced east. The river bosque was brilliant with October sunlight. Clear, Indian summer days, a time of harvest. The fruit stands were piled with apples, chile, red ristras, pumpkins.

In the northern Sangre de Cristos, the aspens were already gold, shimmering with light. Wood piles grew around the houses of the pueblos. In high forests the elk were mating, the bulls bugleing, and people were getting ready to go hunting.

People were storing food, preserving jellies and jams, the sweets of the harvest.

The nights were cool now, not yet freezing but brisk, and the scent of piñon logs burning in fireplaces permeated the valley. It should be a time of peace, a time of home, a time of story-telling. But it wasn't.

In the city of el Duque de Alburquerque, there was only one thing missing from the scene: hot-air balloons flowering in the crisp, October sky.

"Qué piensas?" Lorenza asked.

She had been watching Sonny. As he stood there, looking out the window, she felt his intensity. He sniffed the air, like a coyote who enters new territory. Someone had entered his territory; he was in trouble. Raven's return threatened Sonny's life.

"Thinking about the coyotes." He turned to face her. "I heard a lot of stories when I was a kid. From my abuelos. Old people from the nearby farms would come to visit, and they told the stories. Brujas changing to owls, coyotes, birds. As a kid I believed everything."

"And as a man you put away childish things," she said.

"Why change into the animal form?"

"It's a way to enter the world of spirits."

He raised an eyebrow. "The world of spirits?"

"The soul can travel in many forms. This is just one way. You must learn it because it is Raven's method. He is working through his nagual, so must you. Later you will learn to use your dreams. . . ." Her voice trailed.

He partly understood what she meant. He had to meet Raven on his own terms.

"Use my dreams?" He was puzzled.

"Yes. To create your own dream," she replied. "But now Raven calls the shots. You see, the world of nature is our world. We think entering this age of technology erases the past. It doesn't. Our nature is linked to that of our ancestors, to their beliefs. The surface changes for us, but we know that beneath the surface lies the true world, the world of spirits."

"A world I entered during the ceremony."

"Yes. You found your soul."

Sonny nodded. "Don Eliseo always reminds me of those stories I heard as a child. My abuelos believed in the world of spirits. It was all around them. They were staunch Catholics, and they didn't want to give the stories of the witches too much credence, but they believed."

He paused and looked deep into her eyes, the eyes that fascinated him because he couldn't make them focus to meet his stare. Shaman eyes. One eye the eye of an owl.

"Going into that vision, meeting the coyotes . . . I didn't think it could be done." He shook his head.

"It's as old as the Aztecs. Moctezuma Ilhuicamina sent forty of his brujos, that's the word the Spanish friars used to describe the shamans, to the underworld. They went as jaguars, eagles, birds, other creatures of the earth. They returned to tell their kind that the Aztec empire was doomed."

She paused and poured him a fresh cup of coffee.

The same battle don Eliseo saw taking place, Sonny pondered. It was older and bigger than simple witchcraft games. It involved civilizations. A way of life was ending, a new one was coming into being.

"The Spaniards destroyed the temples. Paganism and the worship of idols, they called the old religion. They saw the skulls of the ancestors on the temple walls and made up stories that the Aztecs were cannibals who sacrificed people. That served their purpose, which was to control the people with a new religion."

"So the experts write that the Aztecs did sacrifice."

"Those people worshiped their ancestors. Just like today, one of the most important holidays is el Día de los Muertos. People go to the cemeteries to be with those who have died. They set up altars, they take food, they have a fiesta. It's a form of remembering the ancestors and celebrating the good they did on earth. Long ago the celebrations lasted longer. The skulls of the ancestors were taken from their chambers where they were kept, they were lovingly cleaned and placed along the temple walls. What the Spaniards called idolatry were days of prayer and remembrance. Days of thanksgiving to the ancestors."

"And the Spaniards got it assbackward," Sonny said.

"They needed to invent stories of idolatry to tear down the temples and impose their religion. Conquerors everywhere have always done this to people they conquer. They make them pagans or subhuman, and they call their beliefs superstitions. They rationalize destruction."

"Yeah, look around you," Sonny mused.

"I was in México on Día de los Muertos. I saw how the people celebrated and honored their ancestors. The more traditional the Indian tribe, the more they understand this connection to the ancestors, and the honor due to them."

"We honor them, too, don't we," Sonny whispered.

Sonny thought of masses for the dead his mother offered at church for his father. The altar she kept at home with the statue of la Virgen de Guadalupe, the Mexican virgin, and statues of the saints. And there on the altar, amid the statues and the burning votive candles, the photographs of her family.

He thought of his father and how almost daily the man was in his thoughts. Even el Bisabuelo, Elfego Baca, the great-grandfather he had never known, was a spirit guiding his life. Yes, he honored them, for their work, for the history, for the traditions and beliefs they had passed down.

"The conquering Spaniards had to make something evil out of the indigenous beliefs," Lorenza said. "So they killed the priests and destroyed the temples. They built their churches on the sites of the old temples, but the people kept their beliefs. Long after most of the Aztec civilization was destroyed, the people knew they moved in and out of the world of spirits."

"And the curanderas helped."

Lorenza smiled. "That's our work. To take people to that world. People go on having soul-troubles, and our work is to help."

She echoed don Eliseo's thoughts, told stories just like the old man and his friends. They whispered their stories around the fire on summer evenings when they sat out to enjoy the cool of night. She could be their daughter. They trusted her; they knew she was one of the few who sought the old indigenous ways.

"My mother used to say I had a guardian angel," he said, "but now I learn I also have a guardian animal? Do you have a nagual?" he asked.

"Yes."

"What?"

"It is best not to speak about it."

"Why?"

"It takes its power away."

"It really does protect you?"

"Yes."

"From what?"

"The evil forces."

"Forces?"

"The struggle has always been between a harmonious universe and one which collapses into complete chaos. Put another way, it's the struggle between good and evil. All resides in our souls, so the energy of evil brujos works to defeat us."

"And this is made clear in the world of spirits," Sonny said.

She nodded. "But we've lost so much of the knowledge of our ancestors."

"It's not just losing traditions," Sonny said. "It's losing a kind of inner knowledge. I see that inner harmony at work in don Eliseo, and I wonder why can't we all acquire the wisdom he has."

"Because we live surrounded by those who don't believe in the old knowledge. The world is full of doubt, and people no longer communicate with their souls. People come here and *feel* this place is spiritual, but they don't go deeper. They stop at the gate."

That's what don Eliseo often said, Sonny thought. The Río Grande valley was the meeting ground of spiritual ways. Hispanos and Mexicanos had learned the Pueblo ways, but the Indian religion had gone underground under the persecution of the Spanish friars. The pursuit of the Franciscans to convert and baptize the Indians was relentless, and the civil authority backing them was as vicious. The esoteric knowledge had been driven underground.

With the coming of the Anglo Americans, the Nuevo Mexicanos did the same. The ceremonies of the church remained in the open, but the deeper beliefs and folk remedies, the stories of the brujos, went underground.

Other communities had gone secret. The conversos, those Jews who converted to Christianity and came to Nueva España to avoid the Holy Office of the Inquisition, had also kept their traditions secret.

The Pueblos went into the kiva and learned the hard way they had to protect the knowledge that anthropologists might misuse.

"A lot of people in hiding," Sonny said.

"A lot of knowledge," Lorenza replied. "We have so much to offer each other. Ways to care for the soul. The ways of our ancestors."

"And fewer and fewer believe in the soul," Sonny mused. "Like me. Have I lost my soul?"

"You had lost the way of knowledge of your ancestors," Lorenza replied. "You remember the stories of your abuelos, but you lost belief in them. Then Gloria's spirit came to haunt you, and you realized you needed help. You've begun your journey."

"I can't do it alone," Sonny said, admitting for the first time that there were *some* things he didn't know.

"Everyone needs a guide. Women have passed the knowledge down generation to generation. Now we have so few who can keep the brujos in check."

"Part of what you do is keep Raven, and those like him, in check?"

"It's what we all should be doing. Raven represents a very destructive evil."

"Yes," Sonny murmured.

He leaned back in the chair, admiring Lorenza's fine-chiseled face, the Indian cheekbones, the flare of her nostrils, the light brown skin. Her brown eyes. Her inner beauty shone on her face, as it did with Rita, don Eliseo, others he loved. A truly positive spirit radiated from within.

"Will I see the coyotes again?" he asked.

"Of course," she replied. "Are you ready?"

"Raven tried to kill me. I need to find him."

"You need to prepare," she said. "Come." She led him into the small consultation room at the back of the house where she had performed the limpieza.

She closed the door. "Unbutton your shirt," she commanded.

Sonny did as he was told, exposing the Zia medallion, a piece of the sun burning on his chest.

"Tamara said it's the only protection I have against Raven," he explained.

"It can be," she said. "But it needs to be blessed. Raven had possession of the Zia symbol on the medallion, and he was using it to carry out his destruction. You must do good work with it. It will fill you with light. Take the medallion and place it at the altar."

He took the medallion from around his neck and walked to the altar and laid it at the foot of the statue of la Virgen de Guadalupe. The gold burned his hand and he was startled. He returned to sit next to Lorenza. She pulled her chair close to his, their knees touched. She reached out and held his hands. Her hands were warm, enveloping. Her fragrance was a mixture of the incense and herbs she used in her healing, and the wax of the candle that burned at the altar.

"Finding Raven can be dangerous," she said.

"More dangerous if I don't."

"Yes," she agreed, and looked out the window toward the river bosque. She appeared irritated for a moment.

"Is anything wrong?" Sonny asked.

"No, it's just that I've had so little time to prepare you. You know Raven has special powers."

Sonny nodded. "Don Eliseo calls him a brujo."

"Yes, a very dangerous brujo. A sorcerer. He draws people into his cult and will not let them go."

"Veronica was one of them," Sonny said.

"Yes, the women killed Gloria, but they don't have his power. He controls them. Raven lives in the world of darkness. He wants people under his control."

"How do you know so much about him?" Sonny asked.

She leaned back. Sonny didn't know the world of the brujos. He had met his guardian spirits, but now he was threatened by his ancient enemy. Now he needed the coyotes, the guardian spirits who could take him into the world of spirits and give him the power to fight Raven. Sonny was awakening from a long sleep.

"Brujo is the Spanish word for witch," she said. "But that really doesn't describe Raven. He's more than a brujo." She paused. "Those of us who guide people in search of their souls know about Raven. He has the power of his nagual."

"Raven can *become* a raven?"

"Yes."

"Then all I need is a raven trap," Sonny joked.

She looked into Sonny's bright, mischievous eyes and laughed. Sonny did have the spirit of coyote. That was good. He was a trickster caught in a dangerous and tangled web, and he didn't know what it held for him, but he could still laugh. He had the spirit to learn and survive.

"Yes, a raven trap," Lorenza said. "His nagual makes him very powerful, and the only way you can stop him is to learn to use the power of the coyotes."

"Why the coyotes?"

"For now it seems that is the energy calling to you. There are other ways, but this is expedient. For now."

"And later?"

"Later you travel through your dreams, later still through moments of meditation, until you can at will step from one world to the next."

"So I'm just beginning," he said. "Okay, let's do it. My abuelo used to tell me, 'Whenever you're in trouble, maybe you have a problem you have to think about, go to the river. Go to that safe place where the coyotes live.' Maybe he knew the coyotes would help me."

"They will help," she said. She took his hand again. "Tell me more about those river coyotes."

"I spent summers with my abuelos. There was an oxbow at the river. The river curved in and out, like a horseshoe. The water was calm, deep. I could fish there, go swimming. I would sit still, and even though the family of coyotes could smell me, would know I was there, they didn't run away. They had their den under the huge roots of the alamo. The cubs played in the shade. . . ."

"How many?"

"Four. Male, female, two cubs."

"The four you saw in your vision."

"Yes. I can see them now."

The vision suddenly appeared, so clear it overwhelmed him. Did it have something to do with Lorenza's touch? Was she hypnotizing him and taking him into his past?

"You are there now?"

"I can see it clearly. . . ."

She stood and moved to the tape player, turned it on, and the drumming began. "Lie here, on the floor," she said. "On your side."

He obeyed, and she lay next to him, along his back.

"Are you sure this—" he started to say, but she cut in.

"Do as I say," she whispered. "Listen to the drumming."

He could feel her warmth, hear her steady breathing.

"Keep the image of the pond clear. . . . You will enter there. . . . Sing your song."

He closed his eyes and began to sing, softly, barely audible, to the beat of the drum. He saw his grandfather's farm, the adobe house, so cool in the summer, the fields of alfalfa being mowed and packed by the men, the summer drone of cicadas, the scattering grasshoppers as he ran through the grass, the call of birds in the orchard, the pungency of the chile verde his grandmother roasted for the noonday meal.

So much of his childhood was smell, touch, sound, dreams.

When did the senses of the child leave off and the dreams begin? Life then had been like a vibration, a steady pulse droning with a strange energy, like a low current of electricity passing through his body.

He felt it all again, so clearly that he felt he could reach out and touch the burst of sunflowers along the irrigation ditch as he ran toward the river, could feel the whip of the wild grasses, the fragrance of the yellow clusters of flowers on the Russian olive trees, the warmth of salty sweat trickling down his cheeks, along the back of his neck.

The river was serene, peaceful. The canopy of the cottonwoods was the underworld of his childhood. He had fallen back to childhood, and there on the damp bank of the pond sat the four coyotes. Two grown ones and two large cubs. It was a family.

He stepped into the middle of their circle. The coyotes stood around him, east, north, west, south. Quiet sentries marking the sacred directions, and he at the center. Their energy flowed to him, filling him with lightness, exuberation. He was running, close to the ground, close to the scents of the other animals, running with the coyotes, free, flying.

He saw a different kind of forest: the Sandia Mountains' pine tree forest where he had first found Raven's compound. The vision dissolved, and the forest became a jungle, people running. Thunderous gunfire filled the air, as did the sound of mortars. He saw a dark shadow rising from the trees, and suddenly helicopters swarmed overhead. People were dying. They disappeared into the smoke of the battle.

"The homeless," Sonny muttered. There was nothing he could do to save the brown-skinned people being slaughtered.

"Raven!" Sonny heard himself shout. He was challenging Raven to come out in the open.

A large moving van appeared. At first he thought it had something to do with the homeless, and then he saw the top of the van open and Raven's dark balloon rise into the sky.

"Ah," Sonny heard himself whisper.

The pounding drum told him it was time to go deeper.

"Go deeper," the voice said. "Go deeper. . . ."

He found Gloria. Her body wasn't cold from death as he had seen her that day in June, but warm, inviting, as she had been the night she gave herself to him.

She put her arm around him, drew him near.

"Gloria," he whispered. Finally she was there in front of him! She had haunted his dreams and waking hours, driving him relentlessly. She wanted revenge for her murder, and she was using Sonny.

The coyotes tugged at him, forcing him to look closely at the woman in his arms. It wasn't Gloria holding him, it was her spirit. He had followed the coyotes into the world of spirits. They had brought him here so he could be released from her.

"Release me," he said, and she was gone. A luminous light moved away from him and he stood alone, gasping for breath. He felt a tremendous surge of energy as the light moved away from him, moved toward the setting sun.

"I'm free," he sobbed. "I'm free. . . ."

The drumming was so low now he could barely hear it. He felt Lorenza rise, heard her praying; then the eagle feather passed across his closed eyes, and he felt the stir of air. She clapped loudly, four times, and gently touched her hands to his eyes.

"Open your eyes. Open them very slowly. Use the coyotes to return to this world. . . ."

He turned from the world of spirits and ran with the coyotes. Ran low to the ground, like them, sniffing as he went, flying as he went.

"Breathe in, deep, then out, slowly. Open your eyes slowly," she said, giving careful instructions, and the glare of the world returned.

He was lying on the floor, Lorenza sitting beside him.

"Feels like I've been smoking pot." He smiled. "Or peyote." He had done the medicine with don Eliseo once. "I thought you were Gloria. . . ."

She smiled. "You called her name. What did you see?"

Sonny told her his vision.

"You are free of Gloria's spirit," she said. "And now we know the guardian spirits will help. Great news, Sonny Baca."

She smiled and walked out of the room. Sonny stood and looked around him. The reality of the room felt so mundane compared to the trip he had just taken. And why could he take such a trip without smoking grass or chewing peyote? Was it that easy to call on the guardian spirits and go to the world of spirits? Or had Lorenza given him something in his coffee?

She returned with two cups of tea and offered one to Sonny. He took it and sipped, enjoying the aroma, the soft, warm liquid silky on his tongue. He was thirsty.

"Do you put something in the drinks?" he asked.

She laughed. "It's all in you, Sonny, all in you."

"I can call the coyotes?"

"Anytime," she said.

"Great medicine."

"It is. Powerful stuff."

"Too bad more people don't know about this." He smiled. "We'd be tripping to the world of spirits all the time."

"No," she cautioned. "It has a very serious purpose."

"I thought Coyote was a trickster."

"He is, but that doesn't mean he's around just to pull pranks. Coyote *is* an old trickster. Sometimes he forgets and turns to beguiling the young women he meets in the bars along Fourth Street. Drink and dance and take them to bed. They love his ways and words of honey."

"That sounds familiar," Sonny muttered, his face growing red.

She laughed. "You're learning. The journey into the world of spirits can be full of danger. At first you don't understand what you see. You took the form of the coyote in the vision and had a very pleasant trip."

"I feel great."

"Ah, good."

"And you?" he asked.

He sipped the tea and looked into her clear eyes. She was attractive, alone, and he knew he pleased her.

"My role is only to guide you," she said. "The journey is dangerous. A lot of spirits live in that underworld, a lot of ghosts live in your unconscious. Right now the goal is to get you in touch with your guardians, your source of power."

"I felt like I was flying."

She laughed. "Brujos fly."

"Me?"

She nodded.

"I wouldn't believe it if I hadn't been there. Yes, it was being there. And the other things I saw?"

"They are signs. Think carefully on them. They are signs."

"Gracias por todo," he said. "And the Zia medallion?"

"It's been blessed by your guardian spirits. It is yours to wear. Now it will protect you."

He went to the altar and retrieved the Zia medallion. For a moment he hesitated, thinking this is what would bring Raven to him, then he slipped it around his neck.

He went to her and gave her an abrazo, feeling again, momentarily, the warmth of her body. "Gracias," he said again, then quickly walked out of the house, not daring to look back.

"Ve con Dios, los santos, y tu nagual," she whispered.

Sonny got in his truck and felt a new mood wash over him. He was feeling stronger. Gloria's dread was lifted from him, and her soul, which so desired revenge, was winging its way to heaven.

Or wherever souls went after their life on earth. Back to the cosmic wind, the light of the universe, as don Eliseo said. Gloria's soul was now following its natural evolution, and Sonny was free.

The guardian spirits helped, he thought as he peered at the edge of the river bosque, where shadows shifted in the afternoon light. The coyotes were close by.

A blanket of light lay across the valley. The slanting rays of October sun suffused the land with the glow of golden pollen. The Sandias were mauve.

Ah, to be able to enjoy the light falling across the land is a good sign.

Before he picked up Peter at the television station, he stopped by the library. Ruth had a few notes on the people he was tracking.

"Not much," she apologized, "but I'll keep digging."

"This is a great start," Sonny said, and thanked her. At TV 7 he found Peter talking to Francine Hunter in the parking lot. She had just wrapped up her report for the evening news and was also on her way home.

"Tough luck," Peter greeted him.

"Hi, Sonny. Anything new?" Francine asked.

Sonny shook his head.

"It's a black eye for the fiesta." She walked to her car. "Are you working for the fiesta board?"

"Yes," Sonny replied.

For a moment her newswoman instincts almost caused her to ask the next questions: Who do you think murdered Mario Secco? And why? But she didn't. "Well, good luck on it," she said. "It's a terrible thing. See you in the morning, Peter. Thanks."

"Be here eight o'clock sharp." Peter waved as she drove away.

"Did you shoot the Secco murder?" Sonny asked as they drove home.

"Yes. Francine is like a bulldog. Worse than that guy Barker. Once she starts on a story, she doesn't let go."

"Did you see anything?"

"No. We were outside the police cordon. They said the killer was in a black balloon. Like the one we saw, I'm sure. So this evil man who haunts your tracks has killed again."

"Yes," Sonny replied.

At Rita's Sonny dropped Peter off in the backyard, where Peewee and Busboy were resting and talking about the day's work.

Inside, Sonny found Cristina trying on the new clothes Rita had bought for her. She was showing them to her father.

"Quíhubole, bro," Diego greeted him.

"Amor." Rita kissed him. "I'm so glad to see you."

"And I'm glad to see you," he said, holding her for a moment and looking in her eyes. He wanted to tell her about his visit to Lorenza, but it could wait. "What's this?" he asked, turning to Cristina.

"My tía Rita bought me these clothes," Cristina said, embracing Rita.

"Beautiful." Sonny smiled, picked her up, and whirled her around.

"And my hair," she said, showing it off. Her glossy black hair was tied in two braids accented with ribbons. "For school," she said.

"School?" Diego looked at his wife.

"Los Ranchos Elementary is close," Marta answered.

"She should be in school," Rita explained. "It might as well be here. I know the principal. A wonderful woman. She'll make sure Cristina will be welcome."

"I want to go, Papá," Cristina said. "I miss school."

Diego looked at his daughter, his wife, and shrugged. "You need money to go to school," he said, "and I don't have a job—" He paused. "I'll check on the boys," he said, turning and walking hurriedly outside.

Sonny started to follow, but Marta touched his arm. "It's not easy for him. We tried to leave the river before, and it never worked out. We always have to return. If he could find a real job, he could make it."

"We'll work on it," Sonny said. "Cristina should be in school." He kneeled and looked in her eyes. "You like school?"

"Oh, yes," she replied.

"Good. Now go get your papá and the others. Tell them we're going to celebrate by having the best meal in town."

Cristina ran outside, calling her father.

Sonny looked out the back window, where the men were sitting. They were laughing and joking, as men will do after a hard but satisfying day's work. It was only part-time work, but it was a beginning. Still he knew he couldn't assure Diego and his family that in a few weeks, when the part-time jobs were over, they wouldn't have to return to the river.

"I heard the news on the radio," Rita said when Cristina was out of the room. "It was Raven?"

"Yes."

"Why?"

"I wish I knew," Sonny replied.

"What now?"

"Maybe just forget about him," Sonny said.

He didn't tell her about the flight scheduled for tomorrow.

"Vamos, let's eat," he said to change the subject.

Rita had insisted it was her treat at her restaurant, and so they packed the women in her car and the men in Sonny's truck and drove to Rita's Cocina.

"First time I ever came into a restaurant to eat and not to wash dishes," Busboy said when they entered.

"First time we've come in the front door of any place in a long time," Diego added.

The story of Mario Secco's death had scared people away; many balloonists were leaving town. The consequences already showed in Rita's place. Last night it had been packed, now it was half full.

Sonny sat across from Diego; they ordered cold Coronas.

"How did you get along with don Eliseo?" Sonny asked Diego.

"Bien," Diego answered. "The old man reminds me of my grandfather. I grew up in a little ranchito like his. Don Eliseo's place needs a lot of repair."

"He needs help," Sonny agreed. "He has a couple of boys, but they live in the Heights. They've got their families, and little time to help the old man. One's a high school teacher—music, I think. The other's an engineer at Sandia. They come around once in a while, try to help, but they only stay an hour. Then they leave. Farming the old ranchito is not their thing."

"Families change, they scatter," Diego said. He understood. "When I came back from Nam, it was like that."

Sonny wanted to know more about the man he had befriended, but he was cautious and did not question him further.

"Nam. Seems like a generation ago," he mused.

"I guess people have forgotten it, but those of us who were

there won't. I never saw action, hell, compared to some of my brothers in the field I had it made. But when I got back, my sister had sold the house, and after my mother died, I had nothing to come back to. I have brothers. Three. One here, two in California. They sold Grandpa's place."

"Did you get anything from it?"

"I didn't want anything. I was burned out. In Nam I was on a Graves Registry detail, picking up and bagging body parts. The guy I worked for was a mortician, not regular army. He turned me on to dope. It was the only way to do the job. . . ."

He sipped his beer.

"All of us should be dead by now. We did things in a crazy way. Charlie would wire the bodies, and we were always so toked up we just ripped in. A couple of the guys bought the farm that way. I was busted for doing drugs, but that didn't mean nada. They needed us. You know, some of the guys were so hooked, they signed on for Graves again. For the dope. I got out when my mother died, started drinking. I lost track of the years. I mean, I was so deep into booze and crap, nothing mattered. I spent five years on the streets of 'Burque, drinking, living on the river. Then I met Marta. She saved me. Helped me get clean. Then we had Cristina. I tried to climb out of the hole, but it's hard. I have no education, no skills. Part-time jobs came and went. We sank, hermano, we sank. The worst curse is to have no home for your kid. You know God is really punishing you when that happens."

Diego fell silent. Peter filled the silence by telling them about his day with Francine Hunter and the Mario Secco murder scene, but Diego's gaze was elsewhere, out the window floating over the North Fourth Street traffic, and beyond. He knew the city, but the city didn't know him. His family had lived for generations in the state, but when the ranchito was sold, he was left hanging, and no one gave a damn how long the family had lived in the valley or how many centuries ago their ancestors had colonized the area.

For Sonny, the night also ended in a somber mood. Rita took Marta and Cristina home with her, and Sonny dropped the

Marta and Cristina home with her, and Sonny dropped the men off at don Eliseo's. Don Eliseo's large rambling house had plenty of rooms where the men could sleep, but Sonny's place had only one small bedroom.

"Hasta mañana," they called. "Thanks for the dinner. Thanks for everything."

"I appreciate what you've done," Diego said, and took Sonny's hand. "Buenas noches, hermano."

Diego's parting words reminded Sonny of his brother, Armando. Mando wasn't homeless, but he was buffeted by fate. He kept trying to start his own car business, and small glitches kept ruining his enterprises.

Qué cosa es el destino, Sonny thought as he dropped wearily into bed. One man succeeds, the other doesn't. One fails, the other thrives. Diego calls me hermano, and I haven't been a very good brother to my own.

He read through Ruth's notes from the library. Hidden in the names, he hoped, was part of the reason the skies over the city had erupted with death. Raven needed money to get his cult back in business. He needed a car, arms, dynamite if he was going to strike again. There were other disturbing things in the files he read. Many people had converged on Alburquerque for the balloon fiesta, and each had an interesting background.

"Everyone has a motive," he remembered his mentor Manuel López telling him. "That's what makes our work so damn interesting."

Sonny dozed but slept little. The night was full of disturbing images, faces of people who peered from the shadows. He was in a hospital looking for a group of Nam veterans. He searched everywhere, until a blond nurse pointed the way. He found the group, hulks of men without legs and arms. Their torsos were buried in the ground in a circle. He drew close. Diego welcomed him in a strange language. The men in the circle were autistic; only grunts came from their throats.

He conversed with Diego, in metaphors, witty wordplay, and each time he outdid Diego, Diego laughed. The dark masses around him didn't seem to care. Finally he was accepted into the circle, he had passed the test. Sit, Diego said, and he pointed to an empty chair next to a young woman. She held many papers. Sophia, he thought. Her face radiated beauty. She smiled and welcomed him.

Some of her papers were on the low chair next to her, and when he sat, he apologized. I'm going to sit on your papers, he said, and she smiled again. Sit on wisdom.

He looked around the circle at the misshapen bodies. That's it, he thought. I am talking to them, but not with words! It's some kind of mental telepathy! I can communicate with them. Not with words, with thought.

He wanted to speak more with those earth shapes, to make amends or apologize for their suffering. Maybe his words, if he could only speak, would allow the bodies half-buried in the mud some rest. They were the bodies Diego had collected in the killing fields. Those soldiers in the field had been killed in the most horrendous ways, instant separation of soul and body. And there was no family to place a descanso cross where they died.

With sadness in his heart, he picked up two pieces of bamboo. Tying the two pieces together with a bootlace, he fashioned a cross and stuck it by the side of the path. There, just like the crosses that dotted the roads of the state where someone had died in a car wreck, the place where all those grunts had died was now marked. *Descanso* meant "to rest." A resting place. The men could rest.

He smiled and rolled over. How reassuring the strange dream seemed.

Rita appeared, rising in a colorful balloon. She was laughing, she waved. Around her dozens of colorful balloons rose like the flowers of her garden. Sonny wanted to be in the balloon with her, but there was no way to climb up. A rope appeared, he climbed, and suddenly a dark shadow blocked the kaleidoscope of colors, and Sonny was falling through darkness.

He awoke with a start to the knock on the door.

Madge. He stumbled out of bed and opened the front door. It was dark outside. He rubbed his eyes. "Come in, come in."

"Brr, it is cold outside." She entered and closed the door behind her.

"You're early. I'll make coffee—"

"There's time," she said, and put her arms around him.

"Raven won't wait," he said, disengaging himself tactfully. "I'll turn on the heater."

She laughed and turned to look around. "As I understand it, we might get blown out of the sky today, and you want to go chaste."

"Yeah, for today." He smiled. "I'll get dressed. Coffee's in the kitchen." He pointed her to the kitchen and hurried to shower.

Damn! he thought as the cold water awakened him. She's about the best-looking blonde in the city, comes hot-to-trot to my door, and I turn her away. Que pendejo! I just hope she realizes what she's getting into. I hope she didn't agree to this because she thought we would get together. Her life could be in danger.

Ah, well, he tried to make the best of it as he toweled and dressed, singing, "Para bailar la bamba, se necesita unas pocas de ganas, por ti seré, por ti seré."

He walked into the kitchen whistling. Madge poured him coffee.

"A beautiful madrugada. Looks great for ballooning," he said, sipping and looking out the window at the gray morning light. It was still an hour before the sun came over the Sandia Mountains. Santo día, the old people used to say, and Sonny wondered if that got abbreviated to Sandia.

"Great coffee."

"It gets the pump going," Madge replied.

"Sorry if I was too brusque."

She shrugged. "If it doesn't work, it just doesn't work. I'm a big girl, I understand. So let's go do the job."

"Got the balloon ready?"

"Just as you ordered. It's the first armor-plated balloon I've ever seen. Will he take the bait?"

"There's a reason for Raven to be disrupting the fiesta. He's taking chances he normally wouldn't take. What is it about this fiesta, Madge?"

She shook her head. "Nothing, as far as I can tell."

"Had Mario Secco flown here before?"

"No. It was his first time."

"And John Gilroy. The ex-CIA man?"

Her brow knitted. "Ex-CIA?"

Sonny nodded. "Was all over the papers when he came to town."

"We don't check backgrounds. He's been flying four, five years. Everybody knows him. What's the connection?"

"I thought you might tell me."

She finished her coffee. "I don't know these people, so I don't know if they're connected. Look, they apply to fly and the applications are processed. They pay their fee, they fly. I don't get involved on a personal level. Not good for business. Come on, let's go get Raven. Maybe he can answer your questions."

"Yeah, maybe."

He took his deer-hunting rifle from the closet, checked it, and filled his army jacket pockets with shells.

As the sun was ready to burst over the crest of the Sandias, they drove into the balloon launching field. Madge's balloon was already inflated and swaying softly in the cold breeze; it had been filled by her assistant, a man Sonny remembered as Tony. Tony was a "zebra," one of those in charge of launching the balloons.

Jerry Stammer also waited near the balloon, shivering in the early morning cold.

"You're late," he greeted them gruffly, plumes of frozen breath spewing out.

"We're okay," Madge shot back, turning away. "Ready, Tony?"

"All set," the assistant called back, handing her a backpack. "There's a good easterly aloft. Exactly like yesterday. You should be over the path you marked at eight hundred feet."

"Maybe we shouldn't go through with it," Stammer complained. "Too dangerous. Maybe we should call it off."

Why so upset? Sonny wondered. Did he have something for Madge?

"You sure this is the only way?" Stammer asked.

Sonny looked at Madge; she nodded. "Sonny thinks so. And I'm the pilot. Unless you want to fly today?"

"You're crazy," Stammer shot back.

Sonny looked around the huge, empty field. At the far end of it sat an unmarked police car. Garcia. Sonny hoped he wouldn't scare Raven away. If he sensed it was a trap, he might not show himself. But Garcia was playing it cool, laying back in the shadows. He was giving Sonny enough room to hang himself.

"Looks great," Madge said. "The easterly will take us over the river."

"Then let's fly," Sonny said, and they climbed into the basket.

He checked the steel plate on the floor of the basket. Enough to deflect even a bullet from a high-powered weapon and give him time to fire back. Today Raven was not going to meet unarmed people in the sky, he was going to meet a flying coyote with a 30.06.

"Cast off," Madge said, and Tony untied the line that had kept the balloon anchored to iron posts in the ground. Madge pulled the burner lever, and a blast of propane, burning blue, rose into the mouth of the towering balloon. They climbed swiftly.

"Toward the river." She pointed as they climbed into the prevailing easterly breeze.

Sonny had kept his rifle wrapped in his parka. Now he slipped it out, put on the parka, and slipped shells into the chamber.

Yes, toward the river, where both Secco and Veronica had been murdered.

The sun came over the mountain, a blinding ball of light. Rita would be waking up about now. He should have told her. Rita was patient and understanding, but when he told her what he was up to after the fact, it bothered her. She had the right to know; after all, they were planning marriage. Yes, he would marry her, settle down, get out of the adventure business.

know; after all, they were planning marriage. Yes, he would marry her, settle down, get out of the adventure business.

"Time for home and children," he whispered.

"What?" Madge asked.

"Just thinking," he answered. "It's cold up here."

His words spewed out in icy vapor.

"It's freezing," Madge said, smiling, "and it gets colder the higher we go. I love it!"

Yeah, Sonny thought, she clearly gets a thrill out of it. He pulled the zipper on his parka and looked over the side of the basket.

The balloon rose over the field and drifted west. Garcia's car followed well behind the chase truck Tony drove. Both would keep as discreetly far away as possible.

"Remember when you went up with me?" Madge asked.

Sonny nodded. "Yeah. Too bad flying never got in my blood. It is spectacular."

Now as he looked down on the checkered fields of the valley, the roads where tiny antlike cars began to move in the early morning, he felt an exhilaration. The earth was beautiful from this height, at this time of day. A feeling of calm came over him; he was no longer earthbound. He had cut the umbilical cord to the earth, and the rush of freedom coursed through him.

"You haven't lived till you've made love up here," Madge teased.

"Doesn't it get cold?"

"It's like having ice cream in your coffee, hot and cold."

Her eyes were gleaming in the morning cold. She was in her element, and she was offering to share it. She smiled and turned to the task of flying the balloon.

Sonny looked west, returning his gaze to her from time to time. She was a woman who enjoyed the quick rush of sex, the more exciting the better. And why not, life was short. Soar as high as you can, rush in and take what you can get, fly in all the hot-air balloon fiestas of the world, because nothing lasts. Todo se acaba, he remembered his father saying. Everything ends.

Looking down at the land from this height made him turn philosophical. Maybe that was the mystery of ballooning, it put earth and space in context. One felt exhilaration up here, but one also felt very small.

They floated slowly westward, over the tinge of gold that graced the river cottonwoods below, keeping just the right altitude. Early on, Madge had struggled to compensate for the added weight in the balloon, but once she had that under control, she relaxed. She took a bottle of champagne from the pack her assistant had given her.

"Will you do the honors?" she asked, and handed the bottle to Sonny.

Holy tacos, he thought, we're flying toward Raven's nest and she wants champagne. Ah, what the hell, maybe she had the right attitude—drink champagne and let the chips fall where they may. Or let the balloons float where they will. He plied the plastic cap off the bottle; it popped, and he filled two plastic cups.

They touched cups. It might be the last sip of bubbly he would taste if he had made a mistake about Raven.

"To us," she said, and drank. "Isn't this lovely."

"It's great," he agreed, and turned to look west toward Mt. Taylor, the old volcano that rose like the breast of a woman into the bright, clear sky. North lay the blue Jemez and the Sangre de Cristos. The tops of the peaks were dusted with snow, the remnants of one early storm.

Around them the sky was like an inverted bowl, a fragile porcelain decorated with wisps of cirrus clouds; below, the earth was a patterned colcha, a quilt like Sonny's mother used to sew.

From up here he could see the earth as the large hawks that climb on thermals to hunt saw it. Or a hang glider who has just jumped off Sandia Crest and is floating, also catching the thermals. Or someone parachuting down.

They swept gently toward the river, the lazy, meandering Río Grande. The great river flowed toward Los Lunas, Belén, and down past Socorro, land of Sonny's ancestors, where his grand-father had farmed, where the Bisabuelo Elfego Baca was born.

He looked east. The Sandias and the Manzano Mountains rose like giant reptiles in the blue haze. The mountains guarded the eastern entrance to the valley. Beyond them lay the land of the eagle and the serpent, the great plains of the eastern Llano Estacado. Ben Chávez country. The writer had warned Sonny, told him Raven's spirit was all around. Embodying the evil in the Coco, he tried to burn it away.

But that didn't work. Raven had to be met head on. Sonny knew that.

"We're floating directly toward where Secco went down," Madge said.

Sonny held his rifle ready.

He was hunting Raven, and that required ready instincts. He wished he was on the ground, where he could smell the odors, hear the crack of twigs on the path, hear the rustle of wings as birds flew overhead. Up here he felt disconnected.

A sound startled him. He could hear the sounds from the valley floor. Dogs barking, a horse neighing in a field below, someone shouting, then they were over the river bosque, and his mood changed from contemplative to attentive.

He felt the hair rise along the back of his neck.

"Get ready," he said to Madge, and snapped a shell into the rifle's chamber.

As he had anticipated, when they approached the east side of the river, Raven's balloon rose to meet them.

14

There!" Sonny motioned, and Madge turned to see the black balloon rise quickly from the river, the white raven emblem clearly visible. Raven had been waiting; he had launched his balloon from a small clearing somewhere in the bosque. That's how he had escaped detection, he hid in the river forest. Now his balloon rose quickly to meet them.

"That's him!" Madge shouted.

Sonofabitch has balls, Sonny thought. He has to know Garcia's nearby. Does he want me that bad to take the chance?

A sixth sense nudged at Sonny. No, Raven would not take those kinds of chances. Keep to your plan. . . . Keep to your plan. . . .

The figure of Raven crouching low in the basket as the balloon rose to meet them had distracted Sonny for a moment. The figure in the basket held a rifle, there was a flash of fire, and the report of a rifle followed. Sonny heard the whining sound of the bullet ricocheting off the steel plate.

"He's shooting!" Madge cried.

"Yeah," Sonny acknowledged, and peered over the edge of the basket. "Take it down!" he shouted. "Take it down quickly."

"Down?"

"Yes, down! Land it anywhere!"

Another shot sounded from Raven's balloon, then another, but Sonny knew it was a decoy. The thud he felt on the steel plate told him the real shot had been fired from the ground. The plate had deflected the bullet.

Sonny spotted a figure in a clearing near the edge of the river. He took aim and fired. The startled figure jumped back as the bullet spat dirt at his feet. Sonny fired again. The bullet exploded a dry branch right above the man who had shot at them. Sonny saw him disappear into the bosque.

"What are you shooting at?" Madge shouted when she saw Sonny wasn't aiming at the black balloon, but down at the river.

"Look!" Sonny shouted, and pointed at Raven's balloon.

It came up fast, and as it drifted alongside them, they could see the figure in the balloon. It was a dummy, a mannequin holding a broomstick. The blast of gunshots that sounded were firecrackers tied to the tip of a broom. Raven wouldn't take a chance on getting caught in a balloon. He had killed Mario Secco from the ground! The black balloon was a decoy.

"It's a dummy!" Madge cried as the black balloon floated alongside them for a while, then began to drop.

"Yeah." Sonny nodded. He was looking down into the bosque where Raven had disappeared. Caught off guard by their response, Raven wouldn't fire on them again.

Raven had anchored his balloon and inflated it. When Sonny and Madge's balloon approached, he cut the line and the balloon rose to greet them, a distraction so he could get a clear shot at Sonny.

Sonny peered over the edge again. Raven was nowhere in sight. His ruse had been found out, and he didn't want to risk a gun battle with Sonny. Maybe it was safe, but up in the air they were sitting ducks. Best to continue down and get on terra firma.

Madge pointed to a sandbar in the riverbed. "Is that okay?"

"Fine," Sonny replied. Without a fresh burst of hot air, the black balloon floated down, toward the same sandbar Madge was aiming for. Sonny wanted to take a look at it.

"He was on the ground, wasn't he?" Madge said.

Sonny nodded. He knew the gun battle had frightened her, and seeing Sonny shooting down instead of at the black balloon had confused her for a moment.

She skillfully brought the fast-descending balloon to a landing on the sandbar.

"Let's anchor it and keep it inflated!" Madge shouted, tossing Sonny the rope and pointing to a large log half-buried in the wet sand.

If she deflated the balloon, they would need a portable fan to inflate it again, and they weren't packing a fan. Sonny tied the balloon down, then ran to Raven's balloon. Luckily there was no wind sweeping across the shallow river, and in the fall and winter the sandbars ran for miles.

He cautiously approached Raven's basket, sure that Raven would have one more trick up his sleeve. The mannequin dressed in black was tied to the side of the basket, its face covered with a phantom-of-the-opera mask. The exploded firecrackers covered the tip of the broomstick. No wonder the witnesses who saw the death of Mario Secco swore they saw the gunfire coming from the black balloon; the firecrackers created a loud noise and a flash of fire.

Sonny noticed a tape player hanging around the dummy's neck. When he clicked it on, Raven's mad laughter crackled. The message was for the police chief.

"Garcia . . . by the time you listen to this, Sonny Baca will have a hole in his head. I owed him one, now I'm even. I owe this fucking state one, and it's going to get it. Bad! You and the FBI boys can't stop me."

There was a pause. "But let's suppose Baca made it out alive.

Sure, that would even be more fun. Tricksters love games, don't we, Baca? Yes, I love the game, but it's coming to an end! You have created the fire of the nuclear bomb, and you will feel its wrath!"

Sonny jumped back as a flash of fire exploded from the dummy, quickly engulfing the basket in flames. The tape player must have been rigged to trigger an explosion after the message played once. Raven had planned everything down to the last detail. The balloon that fired on Mario Secco had also gone up in flames. But the police thought the propane tank had blown up. No, Raven had planned the burn.

The sound of a helicopter made Sonny spin around and aim his rifle up. He relaxed when he saw the TV 7 chopper swooping over the treetops to land on the wide sandbar. Francine Hunter jumped from the helicopter and came scrambling across the sandbar, followed by Peter shouldering a camera.

"Did you get him?" she called as she ran toward the burning basket.

"You okay?" Peter asked.

"I'm okay," Sonny shouted above the roar of the motor. "It was a decoy."

"Get a shot!" Francine shouted at Peter.

Madge came running up, putting an arm around Sonny. "Are you all right?"

"Okay," Sonny answered.

"Why burn it?" she asked, looking at the flames and the column of smoke as the basket quickly burned.

"To burn the evidence," Sonny answered. "Raven likes games."

Francine Hunter shouted. "Peter, keep it rolling, keep it rolling! Get a shot of Sonny. Hold on to his arm," she told Madge, positioning her for the shot she wanted Peter to take. "He's our hero for the day."

She turned and faced the camera. "This is Francine Hunter, reporting from a sandbar on the Río Grande where Sonny Baca and Madge Swenson have just landed after being shot at possibly by the person or persons who killed Mario Secco. The hot-air balloon you see burning in the background belongs to the suspected murderer."

Damn, Sonny cursed silently, and kicked the wet sand at his feet. You advertise and you get what you pay for.

He turned to Madge. "Can we get out of here?"

"Sure," she said.

"Hey! Lemme finish the shot!" Francine Hunter called as Sonny and Madge walked back to her balloon.

Peter turned and very softly said, "Chill, Francine. Don't you see they almost got killed?"

"Oh, yeah." Francine nodded, tossing her hair from her forehead.

"Look!"

A second helicopter swooshed over the treetops and roared to a landing.

"Shit!" Madge said. "Doesn't that goddamned pilot know his draft is murder?" She held the lines of the moored balloon, which swayed precariously from the chopper's gust.

Two men jumped from the helicopter and raced toward Sonny. Sonny recognized Mike Stevens and Eddie Martínez. Stevens came toward him while Martínez ran to check out the burning basket.

"What the fuck do you think you're doing?" Stevens shouted above the roar of the motor.

"Taking ballooning lessons," Sonny replied sarcastically. "Agent Stevens, this is my flying instructor, Madge Swenson."

"I know damn well where you do your flying, Baca." The agent scowled. They had been tailing him, hoping he'd lead them to Raven.

"Glad to meet you, Agent Stevens. What brings you to the Grand Central sandbar on the Río Grande?"

He was in no mood to joke. "Stop the camera!" he shouted at Peter. Then turning to Sonny, he asked: "Did you see him?"

"I got a shot off," Sonny answered.

"You sure it was him?"

Sonny shrugged. The FBI knew it was Raven, they had

known all along. If they weren't sharing information, why should he?

"This was a stupid stunt, Baca, a real stupid stunt!" Stevens shouted.

"If it was so stupid, why didn't you stop me?" Sonny asked.

He knew they hadn't stopped him because they had hoped he would draw Raven out.

"They want to catch Raven, but let you take the chances," Madge said with clear disgust.

"We've got jurisdiction in this case. Getting Sonny to work for you is not a good idea, Ms. Swenson. This stunt was not a good idea. You went to visit Mr. Baca early in the morning, that's your business." Stevens grinned. "Just leave the job of finding Mario Secco's murderer to us. Have a good morning," he finished. "Let's go!" he shouted at Martínez, and together they ran toward the helicopter.

Sonny spotted a man sitting behind the chopper's pilot. A third agent? The FBI chopper rose quickly and disappeared over the trees.

"Did you see who was sitting in the chopper?" Francine Hunter said. She and Peter had stood by quietly, listening to the exchange.

Sonny shrugged. "An agent."

"No," she whispered. "That was William Stone."

Sonny ran the name through his name file, but nothing registered. William Stone was a common-enough name.

"CIA," she said in a tone that said her reporter's mind had sniffed a clue.

"CIA? You sure?" Sonny asked, turning to look after the helicopter. Sonny had noticed the pilot in the chopper, and the big, blondish man in the backseat. For a moment he had thought the man was Jerry Stammer; the glare of the sun made it impossible to see his face clearly. But no, it wasn't, so Sonny dismissed him as an agent.

"CNN did a story on him when Bush raided Panama. William Stone was the top honcho in the CIA group that was sending arms to the Contras in Nicaragua."

"What's he doing in Alburquerque?"

"Wire services say he's in the region visiting the FBI, but they don't say why."

Sonny remembered the CNN story now. Stone had been exposed in the report as the leader of the intelligence unit that was overseeing the Contra supply line. That was right after Gilroy got shot down and busted by his own agency for talking too much. Was he Stone's scapegoat? After the CNN show Stone had disappeared back into the caverns of the CIA. Why surface here, now?

And what the hell was he doing riding around in an FBI chopper with the two agents who were chasing Raven? He looked at Francine and saw her mind was asking the same question. Then he turned to Madge.

She shrugged. "I'm ready."

"What the hell, we might as well wrap up with a shot of these two sailing off into the blue," Francine said to Peter.

Sonny and Madge climbed into the basket, and Peter untied the anchor line. The balloon rose quickly, up and out of the bosque.

"What now?" Madge asked as they flew over Coors Road. She had spotted her chase crew; her assistant drove a bright orange pickup. Now she looked for a clear spot where she could land.

"Back to square one," Sonny mumbled in reply, but his mind was working on the incident with Stone. The FBI wanted Raven because he had tried to blow up a WIPP truck carrying nuclear waste material. He qualified as a terrorist. But why would the CIA be interested in Raven? William Stone wasn't out for a joy ride. Nothing was making sense.

Madge brought the balloon down on the soccer field near St. Pius High School. Tony in the chase truck was right there to help. An angry Police Chief Garcia also came roaring up.

"Did you see him?" Garcia asked as Sonny and Madge climbed out of the basket.

"Yes," Sonny answered. "He was hunting coyotes."

Raven had scored again, the evening news would say. That

is, the murderer of Veronica and Mario Secco was shooting at any balloon that went up, at will, and the police were helpless to stop him. The news would drive a deeper wedge of fear into what was left of the balloon fiesta.

"It was a stupid stunt," Garcia said.

Madge turned on the chief. "He got closer to the murderer than anyone else yet."

The police chief looked at her and glared. "Yeah," he snapped, "and you're lucky you didn't get your ass shot off, Miss Swenson!" He stalked away, got in his car, and churned out of the sandy lot.

Madge laughed. "Yeah, I am." She turned to Sonny. "I'm sorry. I panicked up there."

"Hey, it was a hairy scene. No problem."

"How did you know Raven was on the ground?"

"A friend at the police lab told me the autopsy report on Mario Secco said the bullet entered low in his stomach and exited between his shoulder blades. I knew he was killed from the ground, even though Garcia's boys didn't bother to check out the angle."

They looked at the steel plate that sat at the bottom of the basket. One bullet had made a dent in the steel; the angle at which it hit caused it to glance off.

Tony drove them to the balloon park, and Madge drove Sonny home in her red Corvette. "Thanks," she said at parting, "for everything. About this morning, I promise not to get in your life, unless—unless you call. Then I'll give you a long balloon ride on a calm morning. Do you still work for us?"

"Yeah. I want Raven as bad as you do."

"You know we're running out of time."

He nodded.

She put her Vette in gear and sped away, leaving a cloud of October dust in her wake.

Across the street don Eliseo and Diego were burning the dead grass along the irrigation ditch. They paused to watch the blond woman in the red car deliver Sonny, and when she was gone, they ambled over.

"Hey, Sonny. Who's the blonde?"

"My boss."

"She shows up pretty early." Don Eliseo winked at Diego.

Sonny blushed. If the old man knew, then his friends would know. Doña Concha would kid Sonny; the early morning visit would grow as the story got retold. And sooner or later Rita would hear it.

"I need Diego. Can you spare him?"

"Sure. Just bring him back in one piece. He's the best worker I ever had."

Diego smiled. "Your ranchito is going to look as good as one of those manicured estates on Chavez Road, don Eliseo."

"Don't get it to looking too good," don Eliseo laughed, "or one of those rich gringos will try to buy it from me. Adiós. Mucho cuidado."

"Where we going?" Diego asked as they got in Sonny's truck. Sonny told him what had happened on the balloon flight.

"I need to check out the place," Sonny explained.

"Man, you gotta be careful, hermano," Diego cautioned. "But don't worry, if Raven left a trail, I can find it."

"That's what I hoped," Sonny said.

They drove to the river and took a conservancy road along the bank of the irrigation ditch, toward the place where Sonny estimated Raven had launched his balloon. They came to a ditch chain hung across two posts, blocking the road. Sonny parked the truck and they walked into the river bosque. Sonny carried his pistol; he was taking no chances.

"Around here," he said, and they began looking for traces of Raven. It didn't take long for Diego to find the bullet casings in the clearing. He picked one up with a stick and smelled it.

"This is it. Just fired. He waited for you here. See where he inflated the balloon? Enough space to hide, and just enough for a takeoff." Diego pointed. He picked up a black Raven feather. "Doesn't make sense. The man leaves too many signs."

Yeah, Sonny thought, that's Raven.

"And this?" Diego said, picking up a small plastic sandwich bag. "He snorted while he waited?"

"You sure?"

Diego tasted the white powder residue in the bag. "I know good coke when I taste it, compa, and this guy is doing quality caca."

The Raven Sonny had met in June wasn't snorting coke.

"The man is crazy," Sonny said. "Maybe he's also in pain. After he fell into the arroyo, the water would have slammed him against the rocks and along the gravel bottom. One side of his face was cut to ribbons. He wouldn't have been able to see a doctor. The FBI was still looking for him, making it difficult to get help, so he's been in hiding three months."

"And in a lot of pain, so he took dope," Diego finished. "Makes sense."

"Where does he get it?"

"He has friends."

"He still has to buy it. Maybe with the money they took from Gloria."

"Or he's connected," Diego suggested.

"To the pipeline?"

"Hey, this stuff is pure," Diego said, holding up the plastic bag. "Sabes que, last week I was in town, looking for work, and the word on the street was that a big shipment is coming in. I mean really big."

"From where?"

"Colombia. It's not being brought in by the Mexican mafia. There's a direct line from the Cali cartel to Juárez, but for some reason Abrego's boys in Juárez are not handling this shipment. That means someone is paying a lot of bucks for protection."

"You mean to buy out the Juárez cartel?"

"Yeah." Diego nodded.

"Is the dope here?"

"The drop is this week. Everybody knows, but the people I talked to say very little. The deal is big. In the millions. Many millions. That means they have police protection, all the way from U.S. Customs right to the front door."

"Garcia?"

"Garcia's never taken a bribe. But when it comes to millions

"Garcia?"

"Garcia's never taken a bribe. But when it comes to millions of bucks' worth of coke, I guess you can't trust even your best friends."

Sonny couldn't believe the police chief could be bribed. The man was a sonofabitch, but a good sonofabitch. He was a homeboy from the barrio, in trouble like most kids growing up. But he'd gone into the police academy and worked his way up in the ranks. He loved the city and its people. But would he take a cut if the money offered was enough?

"Not Garcia." Sonny shook his head.

"So they go around the city cops. Sonny, when the big boys cut a deal like this, they go to the top. They buy a Customs agent, and the guys who do radar surveillance along the border, and finally they buy someone in the DEA. To them it's business."

Yeah, Sonny thought, big business.

"Remember last year, during the balloon fiesta? There was talk of a big shipment, but it wasn't coming through regular channels to the dealers in town. It was something new."

Sonny looked at Diego and both connected at the same time.

"You're thinking what I'm thinking?"

"Someone is using the fiesta as cover!" Diego exclaimed.

"Someone like Mario Secco could have pulled it off. Alburquerque becomes a distribution point." Sonny snapped his fingers. "A lot of people in town—to fly balloons, to have fun—except a few of them come to pick up dope. It makes sense!"

"You think they're using the balloons to distribute?"

"Maybe."

"How?"

"Maybe just as a decoy."

"Right! They start a war to confuse the local cops. They can bring it through Juárez if they've paid off the mafia. Then truck it in one big shipment right up I-25. But they still have to distribute it."

"That's where Raven comes in. He needs a cut to bankroll his cult."

"And soothe his pain," Diego added.

"Who fronts the money?" Sonny asked aloud. "Who in the hell would work with Raven?"

"Desperate people." Diego nodded.

"Very desperate. They need workers when they drop the stuff."

"Grunts. Yeah. I can ask around," Diego offered.

"No. Too dangerous," Sonny said.

"Mira, hermano, I know the streets. Most of the homeless just want to exist, but a few know the dope scene. I can find things real quick along Central Avenue. I know my gente; I'll be all right. It's you I worry about. Raven wants to get you for what happened at the arroyo. I say we get him first!"

Sonny dropped Diego off near the El Rey downtown, then drove by the police building to see Howard.

While they sipped coffee in the officers' lounge, Sonny filled Howard in.

"So Raven's dealing, and a big shipment's coming in."

"Colombian," Howard acknowledged in a low voice. "U.S. Customs and the DEA claim they're tracking it. They haven't let the local cops in on much. Pisses Garcia off."

"So the agency knows?"

"Yeah, they always know when something's coming in." Howard leaned forward and whispered. "They track everything. Sometimes they find it, sometimes they don't. When they find the junk, they create a media splash out of it. Most of the time they find nothing. Makes you wonder, huh. The shit hits the streets and the dealers make a few bucks. But the cartels who fund the shipment make millions."

"Cali and Juárez," Sonny said.

"Hey, what the news don't tell you is that there are cartels right in this country. Yeah, people here making as much money as those in Cali and Juárez." Howard nodded solemnly and sat back to sip his coffee.

He was a forensics expert, but he knew the streets. He had come out of the South Broadway barrio, and he worried about his community. Now every politician was worried about illegal drugs, and the white middle class and its professionals were turning on to heroin, but in the final analysis dope still created more havoc and pain in the Black and Chicano barrios. Those who could least afford it looked for the numbness it brought to hopeless lives.

"Why do they keep Garcia in the dark?"

Howard glanced at the door, even though they were alone in the small room. "There's two ways this lays out. One, someone very high in U.S. Customs and the DEA is working for the cartel. So protection comes directly from D.C."

"Or?"

"Or Garcia does know, and he's been bought."

There it was, Howard's theories presented in a matter-of-fact manner, and both were very disturbing. Sonny couldn't believe that. No, not Garcia.

But his old mentor, Manuel López, would say: when it comes to making money, suspect everyone. The old Manuel López rules: Everyone is capable of murder. Everyone is capable of taking a bribe.

What if the junk being shipped in had the protection of someone very high in the DEA. If that was so, they could bypass the local cops. The local narcs looked for drug shipments coming through the city at the train station and at the airport. Once in a while they got a tip and busted someone making amphetamines in a kitchen lab.

But the really big shipments were traced by Customs and the

DEA, and if the DEA didn't let the local police in on what it knew, they had no other way of getting the information.

"Not Garcia," Sonny said.

"I'm just laying out the possibilities," Howard replied. He got up to refill his cup. "I don't like it, either. I trust the man. I've known him since he was a rookie, and he never took a dime."

Howard sighed. "But I've also seen better men tempted. You can't get this size of a shipment in without paying big money for the law to look the other way."

Sonny knew that. The whole thing was getting dirty, very dirty. He rose. "Thanks for the coffee."

"De nada. Sorry I had to give you this stuff, but it's all we got. I think Dolly pours her leftover chemicals in it. Anyway, watch your step, bro. You're being tailed."

"Garcia?"

"Nope. FBI. You're on their list."

"Yeah. They dropped in on me this morning. It's Stevens and Martínez who keep coming around. Bueno, I'm on my way." He shook hands with Howard.

"Watch out for those fancy ladies." Howard winked.

Sonny left city hall and headed for the public library. It's like looking for buried treasure, he thought, and remembered that New Mexico was full of lost gold-mine stories. Fool's gold, the worthless iron pyrite of legend that had led many a man into the deserts to die of thirst.

His great-grandfather had once fallen in with some prospectors who swore they had found a gold mine. Two skeletons in Spanish armor guarded the treasure. La Mina de los Dos Españoles they called it, high on Ladrones Peak, a volcanic heap buzzing with rattlesnakes. They had a map; they swore there was enough gold in the mine to fill a bank vault.

They persuaded Elfego to go with them. They loaded burros with water and food and set out. For two months they wandered around the Jornada del Muerto desert and the surrounding peaks.

Lost, hungry, dying of thirst, the men found nothing. Elfego Baca gave up the search and returned home, swearing he would never leave the confines of the Río Grande valley again. The two prospectors returned soon after, crazy from the search, the pack saddles of their burros loaded with fool's gold. Worthless stones. The assayer in Socorro laughed them out of his office.

For weeks the two were the butt of jokes in the Socorro saloons, but they didn't give up their dream. They kept putting aside supplies until they had enough to start the search anew. Both were gone one early morning in June, walking south, into the heart of the Jornada del Muerto. They were never seen again.

History was full of the stories of men who had come to New Mexico in search of gold. It all started with Cabeza de Vaca, who was shipwrecked in 1528 somewhere near Galveston, Texas. He and his companions traversed the region, lost for eight years, crossing the Río Grande at present-day El Paso and finally heading south into México. His reports told of the Seven Cities of Cíbola, and the gold to be found there.

Gold fever. But it was not the land or the people that had filled him with fever, it was his desire to find gold.

So the first European to set foot on the land had wandered lost in the deserts and mountains of the region, dreaming of gold. Cabeza de Vaca, the first hombre dorado, the man who lost his soul in the desert and reported the Indian pueblos were made of gold and precious stones.

His stories fired the imagination of men in Mexico City who dreamed of finding great riches. The explorations from México began. Fray Marcos de Niza was sent north, and he came back with even more fantastic stories.

Gold fever.

What would it buy: eternal youth, eternal happiness? Once the Españoles smelled gold, there was no stopping them. Wave after wave of the conquistadores came, explorers looking for the Seven Cities of the Antila, the homeland the Aztecs called Aztlán, the paradise where streets were reportedly paved with gold.

They found no gold in the Indian pueblos. The real gold was

in the gift of prayer the Pueblo people practiced in their ceremonies, and this the Españoles were too blind to see. Those
greedy for gold had missed the spiritual fountain that was the
gift of the Río Grande pueblos.

At the library Ruth Jamison had more information for him,
including a small file on Alisandra Bustamante-Smith, the journalist from Colombia. A couple of the other names on the list
he had given her had underworld connections, not big-timers,
but mafia gofers. These are the grunts, Sonny reasoned, the
ants who carry the sugar away to feed the addicted country.

But when would the dope be dropped? Where? Had it already been delivered? And why the air war? Why was Secco a
target? Where did Veronica's death fit in? Those running dope
knew a lot of noise would only draw the cops. Maybe they didn't
care about the local cops; as Howard suggested, their protection came from higher up.

No, nobody in the business wanted the kind of attention
Raven had created.

Maybe Veronica's and Secco's death were simply to throw the
local cops off the dope trail. Create confusion and in the melee,
the shipment was dropped, cut, and distributed.

"What now?" Ruth asked.

"Start talking to these folks," Sonny answered. "How can I
thank you?"

"Stay safe," she said.

"I will," he assured her. He riffled through the papers. On
top was a recent article by Maria Alvarado, a reporter for the
local daily who had done an interview with Alisandra.

"Can I use your phone?"

Ruth led him to an office with a private phone. He sat and
read through Maria's article then called her. "Can you help me
get to Alisandra Bustamante-Smith? I need to talk to her." He
was direct, to the point.

"Heard you were working for the balloon fiesta," Maria
replied.

"Yes," Sonny admitted. It was all over town by now.

"You connect her to the fiesta murders?" Maria asked.

"No. I just need to talk to her. She may know something, that's all. But I need you to introduce me."

"She's not involved, Sonny. It's the farthest—"

"I'm not saying she's involved. I just need to talk to her."

There was a pause; then, "I'll call her."

"Thanks, Maria."

"I owe you one, Sonny. But go easy on Alisandra. She's really a sensitive soul."

Yeah, Sonny thought when he hung up the phone, aren't we all.

Alisandra Bustamante-Smith and her family were staying at La Posada downtown. Sonny lounged in the library until he thought Maria had had enough time to call Alisandra. He scanned books on the CIA's role in the Colombian drug-trafficking fields. The money being made by the drug lords was immense, more than the public could ever imagine. Drug money was buying governments, polluting governments.

He called Alisandra from a public phone outside the library and introduced himself. He told her he was a friend of Maria Alvarado, and Alisandra Bustamante-Smith acknowledged that she had just heard from Maria, but what did he want to talk about? When he told her he was interested in Mario Secco, he heard her voice go cold. She was reluctant to answer questions. She said she had read about the murders, and she understood that time was of the essence, but she knew nothing.

"I have a theory," Sonny said, pushing his luck in order to get to see her. "I think Mario Secco was killed over a shipment of dope coming into the city. I know you fought the Medellín cartel in your country. Any information I can get might stop this shipment from hitting the streets."

He waited. He heard her sigh, then a long, contemplative pause followed by "Okay. I'll meet you."

Sonny suggested the coffeeshop at La Posada.

Fifteen minutes later Sonny sat in a booth having coffee and watching the door. When Alisandra Bustamante-Smith walked in, he recognized her from a faded black-and-white newspaper photo in Ruth's file. But the photo hadn't captured her beauty.

She was a dark, lovely woman. She entered the coffeeshop and surveyed it, lowering her dark glasses. Sonny waved and she walked quickly toward him. He rose to meet her.

"Buenos días, Señor Baca." She smiled and offered her hand.

"Buenos días. Un placer," Sonny answered. Her hand was cool to the touch. She was a slender woman, svelte. Her eyes were dark and intense.

A few years ago she was a knowledgeable journalist who was evidently on the verge of exposing government leaders involved in the Medellín cartel in Colombia, and then came the tragic murder of her husband.

"Please join me." Sonny motioned and they sat. "May I order you something? Coffee or tea?"

"Coffee, please," she answered.

She looked at him intently, and he knew she was wondering how far she could trust him. Was he naive enough to think he could stop a cartel shipment from coming into the States? She, too, had once been the idealist. She had set out to expose those in charge of the drug problem in her country, and she lost. She hadn't talked to anyone about anything associated with her work in years.

"Thank you for agreeing to see me," Sonny said.

"Maria tells me you're a private investigator. A detective. She also told me you're working for the balloon fiesta."

Sonny nodded. "The fiesta wants me to find whoever killed Mario Secco. The publicity isn't good for them. But I have my own motive. The man who killed Secco also wants to kill me, and he may hurt innocent people. With or without the fiesta, I have to get him."

"Maria also told me you don't report to the police."

I'll have to take Maria to lunch, Sonny thought, thank her for the good referral. Alisandra had learned to not even trust the police.

"Why are you here?" Sonny asked.

"My husband used to fly hot-air balloons. We came for the fiesta," she replied. "But you know that." She paused while the waitress served them coffee.

"Not a good time to be a tourist in our otherwise friendly city," Sonny said.

"A tragedy. My instinct was to leave yesterday, but we wanted our son to see the folk art museum in Santa Fé."

"What do you know about Mario Secco?"

"My, you get right to the point, Mr. Baca."

"Sonny, por favor."

"Sonny. I like that. You have anglicized your name."

"The schools do it for us," Sonny answered. "I was named after my grandfather, Elfego Francisco Baca. It was a mouthful for the teachers to pronounce."

"How sad." Alisandra sighed, and sipped her coffee. "You lose your heritage a piece at a time. I read the history of Elfego Baca when I studied in the States. He was a Robin Hood."

"Yeah, a Robin Hood of the Río Grande." Sonny smiled. "We don't have many."

"No, you don't have many. I did my undergraduate work at Yale. There were no Chicanos there, but what your writers and poets were writing interested me. I read all I could."

"We've been here a long time."

"True," she continued, "and the country hasn't yet recognized your potential. Not even México has recognized your power. Men like César Chávez made Latin America aware of your importance."

"And now he's dead," Sonny said. "And there's no one to take his place."

"A leader like that comes once in a lifetime," Alisandra said softly, sipped her coffee, and looked at Sonny. "We are violent animals. If one group acquires power, it will not share it with the other. That is the way of history. You Chicanos will have to take power by force, or you will remain the marginalized 'Other' that the society needs as a scapegoat."

"You, too, come right to the point," Sonny said. The woman knew her history, and she told it like it was.

"In my country we have struggled to change the situation," she replied.

Her voice trailed and Sonny followed her gaze out the window. Second Street was nearly empty. A woman in blue crossed the street, peered into the coffeeshop window, smiled as she seemed to recognize Sonny, then walked away.

"Someone you know?"

"No."

"Were you followed?" The tone of caution went up a notch in Alisandra's voice.

"No, I took care. The call was from a public phone. I parked blocks away, walked here."

She smiled, a brooding smile. "We take all the precautions, and still—" She sighed softly. "So, you want to know about Mario."

"Yes."

"More than the papers report?"

Sonny nodded.

"He has a reputation. He was well known in Colombia. I'm sure the FBI knew he was here. The Freedom of Information Act should get you his file."

"That takes too long," Sonny replied.

He felt her hesitancy, so he took the time to tell her of his connection to Raven.

"So you believe this man you call Raven is involved in this shipment of drugs into the country," she said when he had laid out the bare outline of his theory.

"Raven plots destruction," Sonny said. "Whether it's blowing up a WIPP truck and claiming he wants to alert the world to the dangers of nuclear waste, or selling dope, he craves destruction. Let's assume Mario Secco was in charge of this shipment coming in from Colombia. And further assume that he hired Raven to orchestrate the deal. Why did Raven turn on Secco? Who else is involved?"

He paused. She glanced toward the door that led to the lobby. Cautious, she was very cautious.

"One can never be too careful," she said.

"It's okay," Sonny assured her, and reached out to touch her hand. She was a frightened woman, and she needed to be reassured. She had put her life and the lives of her family on the line, and she had lost.

"In Bogotá I learned this business from one of my colleagues, Emilio Aragon. He knew everyone connected with the cartels. He knew the drug lords of the cartels, the men in government who protected those demons, and he knew the rats in the back streets. Six months before my husband was murdered, Emilio disappeared. We have this new class of people in our country, los desaparecidos. The disappeared. They say the drug lords make people disappear, but the fascists in the police and the military can also make anyone disappear. One of the reasons I was going to publish my story on the drug cartel was for Emilio. They knew we were working on the story together. By disappearing him they hoped to scare me away. I didn't scare, so they killed my husband."

"I'm sorry," Sonny said.

"I think of my husband and Emilio every day. But one picks up the pieces and goes on."

He thought of Diego and his family and other homeless families who were disappearing daily. Not victims of fascist police, but like Diego's family, victims of the society that discarded them.

"It is difficult for me to talk about my situation. After my husband was killed, I realized the police were not to be trusted, and worse, the web of deceit led through the police into the newspaper itself."

"Your paper?"

She nodded. "You see why I have lost my faith. I only want to be left alone. I remarried, a professor where I teach. Thomas Smith, a kind man who knows nothing of the world of crime. I have my child, a good job. I teach in a small community college in Texas. Over half of my students are Mexicanos. I'm content. Maybe there is such a thing as destiny, and to be a teacher here is a good thing."

"But you won't talk to the FBI," Sonny said.

"No, of course not. I have a deal with them."

"A deal?"

"There is a certain photograph—" She paused, looked into his eyes, again measuring what she could confide, then reached across the table and touched his hand. "I have to trust you," she said in a whisper, and leaned forward. "You see, Mario Secco was my brother."

Sonny drew back. Had he heard correctly? Was this *the* Alisandra Bustamante-Smith, once the best-known journalist in Colombia, the expatriate now living in Texas? The story of her husband's death had created international headlines. But there was nothing about Mario Secco being her brother in the papers or in her file.

"Few people know," she continued. "Probably the fact is buried in secret FBI files. Mariano Bustamante, my brother, left home at an early age, traveled to Italy on a freighter. For a few years he worked on these ships. When he could speak Italian, he began to work for a very rich man. An Italian shipbuilder. Mariano was always attracted to money. He wanted to be rich, because for him money bought happiness. Drugs are the false promise for such young men. He returned to Colombia and became a man who delivered drugs to Europe. I found this out during my investigation."

Ah, that was it! Sonny thought. She was going to finger her own brother in her never-published exposé. And worse, her own brother could have ordered, or known about, the hit on her husband. The business was deep and dark and ugly.

"You didn't want to expose your brother," Sonny said.

She shook her head. "The deal Emilio and I made was to expose *anyone* we found connected to the cartels. That's the only way to rid the society of the evil. But after they killed my husband, I feared for my child. That fear was so deep, I couldn't bear it. I could not expose my child to the fate my husband met. I ran."

She paused, and Sonny waited until she spoke again.

"Tomorrow I will be at the services. Mariano will be buried here. No family, no friends have claimed him. The balloonists will bury him as one of their own, but they don't know his past. The women he loved to have at his side have already moved on."

"Then you go home."

"Yes, then my husband, my son, and I return to our small Texas town and the satisfying life of teaching in a small college. I have grown to love that quiet life. One more chapter is closed."

It was a sad story, Sonny thought. Alisandra was no more than forty, intelligent, gifted. The reality of Latin America had caught her in a web and made her pay. Now she spent her life in a small town in Texas and counted herself lucky.

"Why did they kill Mario?" Sonny asked.

She looked puzzled for a moment. "They wanted Mario out of the way. Do you know the name John Gilroy?"

The woman was full of surprises, Sonny thought. "Yes," he stammered, "I know the name. Ex-CIA, supplied the Contras in Nica. Ran the right-wing group called Libertad."

"Good. You've done your homework. During those fitful last days of the revolution, the Contras traded war supplies for drugs. Cocaine was channeled into this country with the blessings of some very important people in the government."

"Through the CIA?"

Her nod was barely perceptible. "I believe Mariano, Mario Secco as you know him, was involved. Probably, he, John Gilroy, and the man you call Raven were hired to bring in the drugs. There are millions to be made in such a transaction, so my theory is Gilroy and Raven killed Mario Secco."

"So now they split the profit only two ways," Sonny said. Alisandra knew the business and what she said made sense.

"I knew men like Gilroy in Colombia," she whispered. "Men with no morals and no compunction about killing. But from what you've told me, I would say Raven is the most dangerous player, and he seems intent on harming you."

"Did you run into him during your research?"

"No. There was another contact. Does the name William Stone ring a bell?"

Yes, Sonny thought. William Stone was riding in the backseat of the helicopter that Stevens and Martínez had landed on the river sandbar!

"Big man in the CIA," Sonny muttered.

"William Stone was in charge of CIA operations in Central America. What he reported to his superiors was one thing, what he did in Nicaragua was another." She whispered. "The photograph I mentioned shows William Stone on the front steps of a cartel building in Bogotá. He is standing beside a drug lord of the Medellín cartel. The Medellín drug lords were in power then. The photograph is of poor quality, shot with a telescopic lense, but—"

She reached into her purse and took out a small, yellow envelope.

"This has been my insurance," she said. "The FBI has a copy, and they know I have the original. I came upon this photograph during my investigations. So both the FBI and the CIA have left me alone. Now, they no longer care. Some of the kings of the cartels have been caught, and the public is lulled, believing the problem is under control. They know the fear and concern I have for my son will keep me quiet. And now, except for Stone and Gilroy, even the players have changed. You have a new administration, a new era of diplomacy with Latin America. But people like Stone are still very powerful inside the CIA. They guard themselves. They can't be reached."

"How did Stone and Gilroy come together?"

"Stone recruited Gilroy to run the bogus operation. A small group of CIA operatives, trading arms for cocaine. At first they were motivated by their right-wing ideology. Then they saw there was a lot of money to be made in drugs. When the Nicaragua revolution was won and there were no Contras to supply, they went right on making money."

"Bringing in dope."

"Yes," Alisandra replied. "They shifted their alliance to the newer Cali cartel and set up a supply line. They are protected at very high levels in the government. But Gilroy became a problem. He talked too much, so they retired him to your fair city. Mr. Stone, I assume, still flies in to see him from time to time. It remains a cozy relationship. The wars subsided in Central America, but these men had addicted a generation to drugs."

"Addicted an entire country," Sonny said.

Alisandra nodded. "In business terms, they created a market, and they could keep on supplying it. But Gilroy is too flashy, too loud. He likes to show off his wealth. I understand Stone's connections in Washington don't like Gilroy."

Quite a story, Sonny thought. The elements were well known; what wasn't known were the people behind the scenes. Alisandra Bustamante-Smith had dug up the facts, she named names in her file, and she had the photograph. But she feared for her child. Now she had told Sonny her story.

Sonny looked down at the envelope on the table.

"Open it," she said.

Sonny picked it up and opened it.

"I've been carrying it with me for years."

Sonny looked at the faded photo. On the steps of a building, near a very ornate door, stood two men looking out at him. One, broad shouldered and tall, was blond. Smiling. William Stone.

"You're sure it's Stone?"

"I'm sure," she replied. "The man on the left is a Medellín operative. They are standing in front of a cartel building in Bogotá. They were flying so high in those days, and they were so powerful, they became arrogant. They were dealing with heads of state, the military, and they thought their cartels were destined to rule Latin America."

"They really thought—"

"Of course they did. They claimed to be fighting communism, but they were really in the process of taking over governments by buying officials high in the government. When key government figures wouldn't deal with them, they created anarchy. Their plan was to step in and rule."

Oh, Lord, Sonny thought, countries ruled not by elected representatives, but by drug lords. It made sense. Wild, but it made sense.

"But you need the photograph," Sonny said.

She sighed and shook her head. "The photo wouldn't stand up in court, and the negative was destroyed long ago. It was insurance for a while, but it no longer matters. The people have changed. Noriega is in jail. The country he ruled is run by the U.S. military, and the military responds to the CIA. Rule by the cartels is now falling into place. Our countries, our people, are dying. This is why I have told you what I know." She shrugged sadly. "Now I must go."

She rose and Sonny also stood.

"If you can get Mr. Stone or Mr. Gilroy, it will be a small revenge for the death of my husband. Gilroy has what you want to know, but," she cautioned, "it is a very dangerous trail. Adiós, Señor Baca—" She caught herself. "Adiós, Sonny."

She offered her hand and he took it.

"Gracias," he said, and she smiled, turned, and quickly walked out of the coffeeshop. She disappeared around the green palmetto plant by the door.

Sonny looked after her, then sat and looked at the photograph. He sipped the last of his now-cold coffee.

William Stone, he thought, a protector of our freedom, a top agent in the agency entrusted to care for democracy's survival had traded drugs for arms, and when the revolutions in Salvador and Nicaragua ended, he went on trading.

Created a market, Alisandra had said. People with power and influence had created a market for cocaine. An old American tradition, the Yankee peddler. Create a market, any market, cokes or cigarettes, and you create dependency. And the biggest dependency? Dope.

These modern-day peddlers dealt in poison. Stone had gone to Central America to do business, and he left his calling card. Right there on the photograph, he had left his smiling face.

Thousands of innocent people had been swallowed up by the wars that were waged in the jungles and in the streets of the small cities of Nicaragua, El Salvador, Guatemala. Los desaparecidos were the legacy of political ideologies and of the fortunes to be made in the dope trade. Business as usual.

Sonny glanced out the window. Alisandra Bustamante-Smith passed by, a reflection of a soul who had seen too much, then she was gone.

She needed to see someone like Lorenza Villa, Sonny thought, to wash away the death images. Or else she would carry the shock of her husband's death all her life. You could not give love if you carried the frightening images, Sonny had learned. And yet she had just given him the only lead he had.

"Damn," he cursed, and felt pity for the woman.

He looked out again. On the sidewalks of the city, workers moved back and forth. It was a normal working day in downtown Alburquerque. Only a handful of people knew about the high-stakes game being played. Big operators dropping off a cargo of dope to be delivered into the country. It had to be a pure shipment, and it had to be big.

What did the local FBI office really know? Too many unanswered questions, Sonny thought, and Garcia's boys weren't even in the ball game.

He stared at the photograph. How in the hell did one get to someone as high up as William Stone?

16

John Gilroy lived in the Milagro Country Club, one of the most expensive subdivisions in the northeast quadrant of the city. The homes were expensive and palatial, extravagant. Here, under the looming presence of the Sandia Mountains, the rambling subdivision, which included a golf course, was surrounded by a winding stone wall that Sonny thought was built on the premise of the Great Wall of China: to keep out the hordes. The hordes were only welcomed if they came to tend gardens or clean houses, and they had to leave by nightfall.

Sonny had been in a Milagro home once, invited to a cocktail party during the recent mayoral campaign. He had just cracked the Gloria Dominic murder case, and for a few weeks he received a lot of invitations to strange places.

The middle-aged couple who invited him had just moved in from California, and they let Sonny know they thought the state was "so mystical." Each week they traveled to Santa Fé to have a New Age healer swing a crystal over them, but, Sonny concluded, they knew little of the deeper spiritual world of the valley.

Ah, to each his own, Sonny thought as he got in his truck and headed toward the Heights. He needed to stake out Gilroy's place then follow the man. And he didn't have much time.

He was sitting at a long stoplight on a street corner decorated with orange barrels. The traffic was moving very slowly so he used the opportunity to call Rita.

"Amor," he greeted her.

"Don't amor me!" she said angrily. "What the hell are you doing flying around with that woman! You could get killed!"

The news was out. People around the city had followed Sonny's exploits with Madge Swenson on television.

"I should have told you, but I didn't want to worry you," he replied.

"Worry me? I'm worried now. We're watching television and all of a sudden there you are! On a playa on the río with, with *that* woman hanging on you. Everybody's calling. Your mother called. Where are you now?"

"On my way to Milagro—"

"Up north?"

"No, the country club."

"What for?"

"I've got to see somebody."

"Are you going by hot-air balloon?" Rita said sarcastically.

Yup, she is pissed off. Sonny shook his head. He should have told her.

"I need to learn more about a man named John Gilroy."

"Elfego Francisco Baca, sometimes I wish you didn't have to follow people."

"That's what my mamacita says."

"I don't want to be your mother, I want to be your wife. I don't like you going up in the balloon with some blonde. She's nice-looking, and I don't trust her motives."

Sonny flinched. Rita's intuition was right 99 percent of the time.

"You say you talked to my jefita. How is she?"

"She's doing great. That woman is tough. A double bypass and she's ready to go dancing. She asked why you hadn't been by."

"I have no excuse. I'm a sinvergüenza."

"Amor, don't say that. I told her about Diego and his familia. She knows you're busy. There's nothing to do. She's fine." Her voice took on a softer tone.

"How about la familia?"

"Everybody's fine. I got Cristina to school this morning. She was excited. Marta stayed home to clean the house, and I took some food to don Eliseo's to feed the men. Diego wasn't there."

"He's okay," Sonny explained. "He's doing some legwork for me."

"Legwork. I wonder what you guys mean when you say legwork. Balloons and blondes don't mix," she reminded him again. "Next she'll have you drinking champagne up there."

Sonny gulped. "Listen, I have to find Gilroy and stick to him. I don't know—"

"You don't know when you'll be home. Okay, but call. You have a phone, use it. Y ten cuidado. I love you. I worry about you."

"I love you, amor. And don't worry. I will call."

"Promise?"

"Promise."

"Adiós. Un besito." There was a soft smacking sound.

"Adiós. Un beso." He answered her kiss with his, a loud smack into the phone. He glanced to the side to see the woman in a Camaro watching him. The woman smiled, a "how cute" smile. Sonny felt his face turn red.

"I do love you, cabrón" were Rita's parting words.

"And I love you," he said, clicking the phone to off and joining the flow of traffic easing away from the orange barrel grove. The city was growing like mad, and orange barrels had been designated the city flower.

He did love Rita, more than any woman. She was good for him, and she was the only woman, besides his mother, who worried about him. But right now he had to tail Gilroy, find out what the relationship of the man was to the battle over the Alburquerque skies.

He turned up the street that led into the Milagro Country Club. There was a guard at the gate. A car ahead of him slowed down and was waved through. Sonny stopped at the gate.

"Business?" the beefy guard asked him.

"Lawn work," Sonny answered. He had no business decal on his truck, so he couldn't even claim the self-respect of a plumber or electrician.

"Address?"

Sonny gave the only address he knew, Gilroy's. The guard looked suspiciously at Sonny but waved him through.

John Gilroy's home was a study in nouveau riche architecture: a three-story mansion with Greek Ionic pillars in a poor imitation of an old southern plantation. The monstrosity was framed against the blue Sandia Mountains. The wide lawn was as big as some of the baseball parks in the poorer districts of the city. On the wide driveway were parked two Mercedes sedans.

It fits, Sonny thought. Some think bigger, louder, and richer is better. Gilroy had become a pillar of the community, a leader in the country club. They didn't know his fortune came from dope money.

Ah-ha, Sonny thought as he drove past the house, I'm not the only one interested in Gilroy.

A cable TV van was parked half a block from the Gilroy place; just about where Sonny had expected the FBI to have a stakeout. They had set up a couple of orange barrels and pretended to be busy at curbside. One tall, one short, Mutt and Jeff. But he didn't recognize the agents; they weren't Mike and Eddie. Did Gilroy know he was being watched? Sonny hoped that a nervous Gilroy was ready to make a move.

Sonny parked down the street. He could watch the house—and the FBI van—from here, but sooner or later he would attract attention and have to move. If he loitered, someone was sure to report him.

He felt his stomach rumble. He had packed a peanut butter and jelly sandwich and coffee. He ate the sandwich and sipped coffee as he read through Gilroy's file. About six feet, the man was big and chunky. Blond hair cut short. A determined jaw. The kind of man who learns to run over people while playing fullback in college.

Gilroy had done a stint at the Air Academy in Colorado Springs. He flunked and was recruited by the CIA. There his paper trail ended, only to resurface on the front pages of international newspapers when he was shot down over Nicaragua and taken prisoner by the Sandinistas. It had been a crippling blow to the clandestine CIA operation supplying the Contras.

Alisandra had connected Gilroy to the Medellín drug cartel, but her story was debunked in Washington. When the Sandinistas turned Gilroy back to the U.S. government, he was given a new identity and told to disappear. But he wasn't the type to disappear.

The phone interrupted Sonny's reading. It was Diego.

"Hey, hermano, I hear you got shot at. You okay?"

"Fine. Raven's a bad shot."

"Don't get careless. Listen, you know the name Gilroy."

"I'm sitting at his front door," Sonny answered.

"So you're ahead of me. My people know very little, but they do know the shipment hasn't come in yet. This man Gilroy keeps his hands clean, but things are hot. He's going to move the carga himself."

"Where is it now?"

"Juárez."

"Anything else?"

"It's a big shipment."

"How big?"

"Biggest one they ever tried. Millions!"

Sonny whistled. Damn. Enough carga to keep the country warm during the winter.

"Something else."

"What?"

"It's not just coke, also heroin. Quick jolts for anyone with a few bucks."

"Heroin," Sonny repeated. Everyone knew it was back, and being purchased by professionals with money. Some holidays at the weekend retreat, something to take the stress out of the dog race.

"Things are really quiet on the street. The Mexican mafia's been paid to keep out. They say it comes from Colombia, and the CIA's involved. This man is connected, Sonny. You gotta be careful."

"I will. Gracias," Sonny answered.

Juárez, he thought. So they paid the Juárez cartel to use their route. Hell, you couldn't just pay off the Juárez boys without big money, a lot of money, enough to buy federal officials in Mexico and in the U.S.

He looked up into the blue sky. It was a perfect day for ballooning, and yet the sky was empty. How much longer would the balloonists hang around before they all packed up and left the city?

A blond five-year-old and his young mother went by on bikes. They looked at Sonny. Sonny smiled, the woman scowled. They would report him, he figured; he would have to move. He started his truck at the same time Gilroy's front door opened, and John Gilroy hurried out, jumped into one of his cars, and shot out of the driveway.

In a hurry, Sonny thought. He waited for Mutt and Jeff to jump into the cable TV van and shoot by, trailing Gilroy, then he followed, straight to the airport.

There was no time for disguise, Sonny thought, as he followed Gilroy into the parking garage, then to the Southwest Airlines ticket counter. He had to hope the two agents tailing Gilroy didn't know him.

His man was in a hurry to catch a flight to Juárez. Sonny cautiously stood a few persons behind Gilroy.

"El Paso, Mr. Gilroy," the agent said, handing Gilroy his ticket. "Flight leaves in thirty minutes."

Sonny searched his jacket pocket and found twenty dollars. He was broke. He handed his credit card to the agent and said "El Paso." He breathed a sigh of relief when the agent smiled. "All set, Mr. Baca. They're boarding now, so hurry."

Mutt and Jeff boarded right behind Gilroy, so Sonny was the last one to board the flight. The door closed, and they were quickly airborne. He checked his wallet again. He hadn't planned on a trip to El Paso, but if the coke was in Juárez, then the coincidence of Gilroy going to El Paso was too close to miss. His credit card would be at its limit now. It was going to be a tight squeeze.

He had friends in El Paso, Joe Olvera and Bobby Byrd, guys he had met while at the university, but he wouldn't have time to call and borrow money. Gilroy was moving fast.

The El Paso airport was quiet. Sonny trailed Gilroy and momentarily lost sight of the two agents. Gilroy signaled a cab, got in, and sped away. Sonny jumped into the second cab that swung to the curb.

"See that taxi," he pointed. "Twenty bucks if you can keep up with it." He was straining his resources, but he hadn't come this far to lose Gilroy.

The dark, mustachioed, pockmarked face of the driver turned and scowled. The man had Asian eyes. "Who the hell do you think you are, Charlie Chan?"

"Twenty bucks," Sonny repeated, and held the twenty in front of the man's face.

The man smiled. "All right, bro. So you're not Charlie Chan," he said, grabbed the twenty, and burned rubber as he left the airport. Gilroy's taxi was in sight, but moving fast.

"You a cop?" the driver asked. "See, if you're a cop, I can break the law, maybe not worry about tickets."

"I'm not a cop," Sonny answered, "I'm Elfego Baca." He smiled into the rearview mirror at the cabbie, while keeping his eye on Gilroy's taxi as they wove in and out of traffic. "And don't worry about tickets."

"Elfego Baca? used to be an old cowboy or sheriff or something by that name," the driver said.

"That's me." Sonny smiled.

"You from New Mexico?" the cabbie asked.

"Yeah. How'd you know?"

"Ah, you manitos are all alike." He frowned.

Where were Mutt and Jeff? Sonny wondered. They couldn't have lost Gilroy, but he hadn't seen them come out to the taxi line.

"What city?" the cabbie asked.

" 'Burque. I'm here on vacation."

The driver laughed. "It's no vacation, bro. You got no luggage, see, and you're following a smart man. The driver knows the area, and he knows how to lose people."

"But he ain't going to lose us," Sonny said.

"Not this dude. Hey, I grew up here. I can stay with him."

Sonny glanced at the driver's plastic card on the sun visor. Marcos Vargas. A homeboy. He was in good hands.

"Hey, bro," the driver said as they drove toward the bridge that crossed into Juárez, "your man's going into Juárez. Wanna follow?"

"Yeah."

"It's extra to cross over," Marcos said, and leaned his arm on the backrest as the traffic slowed down at the border checkpoint. "And I don't do drug deals. I got a family, see, and I've done time. So I want to keep my nose clean."

He turned and looked at Sonny, his coal-black eyes letting Sonny know where he stood.

"I'm following the man because I think he killed someone," Sonny leveled with the cab driver. "You drop me now and the man's free."

Marcos shook his head and hit the steering wheel with the palms of his hands. "Damn! Another wild story. Por qué yo, Dios? Por qué yo?"

Just ahead of them was the border checkpoint, the Mexican agents looking into cars and asking the usual questions.

"And you're broke, right?"

"Right." Sonny shrugged, trying to smile.

Marcos groaned, "I told my old lady this morning, today is

going to be a good day. Why? Because I just feel it in my blood.
Then you show up. Are you carrying contrabanda?"

Sonny shook his head.

"Are you carrying a weapon?"

Again Sonny shook his head.

"Mexican jails are the pits." Marcos swore and drove up to
the Mexican agent. "Believe me, I've been in one."

"A dónde?" the Mexican border agent asked, glancing at
Sonny.

"El señor va comprar pisto," Marcos answered.

The agent smiled. "Cuánto tiempo va pasar en México?"

"Una hora, es todo," Sonny answered.

The agent stepped back and waved them through. Marcos
sped away to catch up with Gilroy's taxi. "Murder," he said as
they veered away from downtown Juárez. "Your man's headed
to the Colonia de los Muertos. The mafia warehouse district.
You sure you want to go in there?"

"I'm sure," Sonny replied. He had come this far, and his instinct told him Gilroy was going to an important rendezvous.
Perhaps to the coke shipment.

They followed the cab along the railroad tracks into a large
warehouse district. Small tienditas and talleres dotted the pot-
holed street; mangy dogs and snot-nosed kids played in the
street. Dark-skinned women who had seen one cab pass now
turned to watch the second one. Two cabs from El Paso meant
trouble. Mothers called from open doors for their children to
hurry inside.

"He stopped up ahead." Marcos pointed as he pulled to the
side of the narrow, deserted street. "These warehouses belong
to the Juárez cartel," Marcos whispered. "Carillo territory. You
don't walk these streets unless you're buying or delivering
carga."

Carillo was Mexico's top cocaine smuggler. His Juárez cartel
had grown as big as the Cali cartel. Carillo bought cocaine from
Colombia, brought it through Guadalajara and Ciudad Juárez
and flew it into the states. The Mexican press called him "Lord
of the Skies" because he used jet airliners to fly coke from

Colombia to México. Looked like now he was expanding into the heroin trade as well.

"The man competes with the Gulf cartel," Marcos said. "He buys for the Tijuana and Sinaloa cartels and runs his show from here. He buys directly from Orejuela in Colombia. But you know that," he said, his eyes boring into Sonny's. "You played games with me. I'm dropping you off and you're on your own."

"I'll level with you," Sonny confessed. "The guy we're chasing is just about to ship a big load of dope up to Alburquerque. I want to stop it."

"But you're not a cop?"

"No. With me it's personal."

He fished in his wallet, turned the flap behind which he always carried a ten. For emergencies, and this was one. He handed it to Marcos. "Can you wait?"

"Wait?" Marcos looked at the ten and laughed. "For ten bucks you want me to wait? You're loco! I come within five feet of anyone doing dope and I'm back in the pinta."

"I came in a hurry, I didn't want to lose the man. It's important," Sonny explained, offering the ten.

"Ay, madrecita Llorona." Marcos shook his head. "Just my luck. I drive dumb tourists back and forth all day, and when I get something exciting, it's a manito who's broke. My wife says I should be in the movies; make more money that way. I could be a bad guy. They're always looking for Chicano bad guys, you know. She says I look like Eddie Olmos." He turned and faced Sonny. "Okay, Elfego, I'll drink a cup of coffee, and when I finish, I call the cops and tell them Elfego Baca is dead in that warehouse. Then I go home. I got a wife and kids to take care of."

Sonny smiled and patted the driver's arm. "Thanks, bro. I don't plan to be dead."

He slipped out of the taxi and scooted between the warehouses to the back. The loading dock was empty. He found a backdoor, but it was dead-bolted. He took out his jimmy set and tried it on the dead bolt, but he couldn't turn the pins. The next best thing was a fire escape, so he climbed the rusty ladder to the roof. He pried open a door with a piece of old pipe and entered the cavernous attic of the dark building.

He made his way through the darkness to a skylight covered with cobwebs and dust. Below him he could hear voices. He wiped away the dust from the glass and looked into the middle of a large room. Under the dim light stood John Gilroy. He was shouting at a man who kept to the shadows. Sonny felt the hair rise along the nape of his neck.

Raven! Gilroy had come to meet Raven!

17

Sonny leaned close and strained to hear.

"I don't give a damn what you say! Why did you go up after Baca? He was baiting you for chrissake!"

"I know he was baiting me!" Raven retorted angrily, turning and facing Gilroy. "Sonny and I like to play games. One of these days he's going to come into my circle. Then!" He slammed one fist into the other.

"I don't give a damn about you and Baca!" Gilroy scowled. "I worked a year on this deal, and I don't want it screwed up! The whole thing was supposed to be a diversion, not a way to get Baca! It's gone too far! The boss is pissed!"

"Fuck him," Raven cursed, and Gilroy, who had killed men with his bare hands, checked himself from striking. "We can make the drop in Alburkirk with or without the balloons! I can hire Mexicans here!" Raven boasted.

"You don't get it, do you!" Gilroy gritted his teeth. "Carillo isn't in this deal! It took me a year to set up this deal, a year to bypass the Juárez cartel! Nobody has ever tried one this big!"

Raven sneered. "Chill, man. We're still on schedule. And Secco's dead."

"Yeah, Secco's dead and I'm in charge. That's the only fucking reason the cartel would insure me! They wanted Secco out."

"Don't forget, I'm the one who wasted Secco," Raven shouted, and approached Gilroy.

The light from the lone bulb fell on his face, exposing the grotesque, red-scarred wound.

"You'll get your cut, Raven, when the dope is delivered and in my people's hands. You get any ideas beyond that, and your life's not worth shit."

From where he watched, Sonny could sense the fury that bristled between the two men. They hated each other, they didn't trust each other, but the deal kept them together. Sonny knew it was always like this; the money to be made on drug deals made strange bedfellows. The hate and distrust grew, and only death could ease the greed that was always part of the world of drugs.

"It works both ways," Raven spat.

"Don't threaten me," Gilroy responded.

"Threaten you," Raven sneered. "You're nothing to me. You're not what I want."

"You want what everybody else wants, the money!"

Raven laughed. "You're wrong. Really off base."

"What then?"

"I want Sonny Baca. The man who did this!" He pointed at the scarred side of his face.

"You can have him," Gilroy replied, "but let's take care of business first. You ready?"

"Yeah, I'm ready. Been waiting all morning for you. There's a few kilos here." He nodded to the stack of packages on the floor.

"Good," Gilroy said, "Let's get out of here. I have to get back."

"What's your hurry? Cops won't come until I call them."

Gilroy nodded. "And when the federales get here, they find ashes of the dope in the fire. We've paid the capitán in charge to say the big shipment burned. He calls U.S. Customs and tells them he found the drugs, the case is busted. The Mexican papers make a big deal out of it."

"And our stash is safe in Alburquerque," Raven said.

"Courtesy of UPS. Cops don't put their police dogs to sniffing UPS trucks!" Gilroy grinned.

Both laughed.

They bought people on the inside of the Mexican police and U.S. Customs, Sonny thought. The UPS trucks will have a day and time assigned to go through the agent who's paid off, and they will be waved through. Then megakilos of coke and heroin go straight up I-25 to Alburkirk.

The Mexican federales will rush to the burning warehouse, find a few kilos of dope, but they would announce to the press that it was the same shipment they'd been following since it left Colombia. The local DEA agent would agree; case closed.

But the shipment will already be in Alburquerque, ready for distribution. The city was still the main distribution point.

It was an elaborate plan. Gilroy was protected by the Cali cartel in Colombia. He had made a deal with the cartel to kill Secco, because Secco was a weak link. They had killed Alisandra's husband to quiet her, but they must have feared Secco would spill los frijoles if he was arrested. If the newspapers in Colombia ever released her story, Secco would be indicted, and he would talk. So they got rid of him.

But Raven must also be marked for death, Sonny thought. Gilroy's connected to the cartel and the military; he has protection. At some point Gilroy would protect his margin of profit— and protect the boss behind the whole deal.

How in the hell was Raven protecting himself? Did he hold a trump?

Sonny heard a noise behind him and turned. In the dim light he recognized the two agents who had followed Gilroy: Mutt and Jeff. Each held a pistol.

Ah. He smiled. "Glad to see you," he whispered, and silently beckoned them toward the skylight so they could look down on Gilroy and Raven. He was surprised when one of the agents reached down, grabbed him by the arm, and shoved his pistol against his temple.

"Get up," the man said roughly. He pushed Sonny away from the skylight, leaned over, and shouted down: "We got a visitor!"

"Bring him down!" he heard Gilroy shout back. He didn't act surprised.

Santo Niño, Sonny groaned. The two cable television repairmen who had followed Gilroy weren't agents; they were his bodyguards. They had followed Sonny from the airport even as he was tailing Gilroy. Now he recognized the short man. Sweatband, Raven's crony who tried to kill Sonny in the kitchen! He and the tall man were Raven's new underlings.

"Down the stairs!" Sweatband pointed, and the two pushed Sonny down a set of creaking stairs and into the large room where Gilroy and Raven waited.

"Meet Sonny Baca," one of the men said.

Gilroy glared at Sonny. "What about the cab, Tallboy?" he asked the gangly man.

"It's gone. The guy cleared out," Tallboy answered.

Gilroy sized up Sonny. "So you're Sonny Baca. Read about you in the paper. I thought you'd be smarter than to get into this shit, Baca. Breaking and entering. I should call the cops." He laughed.

"Be my guest." Sonny smiled. When cornered by mad dogs, a coyote tries to disarm them with his charm, he thought. He knew there was no way out. Four of them and two were armed. To make a fight of it would be suicide. No, it would be ridiculous, and he didn't want to die being ridiculous.

"He's a real smart-ass," Raven said, coming out of the shadows to face Sonny.

Sonny winced. The disfigurement was bad. Even someone in a terrible car accident could be patched up if the doctors got to him in time, did a little plastic surgery. But Raven had lain in the mud and debris of the arroyo for days. Bleeding in the hot, June sun, and later he had to hide in the forest, without medical attention, his face open and festering.

"What's the matter, Baca, can't you stand the sight? You did this!" he shouted, and grabbed Sonny by the lapels. "So look! Get your fill! Look at your work!" he screamed, spewing in Sonny's face.

"You made yourself!" Sonny answered, and jerked his arms up and broke Raven's hold. In the same movement he swung and hit Raven across the chin, sending him reeling against Gilroy. He turned to face the two men with the guns, but too late. One struck quickly, hitting Sonny across the neck with his pistol. The second followed with another blow, and Sonny went to his knees.

Raven's kick caught Sonny across the face and flattened him on the floor.

"Time to die!" Raven cursed. He took a pistol from one of the men and pointed it at Sonny's head. "I could've blown the WIPP truck if it hadn't been for you!" he shouted.

"Wait!" Gilroy shouted, and grabbed Raven's arm.

"Why wait!" Raven cursed, his face red with anger, his temples pulsing with rage.

"Don't ruin the setup!" Gilroy insisted, pulling Raven back. "I've got a better idea. Tie him up," he ordered the two assistants, and they picked up a groggy Sonny and tied him against one of the exposed steel beams.

"He's mine!" Raven protested.

"You'll have him!" Gilroy shouted into his face. "But my way. We follow our plan, torch the place. When the cops find the body, it'll take them weeks to trace him. All we need is two days to finish our work."

Raven relaxed, looked at Sonny. "Burn? Yeah, burn the brujo. Why not. Let the fire burn his soul." He grinned. "You hear that, Baca? We're going to make a bonfire. Roasted Baca!"

He laughed and reached forward to tear Sonny's shirt. He gasped when he saw the Zia medallion wasn't hanging on Sonny's bare chest.

"Where is it?"

"It's safe." Sonny smiled. "It's safe and it's no longer yours. The Zia sun is ours!"

Raven's slap drew blood from Sonny's lips.

"Stupid! You think because you're not wearing it I won't get it? By not wearing it, you leave yourself open to death. Yes, the fire will burn away your soul. You have no protection!"

He stepped back and shouted at Tallboy and Sweatband. "Burn him! Burn him now!"

The two quickly made a pile of old papers and wooden crates. "Dry as kindling," Sweatband said with a grin.

"The floor's saturated with oil. It's going to burn fast," his accomplice added.

Raven laughed, and the fiendish sound echoed in the empty warehouse. He grabbed Sonny's hair and shouted in his face. "A sacrifice to the sun!"

He took a lighter from his pocket and touched it to the pile. It flared up quickly. Then he leaned close to Sonny. "Enjoy, Baca," he said.

He took a black feather from his shirt pocket and stuffed it in Sonny's. "This fire's going to do to you what the arroyo did to me. You're going to feel your flesh burn before you die."

"Come on!" Gilroy shouted, and pulled at him.

The four men turned and ran into the adjoining garage. Sonny heard a car start and roar away; then all was quiet except for the popping of the quickly blazing fire.

He struggled against the ropes, but it was useless. He was tightly secured to the steel beam. In front of him the fire roared up, engulfing the dry wooden crates and filling the room with thick, dark smoke. Then the fire ignited the oil-soaked floor and began to spread, its fingers racing toward him, its black smoke filling the warehouse.

Sonny coughed. The smoke would probably asphyxiate him before the flames got to him. That would be more merciful than burning alive. They had left the garage door open, so there was a draft that fed the fire, and the place was a tinderbox.

Sonny cursed, then shouted for help. He pulled at the ropes again. The thick smoke burned his eyes. In this part of the warehouse district, he thought, people would see the smoke and pretend it wasn't there. In this part of the city, one didn't get involved in the dealings. Even if someone sounded an alarm, it would take a long time for the Juárez fire department to arrive; it would be too late. He shouted again, then closed his eyes and prayed.

"Oh, my God, I am sorry for all my sins . . . and for being such a lousy son. . . ."

He thought of his mother. Was she all right? His mother had pleaded for him to give up detective ways, marry Rita, go back to teaching school.

"You're a good teacher . . . the kids need you. It's steady work, you have the summers free, so what if the kids are wild. They need a strong hand. Quit running around like your brother, Mando."

He had wasted his life. Yes, like his brother he had accomplished nothing.

Diego and his family depended on him. They would have to go back to the river camp.

And Rita. "Rita," he murmured. Lord, he would never see Rita again, never hold her in his arms. He had gambled and lost.

He opened his eyes and squinted through the dark smoke.

"Don Eliseo!" he shouted, coughed. "Where are the Lords and Ladies of the Light? Los Señores y Señoras? I give them my soul! Let them return me to my ancestors."

The old man appeared in the swirling black smoke. "The fire is an element of los Señores de la Luz," he said. "Every element of the universe is filled with light, participates in light, and returns to light."

Too many things left undone, he thought as he inhaled the thick black smoke. He coughed and his head slumped, and just before he passed out, he saw a shadow hovering over him.

"Charlie Chan!"

Rough hands shook his shoulders, he heard the snap of a

switchblade and the ropes fell away. Marcos, the cabbie, draped Sonny's arm over his shoulder and dragged him out of the roaring inferno and out into the street to safety.

"You okay, bro?" he asked as he pushed Sonny over his cab's hood.

Sonny coughed and gasped for air. "Yeah," he sputtered, gulping the fresh air, which cleared his lungs.

Behind them the warehouse was a blazing inferno, the oil-soaked wood burned with fury. Somewhere a siren sounded.

"Let's not wait for the cops," Marcos said, and helped Sonny into the cab. He got into the driver's seat and pulled away, leaving behind them the crackling and exploding fire and a rising column of smoke.

The fresh air revived Sonny. His lungs and eyes felt burned with smoke; he was coughing, but he was alive.

"Gracias, bro," he whispered hoarsely when he caught his breath.

"De nada." Marcos smiled. "They worked you over, huh?"

"A little," Sonny answered, and gingerly touched his neck and the back of his head, where painful lumps had appeared. They hurt, but it didn't feel like anything was broken. "I heard them say you had split."

"Nah," Marcos said, "When I saw those two drive up, I went around the block and parked. When I saw them drive out and saw the smoke, I knew you were in trouble."

"Yeah," Sonny said, and slumped back into the seat to cough out the smoke. He owed Marcos his life, the way his bisabuelo Elfego Baca must have owed Billy the Kid his life the first time they hit Alburquerque.

Elfego and Billy were only sixteen, fresh off the ranch, and they got mixed up with a bad constable in the city. Elfego saw the crooked constable kill a man, and if it hadn't been for Billy, who drew on the constable and made him back off, Elfego, who had witnessed the event, would have been next.

They say that's why he became a lawman later in life, to set things straight.

Maybe I am the reincarnation of the Bisabuelo, Sonny's jumbled thoughts told him, come back to fight on the side of law and order, and Raven is part of the evil we've been fighting all along.

"Checkpoint Charlie," Marcos called out.

The border, la frontera for the teeming millions, the new space known as Aztlán to the Chicanos, and the bridge across the invisible line, México/U.S.A. The bridge binding two nations, and separating them as well.

Hundreds of Mexicans were returning home to the colonias of Juárez; after earning the pittance for a day's work, they returned home to their shanties. Silent masses of Mexican workers hurrying to their homes, the dark faces of the mestizos and Indians returning with one day's meager hope in their pockets.

Sonny blew his nose and wiped the sweat from his forehead. The Customs agent looked mean.

"Citizenship?" he asked, peering in on Sonny.

"U.S.A.," Sonny answered.

"What were you doing in Mexico?"

"Just having a good time," Sonny replied. "I guess I drank a little too much. . . ."

"Got proof of citizenship?"

Sonny dug through his empty wallet and fished out his driver's license. "I didn't know it'd be a hassle just to cross over and have a drink," he protested.

Marcos frowned in the rearview mirror. His look said, Don't you know you're supposed to act obedient. They can make life miserable for you if they don't like the way you look.

"You saying this is a hassle, Mr. Baca?" the agent said, looking up from the license. His voice was cold, his look stern.

"No," Sonny whispered.

"Looks like you've been in a fight, Mr. Baca."

"No, just had too much to drink. I tripped. You know the sidewalks, full of potholes."

He tried to grin, but the agent wasn't buying it.

"Would you mind stepping out of the vehicle."

Sonny stepped out and the agent lifted the car seat.

"Pop the trunk," he ordered Marcos, and looked in. "You bringing in any liquor, Mr. Baca?"

"No, nothing," Sonny answered, and lowered his eyes. Marcos's frown had told him to be cool, play the dumb role.

The agent put his sunglasses back on and turned to Marcos. "Lemme see your license." Marcos flashed his license but said nothing.

The agent flipped the license back, said, "Move on," and signaled the next car in line to come forward.

"Cabrón." Marcos seethed. "They act real macho. Like to make us squirm. Jodidos," he cursed, and drove away.

"Hey, we made it," Sonny calmed him. He didn't like having to play games with the agent, but that's the way it was.

Marcos looked in the rearview mirror. "They tried to kill you. Was it Carillo's boys?"

"No," Sonny replied, "I think even bigger boys."

As they entered El Paso, he told Marcos part of the story.

"So they get the stuff to 'Burque and put it in hot-air balloons. Then what?" Marcos said as they drove into Segundo Barrio. "I don't get it."

"I don't, either. What I'm thinking is that the balloon thing is a diversion. They make a lot of noise, let everyone focus on the balloons, then slip it out some other way."

"Makes sense," Marcos agreed.

"Hey, where we going?" Sonny asked.

"What time's your return flight?"

"There's a flight at four. Gilroy probably made that one. The next is at eight. I'll take that one."

"And you're broke, right?"

Sonny nodded. "I can send you the money when I get home."

"Hey, if I wanted to make money I could do that by pushing the stuff you're trying to stop. Yeah, I did a little of that. But now I'm married, have kids, I straightened out. So we've got till eight. How about a fría and fresh air. The day's shot, man, so let's pick up my familia and go out."

Sonny smiled. He was still clearing out his lungs, and he

couldn't think of anything else he'd rather do than sit back with a cold Corona. "One problem," Sonny added. "I'm still broke."

"Hey, don't worry about it, man. One homeboy helps another here."

Marcos lived in Segundo Barrio, a Mexicano barrio. The streets bustled with the steady movement of people. Sonny recognized the Spanish in the sounds on the street and on the signs above the talleres and restaurants.

Linda, Marcos's wife, was a warm, pleasant woman. Marcos told her the story, and she fussed over Sonny, making sure he drank plenty of water. Marcos's children had just come home from school, five kids ranging in age from six to fourteen, and they also wanted to know about Sonny.

"He's a friend," Marcos explained, "and we're going to take him downtown." The children cheered. Downtown was only for Sundays, a once-in-a-while visit. Today their father had rescued someone from the state of New Mexico, and they were going to celebrate.

Sonny called Rita and explained where he was, and that he would take the evening flight back to Alburquerque. Not to worry, he was in good hands, he assured her. He told her he had followed Gilroy to the warehouse, but nothing about the encounter and the fire. And he told her he was with Marcos and his family.

"Juárez," Rita said, "I wish I was there."

It was one of her favorite shopping places. The Mexican decor in her restaurant came from the Juárez shops. "Next time, amor," he said.

Marcos packed his family into the taxi, and they drove downtown. The October sun was sinking over the Juárez colonias to the west, infusing the barrio with a muted glow. Neighbors visited on the sidewalks in the late afternoon as workers arrived home. Marcos joined the parade of lowriders that crawled down the street.

The people in the barrio knew Marcos, so they waved, called hello. The kids waved at their friends. It was a special occasion, to drive downtown in their father's taxi. A very special occasion they attributed to Sonny.

Marcos drove with a smile on his face. He sank back into the seat and played the role. "Wish I could fix up the car with lifters," he said, "really make it rock and roll."

"Cool, Dad," one of his kids said.

"You're too old to be a lowrider," his wife kidded him.

"Ah, no, vieja, a homeboy's never too old." He smiled, and they all laughed and sank back in the seats to enjoy the ride.

Near the McIlvoy Hotel was a small hole-in-the-wall taquería that, Marcos said, had the best tacos in El Paso. And the coldest beer.

"Sabroso," Sonny kept repeating as he ate the hot tacos. Each corn tortilla was packed with different ingredients: lengua, pork, brains, beef, chicharones, and all liberally spiced with hot salsa. He washed the tacos down with cold beer.

"I like New Mexico," Marcos said as they talked. "The manitos are a little weird, you know, very Spanish, pero buena gente."

"We're okay," Sonny replied.

"Yeah, you're okay," Marcos agreed. "I was in Taos once, met a bunch of locos up there. Called themselves la Academia de la Nueva Raza. A place called Embudo. Sabes donde 'stá?"

Sonny nodded. The old activists from that area had done a lot of community work in the seventies. Now only the *Arellano Newsletter* continued the work.

"Hijo, bro, I had a good time. Stayed drunk for days, danced at Taos pueblo, finally someone put me on a bus and shipped me back home. That's before I was married." He glanced at his wife.

"A real playboy," Linda replied.

"The raza's pretty much the same all over," Sonny said.

Sitting in the small café, enjoying beer and taquitos was the same, the sounds and concerns were the same. He thought of Rita's Cocina. Marcos and his wife would fit right in. So would the kids.

"Come on up next summer. We'll go to Taos or to Jemez, do some fishing."

"Yeah?"

"Let's, Dad!" the kids shouted.

"Sure, just pack the familia in your cab and get on the interstate," Sonny offered. "We'll take good care of you."

"All right." Marcos smiled and gave Sonny a high five, their hands meeting over the table. "We'll do it, bro. Qué no, vieja?"

"Seguro que sí," Linda agreed.

The sun disappeared and the street grew dark.

"Take the kids fishing. Yeah. Blue mountains, big pine trees. The kids would like to play in the mountains. No gangs, no hassle."

Linda nodded. The kids had spread to another table to eat their tacos and drink their cokes. The mood was quiet, pleasant. "It's a dream," she said.

"A homeboy's gotta dream." Marcos smiled.

When they finished eating, they drove Sonny to the airport, parting with the vow to meet again. Yes, Sonny would bring Rita to visit someday, and if they came to New Mexico some summer, they would go fishing in the mountains. In parting they exchanged abrazos.

"I'll look for you in the summer," Sonny promised.

"Hey, stay alive," Marcos whispered. "The boys you're playing with are bad dudes."

"I'll stay alive," Sonny nodded, then hurried to catch his flight.

By nine he was back in Alburquerque and driving to the North Valley, exhausted from the day, but thinking about the linkages in the case. So Gilroy and Raven were in the deal, but who was the boss? Stone?

He dialed Howard and found him home.

"Hey, compadre, where you been?"

"It's a long story," Sonny replied. "What do you know about William Stone?" he asked.

"William Stone?" Howard asked. "The CIA William Stone?"

"Yeah."

There was a pause. "I know he's in town. Por qué?"

"He used to do business in Nicaragua."

"Wait a minute," Howard said. "Let's see what we've got."

Sonny waited. He knew Howard had gone to his computer and was pulling up a file. Howard could mainline right into the city police computer bank.

"Yeah, I remember reading about him. Here it is. 'Code name: Bill Bonney,' " Howard said, " 'Billy the Kid.' He and a few other cowboys used to run with Ollie North. They all took cowboy names. Ollie, as you know, was busted, but they couldn't get to Stone. His group, called the Liberators, or Libertad, traded arms for dope." Howard paused. "Holy mackerel!" he exclaimed. "A big deal's coming down, and Stone just happens to be in the city. Why hasn't someone tied the two together before?"

"Good question," Sonny replied.

"Did you know that during the Reagan years this man had the ear of the president? You're not talking shrimp, compadre. Listen to this. Reported to have taken a Sandinista prisoner up in a helicopter and dropped him into the Managua lagoon, after what was called in those days 'interrogation.' Recalled to D.C. when the Gilroy affair blew up. Too much media pressure. You're onto something, Sonny, but whatever it is is bad news. Do you hear what I'm saying? The man is a heavyweight."

"Anything else?" Sonny asked.

"These are newspaper clippings, man. You can also get stuff through Freedom of Information, but to get the real stuff . . ."

"Right," Sonny replied in the pause. The real stuff lay in top secret CIA files.

"Don't do it, bro. If those boys even think you're after info on one of theirs, they'll shoot first, then ask your name later. To inscribe on the tombstone. That's rule one, Sonny, those boys don't like anyone looking in their files."

"I know," Sonny answered. "Dig some more. Let me know if anything else shows up. Buenas noches."

"Take care," Howard replied.

Sonny said good night, shifted gears, and got off the freeway on the North Fourth exit. Raven and Gilroy had tried to kill him. He had to find them quickly. That meant taking chances. He couldn't go to Garcia. The chief would laugh in his face, call it fantasy, ask him to back it up with evidence. Sonny had not one iota. Oh, he had Raven's feather stuffed in his shirt pocket, but so what?

He rolled down his window and let go of the black feather, releasing it to the cold night and darkness.

"Señores y Señoras de la Luz, protect me," he said.

Now he knew he had to flush out Stone, find out how he was connected to Gilroy, and there was only one way to do that. Tell him he had Alisandra Bustamante-Smith's photograph. Make a deal. Raven for the photo.

He called Rita.

"You're back. Gracias a Dios. How are you? Have you eaten?"

"Marcos and his wife fed me like a king. I'm fine. I want to see you."

Lord, how he wanted to see her. The burning warehouse loomed in front of him. He had come close to buying el rancho. He needed to feel connected. He needed her love.

"And I want to see you."

"I'll come over."

"No, let me come to your place," she said.

He remembered Marta and Cristina were staying with Rita.

"Hurry."

"I'm on my way, amor," she whispered.

Minutes later he drove into his driveway. Across the street a light burned in don Eliseo's kitchen. The old man was still up. Sonny honked twice and a shadow appeared at the window. Waved.

Sonny waved back as he alighted from the truck. The old man was watching out for him, but on La Paz Lane, all was peaceful.

He went in, leaving the door unlocked for Rita, turned on the furnace, and headed for the shower. He stood a long time in the hot water, washing away the smoke smell. It had been a long day, a harrowing day. If it hadn't been for Marcos . . .

He toweled briskly then reached into the medicine cabinet. The Zia medallion lay on the bottom shelf.

An inner voice had told him not to wear it today, and so it was safe from Raven. He put on his robe and stepped out of the bathroom and into the bedroom. He smelled perfume. Rita.

"Welcome home," she said. She was waiting for him in bed.

"God, I'm glad to see you." He shivered.

"Ven," she said, and lifted the covers. He slid in beside her, feeling her naked body as if it was the only reality he really knew. A reality that created a great hunger deep inside, a hunger to be satisfied.

He kissed her and pressed his body over hers, feeling the warmth of her curves, the passion of her kisses.

"I missed you," she moaned.

"And I missed you, amor," he whispered, surrendering to the magic of her love.

Later, Rita rose and tended to his wounds. Then he slept like a baby in her arms.

Before the sun rose, he felt her stir, and reached for her. Her love was the dawn light, a pearl gray in which was born the desire, then the exploding brilliance of sunrise. The satisfaction was so complete, Sonny felt something of a miracle happened between him and Rita.

"Happy, amor?" he asked.

"The happiest," she replied.

They lay quietly under the covers. As sunlight filled the room, he told her about the leads he was following, apologized for not telling her about the flight he had planned with Madge. He didn't want to worry her.

"I worry anyway," she replied. "It's part of love. You care for someone and you worry."

They talked, whispers in the room, then Sonny slipped back to sleep. Sometime later he felt her rise, heard the shower, then she sat by his side. "Sleep, Elfego. And take care of yourself."

He felt her warm kiss on his lips, reached up to pull her back under the covers, wanting her again.

"Malcriado," she whispered, patted his cheek, pulling away. Then he heard the front door shut.

She had work to do, a restaurant to run. All over the city people were going to work. Workers expected their hot coffee, huevos rancheros, hot tortillas.

He smelled the aroma of coffee. Ah, she had made him a pot of coffee before she left. Que mujer. It wasn't just the way she made love, the desire she kindled in him, it was a lot of other things. He was going deeper into her, her love, and it was good.

He got out of bed, put on a terry-cloth robe Rita had brought him for his last birthday and went to the kitchen to drink his first cup of coffee.

He looked out his kitchen window. It was, what day? Tuesday. A crisp, October morning. The air was calm; the brilliant spears of sunlight were breaking over the Sandia Mountains.

"Grandfather Sun," he prayed. "Bless all of life. Fill us with clarity. I offer your light in the four directions, to the world. I wash myself in your light."

It was a prayer don Eliseo had taught him.

The old man called the shafts of morning light the Señores y Señoras de la Luz. The Lords and Ladies of the Light. This was the phrase he used to name the male and female sunlight. He taught Sonny the Lords and Ladies of Light came from the rising sun to give birth to the day, to create the dance of sunlight, a dance he called the dance of life. The sunlight came to create life, to bless life.

This was the vital force of the sun, penetrating the earth. Across the road he could see the shimmering of the sunlight on the leaves of the huge cottonwood, don Eliseo's tree, a tree that had been in the valley over a hundred years.

He stood entranced at the window. The old man knew something. He knew the essence of the light and how it brought things to life. The light played on the leaves—gold that made the autumn green shimmer. A mist rose from the irrigation ditch; the earth sparkled with light; pebbles became diamonds; the filaments of spiders shining in the sunlight equaled the Milky Way with their marvel. It was all the same mystery, one mystery unveiling itself before his eyes, and he was part of it.

Don Eliseo stood in the middle of his cornfield, his arms raised, offering the light of dawn to the world. Praying for peace. Around him the yellowing stalks of spent corn bowed to the ground, the juices of summer gone.

The old man was singing now—his prayers of blessing. The sound carried in the cool morning air. Sometimes Sonny heard old Spanish alabados filter across the street; sometimes the chants were songs don Eliseo had learned from his vecinos at Sandia Pueblo. Morning songs for the sun.

For a long time Sonny watched, and finally don Eliseo became part of the glistening light, the breeze that stirred the leaves, the sounds of morning.

The phone rang and woke Sonny from his reverie.

"Sonny, have you looked out your window?" It was Madge Swenson.

"Yes," he answered. "Looks like it's going to be a beautiful day."

"Sonny! Balloons are up!" Madge shouted into the phone. "But they're not lifting from our field, they're lifting up over the West Mesa!"

Sonny moved into the living room, opened the front door and stepped out. In the west he spotted the colorful dots. About a dozen.

"It's John Gilroy," Madge continued. "He got a bunch of crazies together late last night. They got drunk and he persuaded them to go fly. He called me after midnight, wanted my board to clear it. We can't be responsible, but he got a few crazy cowboys to go up anyway. What do you think?"

Sonny couldn't tell Madge about Juárez, not yet. He had no

evidence on Gilroy, only a scene without witnesses that took place in a warehouse. He had to catch Gilroy with the drugs.

He couldn't tell her that the whole thing was a ruse. First they sent Raven out to raise hell, to kill Secco and fire on Sonny and Madge, and now Gilroy himself had gone up. They wanted to focus as much attention on the balloon fiesta as possible. Let the DEA think the coke would show up there, bring in the police dogs, even stir up the local cops, and in the meantime they slipped around the very net they helped create.

"Can I tell my board it's safe?" Madge asked.

"It might be safe for Gilroy, but there's still a murderer loose, you know that."

"Damn!" Madge swore. "So Gilroy's up there flying, and I've got seven hundred pilots hanging around my office demanding to know if the fiesta is on or off. Jerry Stammer calls me every hour, and you were gone all day yesterday. Where were you?"

"I took a little trip," Sonny answered. There wasn't much he could say, to her or to the Duke City cops. The DEA was following Gilroy, and the FBI was following Raven, and persons very high up in government, or governments, had invested in the shipment and wanted their profit.

"Do you have anything new?" Madge asked.

"No," Sonny answered.

"We don't have much time," she said, clearly agitated. "When I make the announcement in just a few minutes that our pilots can't go up, they know I'm saying it's not safe to go up. Some of them will break with us and follow Gilroy up, but most are going to pack up and leave town. We're headed toward disaster. Isn't there anything you can do?"

Sonny watched the balloons. Dots glowing with color in the bright blue sky. Perfect days for flying were predicted for the entire week, perfect days for balloon games.

Gilroy's move would be seen as a stunt. Like Madge said, a few others might also fly, but it wouldn't convince the majority it was safe, those who flew with their families. There were just too many smart pilots who wouldn't risk themselves, passengers, crews, or their balloons.

Gilroy was only causing more confusion, which is exactly what he wanted to do.

But Sonny knew Madge wanted him to make things right. One word from him, and Madge would clear the pilots for flying; everything would return to normal. He couldn't do it. Gilroy and Raven were going to turn on each other, he was sure. At a certain point the distrust would bubble over and they would have it out. Once the dope was delivered, all hell would break loose.

"Hunches," he said, and shivered. "That's all I've got." He closed the door.

"Come by today," Madge said. "We have to talk."

Sonny walked back into the kitchen and poured a fresh cup of coffee, which he sipped on his way to the bathroom. He took a quick shower and shaved. When done, he opened the medicine cabinet, took out the Zia medallion, and put it around his neck. Today he needed all the power he could summon. As satisfied as he felt after the night with Rita, he still felt a presentiment in the air.

"The change of seasons." He shrugged. Early October would be mellow; the gold would imperceptibly creep across the cottonwoods. Then toward the end of the month, a storm would come roaring down from the Rockies, dispelling the easy mood.

If they were lucky, October weather would last nearly till Thanksgiving, freezing nights of course, but mild days in the sixties. No wonder those from northern climates wandered south in search of homes. Californians in search of a quiet lifestyle. The time was driving people to move, creating great social and cultural changes. The don Eliseos of life had their days numbered.

Not if I can help it, Sonny thought. But what could he do? Marry Rita, preserve themselves, preserve something so lovely it sometimes made him feel like crying.

His thoughts turned to the fire in the warehouse. Near death one moment, and in the arms of the woman he loved the next.

Death and life. Could he go on taking chances and still have Rita?

Don Eliseo would say that death sharpens the senses. Like love sharpens them. Meditating on the meaning of death sharpened the soul, and taking in the light of clarity created peace within.

He was frying eggs and bacon when he saw Diego cross the road from don Eliseo's and knock at the door. "Entra," Sonny greeted him. "Café?"

"You betcha." Diego shivered and rubbed his hands together. "Pretty chilly out there."

"Reminds me of the joke of the Tejano and the Mexicano who went out in the cold night to take a leak, and standing there, the Tejano says, 'It's pretty chili,' and the Mexicano says, 'Thank you.' "

Diego laughed. "So where you been, hermano?"

Sonny told him his story as they ate.

"That was too close," Diego said.

"I wouldn't be here if it wasn't for Marcos."

"It's a good thing the guy wasn't a loco," Diego said. "He might have taken the dope and let you burn."

"And you?" Sonny asked.

"I've been all over town. Nada. Everyone whispers there's a big score coming, but nobody knows where. They're not using local people. So like a good detective"—and here he grinned at Sonny—"I went back to first base. I wanted to get a good look at that place by the river. He had to bring in the balloon in a jeep or a truck. I found tracks, followed them up to the ditch road. Lost them. But I kept looking around. I knew there was a homeless family in that area of the river, and I finally found them. They saw a truck. A UPS truck."

"A UPS truck," Sonny repeated. "Gilroy said the dope would be delivered courtesy of UPS."

"The men I talked to laughed. They'd never seen a UPS truck down there."

"It may be the only lead we have." Sonny slapped him on the

back. "They had to buy the trucks. That means they have to have a garage somewhere!"

"Or rent the trucks," Diego said.

"So we look for a garage, check the car dealers, here and in El Paso." Sonny scribbled his brother's number on a paper napkin. "Armando is in used cars. Give him a call. He can call around and maybe find something on the van. He also knows who to call in El Paso. Pero cuidado. Gilroy and Raven are bad news, entiendes?"

"Ten-four," Diego answered. "Y tú?"

"I've got to see a woman."

"La blonde with the balloon?"

"Yeah, la blonde," Sonny replied. "Can you get downtown?"

"Hey, I own a fleet of city buses. I can take the one I like." Diego laughed, and said good-bye.

Sonny washed the breakfast dishes, then backed his truck out of the drive and headed down the dirt road toward Fourth Street. He called Rita to tell her he wouldn't be coming for breakfast, but she didn't answer. Probably delivering Cristina to school.

On the way toward Fiesta Control he called Howard.

"Did you hear," Howard said, "just came over the wires. The Mexican federales busted the coke shipment in Juárez. The whole thing went up in a blaze."

Sonny told Howard his story.

"Damn!" Howard exclaimed. "It looked good from here. Garcia's bought it, hook, line, and sinker."

"A Juárez capitán reports to Gilroy. He'll let them know there was no body in the burned warehouse. So they will know I'm alive."

An agitated feeling coursed through Sonny. He sniffed the air. Raven was about to strike again, close to home.

"Sonny?"

"Yeah, I'm here." He told Howard about the van.

" 'Bout as good as any other theory," Howard said. "The DEA is definitely following Gilroy, but they're not giving any information to the local cops. Now they're advertising the heat's off."

"Except Raven and Gilroy don't trust each other," Sonny said. "I expect a blowout."

"With Orejuela in jail, the Cali people are running scared. Maybe that's why the shipment is so big, they want to make a big score then spend some time regrouping."

"They'll be back. Their junk buys a lot of silence," Sonny replied. Someone in a very powerful place was protecting Gilroy.

"By the way, the mayor called the chief on the carpet," Howard said. "Garcia is spending a lot of time getting chewed out by the mayor, and Marisa gets hers from the Chamber of Commerce. They don't want to lose the business."

"It's a bad show all the way around," Sonny replied.

"Hasta la vista, Elfego," Howard said. "Remember: a wet bird never flies at night."

"Good advice," Sonny answered.

Trucks and vans were pulling out of the balloon fiesta grounds when Sonny arrived. The dejected faces of the people told the story. Madge Swenson had already announced that in spite of the Gilroy group flying, the fiesta board did not sanction any flights, and it couldn't be sure if anyone would fly tomorrow. The radio and television stations were pulling out their reporters, for the story that might have developed out of the small group that flew that morning was suddenly dead.

Over the West Mesa Gilroy's cowboys had already disappeared from view. The bright and clear skies over the city were empty. Gilroy's stunt had not drawn out an en masse ascension, and that meant he had to try another tactic.

Jerry Stammer met Sonny at the door. "Anything new?" he asked immediately. Sonny shook his head.

"Listen, Baca, we need results. The whole thing is falling apart. We don't have time!"

Sonny's frustration also surfaced. "I know about time. I'm not sitting on my ass! I just—"

He stopped short as Madge Swenson stepped out of her office.

"Look," he said, calming down. "I know the pressure you're under. I've got a few leads."

"That's not enough!" Stammer sputtered. "We need results, Baca. That's why we hired you. This may be our last day. Half our balloonists are gone." He stuck his hands in his pockets and stalked back into the board meeting room.

"Sorry, but we're all bent out of shape," Madge apologized. "Hope is fading. Garcia promises nothing, and it's not because he's not under pressure. Come on in," she said, ushering him into her office.

She looked into his eyes, and Sonny understood that if Stammer hadn't jumped down his throat, it would have been Madge. She was fighting for existence, and because she was a survivor, she would fight with all she had.

"I don't know whether to let Stammer fire you or—"

"Or what?" He could smell her perfume. A very expensive fragrance now mixing with frustration.

"We need to know what's happening!"

He sensed her nervousness. She was in a tough spot, afraid of losing it all. Okay, he would level with her.

"Raven's going to deliver a shipment of cocaine into the city," he said, cautiously withholding Gilroy's involvement, waiting for her reaction.

"So?"

"It's big, really big, and you may be sitting on it."

"Say again?"

"The fiesta draws thousands. The potential for using the fiesta as a cover is there." He said no more.

She had worked the dope fields when she was serving lines to her art clients in Santa Fe. She wasn't dumb. He looked at her and waited.

"Are you saying there's a connection between this drug shipment and the balloon fiesta?"

"Yes."

"How?"

"You tell me."

"You sonofabitch!" she flared up. "You don't suppose for one minute that I—"

She looked into his unflinching eyes and stopped short. Then she pulled back slowly, let out a soft breath. Sonny knew her past; a lot of people knew her past.

"It's not fair," she said, her shoulders sagging. She lowered her gaze.

"So tell me what you know," Sonny said.

She shook her head and walked to the window, which looked out on the field.

"You think because I used to buy the stuff that I'm still in the game."

"Just tell me what you know," he whispered.

"Maybe you're right."

He saw her nod. He walked to her, started to reach out to touch her, waited.

"You know about John Gilroy," he said, and she turned to face him.

"He applied to fly in the fiesta. The board rejected him. His past came up, so some of the board members felt uneasy, but Jerry insisted Gilroy should fly. It was a battle royal, won by Jerry when suddenly a large piece of land was donated to the fiesta board. For our new field."

"Gilroy?"

She nodded. "Anonymous donor as far as the public is concerned. Gilroy has a lot of money."

It fits, Sonny thought. Gilroy needs the cover of the fiesta.

"I know one thing for certain," she said. "We're not connected to the dope deal. If I knew anyone was using us, I'd be the first to call Garcia."

"You knew Gilroy had flown dope from Central America?"

"Yes, I knew. Everybody there knew about the Panama pipeline. It was so obvious it was a joke. When the Cali cartel expanded, Juárez bought from them."

"And you bought from Juárez," Sonny finished.

"My husband, my ex-husband, used to buy his stuff in

Juárez. *Used* to," she repeated. Her eyes were wet with tears. "I've never been a crybaby, but if you think I—"

"I have to know what you know," Sonny said. "Two people are dead!" And they almost got me, he thought.

"I'm leveling with you, Sonny. We're not involved. With all I've got going for me now, would I be so stupid?"

She paused and gathered her resolve, tossed her head back. "If there's anything we can do to help, we'll do it. But Jerry's right, you know. We don't mean to be shitheads, but we just don't have much time left."

"Yeah," Sonny replied. "If anything comes up, call me."

"And you call me."

Ah, he thought, a lot of people have a stake in this game, and it all began with the bundle that fell from the sky. Lorenza Villa loomed in his mind. She could see into things. Could she help?

At his truck he punched his answering machine's number. Garcia's voice message told him to call Rita's home number as soon as he could.

Garcia? Call Rita? He felt goosebumps on his skin. It didn't sound good. He dialed her number and Marta answered.

"They're gone!" she cried. "They're gone! M'ijita! He took her! He took Rita! I can't find Diego! I can't find Diego!"

"Marta, calm down," Sonny answered. He couldn't make sense of her cry for help, but he was already peeling rubber out of the lot, leaving behind a cloud of dust. Marta's frantic voice frightened him.

"What happened?" he shouted into the phone.

"A man came!" she cried. "He took Rita and m'ijita! He tied me up! I can't find Diego! The police are here! Dear God, what am I going to do!"

"Be calm," Sonny answered, "I'll be there in a few minutes. Let me talk to someone."

Garcia came on the line. "He took Rita and the little girl, Sonny. Get here!"

"I'm on my way!" he shouted, and raced to Rita's.

Raven had wasted no time, he had gone for Sonny's soul. If he had Rita, he called the shots.

When he got to Rita's, the place was surrounded by police cars and television vans. Francine Hunter rushed up to him, followed by Peter with his camera.

"I understand Rita López has been kidnapped," she said. "Does this have anything to do with the balloon fiesta murders?"

"I don't know what happened," he replied, and hurried into the house. Chief Garcia met him at the door.

"What happened?" Sonny asked. He could see a distraught Marta sitting in the living room, her head bent over, crying.

"You know this woman?" Garcia asked.

"Just tell me what in the hell happened!" Sonny cried, grabbing the chief's arm.

"She says someone kidnapped Rita ánd her daughter. The description fits Raven. I don't know—"

Sonny pushed past the chief to Marta. She rose and hugged him. "Sonny! Thank God, you came! What are we going to do?" she cried. "Why would they take my daughter? Why Rita? It was horrible!" she cried. "M'ijita, m'ijita."

Sonny made her sit down and held her hands. "Calm down. Tell us what happened. The police can help, but you have to tell us exactly what happened."

He got her some water to drink, and she quieted down. "We were ready to take Cristina to school," she said. "A man broke into the house. Oh, he was frightful. His face was so horrible."

Sonny clenched his fists. Raven had taken Rita, and finding Cristina with her, he had also taken the girl. He left Marta to call the police and describe him. It was stupid and it was desperate, but now Raven was holding a shield, his protection.

"I'll find her, Marta, I'll find your daughter and Rita. I promise you. Diego will be here any moment. He was downtown. Do you understand?"

Marta suppressed a sob, nodded. "Sí."

"It doesn't make sense," Garcia said. "He knows I'm turning

the city inside out looking for him, and now this. The man's crazy!"

"Maybe," Sonny said. "He likes to play games. Deadly games."

He took Garcia aside and told him about his trip to Juárez. When he was done, Garcia cursed.

"And those bastards at the DEA expected me to believe the burned warehouse story!" He sputtered. "They and the FBI still think we're small-town cops who can't be trusted with their info. Damn!"

"At least we know what we're looking for," Sonny said.

"Stolen UPS vans," Garcia said. "And Raven and dope and Rita." He looked at Sonny. "I want you to know my number one concern is for Rita and the girl," he said. "That's what my boys are gong to work on first."

"Thanks," Sonny replied. He watched the chief turn and walk out of the house to his car.

The phone rang and Sonny answered. It was Lorenza Villa. "Sonny," she said in a tremulous voice, "Rita's in trouble!"

"What?"

"I had a dream last night. I didn't call Rita because I didn't want to believe my vision. I didn't want to frighten her. I saw Raven take Rita."

"You saw him?" Sonny asked, and held his breath.

"Yes."

"What do you mean?"

"In my vision Raven was flying in a balloon. He grabbed Rita, and some other person, but when he landed, I could see the streets very clearly. I know where he landed," Lorenza said.

Sonny explained what had happened.

"Madre de los dioses," Lorenza whispered.

"But Raven wasn't in a balloon when he took them," Sonny said.

"No, he wasn't in a balloon, but my vision is *real*. Don't you see, I know Raven can fly, so in my vision I see him in a balloon. I know where Raven took Rita. I saw the streets as the balloon flew over them."

"Do you think you can you find the place?"

"I think so," she whispered. "I saw the streets so clearly, and the roof of the building. It's a warehouse, and the Zia sign is painted on the roof. Somewhere on North Edith. I saw the railroad tracks clearly, and the name of a street. The street name has something to do with the devil."

"Can you hold a minute," Sonny said as he reached for the telephone directory. He flipped to Zia and ran his finger down the long list under Zia. Zia Animal Clinic; Zia Elementary School; Zia, Pueblo of . . . four dozen Zia listings, but not a one had a North Edith address.

"You sure the street was Edith?"

"Yes."

Okay, Sonny thought, she saw the place in her vision, but the only way to find it was from above. She had to look down on the building with the Zia sign, somewhere along North Edith.

"If you were up high, flying over the warehouse, could you recognize the place?"

"From a balloon?" she asked.

"Yes," Sonny answered.

"Yes, it makes sense. In my vision I was flying, so if I was in a balloon, I could recognize the streets. And the Zia warehouse. Outside was a van, a large van, dark colored, like UPS."

"That's it!" Sonny cried. "I'll be right over!"

He hung up the phone. She had described the van Raven was using. But was it possible to spot streets seen in a dream? It was a slim lead, but he had to follow it. Madge would lend him a balloon, but in the balloon they would be at the mercy of the wind.

A helicopter? he thought. Fiesta Control has a chopper, an R-22 Robinson, and Sonny had flown it. Three years ago Tim Lewis, the officer in charge of security at the balloon fiesta, had taught him to fly the two-seater.

He called Madge Swenson and told her what had happened. He explained there was a possibility a woman could spot Raven's place from the air. Yes, she replied, the helicopter would be waiting.

Raven's place from the air. Yes, she replied, the helicopter would be waiting.

As Sonny hung up the phone, Diego came running in. He gathered his wife in his arms. Peter followed him.

"Mi hijita," Marta cried again as she repeated the story of the man with the grotesque face who came to take Rita and Cristina. Diego calmed her and turned to face Sonny.

"Kidnapped mi hija, Sonny. The man's crazy and now he has my daughter."

"Diego, I'm sorry. I'll find them, I promise."

"In the river we had nothing," Diego said with bitterness. "No hot water, cold nights, no school for my daughter. But we were safe. . . ." His voice cracked, his shoulders sagged.

He had thought the danger in tracking Raven would be directed against him or Sonny, and he could deal with that. He had never thought the danger would be turned on his daughter.

"I'm sorry," Sonny repeated. "It's my fault."

Diego shook his head. "Maybe I have done something so wrong that God punishes me." He turned and looked up, and in an agonizing voice he cried out. "God, punish me, not my daughter!"

"Diego, Diego," his wife soothed him, "you haven't done anything wrong. We have to trust in God."

"Trust in God, how can I?" He turned to Sonny. "I'll trust in you. What can we do?"

"Find him," Sonny answered. "Find him fast."

"How?"

"I'm going up in a helicopter with Lorenza Villa." He didn't have time to explain. "Did you talk to Armando?"

Diego nodded. "Three UPS vans were sold at auction last week. In El Paso. Your brother Mando was there. Vans don't interest him, so he didn't bid. But he knew the man who bought them. He used to have a junk car lot on North Edith. Along the railroad tracks."

Zia junked cars, Sonny thought. Maybe that's what Lorenza

saw on the roof of the warehouse. North Edith was full of warehouses, small businesses, small car lots.

"I'm on my way," Sonny said.

"I'll go with you," Diego volunteered.

"No, stay with Marta. She needs you."

"Is there anything I can do?"

"Pray Lorenza can spot the place from the air," Sonny said, and hurried out. "North Second or North Edith," he called to Garcia as he ran for his truck. "I'll be flying the fiesta chopper!"

Lorenza Villa was waiting by her front door when Sonny arrived. She wore jeans, a white huipil blouse, and a bright, embroidered Guatemalan jacket. Her long dark hair fell around her shoulders; her face was drawn. Sonny thought she looked thinner, her eyes dark and focused.

Was she summoning her guardian spirit's strength now? Sonny wondered. What animal from the primal world was working in her blood, her soul, her eyes? He sniffed the air, felt a tingle along his spine and in his guts as her aroma filled the truck.

His adrenaline was flowing, he felt aroused, the chakras from head to sex were strangely alive.

"I feel . . . strange. The coyotes?" he said.

"Yes," she replied.

That's it! He felt as he had when he ran with the coyotes during the limpieza.

"You have learned to summon them at will. That's good. Now it will be like that, a steady flow of energy."

She said no more, but as they drove to Fiesta Control, he told her about Juárez and the kidnapping. She listened attentively.

"Raven always seems to be one step ahead of me," Sonny said. "I had the premonition, but I did nothing. He knew I didn't go up in flames, didn't he?"

"He's been ahead of you because he uses his raven power," she said. "But you're catching up."

No, not catching up, Sonny thought, not if Raven has Rita.

But he said nothing.

When they approached the balloon field, Lorenza turned to him. "Since your limpieza my dreams are about flying. First the falling body, then Raven lifting Rita away. I know about the flight of the soul, but I've never flown in a helicopter."

The woman wasn't invincible after all, Sonny thought. "You'll be all right," he said.

He turned into the balloon grounds and gunned the truck past the empty food and souvenir tents toward the waiting helicopter sitting in the middle of the field. Madge, in flying fatigues and helmet, was standing by the chopper's door; beside her stood her assistant and Jerry Stammer.

Sonny stopped the truck fifty feet from the helicopter, reached into his glove compartment, and took out his pistol. He checked to see it was loaded, then stuck it under his belt. He jumped out and opened Lorenza's door.

"Ready?"

She nodded and stepped out. The blast from the helicopter's blades swept around her and swirled her long dark hair like a mare's mane.

She reminded Sonny of a woman he had known, a woman in a dream. She seemed familiar and strong, like his mother had been to him when he was a child.

Lorenza paused. "Who's the woman?" she asked.

"Madge Swenson. She directs the fiesta. It's their chopper we're using. She volunteered to fly us."

Lorenza shook her head.

"What?" Sonny asked, puzzled.

"It won't work," she said.

Sonny looked at Madge, motioning for them to come forward. Everything was ready.

"It won't work if she flies with us."

"Why?"

"I saw this woman in my vision. She will disrupt my power to see," Lorenza said, without further explanation.

"Do you know her?" Sonny asked.

"Only in the vision," Lorenza answered cryptically.

"Okay," Sonny shouted, grabbing her hand and pulling her across the tarmac to the helicopter, shielding her against the blast of the rotors.

"Who's your friend?" Madge shouted above the roar of the chopper's engine.

"Lorenza!" Sonny replied. "She thinks she can spot the place!"

"How?" Stammer interrupted.

Sonny didn't have time to explain. Besides, how could he explain that he was going up with Lorenza because she thought she could recognize the streets from a dream of warning.

Stammer shook his head. "It's crazy!"

"This thing won't fly three people." Madge frowned.

"I'll fly it!" Sonny said.

Madge paused. "You don't have a license."

"I'll take a chance," he replied.

"But—" Madge paused, looking from him to Lorenza. "You sure?"

"It's the only way!"

"Okay. Suit yourself."

She removed her helmet and handed it to Sonny. "Try this on for size."

Sonny put the helmet on, adjusted the microphone, and gave a thumbs-up signal. He helped Lorenza aboard, then climbed in beside her. He wished he was flying a Bell Jet Ranger with all its power, but the old Robinson would have to do. It was the same one he had flown before. Good. He shut the door.

"Strap on your belt!" he shouted at Lorenza, showing her how he was snapping his on. She nodded and did as he said.

Once the door was closed, the noise inside the plastic capsule lessened. There was no blast of air or dust. Sonny checked the instrument panel. Yeah, he could handle this baby.

He looked at Lorenza. Go, her look said. We have to move fast. Raven will not wait.

She was right. Raven held Rita and the girl; time was working against them.

Sonny drew a deep breath and gunned the chopper, feeling its vibrations, sensing its internal rhythm. He looked out the window and gave the thumbs-up signal to Madge. She returned the signal, then she stepped away.

The chopper lifted as Sonny pulled on the stick, rocked forward, then rocked backward as he overadjusted.

A little rusty, he thought, as he guided the chopper up. He relaxed, getting the feel of the foot pedals, leveled out, felt its lightness and compensated. He lifted it straight up, pushed it forward, and went swooping away, skimming toward the tops of some anchored animal balloons at the far end of the field. He pulled the stick up, and they cleared the balloons by a few feet, then he rolled it sideways and away.

He breathed a sigh of relief; beside him Lorenza whispered a silent prayer.

"Airborne!" Sonny shouted, and headed the chopper toward North Edith.

Lorenza relaxed. The sudden lift had made her stomach queasy. Her ears rang with the roar of the motor, but as they climbed, an inner peace replaced the anxiety. They were going to rescue Rita.

Sonny pointed and she looked out the window.

To the west the Río Grande was a green serpent with golden scales. The river was her main reference point. For her it was like the snake, a symbol of genuine intuitive energy, guidance, clear wisdom.

The valley was her Eden, home to the clarity of thought the serpent represented. The river as serpent was the giver of life, the mother source of water. So the ancient tribes had constructed their pueblos along the river valley. The water nurtured their fields, and they in turn gave thanks to the earth for the richness.

The river winding south was the mud-brown serpent glistening in her dream, a compass. The streets were her second reference. The UPS truck had traveled south, toward the inferno of the railroad tracks and the warehouse district. The devil's street.

"Infierno," she said to Sonny. He didn't hear.

A street called hell.

"Is there a street named Infierno?" she shouted at Sonny and tugged at his arm.

"Infierno? Street?" He thought he knew every street in the North Valley by heart, or so he prided himself. "No, I don't remember—"

Then it came to him. There was a very short dirt road that cut across from Second Street to Edith. It lay on a desolate piece of land that was an old gravel pit. And there was a deserted junked car lot there!

"Yeah! Infierno!"

Raven's nest was in hell.

Sonny leveled off and swept south along I-25, then banked to fly over the railroad tracks. It was a wild chance, but if Lorenza had come up with a street name, then maybe the vision was paying off.

She was looking down, looking for the streets that had appeared in her vision, the infierno where Rita and the girl were prisoners.

"There!" she shouted. "See!" She pointed and he looked down.

He followed the line of the tip of her finger and he saw the warehouse, and Raven's sign. Painted on the roof of the building in faded red was the Zia sign, the round sun and the four sets of radiating lines and the words ZIA JUNKED CARS. Sitting behind the warehouse was a UPS truck. Raven's in there, Sonny guessed. With Rita and Cristina. And the drugs.

"That's it!" Lorenza shouted.

Sonny nodded and touched the gold medallion on his chest. Raven was near, he could feel him, but only from the air could they have spotted the Zia sign. Rita and Cristina were in the old deserted building that lay in a dusty, barren field surrounded by the hulks of scrapped cars and trucks, now useless carcasses stripped of their once-valuable organs.

The lot was surrounded by a windbreak of scraggly, beetle-eaten elm trees. A high chain-link fence, partially hidden by the elm trees, surrounded the lot.

"They're going to hear me land, sure as hell," Sonny cursed, but he didn't have a choice. If he landed outside the fence, he would have to climb it or find a way in, waste precious time. No, he didn't have a choice; he had to set the chopper right down in Raven's nest.

He swooped in to a standstill, then lowered the helicopter to the ground. It rocked sideways, and the rushing ground came up to meet them. A thud greeted them, but not as rough as Sonny had expected. He cut the engine and snapped open his safety belt.

Lorenza breathed a sigh of relief.

"You stay here," he said to Lorenza.

"No," she answered. "I'll go with you."

Sonny shrugged. There was no time to persuade her to stay behind. Raven knew they were coming, and he'd be waiting.

He jumped out of the helicopter, and together they raced toward the warehouse and pressed themselves against the side of the gray tin building.

Can't depend on surprise, Sonny thought, as he reached for the pistol. The .45-caliber Colt felt cold to his touch.

He sniffed the air. It was late afternoon; the golden hue of light was already stirring in the clouds over the West Mesa. There was danger all around him; he felt it.

He motioned for Lorenza to follow, and together they cautiously approached the door. Sonny motioned for her to step back, then slowly opened the door. The room was dark, deserted. The smell of car oil permeated the building.

Together they entered a dust-laden office. The place was undisturbed. The dust on the desk and the office chair was thick. Cobwebs covered the window and the door that Sonny guessed led into the garage. Had they found the right place? Raven was an expert at creating false trails.

Sonny lowered his pistol and opened the door that led into the interior of the warehouse, and as he did, he was assaulted by two dark figures. They rushed at him firing a cloud of smoke.

"Tear gas!" Sonny cried as he inhaled the acrid gas. He pushed Lorenza back as the first man shot a cloud directly into his face.

He coughed, held his breath, and pointed his pistol at the masked men that rushed at him. Somewhere beyond one of the creatures, he heard Rita call his name, and he held his fire. The moment cost him. He felt a blow to his stomach and he went down, his lungs burning from the fumes.

Lorenza didn't go down as quickly. She had cupped her hands over her mouth and nose. She reached up and stripped the mask away from the man who attacked her, revealing a grotesque face. The man cursed and struck at her.

"Raven," she groaned, and fell to the floor beside Sonny.

Loss of consciousness came quickly. For a few dazed moments Sonny felt someone standing over him, and he heard strange sounds, grunts, then felt himself being dragged away. His breathing grew calmer, the burning sensation lessened. He slipped in and out of semiconsciousness, felt his body being tied, then pulled outside.

The cold air filled his lungs, easing the burning sensation. He struggled, but his arms and legs were tied. The fresh air revived him, the sunlight returned. He coughed, sucked for air, felt himself being dumped into a cart.

The cart of death, he thought. La Muerte the Neuvo Mexicanos knew as doña Sebastiana. She came in a creaking cart pulled by the souls of the dead.

Was he dying? Or had they already killed him and Lorenza?

Serves me right, he said to himself. I rushed in like a fool, threw caution to the wind. But he had heard Rita! She had called his name. What difference did it make? Raven had him where he wanted him.

He breathed deeply again. Fresh air. The stinging of the tear gas lifted. He wasn't dead, he was reviving. He felt a tug at his neck and opened his eyes. Through a film of tears he looked at Raven as he pulled the Zia medallion from Sonny's neck.

"Mine!" Raven shouted and held up the Zia medallion to the sun. The gold caught the light. "Zia sun! Now I am complete!" He laughed and slipped the chain around his neck.

He looked at Sonny. "You have nine lives, Sonny. Just like your old grandfather. But I have thirteen!"

Sonny shook his head. The gas they used had burned his eyes, but the cobwebs were falling away. He glanced at Lorenza slumped next to him, then at Raven's assistant, Sweatband.

The black shape of an inflated balloon rose over them. They had dumped him and Lorenza into a balloon basket!

"So you escaped the fire. Let's see how well you can fly!"

Raven grinned, took Sonny's pistol, and emptied the chamber. One, two, three, four, five shells fell to the ground; then he tossed the empty pistol into the basket. Then he turned to Lorenza, leering. "You got him into this. Let's see if you can get him out!"

"Cut the chatter! Let's get the hell outta here!" Sweatband complained nervously. "Cops are on the way!"

Sonny blinked. He was the man who had nearly killed Sonny in his kitchen, the one with Tallboy at the Juárez warehouse.

Sonny flexed his arms and found them tied behind his back. When he moved, the rope around his neck tightened.

Garcia, Sonny thought, where are you when I need you?

He strained again, but the ropes were secure, tied so he couldn't stand up. He struggled and found he couldn't even sit up. Beside him lay Lorenza Villa. She, too, had her hands and feet tied.

"Relax," Raven replied. "We got time." He turned to look at Sonny. "You're going for a ride, Baca. You're going to fly as high as a raven. But you ain't got wings!"

Sonny cursed. Raven was going to kill them by cutting the ropes that kept the inflated balloon moored.

"When this thing lands, you're going to look like me! So's your girlfriend!"

"Let her go," Sonny protested. "She's got nothing to do with this!"

"Oh, she's in on it." Raven cocked his head, turning to Lorenza. "You haven't told Mr. Baca about us brujos? Ah, maybe he's too innocent to know. Maybe your little ceremony didn't work. No coyotes?"

"Don't bet on it," Lorenza hissed.

He turned to Sonny. "So she told you. So what? Maybe she's taken you to visit your ancestors. That's fine with me. So she got you here, now let's see if she can get you out! Let's see if the coyote can fly!"

"You have no power here!" Lorenza shouted.

Raven struck out and slapped her. "I see no brujos!" he hissed.

"Oh, the owl claws will strike!"

Suddenly, Raven clutched at his stomach as if in pain. He doubled over, moaning. "Bruja!" he shouted, stepping back as if to escape Lorenza's stare.

Sweatband, seeing Raven fall back, jumped forward and pulled the rope attached to the lever on the propane burner. When he pulled the rope, the burner spurted a blue flame that fired up into the inside of the balloon, filling its belly with a fresh gush of hot air.

He slipped the loop of the rope over a pin on the side of the basket and threw a slipknot on it. Thus secured, the burner kept firing. The balloon tugged at the anchor ropes that kept it moored to the ground.

"A curse on all your kind!" Raven shouted. "Cut the rope!"

Sweatband bent and cut the anchor lines, causing the black balloon to rise rapidly into the sky. With the burner going full blast, the balloon ascended rapidly.

"Santo Niño," Sonny whispered.

He had gotten them into this. He had sensed Raven's presence, and he had still rushed in. Como un tonto! No, like a pendejo! He hadn't waited for Garcia. He charged into the warehouse like Billy the Kid! His concern for Rita and Cristina had made him foolhardy, and now he and Lorenza were going to pay for it. And there was no sidekick to help him out.

He struggled to get up, straining every muscle to reach the burner rope above his head. If he could pull it off the hook, the burner would stop firing. He strained at his bonds, but the way he was tied made it impossible for him to move his hands without choking himself.

Below him he heard a siren and wondered if Garcia was arriving at the chain-link fence. Too late. Raven would have already slipped out the back way, his UPS truck loaded with Rita and Cristina and the drugs.

Sonny pulled at his ropes again, but it was useless. The balloon was rising rapidly.

"We gotta turn off the burner!" Sonny shouted. "About five miles up, it'll go off! Not enough oxygen! Then we drop! If we don't freeze first!"

Lorenza nodded. He saw her pulling at her ropes, trying to kneel or sit, but it was useless. The ties were expertly done.

Sonny heard a roar louder than the burner and turned to see a DEA helicopter swoop past them, making the balloon tilt dangerously to its side. A warning shot from a rifle exploded in the air.

"They're shooting!" Lorenza cried.

"They think we're Raven! Sonsofbitches think they've found Raven!" Sonny replied.

The chopper made a short circle and came by for another pass. Another warning shot rang out, zinging just past the basket, the whoosh of the rotors again making the balloon swirl and tip in its wake.

They're going to kill us! Sonny thought. They can't see us from the chopper. Or maybe they know who it is, and they're firing anyway.

Sonny struggled against his ropes. The ropes held tight. Not a damn thing he could do! Not sheer strength but craftiness was what was needed.

"If you get on top of me," he shouted, "I can push you up!" He looked up at the burner rope looped over the pin. If they could pull it loose, it would stop the burner.

Lorenza smiled. "Ándale!"

She pushed sideways and rolled on top of him. His feet were bound, but he caught her with his knees and steadied her. It was worth a try. He balanced her as she straddled him; he held her poised for a moment, feeling the firmness of her body, her warm breath on his face. "On three!"

He counted, "Uno, dos, tres!" and on three he shoved as hard as he could. She rose, snapped at the rope with her teeth, missed by inches, and came crashing down on him.

"I almost had it," she said, gasping for air.

Already the cold air was getting thin, and the exertion took her breath away.

"Try again!" Sonny shouted. It was their only chance.

They both knew this might be the last chance they had to reach the rope. Their energy was already being sapped by the cold and lack of oxygen.

"Harder!" she cried, her teeth chattering. High, they were very high and growing colder.

He nodded and counted to three again, thrusting her up, pushing her as far as he could, arching his back and balancing her as high as he could so she could have the height she needed.

She rose, snapping like a drowning woman at a lifeline. Her teeth caught the end of the rope, and she clamped down hard. An excruciating pain shot through her jaw, but the slipknot gave, and as she dropped to Sonny's side, the burner stopped firing.

"Yahoo!" Sonny shouted. "You got it!"

She groaned and lay exhausted and trembling against Sonny, panting for breath, her lips bloodied from the rope. Her face was dark from the cold.

The balloon came to a standstill. Soon it would begin its descent. The DEA helicopter chasing them read the sign as friendly and pulled back to hover at a safe distance.

"Great job, mujer," he complimented her.

"Gracias," she answered.

Shivering from the cold, she pressed against Sonny.

"I don't ever want to see another balloon in my life," she said.

"Yo tampoco," Sonny said.

They floated silently in the high, thin atmosphere, in the silence that enveloped them. They burrowed into each other to ward off the cold as the balloon began its slow descent.

"We have to fire it again," Sonny said when the balloon began to drop too fast. "Slow it down."

She nodded. Now it was easier. Her strength had returned, and the shivering was subsiding. The rope dangling from the burner was within reach, and she took it in her mouth and pulled. The burner fired and slowed the descent of the balloon.

She kept this up during the long descent, firing the burner to slow the balloon, alternating the firing with the long drops.

From the floor of the basket, they couldn't see the ground, they could only guess how close they were. Sonny tried to judge their altitude and the speed of their descent as the gravity of the earth pulled them down.

They didn't know what danger would greet their landing. Were there electric lines, buildings, trees, traffic?

They heard children shouting.

"Where are we?" Lorenza shouted.

"Very close!" Sonny replied. "Give it one final blast."

She fired the burner one last time, and the balloon seemed to sway to a stop, like an airplane flaring as it approaches the runway.

"It's coming down! It's coming down!" They heard someone call.

"Get out of the way! Get out of the way!"

"Awesome!"

Their descent was being followed by children as they chased

after the black balloon. An empty balloon, they believed, because they couldn't see anyone on board. It had come from nowhere, dropping from the sky. Now it was landing by itself, and it was being followed by a helicopter! Cops and robbers! Or maybe a movie!

Sonny and Lorenza felt the ground meet them, a welcome thud that jarred them, and they laughed and shouted at each other in relief and fear as the breeze sent the basket tumbling along the ground until the balloon deflated and folded itself to earth.

The basket tipped on its side and Sonny and Lorenza tumbled out. Sonny groaned. He looked at Lorenza. She smiled at him. What a woman, he thought. Without her, he'd be dead.

They had landed just short of the huge, black boulders of the volcano escarpment on the West Mesa. A dune buggy parked near them, and the kids came running. When they saw Sonny and Lorenza, they were surprised.

A tall, lanky boy said, "Hey, mister, you okay?"

His friend, a curly, blond-haired girl, pushed him aside. "There's a woman!" she shouted. "You making a movie or something?" she asked.

A third face, small and round, appeared, his eyes wide as milk saucers, and gasped, "Totally awesome."

20

The landing of the balloon turned into a major media event. *Sky 7*, a helicopter from one of the television stations, had spotted the black balloon and followed it. They got some great shots of the DEA chopper buzzing and shooting at Raven's balloon.

By the time Sonny and Lorenza landed, the other two TV stations had news crews chasing the black balloon to its final resting place at the edge of Petroglyph Park on the West Mesa.

"What's your name?" Sonny asked the lanky kid who had been driving the other two in the dune buggy.

"Lawrence Marquez," he replied.

"Will you untie me, please, Lawrence?" Sonny said softly. He didn't want to scare them away.

The kid took out a Boy Scout knife and cut the ropes.

"You okay?" Lawrence asked.

"Okay." Sonny nodded, rubbing circulation into his wrists and cutting Lorenza free. He helped her to her feet. "Close," she whispered, and pointed at the mammoth black boulder in front of them. The giant monoliths rose like dark leviathans at the edge of the lava flow.

Carved on the side of the rock closest to them was the figure of a man, a weather-faded character holding bow and arrows who had long ago been chipped into the rock by a hunter of the Río Grande valley. He was aiming at a bird in the sky. Hunting raven, Sonny thought.

On another boulder he saw the faded figure of Kokopelli, the flute player, the humpback who traveled around the land spreading fertile seeds.

Long before there was a Johnny Appleseed, there was Kokopelli, this flute player of the southwest desert. Now he appeared everywhere, on bolo neckties, earrings, cufflinks, and paintings. Southwest chic. But once in a distant time, he was a god of fertility, a Greek Pan of the Río Grande Pueblos, a humpbacked creature of the underworld.

Kokopelli's hump was said to be full of seeds, seeds he scattered on his journeys, the semen of the male principle to be laid to rest in the earth. His flute music soothed the earth, made it ready to receive the seed, as the honeyed words of a man will soothe the woman and make her receptive.

Sonny chuckled and looked up at the crest of the petroglyphs, where two shadows darted. He glanced at Lorenza. She had seen them too.

"The coyotes watch over you," she said.

Sonny nodded and turned to look at the swarm of approaching cars. "God almighty!" he exclaimed.

There were cars, cops, ambulances, and even a fire truck streaming up the sandy slope, threatening desert tarantulas on their way to their winter nests, threatening the West Mesa roadrunners even the developers hadn't been able to wipe out.

The whole thing looked like a circus to Sonny as he looked up at the dark escarpment of the petroglyph park. A few more feet and the basket would have crashed into the huge black boulders. He shivered. As it was, the balloon came down just short of the old volcanic flow and landed on the soft sand dotted with chamisa and sage. They couldn't have asked for a better blind landing spot.

The TV and radio stations had reported the balloon's flight from the time they spotted it. Some who heard the reports had followed the balloon across the river to its landing on the West Mesa. Now a caravan of cars and trucks and lowriders came following the police and television vans up the slope of the hill. Sirens pierced the quiet October sunset.

The children who had untied Sonny and Lorenza were in awe.

"Great landing."

"You guys do this for a living?"

"Is this a movie?" the littlest kid asked.

"Yeah," Sonny answered. "It's just a movie."

A movie, but I didn't rescue my girl and I almost got us killed. He kicked the sand at his feet.

Chief Garcia plowed through the gathering crowd, followed by his lieutenant and two paramedics.

"You trying to get yourself killed?" Garcia shouted

Sonny groaned. He was in no mood to talk to Garcia. "Did you get to the warehouse?" he asked.

"I've got men there. Nothing! It's clean."

"Rita and the girl were there," Sonny insisted.

"Did you see her?"

Sonny shook his head. He was sure he had heard her—that's why he hadn't fired at Raven—but no sense explaining to Garcia.

"The place is clean. You're lucky you're alive, you know." He looked at Lorenza and added: "You, too."

The place wasn't clean, Sonny thought. They had stored the powder in the warehouse. Maybe they had moved it just before he got there, but every time they moved it, they took a chance on getting caught. They had to unload it soon. It was panic time in the drug deal.

The DEA helicopter that had hovered over them now turned and swooped toward the river.

"Who's the DEA agent?" Sonny asked.

"Flannery," Garcia answered.

"Why did they come up shooting?"

"They thought they had Raven." Garcia shrugged.

"Bullshit," Sonny replied. "They knew it wasn't Raven."

"Don't go making up stories, Sonny. How were they to know it was you and your lady friend in the balloon? It has Raven's sign on it."

"You could have told them," Sonny shot back.

Garcia shrugged again. "The DEA isn't exactly in radio contact with me."

Sonny turned, glad to see Howard pushing through the crowd.

"I heard about Rita," Howard said. "Damn, I'm sorry. There anything I can do?"

"You can get us out of here," Sonny replied.

Howard led Sonny and Lorenza toward his truck. His four-wheeler quickly plowed around the traffic jam through the sandy path and to Coors Road.

"Raven?" Howard asked.

"Yup."

"Did you find anything?"

"Nada," Sonny replied. "We ran into an ambush." He looked at Lorenza. "I nearly got us killed."

"We tried," she said. They had been so close to Rita and the girl—and missed.

"I heard her voice," Sonny said.

"Yes," Lorenza agreed, "she was there."

"Thank God, she's alive," Howard said. "That's good news."

"I think the dope was at the warehouse," Sonny said.

Howard frowned. "I hate to think so," he said. "The place was staked out."

"Who?"

"DEA."

"The DEA had the warehouse staked out? You sure?"

Howard glanced from Sonny to Lorenza. "Off the record, but Garcia got a tip on the warehouse, and about the same time he got a call from the local DEA man—"

"Flannery?"

"Yeah. He told Garcia they were on top of everything. They'd take care of it. That's why Garcia's pissed. They're dancing circles around him."

"Or—"

Sonny didn't finish the thought. He looked at Howard, and Howard shook his head. Neither of them could believe Garcia would sell out for a cut. But it sure as hell looked as if a lot of people interested in the dope shipment might be bedfellows.

"Is Flannery calling the shots?" Sonny asked.

"Yup. He's probably working with the FBI on this."

"Have you heard from Matt Paiz?"

"Garcia called him, so he's lending his boys to look for Rita."

Good, Sonny thought. The FBI was looking for Raven, and now they would also be looking for Rita. But the clock was ticking, and there was very little time left.

"How about the CIA?"

Howard's forehead knitted into a question. "You know more than I do."

"Yeah," Sonny whispered. William Stone was in town, and Gilroy had once been connected to the CIA.

"They have to distribute the dope soon," Howard said as they drove toward Corrales.

Yeah, but where? Sonny thought, looking at the Río Grande valley, which lay baking in the mellow October warmth. Across the way the Sandias rose, a pale blue granite face rising up five thousand feet.

The valley was a green oasis in summer; now autumn was creeping in, and in a few weeks the Río Grande cottonwoods would be completely clothed in brilliant gold and yellow.

The fall ushered in a calmness over the land, backyard gardens matured, the cosmos and marigolds overran their plots. The people of the valley began to prepare for winter.

In the orchards, apples took on a crispness with the first

frost. People hung red chile ristras for winter. Kids began to think of Halloween. The warm shirt-only weather would probably last the entire month. Even November would be pleasant if the jet stream didn't dip south. The people of the valley were spoiled by the mellow transition of time. They sighed, a breath of satisfaction as life slowed to a crawl.

Cycles—the seasons of the valley moved in cycles. Each season created its distinct flavors, colors, sounds. The seasons were also reflected in the temperament of the people of the valley. Time was a value to the old paisanos. Time was more valuable than gold, and so it was to be lived fully.

But for Sonny there was no time to enjoy his favorite season, no time to indulge in the final burst of life before winter fell. He had to find Rita; Raven would not play cat and mouse much longer.

They dropped Lorenza at her home in Corrales. Sonny walked her to the door. "What do you think?" he asked.

"It's not good," she replied, confirming his own fears. "Even if you find Raven—"

"What?"

"Don't you see why he can come and go as he pleases? He laughs at the police, and he takes your woman. You and Howard think it's because he's protected by others, by people interested in making money from the sale of the mierda. It's more than that. He is living in the spirit world. He comes and goes as the spirit Raven, and he has taken Rita to draw you to his circle."

Her words were whispered, the tone deadly serious.

"He's looking for a fight."

"Yes. And you must respond!"

Respond? To Raven the brujo? Raven had said, "You haven't told Mr. Baca about us brujos. Ah, maybe he's too innocent." And he'd said Lorenza was "in on it." Were they playing games around him?

"How?" he asked, a tone of irritation in his voice.

"We didn't go prepared," Lorenza said. "We were worried

about Rita and we rushed. We have to think like Raven. Otherwise . . ." She didn't finish.

"Otherwise what?" Sonny asked.

Lorenza touched his arm. "You have to concentrate on Rita. Make a connection to her. Keep thinking of her. She'll answer. Her image will come to you."

"I'll try," Sonny said. "I'll try anything."

"Both of us will," she said, and kissed his cheek. "Call me if you feel she's answering you. Trust her power to come to you." She turned quickly and went into the house.

Howard drove Sonny to his truck at the balloon field. The Fiesta Control building was surrounded by cars and trucks. They spotted Madge Swenson waiting near Sonny's truck.

"Looks like a big party," Howard said.

"Gilroy will be spooked, running. Maybe finding him leads us to Raven."

He looked at Madge. She was a piece of the larger puzzle in Sonny's mind. The dope deal was supposedly worth millions and that was bound to attract cats of every stripe.

"Do you have the time to follow a good-looking woman tonight?" Sonny asked, nodding at Madge as Howard pulled over.

"Madge? You got it," Howard said. "And you?"

"I'm going to hit the bars, take the city apart piece by piece. The drugs have to be somewhere," Sonny replied, and jumped out. "Thanks for the ride."

"I'll call." Howard waved and drove off.

"I heard everything on the radio," Madge said as she approached Sonny. "I'm glad you're alive. What now?" she asked. Her concern seemed real.

"Can you get your chopper back?"

"No problem. The guys are out there already— And Rita?"

"I'll find Rita," Sonny replied.

"I waited to tell you personally that we're going to fly tomorrow."

"You're going to what?"

"Jerry and the board have decided that the only way to save the fiesta is to give the go-ahead and let everyone fly."

"After what just happened?" Sonny protested. "Raven's still out there! Lorenza and I came this close to being killed!"

"That's just it, Sonny. You weren't killed. You should have heard the news! They played it up like a game. Like Chase the Hare. The phones are ringing off the hook, the place is packed with pilots who want to know why you're up there having all the fun and they're grounded. They formed a group to pressure the board, and they won."

"And Stammer?"

"Jerry's with them. He thinks it's safe."

"You?"

"God, Sonny. I just want to save the fiesta. The truth is, Raven isn't out to hurt the fiesta. Whatever happened had to do with the dope deal you suspect. That has nothing to do with us. We're not involved, the fiesta's safe."

"Yeah, and the death of Mario Secco was an accident." Sonny frowned.

Anger rose in him, an anger that had started when he fell into Gilroy's hands at the Juárez warehouse, an anger that came with the fear he felt as Raven's balloon rose into the sky with him and Lorenza in it. But the real cause of the anger was the emotional, gut-wrenching fury that came from knowing Rita was in danger and he was helpless.

"Sonny, the fiesta has nothing to do with the other thing. But I still need your help. The board can still make it worth your while if you go on television. I've got a press conference waiting right now. If you say it's okay, we can save seven days of flying, maybe even add two—"

"And you write in black on the bottom line, is that it?"

Madge stepped back. "Yes. That's my job, Sonny. I have a lot invested in this. And so has the city. We can't blow it."

"If Mario Secco was an accident, what was Veronica?"

"She was a witness. She was killed because she was a witness. It had nothing to do with the fiesta. Look, our pilots have families, but they're convinced the murderers had nothing to do with any kind of terrorism against the fiesta. All they want to do is fly. Can't you see that?"

Sonny leaned against his truck. His entire body felt bruised. The October afternoon carried a breeze; he shivered. He smelled the sweat of fear on his body.

"I feel like a drink," he said.

"Come inside." Madge touched his arm. "I have some good scotch. Wash your face, you'll feel better. Everyone's waiting for you. You're a hero, Sonny. The whole city knows about your flight today. You walk in there and the applause is going to take the roof off the building. Come." She held out her hand.

Sonny hesitated. "I gotta find Rita."

Madge nodded. "And I want to help." She squeezed Sonny's arm. "Come in. Come with me."

He shook his head.

Her shoulders sagged for a moment; then she took a deep breath. "We're going to fly tomorrow," she said. "It's a board decision."

"I've got to talk to Stammer," Sonny replied.

"It won't do any good, but go ahead."

"I'll go by his office."

"He's probably at the lab. You haven't heard. His peers at the hospital just kicked him out. After all these years and he's out."

Sonny shrugged. He remembered his mother, and his promise to call her.

"Can you call him for me? Tell him I'll drop in at the lab?"

Madge nodded. "No problem. But he's really depressed. I don't know if he'll be of much help." She turned and walked quickly into Fiesta Control.

Sonny watched her walk away and close the door behind her. He looked west, toward the West Mesa and Petroglyph Park, where a short while ago he had touched back to earth.

"Rita," he whispered, "speak to me. Tell me where you are."

He listened in the void of silence. In the field the shrill, final cry of a locust sounded. A truck honked as the eager pilots repositioned their vehicles. A breeze stirred the dust. Along the main street the food and souvenir vendors were opening their tents, lending an air of excitement to the afternoon.

Rita didn't answer.

Sonny cupped his hands over his eyes and felt the tears wet his palms. He had been to Raven's warehouse, he had seen the van Raven was driving, he had been so close, and now he had nothing. Not a clue. And Rita and Cristina were still missing.

He got in the truck and called his mother.

"Hijo? Do you want to get yourself killed? We saw everything on television. What were you doing? What are you thinking? Why are you flying balloons? They're so dangerous. And oh, God, why Rita? Why Rita?"

There wasn't much explaining he could do. Rita had been kidnapped because Raven wanted to get to him, but he didn't want to worry his mother. He tried to assure her that things would work out. The police were looking for Rita. He was looking for her. It was only a matter of time.

He had to lie. He thought of her operation, and her alone at home. And he not able to be there.

"Have you seen your doctor?" he asked when he was done reassuring her.

"A Dr. Sanchez is coming by. Not the one who did the operation. I really like him, I can speak Spanish to him. He treats me like he would treat his mother."

"And you're feeling well?"

"I'm feeling great! I feel like going dancing. Max came this morning and brought me breakfast. He stays with me all day. Don't worry about me. You concentrate on finding Rita. I can't believe anyone would wish her harm."

"I'll find her. I'll call you. Don't you worry."

"It's impossible not to worry. Don't be concerned with me. Ay, Dios, I love Rita like a daughter. Hay qué cosas! What is this world coming to?"

"I don't know," Sonny replied, trying to reassure her. "Adiós, mamá."

"Adiós, hijo. Cuídate."

He knew little about Jerry Stammer, so he drove to the public library and had Ruth hustle up every newspaper article she had on the doctor.

Stammer had been considered a young genius in the field of heart transplants. He was driven to score a sensational break-through, but at every turn he had been beaten by other re-searchers in the field. He turned his attention to baboon hearts, hoping to beat those working with pig hearts. It was a race, a very expensive race, with big consequences. Stammer was funding his own laboratory.

Now the small coterie of heart specialists who were the big honchos in the city had just passed judgment: baboon hearts were out of the picture as far as the Alburquerque heart sur-geons were concerned.

As the sun was setting, Sonny started his truck and drove to Jerry Stammer's lab. He drove up Martin Luther King Avenue and turned west. The Stammer Laboratory sat on the hill near St. Joseph's Hospital. He tried the front door and found it open. Inside, the office was empty. No receptionist, no patients, no magazines on coffee tables, no paintings on the walls, no Muzak.

A bad odor hung in the stale air. Baboons, Sonny thought.

He called hello into the dimly lit hallway and waited. Shortly, an exuberant Jerry Stammer entered the reception room and greeted Sonny warmly.

"Sonny, how are you? I heard the good news. We can let our pilots fly. Best news we've had in days."

"I—" Sonny started to answer, but the nervous doctor wasn't listening.

"The pressure's off. I'll level with you, this problem with the fiesta has taken it out of me."

"I'm sure," Sonny replied.

He motioned for Sonny to take a seat, and he sat at the re-ceptionist's desk.

"I've been so damn busy, I can't keep up. I'm going to resign from the board. This is my last year. I love ballooning, but I've served my time. You know we built the fiesta up from nothing. Time for young blood to come on board. And this year, well you know, it's been tough. Really tough. A lot of people don't realize how important we are to the economy of the city. Hey, after the summer tourists and the state fair, we're it. Twenty to twenty-five million a year into the city economy. And we're growing. We're growing. . . ." He paused. "Hey, I've got to slow down. By the way, how's your mom?"

"She's fine."

"Good, good. And you—oh, you really pulled a neat one today. Have you listened to the news?"

Sonny shook his head.

"The modest hero." Stammer smiled and leaned over the desk, a very satisfied expression on his face. "If it wasn't for you, we wouldn't have given the order to fly."

Sonny shook his head. The last thing he wanted was to be responsible for people going up as long as Raven was free. "I didn't—" he began.

But Stammer allowed no response; he continued. "Yes, you. The minute you landed I was on the phone to the board. They were all cheering you. We believe that if you went up and came down safely, so can our pilots."

Sonny groaned. It wasn't what he had wanted at all. He stood, placed his hands on the desk, and stared at Stammer.

"I was almost killed! It's not safe to fly! Not yet. Not while Raven is still free."

Stammer jumped up and began to pace. "I know about the kidnapping, and I wish to hell I could do something about it. But I can't. We have to fly. Don't you understand?"

Sonny closed his eyes. "Yeah."

"I knew you would. Look, I've been on the phone to the mayor. She assures me the police are putting every man they have into the search. They're going to find this lunatic, and your friend, ah . . ."

"Rita."

"Yes, Rita. She's going to be safe. So's the little girl. I have that assurance from the mayor herself."

So the man was trying to be helpful, but he didn't know

what they were up against. For that matter, neither did Garcia or the mayor.

"You know about the dope deal?"

"Yes," Stammer said, walking back to his chair. "Madge told me everything. Told me what she knows."

Stammer's expression changed; he grew calmer. "Ah, I see. You suspect her. Because—" He shook his head. "Because of her past. You're wrong, Sonny, believe me, you're wrong. She left that life behind her, and she's led an exemplary one while she'd been with us. The board trusts her implicitly. Whatever the so-called 'dope deal' is all about, it has nothing to do with Madge or the fiesta."

"How can you be sure?" Sonny asked.

Stammer frowned. "Because I know Madge. And as you know, we have our own internal security. Aside from the guards you see on the field, we have undercover men in the crowd. Granted, somebody could bring in a little grass, but we have dogs that would sniff out even that. A shipment of dope, the kind you're talking about? Impossible! There's no place to hide it."

"Yeah," Sonny said.

"I think you should know," Stammer continued, "when I called Madge this morning, her first response was to take care of you. She remembers you're going to use your fee to help a homeless family."

Sonny nodded.

"Wonderful, simply a fine gesture. The board has voted to help you in your effort, Sonny. So you didn't catch Raven. Whatever his game, dope or whatever, at least now we know it wasn't the fiesta he was after. Anyway, I hope the cops find him and hang him."

He stopped pacing and stood in front of Sonny. "I want to thank you. On behalf of the board, but also for myself. I've been hasty, but God, the stress has been there. Part of it's personal, and I shouldn't let it affect my work for the fiesta. I *do* want it to succeed."

He paused, returned to the desk. "We'll send you a check. Believe me, the board wants to help."

"Thanks" was all Sonny could say.

He felt empty, exhausted. He hadn't come up with anything new, and the hopelessness of the situation gnawed at him. Stammer trusted Madge, they had a tight handle on security, and finally, there *really* wasn't anyplace to hide the drugs if they were brought to the balloon fiesta field. *If?*

He reached for his chest, where he had grown accustomed to touching the medallion, but it was gone. Was his power fading?

"Thank you for coming. My door is always open," Stammer said. "Believe me, we're going to make a go of it."

"Yeah, sure." Sonny started for the door.

"Anything I can do," Stammer called after him, "just call."

Sonny got in his truck and drove into the valley. There's got to be a leak somewhere, he kept thinking. An answer. Someone out there in the city knows what's coming down, knows the connection. In the night, in the streets, in the small cantinas of North Fourth and the South Valley and along Central, wherever the denizens of the night congregated, there would be rumors, maybe an answer.

It was time to go from bar to bar and hope that somewhere someone would let slip the clue he sought.

He drove to the Fiesta Lounge, but the place was dead, then on to the Fourth Street Cantina, where he ordered a beer. It warmed him, relaxed the tension that was knotted in his muscles. It would take many more to ease the loss he felt in his heart.

Maybe Raven *had* beaten him. He hadn't recognized Raven's real powers, this ability to travel as a raven, a spirit raven.

And he had taken Rita for granted. Over the past two years, she had become part of him, not only his lover, but someone more important. With her gone, he felt empty.

Was it his destiny to lose those he loved? Fate had beaten him before. His father died, a man in his fifties, still young, and there wasn't a damn thing Sonny could do. Gloria had been brutally murdered, and only Veronica had paid for it. Others close to him had died. The image of his childhood friends rose before him.

"Bolsas?" He whispered the name. Lord, he hadn't thought of Bolsas in a month of Sundays. Still, it was the image of his boyhood friend that now appeared in the mirror over the bar.

Bolsas and Ray. As kids they were compas, friends for life. They had tattooed the wicked cross of the pachuco on their hands, right between the thumb and the forefinger. Imitating the way of some of the old pachucos of the valley.

Sonny looked at his hand for the India ink cross on his brown skin. His never took. A few faded dots were all that remained of the boyhood experiment.

Ah, but there were a lot of good times growing up. School, the river in summer, baseball afternoons, football, their first dance in the eighth grade—then the roar of the pistol erasing everything good.

A dark room. They had taken the pistol into the dark room and put one bullet in it. It was Bolsas's idea. He was always pulling something crazy. But Sonny and Ray were as much to blame: they had gone along with him.

Bolsas—snot-faced, bucktoothed, troublemaking Bolsas, who always had his pockets full of nuts and bolts, a pair of pliers, a slingshot, popsicle sticks, Mexican coins, a rabbit's foot, pictures of the bunnies he cut from the *Playboy* magazines, and a million other things he carried in his bulging pockets. Crazy Bolsas had dared them.

The explosion of the pistol had made them jump. Somehow they hadn't expected it to really go off. Neither had Bolsas. Sonny remembered Bolsas's startled eyes as he jerked back, the splash of blood spraying out the back of his head.

Russian roulette. They had dared each other to play Russian roulette.

What pistol had they used? Sonny had blocked that out, but it must have been his father's pistol. Elfego Baca's old, trusty Colt .45, the same pistol Sonny carried in his truck. Is that why he couldn't fire the pistol?

Had they sneaked into his parents' bedroom and played with the pistol there? Had Bolsas been sitting on his mother's bed, splattering the bed with blood? He couldn't remember. There were parts of the incident he had blocked out, forgotten forever.

Bad memories, Sonny thought. He paid for his drink and left the bar. One drink was enough, he didn't want to drive drunk. He headed toward Central. There were a few bars along the strip that served lines in the back rooms, lines for special customers.

Special. "You're special," don Eliseo had told him.

How was he special? " 'You haven't told Mr. Baca about us brujos,' " Raven had told Lorenza.

Me, a brujo? Sonny thought. What does it mean? A brujo is a witch. No, a brujo is also a shaman, a man who can fly. A searcher after souls.

"There are many ways to enter the spirit world," don Eliseo had said. "Some people pray and fast, others meditate, some go in search of a vision, others use dreams. Some can just will it. Like that!" He snapped his fingers. "Some enter the consciousness of someone they know, and they travel to the spirit world, for healing. Lorenza will teach you to use your guardian spirit. Raven is an evil brujo who uses the power of his nagual to gain control over others. He uses the spirit of the raven. But he misuses his power."

Ah, he hadn't listened closely to the old man. Thought the old man's rambling were just old stories, old memories. Yes, the old man had at various times told him of the power of brujos, the evil ones and the good shamans. Don Eliseo spoke of the journey to the world of spirits, the preparation.

"What can I do?" Sonny had asked, and don Eliseo's answer came back: "Use the power in you, the power of your soul, whose essence is connected to the world. The guardian spirit resides in you, the power to move into the world of spirits resides in you."

Exactly what Lorenza had said.

Sonny shook his head and spit out the window. Enough of these crazy thoughts. Manuel López would say "Go for the facts." Stay on the trail like a bloodhound, not a coyote. Coyotes are playful, they're tricksters, they're too easily distracted. The world of spirits is for philosophers like don Eliseo, not for a detective on the trail.

But wasn't Raven a trickster, one who loved games?

Faces appeared in the swirling darkness of the bars he entered, old friends who had heard of the landing on the West Mesa, who knew Rita was missing. They offered to help, but they didn't know Raven or his gang. No one involved in the dope deal was dropping in for a drink and company. They wished Sonny good luck and moved on.

The swirl of dancers, strobe lights, smoke, and Tex-Mex music drowned the whispered words. People drank, danced, and had a good time while inside Sonny grew more frustrated, more depressed.

Sure the vatos locos knew about the shipment, all the old veteranos knew, and they also sensed it was not the usual thing. It was big, and it was dangerous. Best keep quiet and keep away. Something like this came around only once in a long while.

Finally, at the Puro Pedo Bar on Coors, one old veterano from the fifties, a vato Sonny had helped get on a methadone program, whispered the clue.

"You want to know the score on drogas? Pues, go to Turco, ese. Check out Turco. Ese vato sabe todo. Te das cuenta?"

"Turco? He's still alive?" The Juárez cartel had been looking for Turco since he ran off with their money in June.

"Simón, ese. Turco knows. Pues, he's the Juárez connection."

Yeah, por qué no? Sonny thought, and flipped some bills on the bar. Turco must have cut himself a sweet, if dangerous, deal to work off his debt.

"Gracias," he told his old friend, and hurried out.

The night had turned dark and cold. A wind blew in from the west, the streets of the city emptied, and only a car or two occupied the parking lots around cafés and bars.

Turco Dominguez was the head honcho of the South Valley drug trade. But working with Juárez would be a big step up. And Turco was his cousin. A cousin he hated to the core for what he had done to Gloria, but a cousin nevertheless.

Yeah, it was time to pay Turco a visit. Time to check out his hangout in the South Valley.

21

It was after midnight when Sonny entered the Aquí Me Quedo Bar.

Two flashily dressed Juárez mafiosos sat at a table near the bar. Near the jukebox stood three brightly dressed Mexicanas, ladies of the Juárez men. They were arguing over which song to play. Otherwise the place was dead.

Three women, two men. "Turco's here," Sonny whispered, and sat at the bar. The mafiosos glanced at him, returned to their quiet conversation.

"Hey, compa," Sonny greeted the bartender. "What are you running? A funeral home? Gimme a Bud."

"Sonny, haven't seen you in a long time," the bartender said, sliding a beer across the bar.

Sonny peered at the man. He knew him. From where?

"Manny Arroyo. Mama Lucy's boy. I used to be in politics."

"Órale!" Sonny said, and extended his hand. The guy represented the South Valley till the governor put him on his hit list.

"How's business?" Sonny asked.

"Slow. I heard about Rita," Manny said. "Sorry."

Sonny shrugged. "So what's coming down?"

"Nada," Manny replied. He knew Sonny was referring to the three men. "I keep my nose clean."

"Give me a shot of whiskey," Sonny said, dug into his shirt pocket, and tossed a ten on the bar.

He looked at the three women at the jukebox. Two of them were Freddie Fender groupies, ragged at the edges, but the third was a beauty, a Pedro Infante type. She had to be Turco's woman. He thought he recognized her from his last run-in with his cousin. This was Turco territory, and the two men from Juárez were not at the Aquí Me Quedo to party. They were waiting. Waiting meant a deal was coming down.

"I feel like dancing!" Sonny said loudly. It was time to make trouble, time to rouse Turco.

The women turned to look at him.

"Esas jainas," he shouted at the three women by the jukebox. "Vamos a bailar!"

"Órale!" Turco's woman shouted back aggressively. "Why not?" Maybe the young, handsome vato was crazy. He had to know they were with their men. Or he had a lot of huevos, and they admired that.

The two men at the table turned and glared at Sonny, but made no move.

Manny served Sonny's drink and placed his hand on his arm. "Take it easy, Sonny. I want no trouble."

"Hey, I'm here to have a good time." Sonny smiled and tossed down his drink. He looked at the two men. "Dónde está Turco?"

They didn't answer, but the menacing look in their dark eyes told him he was pushing his luck.

The women at the jukebox grew quiet. The young man who asked for Turco was looking for a fight, and he didn't have the brains to know their men were armed. He had just signed his death warrant.

One of the two men stood. "Qué quieres con Turco?" He slipped his hand into his jacket pocket.

But he didn't come at Sonny. They didn't want a fight, because then the bartender would have to call the cops, and just then, they didn't want the cops. The man was giving him a chance to back down. If Sonny said no, he wasn't looking for trouble, and turned away, he could just leave quietly. All was cool.

"Solamente para saludarlo," Sonny answered.

"Quién lo busca?" the man asked, his voice cold.

"Su primo," Sonny answered. He hated to call Turco his cousin, but so it was.

The bartender groaned. There was going to be a fight. He had gone a week without a fight, a near record.

The deadly silence was broken by the creaking bathroom door. It opened and out stepped a heavyset man who weighed over two hundred pounds: dark, pockmarked Turco Dominguez. He stood resplendent in a dark violet suit. Diamonds glittered from his fingers as he slicked his hair back. His sensuous nostrils seemed to sniff the air as he looked at Sonny.

"Hey, primo." Sonny smiled, stepping forward. "How you been?"

"Qué chingaos quieres, Sonny?" Turco replied, glancing nervously at the two men at the table. He was in no mood to greet Sonny, or anyone else for that matter. The two men with him weren't his South Valley boys, but Juárez mafia, men sent to make sure whatever deal they were working went right.

"Is that any way to treat a primo?" Sonny asked, smiling. "Let me buy you a drink."

"I got no time." Turco scowled, glanced at his woman, and went to sit down.

"No time for familia? 'Stá bien," Sonny said, following him to the table. "But you know my lady's missing."

"That's got nothing to do with me," Turco replied.

"I hope not, ese, because if it does—" Sonny leaned over the table, his gaze boring into Turco.

"Qué dices?" Turco asked, anger flashing across his dark face. Had he heard right? The puto was threatening him.

"You heard," Sonny said softly, the muscles on his face tensing.

"Don't threaten me," Turco hissed, his eyes as intense as a jungle cat about to charge, his neck bulging.

Sonny pulled back. Turco had to be armed, and he had two pistoleros with him. A fight wasn't going to get him information. He needed to know what Turco knew about Rita.

"Hey, primo, easy. I'm hurting. You know—"

Turco shrugged. "I told you, that has nothing to do with me."

"Anda, let me buy you a drink." Sonny smiled. "Cantinero! Drinks for all my friends." He bowed to the women at the jukebox, and they returned the compliment with smiles. Turco's woman, the one in the red satin dress, had come to stand by Turco.

"I remember you," she said in halting English.

"Morenita, I would never forget you," Sonny replied.

She laughed. "I like your primo," she said to Turco. "He is muy guapo y muy valiente."

"Siéntate!" Turco snarled, and pushed her toward a chair. "I don't have time for a drink," he said to Sonny. "I'm with friends. So push off, Sonny."

"You don't have time for familia?" Sonny said, acting incredulous. "Okay. Maybe you have time to arm-wrestle," he said, slipped off his jacket, and began to roll up his sleeve, challenging Turco.

"No," Turco answered angrily.

"Come on, prim', I'll arm-wrestle you for a drink." Sonny edged him on.

Turco's chest was as round as a barrel, and although his touch was soft and damp, his arms were thick. He was unbeatable in the South Valley. And he could never resist a challenge.

" 'Stás loco?" He tried to dismiss Sonny.

"No, come on, I'll arm-wrestle you. Loser buys drinks," Sonny said, rolling up his sleeve.

"Shit," Turco cursed.

He looked at the two men. Anda, their expressions said, put down this puto primo of yours so we can get on with our business. Now he couldn't back down.

"Órale." He nodded, slipped his jacket off, and handed it to his lady.

"Cuidado." She smiled, her white, even teeth a row of pearls behind her dark lips. "He looks muy fuerte."

Sonny smiled at her. It was time to rile Turco. "Hey, morenita, maybe the winner can take you home."

"Hey! You don't mess with my woman!" Turco responded, and with a sweep of his arm he cleared the table, sending bottles and glasses flying. Now he was angry. His lady had been insulted, or at least made part of the deal by Sonny. Machismo dictated that he stand up and fight.

Turco tore the gold cufflink off his shirt and began to roll up his sleeve. "Te voy a quebrar el brazo," he said to Sonny. Yeah, to rescue his honor he was going to break Sonny's arm.

The two men nodded approvingly. Turco's woman smiled. "Ay que macho," she crooned.

"Cállate!" Turco shouted. He flexed his right arm. The fat rippled to life.

Lord, Sonny thought, turning Turco's arm would be like trying to roll over a tank.

"Hey, Manny," he yelled at the bartender, "call the paramedics."

"Yeah, call them." Turco grinned and placed his arm on the table. "Sonny boy's gonna need them."

No one laughed.

Sonny pulled up a chair and sat across from him. The two men drew back.

"You gonna miss your deal," Sonny whispered, leaning across the table, looking into Turco's eyes.

Turco smiled. "There's no deal, ese. Just having a good time with the compañeros."

Sitting there Turco was the Olmec Turk, a fat, squat man who was nothing like his sister, Gloria. Nothing like tía Delfina, his mother, a high-spirited, good-hearted woman.

Turco had none of their class. His eyes held the gleam of coke he had just snorted in the bathroom. For the moment, energy was flowing through his blood.

"Bullshit," Sonny replied. "There's a big deal coming down. You know and I know," Sonny whispered, resting his arm on the table. Both drew forward and clasped hands.

"If you know so much, you know it's not ours," Turco replied.

Sonny felt the strain on his arm as Turco's hand tightened over his and he began to push.

"Whose?"

Turco laughed, a hoarse, low laughter of contempt.

"You're talking like one of Garcia's narco putos. Anda, vato, get serious."

Sonny tightened his grip, feeling Turco's soft flesh, but recognizing the strength of the arm, the massive chest that held the power.

"They've got my woman," Sonny replied, "and I don't have much time. . . ."

Sweat popped on Turco's forehead as he pushed. His voice grew strained as they locked hands and slowly tested each other's strength. Sonny felt his muscles come alive, felt his arm tense and bulge as he held against Turco's weight.

"It's not our deal—"

"Who?"

"Big men, big money," Turco replied, his breathing heavy.

"Gilroy?"

They strained against each other, the energy of the two men vibrating as they locked in battle, muscles flexed to the breaking point.

Sweat broke on Sonny's forehead, his jaw tightened as he strained to hold back Turco's massive weight and strength. Every tendon, every muscle swelled, making his arm, neck, and shoulders tremble with effort.

"Anda, honey," Turco's woman encouraged him, massaging his shoulders.

Turco grinned. He strained, breathing hard, slowly beginning to push Sonny's arm down toward the tabletop.

Turco was thick and heavy, but Sonny was muscular. He held against Turco and slowly lifted his arm upright, held it in that precarious position a second, then slowly began to put the pressure on Turco.

"What about Gilroy?" Sonny asked through clenched teeth.

His anger and need to get to Rita was his advantage, and Turco's flush of coke was gone. His stamina was failing, the kill had not been quick. But Sonny would let him win if he divulged names, and in front of the men from Juárez, he had to win.

"Tell me and you can break my arm," Sonny whispered.

"No sé!" Turco cursed, drenched in sweat, his arm beginning to spasm.

"Who deals with Gilroy?"

"No sé." Turco grimaced.

"Tell me, cabrón!" Sonny cursed through gritted teeth, and Turco knew he had lost the advantage.

Turco groaned, his strength sapped. His tobacco-stained lungs didn't have the air. With one final wrench Sonny slammed Turco's arm against the table. The big man cried out as his shoulder popped.

"Hijo de la chingada!" he cursed in pain.

A switchblade snapped open and Sonny jumped up to face Turco's companions.

Turco groaned, pushed his chair away, and stood. "Mátenlo!" he shouted.

The Mexicanos circled Sonny slowly, holding the knives low, making Sonny back up against the bar. He grabbed a beer bottle from the bar and waited for them to make the move. He could take one down, but the second one was going to cut him. It was only a matter of how bad, he thought.

Just then the door swung open with a bang, and all turned to see Diego. In his hand he held Sonny's Colt .45.

"Órale," Diego said, like he was surprised he had run into a fight. His voice soft, so as not to make anyone overreact. He aimed the pistol. "Mucho cuidao con las filas," he warned the men holding the knives.

"Quién eres?" Turco asked and peered at Diego.

"Un compa," Diego answered, moving slowly toward Turco, holding the pistol so the two men could see it, until he was beside Turco and held the pistol to his head.

"Tiren las filas," he said. Turco nodded, and the two dropped their knives on the floor.

Sonny leaped forward and grabbed Turco by the lapels. "Where do I find Rita?"

"I told you," Turco groaned, reaching for his aching shoulder with his good arm. "It's not our deal!"

"Tell me where she is!" Sonny shouted, his anger rising like a dark night crashing down on him. He was tired of playing games. Time was against him finding Rita and the girl. "You know Gilroy! He's behind Raven, and he's got Rita!"

"Sí," Turco cried, struggling to pull back, trying to relieve the pain in the arm. "Ask his woman," he cried.

"Who?"

"The big shot who runs the balloons, pendejo!" Turco snarled, wrenching free from Sonny's hold.

"Madge," Sonny whispered. What the hell did Turco mean? Madge and Gilroy? So that was the link.

Turco laughed. "Yeah, it's la blonde you work for! She belongs to Gilroy! Always a woman, qué no?" he said, looking at his own woman standing beside him.

He spit on the floor. "You come here acting so big, vato, and you're looking in the wrong place! They played you for a pendejo. You're out looking for Gilroy, and the balloon lady delivered the drogas under your nose." He turned to his men and said, "Vamos."

"Hasta pronto," one of the men threatened as he walked past Diego. We'll even the score some other time, his look said.

The door slammed shut and the bar fell silent. Sonny glanced at the bartender, who shook his head, wiped sweat from his forehead, and poured himself a drink. "Chingao," he mumbled. Tonight they were lucky: no blood on the floor. He would close up, go home to a quiet sleep, and thank the saints.

Sonny turned to Diego. "Gracias, compa."

"De nada." Diego smiled. "You okay?"

"Yeah, okay."

"I found Gilroy," Diego said.

"Where?"

"I was checking the Central bars, and I dropped into the El Rey. I met an old friend, Chanclas. Maybe you know him. He's in computers."

Sonny nodded. Joe Chávez came from a poor family in the valley. The soles of his shoes were always loose and flapping, so the kids called him Chanclas. He joined the army, learned computers, came back and set up a store, and made a fortune. Money went through his hands like sand; he liked gambling at the new Indian casinos. Gambling became his obsession, so his old lady split. End of his millions. Now he had a small business, customized computers. Sonny sometimes ran into him at Epi's, drinking beer with the compas.

"Chanclas was talking about this house he had wired in the Milagro Country Club. The man bought the best and fastest— enough, Chanclas figured, to communicate with the most sophisticated systems in the world. Yesterday the guy moved out and left Chanclas holding the bag. The man is John Gilroy."

"Chanclas told you?"

"Yeah. And there's more. Gilroy moved into the Pyramid Hotel. I couldn't get hold of you, so I took a bus up to the Pyramid. I was just stepping off the bus when the balloon fiesta lady drives up in her Vette."

"Madge?"

Diego nodded. "I followed her in, and in the bar she meets—"

"Gilroy."

"Right."

"Ah," Sonny thought, so Turco was right!

"They had a drink, and I can tell she's madder than hell. So they leave the bar and go up in the elevator. I watch for the floor, then I go up the stairs, walk down the hall until I hear them shouting. Really mad. It sounded like a double cross. She's telling him to get the hell out of the city. Warning him. He shouted back that it's none of her business. 'I don't want you near the field!' she said. 'There's nothing you can do about it,' he answered. And then a security guard came down the hall and I had to get out. That's all I heard. I called Peter. He and Peewee are outside now."

"You did great," Sonny said, putting his arm around Diego's shoulder, and they walked outside. "I owe you. How'd you find me?"

"Hey, bro, I told you I know the streets. I couldn't just sit and do nothing, so I hit a couple of bars. Pues, you left a trail a mile wide."

Sonny smiled. Thank the santos; thank the coyote spirit.

Diego handed Sonny his pistol. "When I drove up, I spotted your truck and the Cadillac. Turco's the only man in the South Valley who drives a purple Caddy with gold trim. Bad news, I thought. I knew you carried the pistol in your truck. Is it loaded?"

"No," Sonny replied.

Diego grimaced. He had picked up the pistol in a hurry and hadn't even bothered to check it. He had faced Turco's bodyguards with an empty pistol!

"Chingao," he said, and they laughed. "Load it," Diego warned him. "These people are playing for big stakes, and it's nearly payoff time."

"Yeah," Sonny agreed. "I will."

The glass-littered parking lot was deserted; the cold wind had stopped blowing but the air was still chilly.

According to weatherman Morgan, tomorrow would be bright and clear, Sonny thought. Perfect ballooning weather. The UPS van and the balloons would connect somewhere, the illegal parcels would be dropped to the chase crew trucks, then those trucks would head out of town. East, west, and not a state cop in the world would stop to check trucks carrying balloons out of Alburquerque. The red-blooded American boys would be going home from the big Alburquerque fiesta. Families enjoying one of the hottest sports in the country. The cops would wave them through while Gilroy and Madge sat somewhere in the city dividing the money and laughing their heads off.

"Thanks," Sonny said. "Right now you better get some sleep."

"And you?" Diego asked.

"I'm going to pay Madge Swenson a visit. And what room was Gilroy in?"

Diego reached for a crumpled note in his jacket pocket and handed it to Sonny. "I marked it here. Be careful."

Sonny nodded. He watched Diego drive away in the borrowed TV 7 van. Then he started his truck and headed for the West Mesa. On the way he dialed his answering machine at home.

Messages from a salesman selling aluminum siding, and his mother saying she was well and asking if there was any word on Rita.

At the end of the tape, Howard: "I lost her, Sonny. Damn! I lost her! She opened up the Vette on the freeway and she was gone! She knew she was being tailed!" There was a pause, then: "Sorry. I'll head home. Call me."

So Madge knew all along she was being followed, Sonny thought. She hired me, made it look like a big investigation was going on. She hooked me up with the helicopter and sent me and Lorenza right into Raven's nest. She made her own deal with Gilroy. Had the deal gone sour? And where in the hell was Raven?

Madge Swenson lived in a condo in La Luz on the West Mesa. La Luz was one of the first new Pueblo-style compounds in the city. The townhouses snuggled against the slope of the mesa near the river bosque—adobe-style living for those who wanted to get away from the hustle of the city.

But the West Mesa, too, was filling up. From the Río Grande to the Río Puerco, the developers were building hundreds of tract homes on the sand hills. The West Mesa was already looking like the Heights, full of traffic jams and shopping centers. The peace and quiet were gone, and if Frank Dominic had his way, even the river bosque would teem with hotels and gambling casinos. The natural landscape that made the city and the river valley distinctive would be gone.

He turned into La Luz and parked against a row of Russian olive trees. The West Mesa was quiet, asleep. The moonlight wove magical shadows into the dark blue of early morning. Near the river a pack of coyotes cried. From Suzy Poole's rambling adobe estate a dog answered, then all was quiet again.

Sonny ran to the wall of the compound and pressed himself against it. He had been to a party at Madge's condo when he had worked for the balloon fiesta. He knew there was a security guard on the grounds, so he had limited time before his truck was spotted.

He located Madge's patio, leaped the wall, and crouched against it. There was a light on in the upstairs window. Her bedroom? Was it possible Gilroy was here? When Diego returned the pistol, Sonny had slipped it back into the holster and put it in the glove compartment. Now he wished he had kept it. It was too late to return for it. He didn't have much time.

He moved toward the sliding glass door of the patio. It was locked, but when he pushed and lifted, it snapped open. He slipped quickly into the den. Jazz music floated through the house. Gillespie, Sonny guessed. A light shone in the upstairs area. Slowly Sonny made his way up a flight of polished wood steps. The faint light cast shadows on the paintings and rugs on the wall, on the steps.

The bedroom door was open; the light and music from within flowed softly into the hallway. Sonny waited, listening for sounds he might recognize, but there were none. She was alone. He approached the door and looked in.

Madge Swenson was sitting up in bed, reading. A lighted cigarette sat on the ashtray of the bed table. Beside that, a bottle of white wine and a half-empty glass. She was engrossed in the book. Her short, blond hair fell around her cheeks; her breasts rose and fell beneath the silk gown.

Sonny stood watching her until she felt his presence and looked up. She gasped, reached for the night table, then smiled.

"Sonny. You scared the shit out of me. Forgot your manners?" she said.

"I'm in a hurry," Sonny replied, and stepped into the room.

Madge put the book aside, patted the bed, and asked: "Glass of wine?"

"You know why I'm here."

"To make love, I hope," she answered, and stood. Her silk gown revealed her figure against the light. Her warm breath was tinged with wine. Her blue eyes were also warm—small crystals that reminded Sonny of the blue cat's-eye marbles he had treasured as a kid.

"First, why don't you tell me about you and Gilroy?" he said.

"Nothing to tell," she replied, a frown crossing her face.

"Level with me, Madge!" Sonny's voice rose with anger. "You were in Gilroy's room at the Pyramid! The man is running the dope! Two plus two is four!"

"You have no right to insinuate—"

"Yes, I do!" Sonny shot back. "Remember, I was hired to find the killer! I nearly got fried to a crisp in Juárez by your friend Gilroy! And then nearly frozen or crushed chasing after him and Raven!"

"Stop!" she shouted, and slapped at him. He grabbed her wrist and held her, felt her trembling rage.

"You're running dope and you hired me to take the heat off!" he shouted in her face.

"I'm not in the deal!" Madge shouted, trying to pull out of Sonny's grip.

"Prove it!"

"I was with Gilroy tonight," she responded, her eyes brimming with tears as she stopped struggling. "But I swear, I'm not in the deal."

"You knew about it!" Sonny insisted.

Madge nodded, her body went limp. Sonny let go of her hand, and she sat on the edge of the bed. A mixture of anger and arousal swept through Sonny as he looked down at her.

"Yes, I knew." She nodded. She reached with a shaking hand for her glass of wine and took a sip.

"I don't have much time," he said, thinking of Rita and wondering how long Raven would keep her and the girl alive.

Madge nodded. "I didn't want to see John tonight, believe me, I didn't!" Her eyes filled with tears. She reached out and took Sonny's hand.

"He and my ex used to do business. John flew in coke, and everybody was happy. I was using it, too—high like everybody else." She paused. "Until I woke up and left. I thought I could just walk out, but it wasn't that easy. Gilroy had his claws in a lot of people, including me. My ex wasn't completely stupid. He had made me do the buying. Gilroy is not stupid, either. He recorded the buys. Blackmail, Sonny, blackmail. He's got his claws into me."

"So you made one last deal."

Madge shook her head. "No! Maybe I should have," she whispered. "It's a big shipment. But I said no."

"And Gilroy doesn't take no for an answer," Sonny thought aloud. Could he believe her?

"He's got a lot of people on his string, Sonny. People in power in Santa Fe. He's running the high-quality stuff into the state and even the drug boys stay away from him."

"Because of his old CIA connections?"

She nodded. "I knew he was using the balloon fiesta, but I didn't know how. I didn't want to know. That's my only sin. I turned my back and pretended he wasn't there. You have to believe me." Her voice was soft, pleading.

"I need something to go on," he said.

"If I knew anything, I'd tell you. I can only guess that whoever buys the drugs from Gilroy is here. But I know it's not a balloon pilot."

"You checked through your records?"

"Jerry and I checked every single entry. We know our pilots."

"But anyone can register."

"True."

"How many balloons are going up?"

"Seven hundred."

Like looking for a needle in a haystack, Sonny thought. "What time?"

"Takeoff is seven-thirty."

Sonny glanced at his watch. He had three hours. "The FBI knows about Gilroy, so does the DEA. What are they doing?"

"Just to be on the up-and-up, we permitted agents with their drug-sniffing dogs on the field. No one with drugs can get past them."

"Yeah," Sonny answered. Maybe Raven was no one, no man.

He looked across the room to the painting on the wall. A nude woman reclining on a Navajo blanket spread out on the dry grass of the West Mesa. In the background was the brilliant gold of the river cottonwoods in their fall dress. Beyond the yellow of the river bosque lay the blue outline of the Sandia Mountains, and in the wide, blue sky a hundred colorful balloons rising.

The nude was Madge, staring not at the balloons, but out at the viewer. Her eyes held Sonny.

He rose and walked to it. Something in the eyes of the nude beckoned him. He drew close and saw that the artist had painted two dark balloons as irises. He turned and looked at Madge. Was she telling the truth?

She pulled the belt of her gown and let it slip to the floor. "I want to help you," she said softly. "Stay with me."

Sonny shook his head, turned, and walked out of the room.

"Damn you!" he heard her cry.

He was quickly down the stairs and out the patio door, running as he leaped over the patio wall. He turned back. She had parted the curtains to the upstairs bedroom; she stood outlined against the light, her body sharp and clear.

He turned and ran to his truck, then gunned it out of the compound, north on Coors to the Paseo del Norte bridge and across the valley to the Pyramid Hotel, hoping Gilroy was still there.

22

Sonny drove into the parking lot of the Pyramid Hotel, or as some of la gente called it, the Peso Pyramid, referring to its supposedly Mayan inspiration.

This was definitely not a place to plot the course of the moon at night as the Mayans had done with their pyramids for hundreds of years, not a place to worship the sun as it came over the Sandias, following its diurnal course. On June 21, the sun rose over Sandia Crest; on the winter solstice it rose over Tijeras Canyon.

Then the people from the pueblos would pray for the return of the sun; there would be a cycle of ceremonies and dances. Prayers and ritual. That's what sustained the life of the old inhabitants of the valley, prayers and ceremonies. A belief that they were intimately connected to the earth, to the course of the sun, moon, and planets.

Last Christmas Eve Rita had invited him to la misa del gallo, midnight mass at the Old Town San Felipe de Neri Church. Then they went to his mother's home to eat posole. After a few hours of sleep, they drove to a deer dance at Jemez pueblo. The spirit within was fulfilled in those ceremonies. But the kids Sonny had taught at Valley High weren't into the old ceremonies anymore. On Christmas day they headed for the malls. Days of worship gave way to shopping and football games.

Would Rita be with him this winter solstice to pray for the return of the sun? he thought as he walked into the deserted lobby. Yes, she will, he answered himself. I'll make sure.

He flexed his arm. Tomorrow it would be sore, maybe swollen, from the strain of his bout with Turco.

He paused, sniffed the air, and was met by the sweet smell of roses. He remembered the lilac fragrance that had permeated the dead body of Gloria Dominic, and for a moment he felt his stomach churn. He glanced into the lobby area and saw dozens of flower stands; little carts with awnings surrounded the lobby. The conference schedule board announced the end-of-season meeting of the New Mexico Flower Society. Displays of October flowers and roses filled the stands.

A huge balloon made entirely of flowers graced the middle of the lobby.

Sweet old ladies, Sonny thought, and some sweet old guys, having a ball showing off their prize flowers, dreaming sweet dreams of this year's prize Peace Rose or next year's red hybrid tea.

Sonny turned toward the deserted reception desk. There were two ways to get into Gilroy's room: bluff the desk clerk or steal a key. He glanced over the counter at the reception desk. A light shone from the room behind the counter. It was four in the morning and a sleepy night clerk was probably watching television.

Okay, Sonny thought, just do it! There was sure to be a security guard or two roaming the balcony areas that looked down into the huge, empty lobby. Break and enter. If he got caught,

Garcia would probably let him rot in jail, but he was going for broke. Going for Rita.

He hurried around the counter, riffled through the key slots, found the electronic key for Gilroy's room, and stuck it in his pocket.

At the elevator a security guard appeared out of nowhere and stood in front of him. His stern look said, What the hell are you doing out this time of the morning?

Sonny put on his innocent smile and blurred his voice. "Late party," he mumbled, "gonna be hell to fly," and he walked past the guard and into the elevator. He pushed the button, and when the door closed, he breathed a sigh of relief. The elevator rose quickly, the glass pane allowing him a view of the lobby below.

On the sixth floor he stepped out and quickly walked down the deserted balcony, found the room, and stuck the card into the slot. He opened the door and stepped into the anteroom, closing the door quickly and waiting for his eyes to adjust to the dark. There was someone in the room; he could sense a presence. Someone asleep? A hallway led from the anteroom to the bedroom beyond, going past the bathroom to the side.

All was dark. A sliver of moonlight through the dark curtains was the sole illumination in the bedroom area.

West side, Sonny thought. If he opened the curtains the view was toward the balloon field. Beyond that, the lights of the sleeping city.

But what of the presence he felt? Sonny wondered as he moved cautiously, past the bathroom, into the bedroom. He held his breath, peered in, the bed was empty. John Gilroy was gone. Sonny breathed easily. The bed was made. If Gilroy had been here, he hadn't slept here. Sonny flipped on a bedside lamp.

On a glass-topped table beside the bed sat a bottle of scotch, two glasses, and faint traces of coke lines. Gilroy had partied before he left. Maybe partied with Madge; maybe they toasted each other and laughed at Sonny Baca, the dumb private dick they led by the nose.

But there was no trace of Gilroy. Had he flown the coop after he argued with Madge, or was he already at the balloon field orchestrating the distribution? Sonny turned to leave when his "cuidado" sense told him the presence he had felt was still in the room.

He felt goosebumps along the back of his neck. Be alert, he told himself, like the coyote. Go slow. There's danger here. Blood? The scent of blood!

The bathroom, he thought as he paused at the door. I didn't check the bathroom! That was a stupid move. He pushed the bathroom door open slowly, then flipped on the lights.

He shuddered. The large, white-tiled room was splattered with blood. Lying in the bathtub lay the body of John Gilroy, partially covered by the shower curtain he had grabbed as he fell. His vacant eyes were open, staring up at Sonny. Blood soaked Gilroy's clothes and streaked his face.

"Damn," Sonny cursed. He felt for a pulse but found none. The body was still warm. He had come too late. Someone had just axed his prime suspect. He had missed the killer between the time Madge left Gilroy and the time it had taken Sonny to get here. Unless Madge . . .

Sonny felt his stomach turn queasy, but he forced himself to look closer. Yes, it was Gilroy, and the way he lay told Sonny that Gilroy had known his murderer. There were no signs of struggle, no torn shirt. Perhaps they had just done a line of coke together, then Gilroy got up to go to the bathroom and was taking a leak when "his friend" cut his throat from behind. Gilroy turned, received two more stabs across his carotid artery, grabbed for the shower curtain, and toppled into the bathtub. It took only seconds.

Madge was the last one with him. They were arguing, Diego said. Shouting at each other, fighting over the money that would be paid in a few hours when the dope was delivered. Madge was strong, Sonny knew, but could she wield a knife? Could she deliver a deadly blow? Gilroy was a big man, a cautious man, and a highly trained CIA operator. Could coke put him so off guard?

No, it had to be someone stronger than Madge. Sonny covered his mouth and nose and leaned closer. If it was Raven who'd rubbed out Gilroy, he hadn't left his calling card. There were no black raven feathers on the body.

A tingling sensation ran along the back of Sonny's neck again, and in that instant he knew he had made a mistake. He'd never checked the closet. Raven hadn't had time to leave his calling card! He was still in the room!

Sonny cursed and turned quickly just as the bathroom lights went out and a dark figure leaped forward. Sonny lifted his arm as Raven struck. The knife came slicing across Sonny's left arm, missing Sonny's neck by inches, but cutting through his leather jacket.

Sonny countered with a right cross that smashed into Raven's chest, a blow not strong enough to stop Raven's rush, but enough to slow the second strike.

The onslaught sent Sonny crashing into the wall. Sonny pushed back, and they tumbled into the dark anteroom. In the struggle Sonny grabbed at Raven's right hand, twisting away the knife. Raven let go of the knife and at the same time brought his knee hard into Sonny's groin. The blow made Sonny stagger, and a second blow to the face sent him crashing into the divan.

Raven turned and ran out of the room, followed by a dazed Sonny stumbling after him. Raven was halfway to the elevator when it opened and Chief Garcia, a hotel security guard, and two cops jumped out.

"Freeze!" Garcia called, and all four drew their pistols and aimed at Raven.

Raven turned to face Sonny.

"Where's Rita?" Sonny gasped, the fury in the voice echoing into the atrium's open space.

"Stay where you are!" Garcia called again. "You move and you're dead."

Raven looked at the cops, then at Sonny.

"Where's Rita?" Sonny snarled, advancing on Raven.

"She's mine!" Raven cried.

"I'll kill you," Sonny swore.

"No!" Raven snarled back. "It's you that dies!"

"You're surrounded," Garcia shouted, and he and the cops advanced slowly with drawn pistols. "Get down on the floor! Facedown! Down on the floor or we shoot!"

Raven knew he was trapped. He looked over the edge of the balcony to the lobby six floors below.

"Get down!" Garcia repeated as they closed in. "Sonny, you too."

"You're too late," Raven said, and disappeared over the side of the balcony.

The startled security guard leaned over the railing and got off one quick shot; an explosion that echoed through the atrium.

"Don't shoot!" Garcia shouted. "You don't know who else is down there!"

Sonny rushed to look over the railing. He expected to see Raven smashed to the lobby floor below. What he, Garcia, and the cops saw was a collapsed flower cart where Raven had landed, the awning crumpled.

"Sonofabitch jumped!" Garcia swore. "Hope he broke his neck!"

"Come on!" Sonny shouted, and rushed to the elevator, followed by Garcia.

"Check the stairs!" Garcia shouted, and the cops went for the stairs. "What were you doing here?" Garcia asked as he kept punching the lobby button.

"Looking for Gilroy," Sonny answered.

"Find him?"

"He's dead," Sonny answered.

"Raven?"

Sonny nodded.

The elevator opened at the lobby as Garcia's men burst out of the stairwell. They all rushed toward the cart where Raven had landed, Garcia shouting instructions to his boys. "Surround it! Go in slow. Sonofabitch has more lives than a cat!"

Above them, guests had come out of their rooms to lean over

balconies and look down. A woman screamed, "He jumped! I saw him jump!"

"What's going on?" someone shouted.

"Police! Stay in your rooms!" one of Garcia's officers shouted back. "Everything's under control, stay in your rooms!"

Outside a siren wailed.

"Did you leave someone at the door?" Sonny asked.

Garcia looked at him and cursed. He pushed one of the cops. "Cover the door! Go on! Cover the fucking door!"

They approached the cart cautiously, expecting to find Raven's body in the tangled awning and spilled roses. Sonny pulled away the awning, revealing broken pots and smashed flowers. He tossed the awning aside and looked up. Six floors—but the awning and the cart had broken Raven's fall, and the brujo who could fly had gotten up and walked away.

Raven is a brujo, an evil shaman who can fly, both don Eliseo and Lorenza had warned Sonny.

"Okay," Sonny whispered, "I believe you now. He can fly."

"Sonofabitch!" Chief Garcia cursed. He vented his anger on his assistants. "Get out there! Seal off the parking lot! Check the entire lobby! Go! Go! Go!"

The cops and security guards ran to do his bidding.

"Do you believe this!" a frustrated Garcia turned to Sonny. "Do you frigging believe this?"

"Yes," Sonny replied.

Raven had been washed down the worst arroyo flood Sonny had ever seen, and he had lived through it. Now he had jumped six floors and was nowhere to be found. He had many lives, one for each step to the underworld.

Garcia turned to greet two DEA agents coming through the front door. "If it isn't Police Chief Garcia," one of the agents said. "Out partying, Chief?"

Sonny recognized Joe Flannery.

"Raven just flew," Garcia answered.

"Raven?" Flannery acted surprised. "Is Matt here?"

"No," Garcia replied. "The FBI didn't find Raven, Sonny found him. This is Sonny Baca." He motioned. "Joe Flannery."

"Mr. Baca"—Flannery grinned—"you seem to have a knack for being in hot spots. Frisk him," he snapped at his assistant.

The agent with Flannery put his hand to his pistol and snapped at Sonny. "Turn around and put your hands against the wall!"

Sonny blew him off. "Are you for real?"

"Yeah, we're for real," a very irritated Flannery replied, drawing his pistol. Garcia jumped in front of him.

"Easy, Joe! You're pissing up the wrong tree!"

"We got a call! Baca was described!" Flannery grunted.

"I'm in charge here, and I say back off!" Garcia shouted.

Flannery fumed but nodded at his partner.

"This guy's bleeding," the agent said.

"Did he get you?" Garcia asked.

Sonny held up his arm. His shirt sleeve was dark with blood. During the excitement he hadn't felt the cut. "He had a knife."

"Better get a doc to look at that."

"Later," Sonny said.

"Okay," Flannery grunted, "so why in the hell are you here, Baca?"

"I got a call, saying you'd be here," Sonny retorted.

"Not funny," Flannery replied. "I'm up in the middle of the night chasing ghosts, so can the humor."

Sonny shrugged and removed his jacket. The leather jacket had saved him from a bad cut.

"Never can tell about a knife wound," Garcia said. He handed Sonny a handkerchief, which Sonny wrapped around the wound. "One of my boys can patch you up for now."

"I'm okay," Sonny insisted. "The guy that's not okay is Gilroy."

"Show us the body," Garcia said.

"Body?" Flannery asked.

"Baca says we've got homicide."

They took the elevator up and entered Gilroy's room. Garcia flipped on the light.

"In the bathroom," Sonny said, and the chief flipped on the bathroom light.

Garcia and Flannery peered in.

"Holy mother of God." Garcia whistled. "It's Gilroy, and he is dead as a doornail all right."

"Whoever got him is good with a knife," Flannery said, reaching for a cigarette as he looked down at the body.

"Raven."

"You're lucky, Baca," Flannery said. "A slice like that will definitely take you out."

"Maybe that's why you were called," Garcia said, following him into the anteroom.

"We've got nothing on Gilroy." Flannery shrugged.

Sonny bit his tongue to keep from challenging. Of course the DEA knew Gilroy's past! The whole world knew his past! He had been sheltered by the government, and now he was dead. So much for government protection!

"Really," Garcia grumbled. He, too, was angered that the DEA wasn't leveling with him, and he had had enough run-ins with the arrogant Flannery to develop a healthy dislike. "I thought he was one of your undercover agents."

"No way." Flannery grinned.

"Come on, Joe, everybody knows Gilroy worked for you," Garcia insisted.

"Maybe for Matt, not for us!" Flannery replied, his anger flaring for an instant. "Anyway"—he shrugged—"if you believe Baca here, I would say you just solved your case. Raven's been terrorizing the fiesta, right? And he just killed Gilroy, right? Get Raven and it's all over." Flannery turned to Sonny and smiled. "So, Baca, you can go back to your people and tell them it's safe to fly. Raven's on the run. I'm sure Garcia here will have him corraled in no time. Yeah, it's safe to fly," he chuckled, and went out smiling.

Garcia cursed. "That's one arrogant sonofabitch!"

"They know about Gilroy."

"Of course they know him! What do you take me for? A pendejo?"

"So why lie?"

"They're trained to lie! They want to do the bust! Won't give the local cops any information!" He glared at Sonny. "Why don't you get the hell out of here!" He was pissed at Flannery and taking it out on Sonny.

"What about Raven?"

"We'll get Raven," Garcia muttered. "And we'll find Rita. Now get a doctor to look at the cut."

Sonny nodded. Rita. Raven would be out in the open, maybe make more mistakes. But that would also increase the danger for Rita. Raven was still holding the prize.

Sonny walked out of the crowded hotel lobby into the mellow, suffused light before sunrise. There was a chill in the air, but no frost. The Sandia Mountains stood outlined against the very soft pearl blue of the east. He looked at his watch. Wednesday. Within the hour the sun would rise, and with it, hundreds of balloons.

He got into his truck and drove to a Pres Hospital emergency room just blocks away. A doctor washed his wound, stitched it, and gave Sonny a prescription for antibiotics. When asked how he got the cut, Sonny answered, "Bar fight."

"Have your family doctor check this out in a week or so. He can take out the stitches," the doctor said. "And just to be safe, you might want to get tested for HIV."

"Sure," Sonny replied. Family doctor? He didn't have one. What would he say to one if he did have one? "I've got this problem. A man trying to kill me takes the form of a spirit Raven. An evil one, not a friendly raven. He kidnapped my woman, and he wants to kill me. My friend the curandera says Raven is now in his circle of power. So he's invincible. If I go there, I may die. But I have to get Rita back. And for that I need my nagual."

"Nagual?" the doctor would ask.

"Yes, the coyote, my guardian spirit. You see, the only way I'm finally going to be done with Raven is to fight him on his own terms."

"Raven?"

"Never mind," Sonny would say. It's too much to explain. Science had no world of spirits, and there was no time for doctors. Right now his only concern was Rita. And he was sure Lorenza could help.

He thanked the doctor and hurried to the balloon field. Alameda Boulevard was already choked with traffic. There were cops directing traffic into the parking lots, and at the main entrance sheriff's deputies on horseback. A sense of excitement rippled through the bracing-cold air as families hurried onto the balloon grounds.

This was mass ascension day, hundreds of balloons rising, a cause for happiness after the damper the murders had thrown over the festivities. Thousands of people were converging on the grounds to enjoy the fiesta, thinking all was safe.

Sonny turned into the main gate. One of the deputies on horseback leaned in his saddle. "Hey, you can't—" He recognized Sonny. "You still working here?"

"Hope so," Sonny replied.

The deputy waved him through.

Sonny turned toward Fiesta Control, skirting the long line of tents that lent a carnival atmosphere to the fiesta. Already the tantalizing aroma of morning burritos and brewing coffee filled the air. Later in the morning the hungry fiesta-goers would flock to the tents to eat a variety of food, from pizza to tacos.

Beyond the tent street lay the balloon field, eerie in the predawn light. Row upon row of trucks lined the field. Crews gathered around their balloons, readying for flight. The first rows to the south would take off first, and there crews were already inflating their balloons with portable fans. Filled with hot air, still tethered to the ground, the balloons dotted the landscape like bright desert flowers.

Blossoms of cactus flowers, Sonny thought, some deep purple, some red, some yellow. A field of many colors. The Chinese lanterns that Ben Chávez had once predicted would dot the New Mexican landscape.

Loudspeakers from a radio station announced the beginning of the festivities. Other radio and television stations beamed out the news from their tents: the fiesta was back on schedule. The balloons were flying today. The entire city was awakening with a sense of joy. Today on the way to work, thousands of motorists would once again see the balloons over the skies of Alburquerque.

Sonny thought of Lorenza, and their near-death ride. He remembered what Lorenza told him. Communicate with Rita. Send the coyote thoughts her way, let her answer. A couple of times he thought he had heard her. He could see her in a dark room, almost a cave. He could see two forms huddled on the ground, holding each other. Rita and Cristina. They were still alive; there was still time.

Instead of going directly to Fiesta Control, he parked and wandered out onto the field. Crews and onlookers looked like bundled spirits in their parkas, scarves, and caps. There was no breeze, so the dust of the valley hung close to the ground. The loud blasts of the burners roared in the muffled morning silence as the kachinas of flight waited for the signal from Fiesta Control to rise into the sky.

Did the Hopi have a kachina of flight? Sonny wondered. He had yet to see one with wings. Maybe they had never had the yearning to fly, never the desire to leave Mother Earth. The gods came to visit the pueblo, and so flight was for the gods, not for man. It made sense.

It was cold, near freezing, and Sonny shivered. The scene

was lighted in an eerie predawn glow, but the crowd and those flying today were in a cheery mood.

The crowd would feel joy when the release came and the colorful balloons ascended, but Sonny wouldn't feel it. He saw instead a wasteland, shadows crawling around the balloons that glowed colorfully when the propane burners fired. He felt the eagerness of the people, most with cameras poised, drawing close to the balloons to take the perfect picture. All wanted to share in the magic of those who would rise and fly.

Sonny paused. Around him the blue burst of the burners going off intermittently filled the air with loud whooshes, the hot air inflating the colorful balloons until they appeared to be giant luminarias, the farolitos of October. Within the hour the ascension would begin.

Already the "zebras," men and women dressed in black-and-white striped outfits, ran up and down the first row, shouting instructions, double-checking instructions on their mobile phones. The zebras were in charge of the ascension, coordinating the liftoff.

Sonny turned quickly and headed for Fiesta Control. He was sure the dope was in the city, courtesy of Gilroy, and some of it had to be here on the field. That was their plan, to draw every DEA officer and his mother to the field. Bring them in to a nonperformance.

He spotted a couple of DEA agents with dogs. They were moving slowly across the crowded field, the dogs sniffing the baskets, but Sonny knew the dogs weren't going to find anything.

The Fiesta Control lobby was packed with reporters. Sonny pushed his way through and entered Madge's office. Madge, her two zebras, and Jerry Stammer were huddled over a map. One of the zebras was reviewing wind-aloft speed and direction. Today, the Alburquerque box was perfect for flying. A soft breeze would carry the balloons south, and when they went higher, another breeze would return them to the field.

Madge looked up. Stammer also turned.

"Our wayward detective," Stammer said. "You gave it a good run, buddy, but you came up empty-handed. Today we fly."

The two zebras, sensing the tension, drew away to refill their coffee cups.

Sonny's gaze remained riveted on Madge. She looked back at him, revealing nothing in her blue eyes.

"Gilroy's dead," Sonny said.

"Garcia called." Madge nodded.

"It's in the news," Stammer added. "Too bad, but it means nothing to the fiesta."

"It means an obstacle has been eliminated," Sonny replied.

Stammer relaxed, then smiled. "See, I told you," he said to Madge. "The crazies have eliminated each other. I said all along, the fiesta is as safe as a Sunday picnic. We're go!" he turned to the zebras and gave a thumbs-up signal.

"It's not that simple," Sonny cautioned.

"The hell it ain't," Stammer responded. "You just said the last obstacle's been removed. I'm sorry about Gilroy, but whatever he was involved in had nothing to do with us!"

"Yeah, it does," Sonny said. "Whoever killed Gilroy is flying the dope today."

"You still believe that!" Stammer laughed. "Hear that, Madge, we're flying dope. It doesn't play, Baca! It just doesn't wash!" he said in anger. "Anyway, for your information, there are DEA agents on the grounds right now! I personally invited them here."

"But they're not going to find anything," Sonny shot back.

"Right." Stammer drew himself up. "Because there's nothing to find!"

Madge stepped between them and looked at Sonny. "I can't say I'm sorry about Gilroy," she said flatly. "I suspect whatever that was all about is done."

"I've got a hunch," Sonny replied.

"A hunch!" Stammer responded angrily. "You come to us with a hunch! You make me laugh, Baca!"

"Only a hunch." Madge glared. "I agree with Jerry, that doesn't help! Look, if you've got any information, tell us, or tell Garcia. We want to help."

"The coke and the heroin are here!" Sonny shivered, his voice a whisper, his eyes darting from Madge to Stammer. "I know it's here! I can feel it."

"He can feel it!" Stammer shook his head in disgust and turned away. "You talk to him Madge."

"Sonny—"

He grabbed her arms and looked into her eyes. "I know it's here! I've followed it around the city, and now I'm this close to it." He made a sign with his fingers. "This close!"

"Where?" she shouted.

"Ah, Lord," he groaned, and turned away, looking out the window at the sun, which was just about to burst clear of the mountain's crest, a golden orb, the fire balloon of the gods coming to grace the valley. The grandfather kachina.

In his withered field of corn, don Eliseo would be praying in the morning light, lifting his arms to the sun, Grandfather Sun, the bringer of all life. "Bless all of life," the old man would whisper, and with those simple words he would embrace the earth, planets, and cosmos.

In the river bosque the coyotes were calling, moving as a family down the well-worn paths, shivering in the cold October morning, their night hunt done.

I'm sweating, Sonny thought, rubbing his dirty hands on his jacket, looking down at his wrinkled jeans. The cut on his arm throbbed. He was sweaty, tired, exhausted. Maybe not thinking straight. Maybe I've lost it, he admitted.

The others in the room looked at him with furtive glances. Yes, he had lost it. They felt sorry for him, embarrassed. He hadn't shaved, or combed his hair, and his arm hung loose in the torn spotted sleeve. It was clear he was in pain, coming apart. He had nothing to go on.

"It was shipped in," he whispered, and saw in his mind's eye the UPS truck lumbering out of Raven's nest, the deadly cargo in its belly.

"What?" Madge asked.

Sonny turned to the two zebras. "Did you receive a large UPS shipment recently? Yesterday? Or early this morning?"

"Yes," the woman answered tentatively, glancing at Jerry Stammer. "This morning."

"What was in it?"

"Normal stuff. A lot of extra propane tanks, repair materials, some flight maps, even a new balloon—" She laughed nervously and again looked from Madge to Stammer.

"You're fishing!" Stammer interrupted. "That's been the problem all along, Baca! You don't know a thing, and you go fishing. Enough questions!" He turned to Madge. "Launch time!"

Madge looked at her watch, turned to Sonny. "We have to—"

"If you're going to stay here and chat, I'm giving the signal!" Stammer growled, starting out the door.

Madge grabbed his arm. "Hey, you may be chairman of the board, but I'm in charge of the flight!"

Stammer glared back at her. "You may not be in charge for long!" he rejoined. "It was your idea to bring Baca on board, and nothing has been solved. Okay, go along with him. But get those balloons in the air on schedule!"

Having delivered his ultimatum, he turned and walked out of the building.

"What about the propane tanks?" Sonny asked the woman.

"The pilots fill up here, so I wondered who would be ordering propane tanks full of gas. We received enough extra propane tanks to fly a balloon from here to Miami!"

"Yeah!" Sonny hit the table with a closed fist. "The tanks. Sealed tanks! The dogs can't sniff it! Who are the tanks for?"

"I've got the invoice here," the woman said, and flipped through her notes. She removed the UPS delivery invoice and handed it to Sonny. "This is the name of the pilot who received the propane. And it's funny, because he was here this morning, waiting for the delivery."

Sonny turned to Madge. "That's it! The delivery! Can we stop him?" he said, shoving the list into her hands.

"Sonny, are you sure?"

"Why would anyone bring in that many extra propane tanks?"

Madge shrugged. "Christ, if we stop them and there's nothing to it—"

"Madge!" Sonny slapped the invoice he held. "This is it!"

Madge turned to the zebra. "You're sure you know who picked up the tanks?"

"Yes, that's the name of the pilot and the number of his balloon on the invoice," she replied.

"I can ground him," Madge said, "but Jerry won't—"

"Do it!" Sonny shouted. "If I'm wrong, I'll take the heat."

Madge hesitated. She was caught in the middle.

"All right, we can check it," she replied. She looked at the list. "Number forty-seven."

She handed the list back to the zebra. "Have security ground this balloon." She turned to the man. "Get on the PA system and delay the flight. Don't let those balloons go up! Let's check number forty-seven," she said to Sonny.

They hurried out, jumped into her golf cart, and shot toward the field. Startled spectators jumped aside.

Near the large KRQE announcing stand the first wave of balloons were ready to fly. Propane fires glowed blue as the pilots of the balloons shouted instructions to their ground crews. It was a festive day, a Mardi Gras of flight.

Today the modern-day Icarus, bored with the weekend football games and family trips to the shopping malls, dared to sprout wings over the desert landscape of the Río Grande basin. Flight into the golden dawn, flight over the shimmering cottonwoods of the river, flight over the serpentine river.

Then a voice boomed over the loudspeaker, across the huge field, holding the flight. Faces turned in the direction of the loudspeaker as a collective groan of disappointment went up.

"Here!" Madge pointed. "Forty-seven. Bobby Lee, from Dallas. . . ."

The bright red balloon carried the name *Avenger*.

A freckled young man in a red parka, another young man, and two young women had just finished firing up the balloon.

They were laughing, having fun, clearly juiced up on morning margaritas.

"Morning, y'all," the lanky Bobby Lee said with a smile as Madge and Sonny pulled up. "You better stand back, we're ready for liftoff!"

"Bobby Lee?"

"At your service, ma'am."

"I'm Madge Swenson, flight control. Your flight is canceled!"

"I heard the announcement, lady, but I came to fly, and I'm flying," Bobby Lee replied. His friends nodded and drew close.

"You're not flying today," Madge repeated.

"Bullshit, lady!" Bobby Lee's voice grew mean. "I've been waiting all week to fly, and nobody's going to stop me!" He turned to his friends. "Are we flying?"

"We're flying!" they shouted back, laughing.

"We're grounding your balloon!" Madge said forcefully. "I'd appreciate it if you'd stand back—"

"You can't ground me, lady," Bobby Lee snarled at her.

Sonny stepped in front of him. "You heard her. She's the boss. You do what she says. Just step back, real nice and easy."

Two security guards appeared behind Madge, and Bobby Lee drew back.

Sonny looked into the basket. It was loaded with five propane tanks. He looked closely at the tanks and lifted out one with traces of white powder around the valve.

"Why so much extra gas?" Sonny asked.

"You have no fuckin' right to take that tank from my basket!" Bobby Lee yelled. He looked at his friend and the women, but they were backing away. They had seen the DEA agents with dogs cutting through the gathering crowd to get to them. They turned and ran.

"I have the right," Madge interrupted. "That's in your contract."

Sonny tapped the tank and smiled. "Sugar?" he whispered. He grabbed a wrench from the basket and started unscrewing the tank's cap.

"Hey, mister!" one of the zebras called. "Don't do that without releasing the gas pressure! It's gonna blow!"

Sonny finished unscrewing the valve, and it fell to the ground. White powder spilled out of the tank. Nearby one of the DEA dogs growled deep and pulled at its leash, trying to push through the crowd that had gathered.

"Sugar," Sonny said, looking at Bobby Lee. "Now why would a young man like you be carrying sugar? You can't burn sugar."

Sonny wet his fingertip with saliva and touched the powder. He tasted, then spit. "Uh-uh, Bobby Lee, that ain't sugar, that's pure coke. Enough to make you fly all the way to Dallas—"

"You sonofabitch," Bobby Lee cursed, and hurled himself on Sonny.

Sonny blocked Bobby Lee's blow and hit him as hard as he could in the stomach. He hit him again, and the fight went out of Bobby Lee. "Where's Raven?" Sonny shouted, grabbing the man by the collar and slapping him hard. Blood spurted from Bobby Lee's mouth.

"Don' know no Raven!"

"Where's Raven?" Sonny shouted, and hit him again, pushing him against the basket.

"Don't know what you're talking about!" Bobby Lee cried.

"Where's the woman and the girl?" Sonny shouted, and hit the man again. "Answer me!" Bobby Lee fell into the spilled cocaine and Sonny landed on top of him. The DEA dogs growled and pulled at their leashes.

"Where's Raven? Where's Rita?" Sonny shouted as he grabbed Bobby Lee and shook him.

The startled crowd pressed in to see the fight. The DEA agent with the dog was on top of them, and now the dog was snapping and barking.

"DEA officer! Stand back! Stand back!" He pulled his pistol.

"Sonny, stop!" Madge called.

"Where's the woman?" Sonny shouted as he hit Bobby Lee again.

Only the powerful hands of Chief Garcia and one of his assistants were able to pry Sonny away from the man.

"Take it easy, Sonny, easy," the chief said as he pulled Sonny back. "We need him alive."

"He's working for Raven! He can tell us where to find Rita!" Sonny gasped for breath.

He had snapped. Now as he stood back catching his breath, he knew he might have killed the man. He was trembling, feeling a stab of pain shoot up from the cut in his arm. He had reopened the wound.

Garcia leaned over the groaning Bobby Lee. "Tell me where they're hiding the woman or I'll give you back to him," the chief threatened.

"You fuckin' crazies," Bobby Lee cursed. "I don' know about any woman!"

"You know Raven!" the chief shouted.

"I don' know Raven! I don' know the fuckin' operators!" He groaned. "I get paid for delivering this to Dallas. That's all."

Garcia pulled back. The man was probably telling the truth. He had been hired to fly the coke out of the field, load it on his waiting chase truck when he landed, then drive to Dallas and deliver it.

Bobby Lee was just a delivery boy, he didn't know the players. The deal could have been arranged on the phone, or arranged by one of Raven's boys. Bobby Lee had never met Raven, and he didn't know about Rita.

He turned to Sonny and shrugged. "He doesn't know, Sonny. He's a delivery boy. You found the dope, but he doesn't know Rita or the girl. . . ."

"Sonofabitch knows." Sonny lurched forward, but the chief stopped him.

"Sonny, you know better! These guys do the delivery, that's all! You know how it works!"

Sonny felt a shudder go through him, and suddenly he felt very weak. Garcia was right, the gofers usually knew very little.

"Two ran," he said as he watched two cops put handcuffs on Bobby Lee.

"We got them," Garcia answered, and turned to Madge. "I'd like to pull them into your office, do some questioning right away. There's a small chance one of them might know a place, a location. It's a slim chance, but it's all we've got."

"Sure," Madge replied. She looked at Sonny. "They *were* using the fiesta. And I doubted you. I'm sorry—" She reached out to touch Sonny, but he drew away.

"Bring those tanks in," Garcia snapped at his officers. Sonny recognized Jerry Candelaria, the undercover narc he had met at Veronica's death scene. Candelaria nodded but said nothing as he gave instructions for the tanks to be pulled from the basket.

Madge turned and led Garcia, his cops, and the handcuffed Bobby Lee toward Fiesta Control.

Sonny rested against the basket. The city cops were cordoning off the area, moving the crowd back.

The DEA knew all along, Sonny thought. They knew a big shipment was coming in.

Sonny turned to look at the inquisitive crowd. They, too, thought the dope had been found, all was well. The cops scored again. Some began to take pictures. This was great, a dope bust right in front of their eyes. Uniformed DEA agents and their dogs. And Sonny Baca. They had seen him catch the dopester and beat him up. Great!

"Sonny!" Francine Hunter called. She was pushing through the crowd. The harried Conroy Chino was right behind her, both trying to scoop the story.

You're on the wrong trail, Sonny thought. Raven and Gilroy and whoever else was in the deal had played it smart. The delivery boys were hired to do the job, but they had no inside information.

The Juárez mafia and the Colombian cartels had spread like a web throughout the land. They could buy anything, anyone. Hell, if presidents in Latin America could be bought, if insiders at the CIA could be bought, then scum like the Bobby Lees of the world numbered in the thousands. Bobby Lee would deliver enough dope to Dallas to keep the city afloat for a day, then it would start all over again. The web was huge and intricate and well financed.

Bobby Lee, the lanky young man with a friendly smile, freckles across his face, and a soft Texas drawl would be out on bail tomorrow. Ready to become the new Gilroy. Ruthless, in command of dope and power, and willing to kill to stay in charge. It was greed and need that fed the process.

Bobby Lee was a pawn in a big money game he didn't yet understand. He was a young man looking for good times, fast money, fast women, the thrill of ballooning, the thrill of life on a fast track. And all of that cost money.

There were thousands of Bobby Lee's out there, of all colors and from all walks. They had acquired a taste for expensive things, expensive habits, and drug money was a quick way to buy instant happiness. They had been brainwashed into the system, brainwashed into delivering crack into their own neighborhoods, their own families. And as small and petty as each one of those dealers might be, each helped build and sustain the web.

At the center sat a fat spider. Who? Who was the weaver of the web?

Sonny looked at the television cameras in front of his face, and he squinted at the bright lights.

You should be aiming your cameras at the source, he thought. The real dope ain't here.

The crowd suddenly drew back and looked skyward. The tension of days waiting to fly could no longer be contained, and all around them the balloons began to rise. They rose in waves, according to the flight plan, a bustle of balloons, the zebras whistling and rushing, trying to keep order, shouting instructions as row upon row of the hot-air globes was released from the bond of earth, exploding into a kaleidoscope of colors against the bright, blue sky.

Pregnant with the hot-blue burning propane, the balloons rose suddenly into the open sky. Baskets swung free of tethered lines, carrying pilots and passengers upward. Excited crews left behind shouted hurrahs as the balloons rose, and the crowd of thousands joined in the shout, a salute to the flight. Shouts of joy, amazement, and exclamation vibrated across the field, making the earth tremble. The echo swept across the dusty field and rose up and away with the balloons.

In the dazzling glory of sunrise, the flowers had exploded, blossomed, and were now rising. The beauty of the mass ascension left everyone dumbfounded.

When the sound died away, like thunder dying away as it rumbles in the summer thunderstorms, it was replaced by gasps of awe, the click of camera shutters, mothers calling to children to get a better view.

Amid the regular pear-shaped balloons rose the unique ones, those in the shape of a cow, an Uncle Sam, a Mickey Mouse, and other creatures from American mythology. A balloon in the shape of a bottle of scotch, a Pepsi can, a roll of film, a dinosaur, and other huge, fantastic shapes.

The children pointed and waved at the passengers in the tiny baskets who were suddenly out of reach, rising into the cloudless sky. They called good-byes, wished them a safe flight, cried "See you later alligator," shrieked and laughed and ran, following the flight of the quickly ascending balloons.

Those lucky enough to be flying smiled and waved down at those they left earthbound. They, too, shouted good-byes, then turned their attention to the huge panorama of sky around them, land below them. This was it! The climb to catch the prevailing wind! The excitement of flight!

The loudspeakers announced the pilots of the balloons as they passed over the television stand. For those at home the mass ascension was being televised and radioed into homes throughout the city.

Sonny looked up. The excitement brought him no joy. Raven still held Rita. Finding the tank full of coke had been a lucky guess, perhaps too easy. Madge was too cooperative. Something was missing.

Joe Flannery approached Sonny.

"You helped us bust a big one," he said. "I personally want to thank you. . . ." He held out his hand.

The newspeople swarmed around them, pushing up against Sonny, firing questions. Each wanted the scoop of reporting that a stash of cocaine had just been found at the balloon fiesta. Cameras focused on the spilled cocaine.

"How'd you know?" Francine Hunter called.

Sonny looked at Flannery. Could he really trust the sonofa-bitch? He didn't mind who got the credit for finding the coke; all he had wanted was a lead to Rita.

"Forget it," Sonny said, and pushed by Flannery.

"Sonny!" A harried Francine Hunter followed him. "How did you know? How big is the bust? Can I ask you a few questions? Peter, get a shot—"

"I can't talk," Sonny replied.

"How'd you know the dope was here?" she repeated, push-ing the mike closer to Sonny.

"There is no dope here!" Sonny snapped, walking away.

"But we heard the coke was brought in by the Cali cartel. Does this mean they have a foothold in New Mexico?"

Sonny spun and faced her. "Foothold? They own the state! They own the country! They make crack for the barrios and make slaves! Where in the hell have you been! Now get off my back!"

"You're pissed," she responded, still holding the mike for-ward. "I understand that, but this is big! I've got to get this story!"

Peter had stopped shooting film. "Give the man a break," he said softly. "He's got other things on his mind."

Francine looked from him to Sonny. "Yeah, right. Sorry—"

Her words lingered in the air as Sonny hurried away.

At Fiesta Control a jubilant Chief Garcia came forward to greet Sonny. "We got every single tank on the list! We got 'em cold. Thanks to you." He smiled magnanimously.

"You got nothing," Sonny replied.

"What?"

Sonny shook his head. "It was too easy." Number 47 had been moored too close to Fiesta Control. Too convenient. One of those false clues Raven loved to set.

"Come on, Sonny. Whaddaya mean?"

Joe Flannery and two of his agents had followed Sonny into the building. Now he stepped forward.

"You keeping something from us, Baca? 'Cause if you are—"

"Open the tanks," Sonny answered. A gnawing feeling tore at his empty stomach. A link was missing in the operation. The DEA had stepped in only after Sonny busted Bobby Lee, and the FBI was hanging back. Not a single agent in sight. Why?

He looked at Madge. She stared back, her cold blue eyes hiding what she really knew.

"I'll take the tanks downtown," Flannery said, "have them opened in our lab—"

"Open them now!" Sonny insisted.

"Sonny," Garcia said sternly, "it's his jurisdiction. I want to talk to the people we've arrested. There's a chance they know something about Rita. That's my concern right now."

"They know zero," Sonny responded. He grabbed a pair of pliers from a nearby tool chest and opened the safety valve on the nearest tank. The rotten-egg smell of propane filled the air. Sonny opened another and again the gas shot out.

"Gas!" Flannery shouted, a surprised look crossing his face. He looked at Garcia. "Fucking tanks are full of gas!"

Madge moved forward to shut off the tank valves. "There's no dope," she whispered.

"Damn!" Garcia cursed and looked at Sonny. "We've been had!"

Flannery looked at Sonny and almost grinned. "Looks like my congratulations came too early." He shrugged. "You found a kilo of coke, that's all. The rest is gas. So where's the big shipment you had us chasing?"

"Don't you know?" Sonny replied, tossing the pliers so a startled Flannery had to catch them.

"Listen, Baca, I don't like the insinuation," Flannery snarled, stepping forward. Then he eased back. "Ah, what the hell. Think what you want! What we've got here is a kilo of coke, nothing more."

He turned to Madge. "Might as well let the press in. What we've got here is a small bust. No big deal. Sonny Baca's been wasting our time. I'd like to use your office."

She nodded. Sonny, the chief, and Madge stood in silence,

watching as one of the agents let in the herd of reporters who had waited impatiently outside.

"I told you we were clean," Madge said. "Whoever did this wanted the fiesta to get a black eye. One guy brings in a little coke, we get a bad rep. But we're clean."

"What the hell is going on?" Garcia asked in exasperation. He had made a fool of himself in front of the news media, talking about this arrest as if it were the bust of the century, and he didn't appreciate thinking about his next "meet the press" with only a kilo.

"While we were chasing balloons, the shipment was delivered," Sonny explained.

"What?" Garcia muttered.

"It was never meant to come here," Sonny said, looking intently at Madge. "This was a decoy. They planted enough clues to lead us here. They let us bust Bobby Lee, who will be out on bond tomorrow. In the meantime, the drugs were delivered. Courtesy of UPS."

Garcia moaned. "If you're right, there's a hundred ways to get it out of the city. Once the shipment is split up, they're safe!"

Madge turned to Sonny. "Look, I'm sorry your plan didn't work, but it proved what I've said all along: we had nothing to do with it."

"Rita's what's important now," Garcia said.

Sonny shrugged. "Raven's made his deal, he's got the money."

"So he can try to blow up another WIPP truck," Garcia moaned.

"No." Sonny shook his head. "This time it's going to be bigger." He looked at the police chief. "How far do you trust Flannery?" he asked, and Garcia winced.

"They've kept me in the dark," the police chief replied. "Right now I trust no one."

"It's about time they talked," Sonny said through gritted teeth. He was angry because the drugs had sifted through his hands; angry because once the dope was on the streets, it would poison all the poor neighborhoods of the country. And he was really angry because the chase had taken his time, time he needed to find Rita. The sonsofbitches had led him to another dead end.

"Where's Stammer?" he asked Madge.

"He's gone. Probably at his lab. Look, the man's under a lot of stress, overworked."

"Yeah, tell me about it," Sonny replied, and walked to the door.

"Where are you going?" Garcia called.

"To church," Sonny replied.

Whoever had sliced Gilroy's throat was an expert. First Veronica, then Secco, then Gilroy. Deaths they wanted him to connect to the balloon fiesta, but which really had roots in decades of drug trade.

Yeah, everything had been orchestrated, everything in place, everything calculated to lead the local law and Sonny down the wrong avenues. And it had worked. Now it was time to go to the source!

In his truck Sonny dialed home and listened through the messages on his machine. One was from Diego. Sonny dialed him.

"Sonny, glad you called," Diego answered. "I've been on the phone, calling old friends. The deal was made! The dope's in the city by now."

"Yeah," Sonny acknowledged. "I know."

"And no word on Rita and my hijita. I feel useless as hell sitting here. I'm afraid, Sonny. I'm afraid for my little girl. And her mother's a wreck, too."

"Hang in there." Sonny tried to comfort his friend. "I'm going to try something. I'll check with you later."

"Cuidado," Diego said.

"Don't have time to be careful," Sonny replied.

He had been thinking of the move he had to make. There was one man in town who knew all about the old CIA connections in Central America. One man who knew Gilroy, who knew the games that U.S. Customs and the DEA were playing. William Stone.

He called Ruth Jamison at the public library.

"Hi, Ruth. Sonny Baca."

"Sonny, are you all right?"

"I'm fine. Listen. I'm in a hurry. What did you find on Stone?"

"Only the newspaper and magazine clippings. There are FBI and CIA files that would be very interesting, but that takes time through Freedom of Information. And files like that get purged. What I have are mostly articles from the *Washington Post, The New York Times,* et cetera. Stuff most people know."

Over the phone she sketched out Gilroy's and Stone's involvement.

Unlike Gilroy, Stone was a smooth operator. Educated in the Ivy League, he had worked in the foreign service before transferring to the CIA. He had made a name for himself during the Sandinista takeover of Managua. Some said it was Stone's helicopter that flew Somoza out of the beleaguered capital as it fell. After that the White House gave him the go-ahead to carry out covert operations to supply the Contras.

The right-wing Libertad commandos' murderous methods of extracting information from the Sandinistas were reported in the papers in Latin America. Not a word of Stone's activities was reported in the North American papers.

Sandinista prisoners were taken up in helicopters, questioned, made to confess, then pushed out. But the murdering ways of a covert war gone sour began to tarnish the image of the Contras and their Washington backers.

Then the Gilroy incident broke. Reporters began to dig into Gilroy's past, and the chief operator of Libertad was revealed: William Stone. Those senators who had approved of the clandestine operations to fund the Contras protected Stone and turned on Gilroy.

"The best I could do," Ruth said, "is find his phone number."

"You got his *number?*" Sonny said.

"A friend at US West," she said. "Stone is staying with friends. Very rich and conservative folks who fund right-wing militia groups in the state," Ruth whispered, and read Sonny the phone number.

"You're great," Sonny said.

"Anytime," she answered. "I hope you find Rita soon," she added. "I'm praying."

"Yeah," he whispered, "me too."

He hung up and dialed Stone's number.

Overhead the sky was clear. Most of the balloons had landed safely. Nobody shot, no accidents, the fiesta board was in charge again, the fiesta could be saved, the money would flow safely into the cash registers of the city after all.

There was only one more thing to do: find Rita and the girl.

A man answered.

"Billy the Kid?" Sonny said.

There was a pause on the other end. Then, "Who is this?"

"Juan Libertad," Sonny replied. He knew he had to get Stone's interest quickly.

"You've got the wrong number—"

"Come on, Billy, I've got the right number."

There was only a slight pause, then: "Are you a reporter?"

Sonny laughed. "Would a reporter named Juan Libertad call you? No, I'm not a reporter, but I know who killed Gilroy."

"Then go to the police," Stone answered.

"You don't really want me to do that, do you? Names will begin to fly, and yours might come up. No, I need to talk to you in private, Mr. Stone."

Sonny hoped he wouldn't spook the man and lose him.

Stone laughed. "You don't make sense, Juan. What is it you want?"

"I want to sell you information. You should talk to me."

"Who are you?" Stone asked.

Got him! Sonny thought. He's interested!

"I told you, Juan Libertad," Sonny replied.

He paused, waited. Would Stone really take the bait? He was a pro, and no fool. He had survived the intricate plots before the Cold War ended, survived Nicaragua, and now, if Sonny was right, he was surviving as an insider in the cartels that provided the world its daily fix.

It was Stone's turn to appear disinterested, cool. He laughed again. "I don't know a Juan Libertad. Exactly what is it you want?"

"I want to talk to you."

"To sell information." Stone chuckled, still being cautious. "I'm not in the market. If you really know who killed Gilroy, go to the police."

"I have a photograph," Sonny interrupted, knowing he was on the brink of losing the big man.

"Photograph? So."

"In the picture you're going into a building in Bogotá. A brick building. You're being met on the steps by a man known to be a cartel boss."

Sonny described the building, then held his breath. It was his last trump. Stone also held his breath, or at least he waited a while before he responded.

"I took a vacation in Bogotá," he said. "Anybody could have taken a photograph."

"It's one of a kind," Sonny cut in. "Even a vacation photograph has some value. For the family scrapbook."

Stone laughed again. "Yes, to keep the album complete. You've twisted my arm, Juan. I'll talk to you. Where?"

"Old Town," Sonny replied. "In the church at twelve. Sit ten pews from the front. You are there praying. Don't bring anyone with you."

"I'll be there," Stone replied, and the phone went dead. Sonny breathed relief. Ah, the man had taken the bait, was hooked, and hooked men always had something to hide.

Sonny glanced at his watch. Where was Raven now? Where was Rita?

25

Just before noon Sonny drove into Old Town Plaza, circled the plaza twice, then luckily found a parking place on the south side. He watched the traffic. The plaza was packed with tourists. Most were families who had come to town for the balloon fiesta. They strolled in the sun, enjoying the clean, brisk air.

October was the perfect month in New Mexico. The trees around the gazebo held just the slightest hint of autumn gold. Beneath the east portal the jewelry vendors sat in the shade, their wares spread out on blankets in front of them. Indian craftsmen and -women from the pueblos who practiced the art of silver and turquoise, basketry, and potmaking sat next to one another. Business was brisk.

On the north side of the plaza, the twin aluminum-coated steeples of the San Felipe de Neri Church rose in the clear, cobalt New Mexican sky. This was one of Sonny's favorite places in the city. Many a time he wound up in the plaza, just to sit and talk to the old-timers from the area who spent their time on the benches under the shade trees. They told stories as they watched the tourists stroll around the historic area.

Old Town was a peaceful place, one occupied by the Nuevo Mexicanos since the 1600s, but if the dope dealers had their way, their poison would affect even this quiet neighborhood. The kids wouldn't just be sneaking a marijuana joint, they'd be puffing on crack. Gang-banging.

Sonny glanced at his watch. A quarter to twelve. He had to wait. He reached into his glove compartment and took the old, worn leather holster with the .45 Colt in it. A few weeks ago he had rubbed the holster with saddle soap. The old leather felt smooth and held a sweet fragrance.

Elfego Baca had once strapped on this pistol. He had put on a sheriff's badge when others were too afraid to do so, and he had shot it out with a bunch of drunk cowboys from Texas. Taught them to respect the Mexicanos from Socorro County. His escapades were numerous, including a run-in with Pancho Villa in Juárez.

Pancho Villa had arrived in Ciudad Juárez, a victor of the raging Mexican Revolution. Porfirio Díaz, the dictator loved by the imperialist U.S. corporations because he sold so much of his country to them, had been overthrown in 1910. One of the greatest sagas of the twentieth century began, a civil war that was to change the course of history, both for México and the United States.

War ravaged México; Huerta came into the presidency. There were many opponents, including Pancho Villa, whose troops controlled the state of Chihuahua.

Sonny knew a little of Alburquerque history. In 1914 José Salazar, a Huerta general, had lost a battle to the Villistas and escaped into the United States. He was arrested by the U.S. government and put in jail in Alburquerque. Huerta needed his general back, so he hired Elfego Baca as Salazar's attorney. In November, in an espionage case that became a classic for the sleepy town of Alburquerque, two of Huerta's secret agents arrived in the city to spring Salazar from the Bernalillo County Jail. It was rumored that Elfego Baca helped in Salazar's escape.

So my bisabuelo played both sides. Sonny smiled as he slipped cartridges into the pistol. Six.

A lot of history here, he thought as he looked for William Stone's car to appear. If only the walls of the old church could talk; if only the dark silence of the confessional could give up the record of the sins it held.

In 1706 Francisco Cuervo y Valdés, the governor of New Mexico, had the gall to proclaim the farming community that clustered around the church a villa: la villa de Alburquerque. The good governor thought the miserable kingdom of New Mexico deserved another villa. He looked south at the farms and adobe huts peopled by Mexicanos, mestizos, and Indians, and he decided that the families clustered around the farm of doña Luisa were the perfect foundation for a villa.

Ah, but he had to play politics. One way to get a small village of mud huts designated a villa was to please the viceroy in Mexico City, who in 1706 happened to be a direct descendant of the Alburquerque family from Badajoz, Spain. So he named the villa after the viceroy.

The viceroy was pleased, and the junta appointed by him recommended the villa be called San Felipe de Alburquerque, a politically correct decision that honored both Felipe V and the viceroy.

Governor Cuervo, the father of all future New Mexican politicians, rejoiced.

But who would be the patron saint of the new villa? Governor Cuervo's patron saint was San Francisco Xavier, but the junta had decided on San Felipe. The Mexicanos of the new villa went on calling the villa's church San Francisco Xavier.

It was not until 1776, at a time when the thirteen colonies were fighting their war for independence a long way off, that a new priest to the parish found an old, tattered painting that depicted San Felipe de Neri hidden behind the altar. The new patron saint became San Felipe de Neri, and thereafter that's what the paisanos from la Plaza Vieja called their church.

Now, sitting in the plaza founded almost three hundred years ago, waiting for Stone to appear, Sonny wondered about the workings of the man's plans. How had he acquired so much power in Central America? Why had he used his position to help Gilroy? Greed. Money. It all boiled down to how much money a man could get in his pocket, and how much power that bought.

If William Stone had information about Rita, Sonny was going to get it from him, one way or the other. He stuffed the pistol under his belt and waited.

At five till twelve a black BMW with tinted windows drew into the plaza and circled slowly.

William Stone has come to pray, Sonny thought, and leaned back in his seat. The BMW slid into a parking place in front of the church, and a tall, distinguished man in a dark suit and sunglasses got out. The man looked around, then strode quickly into the church.

Sonny waited, watching the traffic for signs of Stone's agents. The man wouldn't come alone. But the traffic on the plaza seemed ordinary, slow moving. It was a perfect day for shopping; the Old Town stores were doing a thriving business. The morning's flight had gone well, so all was well with the world.

Time to move, Sonny thought, and he stepped out of his truck. At one corner of the plaza, a parade appeared. As he walked across the center of the plaza toward the church, he saw it was a religious procession. Old women and a few young girls dressed in blue, singing songs to the Virgin Mary, led by Father Luna, the priest of the church.

Sonny knew Father Luna. They had played football against each other in high school. Sonny met him at one of the summer training camps the coaches held at the university. Even then, José, the young man who was to become Father Luna, was tough. When he tackled you, you didn't forget. He was also very handsome. The girls loved him. Sonny remembered, the state cheerleaders' convention was being held on campus the same week. They came around to the field to watch the guys practice, dates were made, and Sonny wound up on a double date with José.

José dated a different girl every night that week. They really went for him. But the guy wound up in the seminary in Santa Fé. Gave up the ways of the flesh. Why would a guy like that turn celibate?

To each his own, Sonny thought.

Father Luna was leading a sodality, the Blue Angels, a group of women who took care of the church. They had been praying at the Virgen de Guadalupe Chapel, and now they entered the patio of the convent to pray. Tourists quickly gathered around them to take pictures.

Sonny hurried through the arched doorway of the church courtyard, took one final glance around, then entered the quiet church. The muted light inside contrasted with the bright glare of the October sunlight outside.

A few tourists moved in and out of the church, whispering, gawking, and wondering if they should take pictures, feeling the presence of history and the souls buried beneath the floor and all around the church—souls of the Tiguex Indians, whose pueblos had dotted the Río Grande when Coronado first came up the river in 1540. Souls of the Spanish and Mexican colonists who later settled the region to plant corn, squash, chile, beans, grapes, and fruit orchards.

The altar was brightly decorated. Candles burned, tingeing the air with their fragrance. Sonny, pressed against the back wall, took in everything. The dark-suited man seated in the tenth row was William Stone. He had come alone, or so it seemed.

Sonny took out the photograph Alisandra Bustamante-Smith had given him and looked at it. The blurred image of a tall, blond man with his hair cut short stared back at him. It was the only one of its kind, the only piece of evidence linking Stone to the drug cartels, and Stone wanted it bad enough to come for it.

Sonny felt the pistol tucked under his belt, pulled his windbreaker over it, and started forward. As he passed the font filled with holy water, he instinctively reached out and wet his fingers to make the sign of the cross. Years of going to church with his mother when he was a kid had ingrained the habit.

When was the last time he had been to mass? Last Christmas Eve, with Rita, here at San Felipe. The church and the plaza were decorated with farolitos, the luminarias of Christmas. Those plain paper bags with the candle inside were a New Mexican tradition. Rich or poor, all could afford to light their driveways on Christmas Eve.

For Rita, midnight mass was related to the winter solstice, a time for prayer. For her the santos of the church were like the kachinas to the Pueblo Indians, ancestors one should honor.

Sonny slipped into the pew behind William Stone.

"Don't turn around," Sonny whispered as he knelt. He put the barrel of the pistol to the back of Stone's neck and covered it with his left arm.

"Where's Rita?"

Stone stiffened. "Pulling a gun is stupid. We can talk—"

"I'm not here to play games, you sonofabitch!" Sonny hissed. "I want my woman! You know where she is!"

He paused as a man, woman, and child walked down the aisle. The eight-year-old girl glanced at Sonny. She saw the pistol.

"That man has a gun," she whispered to the mother, and the woman, who was busy looking at the altar, shushed her daughter, took her hand, and pulled her along.

"Watch Daddy," the mother said, and the father, with camcorder in hand, kept the camera rolling to record every last bit of detail on the walls of the old church to show family and friends back home.

"I don't know about your woman," Stone said.

Sonny cocked the pistol. "I'm going to count to five—"

"Don't be a fool!" Stone replied.

"One—"

"Look behind you," Stone whispered.

Sonny turned slowly, keeping the pistol at Stone's neck. A

man wearing sunglasses and a dark suit stood by the door. The bulge under his jacket told Sonny he was carrying an automatic or an Uzi. Another had come up the side aisle and stood almost directly across from Sonny. They must have waited in the car until they spotted Sonny. Now they had him in a crossfire.

"They move one step and you're dead," Sonny said.

"Then you're dead, and a lot of innocent people are dead. Maybe even the priest," Stone replied. "Is that what you want?"

"Just like Nicaragua," Sonny spit out.

"But we don't want innocent people here hurt, do we?" Stone asked.

Sonny's grip tightened on the trigger. The anger and frustration he felt made him shudder, a bitter wave washed over him; he uncocked the pistol and drew it away.

"That's better," Stone said confidently. "You've never killed a man, have you?" he said.

"I never dropped innocent men and women from helicopters," Sonny answered.

Stone shrugged. "The stories are exaggerated. There was a war going on. Our country had a vested interest."

"Like bringing back planeloads of coke?"

"The stuff of fantasy and romance." Stone chuckled. "Look, Mr. Baca. Or do you still insist I call you Juan?" Stone asked, and laughed softly.

The sonofabitch knows me, Sonny thought. The agency hadn't lost its touch. One false move from me and his agents move in. He felt his hand sweaty on the pistol.

"Rita," Sonny snapped. "That's all I want!"

"I don't make mistakes, Baca. Holding the woman would be a mistake!" Stone turned slowly, his blue eyes as clear and cold as the winter sky. His hair was thinning, his face wrinkled.

Sonny felt a chill. Stone's face was the mask of death. The man had killed a lot of people, the man had no soul. He was the hombre dorado who had looked for the fountain of money in the poor countries of Central America and found it transporting coke, found it by torturing people for the Somoza regime, and later for the Contras, and later for Noriega.

"You're not very smart, Baca." Stone smiled. "If you were, you would know I've never taken hostages. You can't transport hostages in the jungle. You interrogate, then—well, you know the rules. If the woman you seek is alive, Raven has her."

"Where is he?"

Stone seemed surprised. "I wish I knew," he replied. "Raven double-crosses people. He's here now, gone the next moment. We're on the same side, Baca. We both want Raven. You for the woman, me for—other reasons."

Sonny heard the hate in Stone's voice. Raven had crossed Stone! Raven took the dope!

"You see," Stone continued, "we both have something in common."

"No," Sonny replied. "We have nothing in common."

At that moment the bells of the church began to ring for midday mass, and two altar boys swung the front door wide open. Father Luna, in full vestments, appeared, holding a prayer book, the two altar boys by his side, one holding a tall cross of brass, the other an incense container. Behind them, adding to the clamor of the bells, came the army of women, the Blue Angels dutifully following the priest and singing a prayer.

"Bendito, bendito, bendito sea Dios . . . Los angeles cantan y alaban a Dios. Yo creo, Dios mío, que 'stás en el altar. . . . Los angeles cantan y alaban a Dios—"

Father Luna, head bowed, lips intoning prayers, walked down the aisle. A large crowd had gathered behind the women in blue, and now they came streaming down the center aisle, tourists with cameras and camcorders who rushed to get the best shots possible.

"Yo creo, Dios mío, que 'stás en el altar," the high-pitched voice of the women filled the church.

As Father Luna drew close, he glanced at Sonny. He stopped and the entire line behind him came to an abrupt stop.

"Sonny." He smiled. "Sonny Baca. I'm glad to—" He stopped, seeing the pistol, and frowned. "Why?"

Sonny looked up at Father Luna, then down at the pistol. "I—"

"You know I don't allow guns in the church." Father Luna reached out and touched Sonny's shoulder. "Now put it away. I'm surprised you would come to church with a gun." He pulled at Sonny, as if to take the pistol.

The interruption was enough for Stone to slip away. When Sonny turned, the man was already hurrying up the side aisle and toward the front door.

"Good to see you, Father! I'll explain later!" Sonny shouted as he ran after Stone, pushing through the thick crowd to get to the door.

"He's got a gun!" someone shouted.

"Wait!" Father Luna shouted after him. "Whatever you've done! We forgive you! Come and pray with us!"

"A gun!"

"Stand back!"

"Is this for real?" a startled tourist cried.

A flashbulb burst in front of Sonny as he pushed through the door, temporarily blinding him. He ran through the courtyard gate in time to see one of Stone's bodyguards hustle the man into the black BMW. The second one jumped behind the wheel and shot out of the parking place, rubber burning and screeching as the car hung a wild right on Romero Street, leaving a cloud of exhaust hanging in the air. Gawking tourists looked after the car, then at Sonny.

"Hey, mister, is this a movie?"

It was the little girl Sonny had seen inside the church, tugging at his sleeve. Her anxious mother wore a look of consternation; behind them the father kept his camcorder rolling.

"Yeah." Sonny tried to smile. "Just a movie." He stuck his pistol under his belt.

"Where's the cameras?" the girl called out as Sonny hurried to his truck.

"Your father's holding it," Sonny replied, "see?"

The little girl turned to look at her father. "Oh, yeah." She smiled.

"Ah, tourists," Sonny muttered, and walked quickly to his truck.

He jumped in the truck and wiped his forehead. It didn't make sense to chase Stone.

Damn! He hit the dashboard in frustration. He had been close and lost it. But Stone had given him some information. Raven had double-crossed everyone!

The photograph? He had stuffed it into his jacket pocket when he rushed out of the church. He took it out and stared at it again. He shook his head. It was worthless. There was no negative, and the face in the photograph was so creased and tattered, there was no way of telling if it was Stone or not.

Stone hadn't come for the photo; he wanted whatever Sonny knew about Raven. It was Raven he wanted, and the drugs.

Sonny looked out across the plaza. Yeah, the man was well connected, and therefore protected. He had earned his badge of evil in clandestine operations with the Contras in Nica, and that meant his hands were bloody. Very bloody.

Hell, putting the pistol to Stone's head just brought back all the survival instincts the man had honed to perfection in the Central American jungles. He wasn't bluffing when he said he would give the signal for his bodyguards to open fire. Innocent bystanders be damned. That's the way they operated.

Stone, alias Billy the Kid, had been Gilroy's boss, Gilroy's alias was Juan, and the CIA right-wing group Libertad took care of its own.

Stone was an untouchable. Too many shredded files protected him. Maybe Noriega would name names, shed light on the atrocities that had been committed in those countries in the name of "America's vested interests." Or maybe someday the Justice Department would make the Cali bosses talk, find out exactly who that money bought.

Just *maybe* there was hope in the system.

He and Howard had spent many a Saturday afternoon watching football games on TV and discussing the U.S.'s role in Central America.

"The U.S. needs the Panama base to springboard into South America," Howard said. Howard analyzed events in terms of a world context. "That's why we created a puppet government in Panama. To keep our base there, to keep the canal. Does the U.S. need the base because it fears the military might of Latin America? Hell, no! The big boys need to be poised for the new impending war for the control of the vast 'cocaine fields' of South America. Those who control the coke control the money, and therefore the governments. The cartels are not only buying governments, they are *becoming* governments. And why do the big boys need the coke?"

Howard answered his own question. "To create a chemical dependency in this country. Give the colored people enough crack to keep them poor and in misery. Fill the jails with them and convince the whites that all people of color are their enemies. Their object is to divide and conquer. Keep the colored people separated from the white world. Yeah, that's what they're doing, cranking up the fear level between blacks and whites. As long as they keep the country divided, they stay in power. A complex formula, but it's working! Damn if it ain't working! Prejudice has *not* gone away. The rise of militia groups in this country is part of the plan. Fear of the colored people. Now they're turning on the Latinos crossing over the border. Of course they don't want to get rid of the so-called drug problem! *They* created it! It creates power for those who want to stay in power!"

Exactly what Alisandra had said: the cartels control the drug trade and drug routes, and now they also control governments.

Sonny groaned. Lord, I don't want to solve world politics, I just want to find Rita. Let people like Stone control the killing fields of cocaine, let him be the man without a soul, just let me find Rita!

He felt helpless. A gnawing feeling knotted his guts, then flowed through his blood like a cold transfusion. He had come to the end of the rope. When had he eaten last? When had he slept? The day was so peaceful and beautiful, while he felt only the torment of failure.

He was like a drowning man reaching for a lifeline. He needed help. Fast. Raven wouldn't wait. He dialed Lorenza Villa's number.

"She's alive," Lorenza said. "I've been meditating all morning, and I know she's alive! I saw the place!"

Sonny listened intently. He knew her meditation meant fasting, maybe the sweat lodge. Prayer meant vision. And she had been right about the warehouse.

"What did you see?" he asked and held his breath.

"I saw a cemetery. . . ." Her voice trailed, fear in its tone. "There are skulls, feathers, black birds. . . . She's in danger, much danger. . . ."

"A cemetery," Sonny repeated. The black birds meant Raven, but the cemeteries around town had no skulls to mark the grave sites.

Lorenza seemed to read his thoughts. "Raven has grown very powerful. Even if you found him, there is extreme danger. He's at the center of his circle, his entry to the underworld."

"His circle of power?"

"Yes."

"And Rita?"

Lorenza hesitated. "He needs a woman. . . . There will be an initiation. . . ."

Dread coursed through Sonny's blood. Lorenza needed to say no more. Raven no longer needed Rita as protection, but he did need her as an ally. His woman in a world of evil. Raven's plan was to take Rita into his world of spirits, to transform her, make her enter the nagual of the raven. If he could do that, there would be no return for Rita.

"Nothing can touch him," Lorenza said. "The only way to get Rita back is to enter Raven's world." Her words held a sense of finality.

She was warning him, but he didn't understand what she meant by "nothing can touch him." A bullet would put a stop to him, even if he had to etch a cross on it. A bullet with a cross on it would kill even a brujo like Raven.

For the first time he realized he was truly capable of killing a man. To save Rita and the girl, he would kill Raven.

"Where are you?"

" Old Town," Sonny replied.

"There isn't much time."

He knew. With the dope delivered, Raven would move, and like William Stone, he would not take hostages with him.

"She's trying to reach us, that's why she appeared to me. Call to her," Lorenza suggested.

"What?"

"Call her name. Do you have anything of hers with you? A photo?"

"Yes." Sonny reached in his wallet and took out her picture.

"Call her name. Use your song to call her."

Sonny felt awkward. Looking down at the face in the photo, he thought of Rita. He loved her; he wanted her back, and he would tear the city apart to find her. Cold sweat broke out on his forehead.

"Rita," he whispered.

The drone of the October day filled the space of the cab. Children called from the grassy area of the plaza. They ran around the gazebo. Sonny felt isolated, alone in the stream of time that swept around him. He thought he heard Rita's voice, saw for an instant the image of her face, her frightened eyes.

He swayed softly, back and forth, sang his song: "To Grandfather Sun I send my prayers. To Tata Dios y los santos I pray. To the four sacred directions I send my prayers. I pray to the spirits of the mountains. May the power of my ancestors fill my soul. Guide me on the path of the sun. Fill me with clarity and goodness."

He prayed to the brilliant sun that even now stood poised over the earth at its zenith point, sending its rays in the four sacred directions. The four sacred mountains were the homes of the spirits, the ancestors. Mount Taylor to the west, Sandia Mountains to the east, the Sangre de Cristos to the north, and the Manzano Mountains to the south. These mountains encompassed Sonny's world, the world of his ancestors.

The coyotes appeared, and he ran with them through a dark forest until he heard her voice.

"Sonny," Rita called in the October rustle of leaves, "don't come, don't come!"

She didn't want him to find Raven's place, even if it meant her life. It was a trap for him. He saw the flutter of black birds, dark gigantic wings circling around the Zia medallion. He heard Raven's laughter, then the alluring voice of Tamara Dubronsky.

"Come to me," she said. "You are an old soul, a lover from my past. You have found your way to my heart. I am with you."

Then the coyotes withdrew and the image was gone.

The brief flash left Sonny with vertigo. He opened his eyes, tried to focus, looked out the truck window. No, the world had not gone away, it was still there, humming its ordinary hum of being. But beneath the ordinary world lay the images of the world of spirits.

"What did you see?" Lorenza whispered.

"I heard her, but I didn't see the place. She doesn't want me there."

"Because it's dangerous for you," Lorenza said.

"Then Tamara entered the vision. Why?"

"You are connected not only to one person. You are connected to many. I cannot tell you what this will mean in the future, but for now she pulls power away from you. She knows where you are."

"Knows where I am?"

"No time to explain. You need to focus on Rita."

"Yeah," Sonny answered. "And I know where to look."

"I'll go with you," Lorenza said.

"No."

"You need help."

"It could be dangerous."

"I went up in the balloon. What was that?"

"Okay," Sonny agreed. "I'll pick you up."

"I'll be ready."

He turned off the phone, started the truck, and headed out of the plaza, north on Río Grande toward Corrales.

He dialed Howard's lab number at police department forensics.

"Sonny? Where have you been?"

"Church," Sonny replied.

"What?"

"Talking to Billy the Kid."

There was a pause, then Howard's low, measured voice: "You talked to— Hold on."

Sonny waited, heard a door close, a urinal flushing, then Howard's barely audible voice. "What did he say?"

"Raven's flown with everything."

"Double-crossed Billy the Kid? Damn, the man's loco. Doesn't he know the CIA protects Billy?"

"And who protects Raven?"

"Ah," Howard intoned. "You need backup?"

"I'm okay. Have you heard from Diego?"

"He called earlier. He's staying by the wife. It's really been hard on them. I told him to hang in there."

"Good. Okay, I'm going to Lorenza's. Call you later."

"Hey, if I can help."

"Hang loose."

"Will do," Howard replied.

Sonny clicked the phone off. According to don Eliseo, the evil sorcerers of the world had been around since the beginning of time. Their power was incredible. And now Lorenza said that Raven was at the center of his world, transformed into his Raven guardian spirit. Unstoppable.

What is this all about? Sonny wondered. Then he remembered something don Eliseo had told him as they sat sipping wine one evening under the old man's cottonwood, shortly after Gloria's murder.

"There is the path of light," don Eliseo had said, "and there is the path of evil. Some souls chose the path of evil. They became the sorcerers. Yes, they are men and women who can fly, but they fly not to liberate the soul, but to draw it into their web. They are the sorcerers who eat souls."

Fly to devour souls. Old sorcerers from the ancient past, walking the earth, destroying the positive symbols of the soul and creating weakness. And he, Sonny Baca, had not thought of his soul since childhood. Since Bolsas died.

His mother had initiated him into the world of God and the saints, and so as a child he followed that strict path. Never scored with a girl while in high school, bragged to his friends that he had, but he hadn't. His soul was to be kept pure. For what? To enter heaven. Ah, he lost faith when his father died. When Bolsas died.

With Gloria's death he had been thrown into the world of soul-devouring sorcerers. But Raven's flight was not just the burst of a cocaine snort, his was the flight of evil.

"How did I get into this?" he had asked don Eliseo.

"Ah, Sonny, you, too, are an old soul," the old man answered. "You have it in you to be a man who can fly."

"Me, a brujo?"

"A good brujo," don Eliseo said, laughing. "Listen to Lorenza, she can help. The greatest danger is to allow the darkness of evil to consume you. Do not allow the sorcerers of evil to devour your soul. You must find your own power within. Find the good brujo."

Yes, Sonny thought as he turned down the dirt road that led to Lorenza's house. I didn't listen to the old man. I didn't know about the coyotes, didn't know the kind of power we have inside. To fly, to enter the world of spirits.

Maybe he hadn't paid attention to the old man or to Lorenza. She had guided him into the underworld with the help of the coyote spirits. Their strength had been with him these past few days, he realized that now. He had to learn to trust it, to use it.

There was a further step to take, and that was to the center of Raven's world. A dangerous step. Yes, he needed Lorenza's help.

"You have two handicaps," Manuel López, the man who taught him the vagaries of detective work in the city, had told him. "You've never aimed the pistol at a man, and someday that might get you dead. And you think too much. Philosophers don't make good detectives."

Okay, Sonny thought, it's time to act.

In a small, sunny clearing in the bosque sat Lorenza's house. She opened the door and greeted him.

"I'm glad to see you," she said, and embraced him.

It was the first time she had greeted him with an abrazo, a common greeting among New Mexicans. Sonny had seen her embrace Rita, as a greeting or in parting; the abrazo was part of the warmth of friendship. Coming from Lorenza, the abrazo was a flow of energy mingling with the aroma of her body. It left Sonny breathless.

"Gracias," he said.

"Por qué?"

"For all you do—"

"Rita is a sister," she said. "And Raven is an evil force. Come, we have a lot of work to do."

She led him to her consultation room and made him lie on the small cot.

"Do we have time?" he asked, eager to be off to find and rescue Rita and Cristina.

"We must take time," she replied. "Raven has gone to his circle. You must meet him there. To be unprepared means death to you. Let's begin with you describing Raven's place."

He closed his eyes and described Raven's compound in the mountain. It was surrounded by a circle of white stones and poles with feathers.

When he was done, Lorenza said, "Ah, so that's the place I saw in my vision."

Sonny nodded. "I was there this summer. He was living there with his four wives, but they've scattered. So he went back, a perfect place to hide."

"And dangerous," Lorenza warned him.

Sonny knew. Within his circle Raven was supposed to be invincible.

"Can I meet him there?" he asked.

"You have no choice," Lorenza replied. "He calls the shots, he has Rita. You have to go to him. He knows that. He'll be waiting."

"I'm ready," Sonny said.

"He's a brujo," she said softly. "Not in the sense the people usually understand the word. Most people say *witch* and think of old women gathered around a cauldron. In the old-world religions, the women were priests. As they lost their power, their ceremonies to the earth and the moon were banned. They began to be called devil worshipers."

"What do *you* mean by brujo?" Sonny asked.

"Brujo is not a word from the Nahuatl language of the Aztecs. The word is Spanish, so it has meaning to the beliefs of the Catholic Spaniards who settled here."

"What's the word in Nahuatl?"

She looked at him. It was time to reveal to Sonny things she had not revealed to anyone. She had told Rita a few of her experiences, but it was Sonny who had to know. He had gone through the first phase of initiation. He had met his guardian spirits, but now he had to meet Raven. There wasn't time for slow preparations. He must realize his potential now; he must know his nagual before it was too late.

"When I was in México, I lived in a village near Tlaxcala. At the foot of the mountain la Malintzi. An extinct volcano, a place of magic. The people there have believed in "witches," people with special powers, long before the Españoles arrived. Their brujos can transform themselves into their animal forms. In the Nahuatl language they call them *tlahuelpuchi*."

"*Tla-huel-puchi*," Sonny repeated the word. He had never heard it.

"They can change into luminous balls of fire. They can change into their nagual."

Sonny waited.

"Raven is one," she said.

"He studied, like you, to become—"

She smiled. "You don't study to become a *tlahuelpuchi*, you are born one."

"Like a curse?"

"One is what one is from the beginning of time." She looked at him and her eyes made him shiver. "You see, evil was born at the beginning of time. All legends tell of the evil germ within the apple or the ear of corn. The legends warn us that evil keeps us from fulfilling our human potential. It is there in the heart of every person."

Sonny nodded. "Are you *tlahuelpuchi?*"

"No. I can call my nagual, but the transformation is not evil. The anthropologists call us transforming tricksters." She laughed. "As if the label explains us away. We are not evil."

"So Raven is one of these *tlahuelpuchi?* He did the murdering all along?"

"Probably."

"And I thought he was controlled by those in the drug ring."

"No, he is a lord from the underworld," Lorenza replied.

And he's got Rita, Sonny thought.

"What now?"

"Now you enter your nagual," she said. "Now you will truly acquire the power of the coyote, so when we go to the mountain and meet Raven, you will be his equal. Now we will go into the world of spirits. Sing your song."

She turned on the tape with the drumming, and Sonny closed his eyes and repeated the words of his song, chanting softly to the drumbeat.

As the sun moved westward, she led him into the underworld, the world of spirits, where Sonny was able to acquire the strength of the coyote.

They practiced, until he understood that the power of the coyote was something inherent in his body and soul. He learned that he could move at will from this world into the parallel world of spirits.

When he finally opened his eyes, the room had grown dim.

"I see," he said.

"Now you're ready." Lorenza nodded.

27

R̲aven's place is just beyond La Cueva," Sonny explained as they drove through Tijeras Canyon, then turned north toward the village of La Cueva.

He described again the mountain clearing, Raven's ceremonial circle of rocks in the form of a Zia sign. Around it, the poles from which hung cow skulls, bones, feathers. He remembered the dread that seemed to permeate the isolated spot in the pine forest.

"The *tlahuelpuchi* uses a secret place to change into his animal form," Lorenza said. "Raven uses the circle as the center of his power. But it's a cemetery. He holds lost spirits in captivity, sucks their energy. It's the place where he enters the world of his nagual."

"Lost spirits?" Sonny questioned.

"That's his business, to imprison souls. It's his way of upsetting the world. A way of returning to chaos."

And Rita was to be yet another sacrifice. Blood and sacrifice formed Raven's world.

"What is Raven's past?" Sonny asked.

"The same as ours," Lorenza replied. "The dark side of our nature has always been with us."

"Yes, but Raven's been around a long time, hasn't he? Was he there, in Tlaxcala?"

"Yes. The power of the *tlahuelpuchi* is very old."

When she didn't continue, Sonny asked: "Why did he come here?"

"Because this is sacred space."

Sonny nodded. Yes, don Eliseo had explained the valley of his ancestors in such terms.

"But why start the Zia cult? The sun worship?"

"They don't worship the sun. Quite the opposite. They want to bring down the sun. That's a part of Raven even Tamara doesn't understand."

"Bring down the sun?"

"This era of time is ending. As don Eliseo has instructed you, there will be violence as the Fifth Sun dies. Raven is one of those who thrive on chaos. His motive is simple: he wants to rule the new time born from the ashes of the old."

"So he creates the violence we are living through," Sonny said.

"And each one of us helps," Lorenza reminded him. "When we give in to that part of our nature that brings destruction, we join the forces of the brujos like Raven."

"What's Tamara's role?"

"He uses her. Tamara didn't know what she was getting into when she joined Raven. For her it was a game, a way to join the sun cult she thought she could control. She wanted to be the Zia queen, a sun queen, and Raven held the prize up to her."

"Then they split up. Why?"

"Because of you," Lorenza replied.

"Me?"

"Tamara really cares for you. She knows you are equal to

Raven. You might say, she sees the *gift* in you, the potential of the nagual. When she discovered Raven's real power, she realized she was in danger. You have similar power, but without the danger."

"She believes I'm an *old soul* from her past lives," Sonny mused.

"You are," Lorenza whispered.

Ah, so even Lorenza allowed the possibility of past lives, Sonny thought. "Are there are others like Raven?"

"Yes. Brujos who believe only in fear, violence, wars, and famine."

"Sounds biblical."

"Every age and every country has had its prophets describing the end of time. Time comes in cycles, and each era ends. It's at that ending of an era that we can choose to move on with our development, our goal, or return to chaos. Like all ages of transformation, this is the time when we are most vulnerable."

"And they use that vulnerability against us," Sonny said.

Raven didn't work alone. There were other sorcerers who had been around since the beginning of time. Time itself was born and moved to completion, collapsed, and from it was born a new era. It was during the collapse, or end, of an era that the negative forces of the universe worked to create the new cycle of time in their image. That negative power—a germ present at every creation—did not die. Its sign was violence.

"That's the way it's always been," Lorenza said. "Civilizations end, the world is destroyed, and out of that violence something new is born. There is a struggle between good or evil. The Aztecs described our present time as the world of the Fifth Sun. Four prior worlds had been created, then destroyed."

"Go on." He nodded, thinking of Rita as he looked down at the speedometer. He was going as fast as he dared. To get stopped by a state cop now would serve no purpose.

Lorenza continued. "Their legends say Quetzalcoatl created people out of ashes during the world of the First Sun, which was called Water Sun. A flood came and swept away the people, and they were turned into dragonflies and fish.

"The Second Sun was called Jaguar Sun. The sky fell from the heavens, and the sun could not continue its journey. Darkness came at midday, and the people were eaten by the monsters of darkness.

"The Third Sun was called the Rain Sun. Fire rained down and the people were burned. Burning rocks and lava fell from the sky, and the red rocks were deposited on earth.

"The Fourth Sun was called the Wind Sun. In the end the people were blown away by a ferocious wind, and they were turned into monkeys. They were called the monkey people.

"The Fifth Sun, our sun, is called Movement Sun. And the legend holds that the people must pray each morning that the Fifth Sun follow its journey, or it will fall and earthquakes and famine will destroy the people. . . ."

She paused.

Sonny glanced out the truck window at the setting sun, the Fifth Sun of Lorenza, the Grandfather Sun of don Eliseo. For Lorenza the age of the Fifth Sun was ending. The evil in the universe was bringing down the sun.

Everywhere nation rose against nation, people against people. The abuse of drugs and violence were symptoms of a far deeper phenomenon. Sure, the drug cartels wanted control, so drugs were being used to sap the soul of people, to make them sleep. But every person or organization or government who practiced control used the same techniques. Evil was loose in the world, and the morality that described humanity had been sapped.

At that moment, when an old era was dying, the people had to decide which way to turn.

They passed the village of La Cueva, and Sonny turned off the paved road onto a barely visible dirt road that led to Raven's compound. Around them the pine forest and brush grew dense and dark. When he was as close as he dared to be, he turned the truck off the road and followed the vague outline of an old lumbering road into the forest.

He stopped, turned off the ignition, and listened. Around them the forest was ominously quiet. On the east side of the mountain the afternoon shadows were deep; the sun had already gone over the crest of the mountain.

He reached for his pistol. With his thumbnail he scratched a cross on the soft lead of a bullet and fed it into the empty chamber.

"To kill a brujo," he said.

Lorenza shook her head. She didn't believe in the power of the pistol. "Trust your medicine," she said.

Sonny reached under his shirt and pulled out the leather pouch that Lorenza had given him. Coyote medicine.

"Good." She smiled.

They slipped out of the truck and headed into the forest. Raven's place was not far away.

The dusk grew thick. Sonny stopped to listen. He motioned for Lorenza to stop. He had felt a presence in the brush. He sniffed the air. Coyotes. Yes, three or four coyotes were following them in the dark.

He motioned again and quietly moved forward through the pines and scrub oak, every sense now alert. He was moving like the coyotes, stealthily, aware of the danger nearby. They continued deeper into the thick forest until they came to the edge of Raven's circle. This was it, Raven's center of power. The small meadow was surrounded by dense pines.

"Here," Lorenza said.

"You know this place," Sonny whispered.

Lorenza nodded. "I have been tracking the *tlahuelpuchi* a long time," she replied. "We know of this evil place."

She turned and faced him, and in the shadows of the tree branches, Sonny saw her owl eyes shining. Yes, she, too, was becoming her nagual of the spirit world.

"Raven moves like a trickster. You know by now he leaves many signs, many clues. Don't you see? He has drawn you to him."

Sonny shivered. Across the circle he heard a dry branch crack; overhead, he heard the flutter of wings.

He looked up to see the gathering of ravens in the pinetops.

Wind chimes made of dry bones swayed in a gust of wind

that swept across the clearing, lending their mournful clacking to the screech of the large crows overhead. Bleached ribs hung from long poles, tibias knocking against large hip bones. Black feathers were hung everywhere, the dull feathers of vultures, the jet-black feathers of crows, and the taboo owl feathers.

Animal skulls decorated the tops of the piñon poles. White, vacant-eyed skulls of cows, sheep, and the smaller skulls of raccoons, skunks, foxes. Bird skulls. And since there had been no rain recently, everything was covered with a thin coat of dust.

Large, chalky stones formed the large outline of a Zia circle, a cemetery for the forsaken. Here Raven and his followers performed their perverse ceremonies to bring down the sun, and here, perhaps, lay buried the bodies of past victims. If not their bodies, their spirits, for Raven's goal was to capture and hold the souls of those who stood in his way.

Sonny sniffed the air. Raven was nearby! Waiting.

Overhead, the cries of the ravens grew stronger, the flutter of wings no longer a presence felt, but shadows that came swooping out of the sky, stirring the dusk. Mountain ravens, dozens of them, their dark eyes fierce as they circled the clearing.

Sonny peered into the afternoon darkness. There, across the clearing he spotted a dark figure. Raven standing in the shadows of the pines. His visage dark, his eyes burning with hate.

"Raven," Sonny whispered.

"Yes," Lorenza replied. "He is waiting for you. Remember, he wears the Zia medallion. It gives him great power. Don't allow him to draw you into the circle. In the circle he can transform himself. He is a trickster, don't let him trick you. You are in your nagual now, the spirit of the coyote is in you."

Sonny felt the bristle of coyote hair along his arms and legs.

"Use the coyote medicine," Lorenza said. "Become coyote!"

He pulled out the leather pouch and began to sing the words of his song.

When he was ready, Lorenza called. "Call coyote! Become coyote!"

Sonny held the leather pouch with the coyote hair aloft.

"Coyote!" he called to his brothers and sisters, and the guardian spirits replied.

In the forest a coyote barked, then another. They were answering the call. First one appeared, then a second, until the thicket around them was full of their shining forms, their fur reflecting the dim light of the moon rising over the Estancia Valley. Luminous in the dark, a circle of protection, they surrounded Sonny.

"You are ready," he heard Lorenza whisper. "Remember, in your vision you have power. In his circle the power is his."

He nodded. Around him the coyotes of the forest moved like shadows. The ravens in the trees cried a warning but did not drop to do battle.

Sonny's eyes glowed bright. Suddenly the world of the forest was no longer dark, but glowing with light. The shadows that moved were distinct, like he remembered the animals that came when he had done the peyote ceremony with don Eliseo. That had been a way to enter the nagual, he knew that now, but he had not followed the peyote path. Now he had this power, to tap the resources within, to enter Raven's world.

He felt the danger inherent in the dark world of spirits. Here life and death met. Raven could not have Sonny as his ally, so he must kill him. And only in the circle of evil could he kill Sonny's old soul.

Again Sonny sniffed the night air. He looked up. Overhead the ravens called, coal-black eyes staring down at the intruder, but they did not attack. In the dark the coyotes protected Sonny.

He moved like a shadow, circling, not entering Raven's trap but staying hidden in the bushes. He moved quickly, with something like the rush of adrenaline flowing through him.

Beneath him the earth held the scent of people. Men had passed through here, and a woman. More than one woman, but there was one distinctive fragrance. Her. Rita.

He moved cautiously, in an arc toward Raven. He felt strong, his movements liquid. Rita's scent was faint, but lingering on the trail nevertheless, brushed against the bark of a tree where she'd steadied herself when she stumbled, clinging to the tips of dry grass. Raven had brought her through here on the way to his compound.

Overhead he heard an owl, its cry echoing in the dark forest.

He paused, sniffing the night breeze, alert, every muscle tense, his heart pounding. A hush came over the ravens in the treetops as the dark grew almost complete.

Raven had also moved forward, now he stood waiting in the center of the clearing. Raven had chosen his circle of stones for their meeting, the evil circle of transformation that was his advantage. He was daring Sonny to meet him in the center of his power.

The test between the two had come, and with it a sense of finality. The call of a raven filled the night; it was answered by the hunting cry of a coyote.

Behind Raven stood the adobe compound, Raven's nest. In one of the rooms, Rita and Cristina would be huddled in fear. Only the dark figure of Raven stood blocking the way.

Sonny uttered a low, savage snarl. The cries of the coyotes surrounding the circle echoed his call.

He hunched his shoulders; his body hair stood on end. There was only one way to take on Raven. The time for being cautious was long past; now he had to rely only on his strength, the animal power of the guardians around him, the newfound power of the coyote spirit coursing through him.

"Rita!" he cried, and charged across the clearing.

Raven turned in surprise. What he saw startled him. He had not expected Sonny's power to come from the world of guardian spirits, and yet the dark figure bounding toward him was clearly the spirit of Coyote. The man he must kill tonight had entered the world of the nagual.

"So be it," he said.

Sonny's attack knocked Raven backward, to the edge of the circle. Raven jumped like a startled bird, high in the air, his cry of defiance filled the night as he struck back.

Sonny moved quickly and escaped the blow.

"Rita!" he cried.

His only thought was to save Rita. That was his advantage. He struck at Raven, and the blow sent him reeling out of the circle.

Raven cried a warning. Out of the circle meant a lessening of his power. Now he was vulnerable.

"The winner takes her," Raven taunted, brandishing a weapon, a shining scimitar that glistened even in the dim light.

He struck at Sonny and Sonny stumbled back into the circle. Raven raised the curved blade to strike.

At that moment an explosion filled the night. The rabble of ravens in the trees rose in a clutter of fear.

A surprised Raven dropped the blade, grabbed at his chest, and looked up. At the edge of the clearing stood Lorenza, Sonny's smoking pistol in her hand.

"Ah, bruja," Raven cursed, and fell backward.

Sonny jumped up, prepared for an attack from the spirit ravens, but they rose and disappeared into the evening dusk.

He stepped cautiously toward Raven's body. The man Lorenza called a *tlahuelpuchi* had more than one life. Even wounded, he was to be approached carefully. In the dim moonlight something shimmered on Raven's chest. Blood? No, the Zia medallion. Sonny reached down and tore it from Raven's neck.

He turned to Lorenza and held the medallion aloft. Now the full October moon that rose over the top of the pine trees shone on the clearing. Its pale light glistened on the gold medal.

"He's dead," Sonny said.

"No." She shook her head. "The ravens have taken his soul, but only for the moment. Quickly," she warned him. She took the medallion and placed it around Sonny's neck.

"Now the Zia medallion is yours. Its energy can return you from the world of the guardian spirits."

The Zia medallion had been Raven's way to his nagual; now it was Sonny's. Knowing this, Sonny could return from the world of guardian spirits, the world of Coyote, more easily, without the help of Lorenza's preparations.

He looked around him and sniffed the air. The smells he had so thoroughly distinguished moments ago now blurred, losing their individual pungency. The luminosity in the trees was replaced by dark shadows. He looked at Lorenza, reached out, and touched her.

"Gracias," he said.

"Rita," she said. "We have to go quickly." Her voice told him there was still danger around them.

Sonny followed her out of the clearing to the house. A dim light shone at one of the windows; otherwise, the dark, ominous building appeared deserted.

Sonny didn't hesitate. Using the coyote power he felt ebbing from him, he lunged at the door. Under his weight the dry wood around the lock splintered and the door sprang open. There in the center of the room, lighted with a kerosene lantern, arms and feet tied with ropes, huddled Rita and Cristina.

"Sonny!" Rita cried, and Sonny was at her side, gathering her in his arms, untying the ropes, kissing her face, and tasting the tears that streamed from her eyes as she cried his name over and over.

Lorenza swept up Cristina and comforted her as she untied her.

"How did you find us?"

"It's a long story," Sonny replied.

He pulled Rita up and helped her stand on her weakened legs. "You okay?" he asked Cristina as he pulled her into an embrace.

"Yes," the girl sobbed.

"Gracias, gracias, gracias," Rita cried, embracing Lorenza. "God, I thought we would never—"

The four stood in a close abrazo. They were safe now.

"I knew you'd come," Rita whispered.

He took her hands in his, examined the swollen, purple bruises on her wrists. He looked at Cristina cradled in Lorenza's arms.

"How are you, m'ijita?"

"I'm fine," she said through tearful eyes. "I want my mamá and papá."

"Your daddy and mother are safe. They sent us for you. Can you walk?"

"Yes," she said with a sigh of relief.

"Good girl." Sonny tousled her hair and turned to Rita.

"We have to hurry," Lorenza said. Sonny nodded and Lorenza led the way out, holding Cristina closely. Sonny's arm was around Rita. They followed the dark trail back to the clearing. There Lorenza paused and motioned to Sonny.

Raven's body was gone.

"Damn," Sonny cursed. He peered at the ground where Raven's body had fallen. There were no tracks. Flown again. The brujo could not be stopped by a bullet.

"You hit him, I was sure you hit him," Sonny whispered.

"I tell you, bullets cannot kill him," she replied.

"Sonny? What is it?" Rita asked.

"The magic of a sorcerer," he answered.

He felt the medallion on his chest. In the middle of the medallion was the dent the bullet had made. He held it up in the moonlight for Lorenza to see. Her shot had struck the medallion and saved Raven's life. The force of the shot may have knocked him out, but he sure as hell wasn't dead.

"Outside his circle he lost some of his power," Lorenza whispered, "but bullets can't kill him. Come."

They turned and hurried Rita and the girl past Raven's evil circle and down the dark forest path to the truck. The gathering night was cold on the mountain. The shivering Rita and Cristina bundled up with the seat blankets.

Sonny started the truck and found the road that would take him back to the highway, back to a world he knew and recognized. Rita, exhausted, fell asleep, leaning her head on his shoulder. Cristina, too, was instantly asleep on Lorenza's lap.

Suddenly he, too, felt exhausted. The world of the truck was new to him. He touched the steering wheel and listened to the sound of the motor beneath the hood. The headlights illuminated the darkness. How strange this world of metal and motors seemed. How weak and fragile.

It could carry him away, as an airplane might carry many people through the air, but the power did not pass to the body or soul of a person. The energy of gas, oil, and metal was an illusion.

In the world of the nagual, he had felt a new kind of strength. He had felt the transformation in his body and soul. The animal guardian spirit was there, lurking around the corners of the world of metal, waiting to teach each person a part of an ancient inheritance.

Once upon a time, in the world of Mesoamerica, in the world that stretched north along the Río Grande, in the primal world that later came to be known as the Americas, men and women had conversed with the world of the spirits. Lorenza had said there were many ways to enter that world. And what was that world but a deep kinship to nature? A deep kinship to one's inner self.

What the Franciscan friars had called the evil of the shaman was really the potential for uniting the human soul with the soul of nature. Tonight, Sonny had felt that unity.

I have walked in the path of Coyote, Sonny thought, and so I am Coyote. I have used the power of the guardian spirit and freed Rita. That power of the brujo can be used for good.

He thought he heard don Eliseo chuckle, then say, "Hijo, you will make a good brujo."

Exhaustion drained him, but he still felt the vibrations of the coyote spirit in his blood. He had wanted only to find Rita and the girl. To protect them he had to take the coyote body, the coyote spirit. But something else had happened, something that he was sure would only reveal itself slowly in the future.

In the dim light of the truck he looked across at Lorenza.

"Gracias," he said.

"De nada," she answered, smiled.

"I feel like . . ."

"A smoke?" she finished.

"How did you know?"

"A good smoke cleanses the evil we picked up from Raven. If we had the time, I would have burned incense there where you met Raven. But the safety of Rita and the girl is more important now. Now we can smoke."

Very carefully, so as not to awaken the girl or Rita, she reached into her bag, took out some tobacco, and rolled it in tobacco paper. He pushed in the cigarette lighter, then handed the glowing ember of metal to her. When the tobacco caught, she offered the smoke in four directions, cleansing the people huddled in the small cab of the truck.

Then she passed the cigarette to Sonny. He had never tasted sweeter tobacco.

"Your own mix?"

"My own mix," she said.

"Good." He nodded. The smoke cleared his mind.

"Good," he repeated, turning onto the paved road, and headed for Tijeras Canyon and the interstate that would lead them home.

His nagual spirit had entered the world of the brujo. Now he believed that perhaps both don Eliseo and Lorenza were right. He, Sonny Baca, was also a brujo.

When your boss, la blonde, pulled up at the Pyramid Hotel, she parked next to a Mercedes," Diego said. "She looked at it like she recognized it."

"So who does it belong to?" Sonny pondered as he and Diego sat in the kitchen having their morning coffee.

"After she met Gilroy, I figured it was his."

"No, not his," Sonny replied, and gazed out the window toward don Eliseo's place.

The old man was up early, as always, to greet the sun, to work. Today he was raking up the huge gold leaves that had fallen from his cottonwood.

Madge, Sonny thought, Madge. You double-crossed me all along. Led me by the nose. Maybe money and dope had always come hand-in-hand for her, a past she couldn't shake loose.

Sonny sipped his coffee and watched don Eliseo raking. The

gigantic hundred-year-old tree had bloomed late in June. Now it was turning golden, dropping its leaves, ready to rest.

A new season was settling into the valley, and those who still farmed had brought in the harvest of the land. Red chile ristras hung against adobe walls. The warm October air, crisp at forty degrees in the mornings, warmed into the seventies by midday. The hot, dry weather slowly dried the chile and turned the pods from a glistening bright red to dark reddish brown.

Red or green? Sonny thought. It was the most-asked question in New Mexico. The next: hot, medium, or mild?

"Damn," Diego groaned. "I should have taken the license plate number."

"Madge knows who the Mercedes belongs to," Sonny said, fingering the gold medallion on his chest. He turned his head to stretch his neck muscles. He was sore and bruised.

He felt like sleeping for a week. Last night the fits of sleep had been cluttered with images of Raven.

Lorenza had taken Rita and Cristina home with her. "They need to sleep," she said. "Rita is strong, but the little girl is frightened. I can help, but right now it's the presence of her mother that will reassure her."

Sonny and Diego understood. It had been a time of terror for Rita and Cristina, a time when they feared for their lives. Sonny knew the shock of a trauma, if not treated, could get worse. They were safe and that was what mattered, but they needed Lorenza's healing ways.

"That woman is incredible," he said.

"Which one?" Diego asked.

Sonny smiled. Diego's wife for the struggle she endured while keeping her family together. Rita and Lorenza. Women warriors, like the curanderas of the past. Strong women. Mentors. Yes, like don Eliseo, these two women were guides, and more was yet to be revealed. Sonny Baca's journey to the world of spirits was just beginning.

"All of them," Sonny replied.

"You betcha." Diego winked.

The phone rang and Sonny rose to answer it.

"Sonny?"

"Yeah."

"Doesn't sound like you. Garcia here."

Diego had called the police chief last night and told him Rita and Cristina had been rescued.

"What's the matter with your voice? You got a cold?"

"No," Sonny replied. Had his voice changed?

"How's Rita?"

"Resting. She's going to be okay."

"And the girl?"

"Fine, just fine."

"I don't know how you did it, Sonny, but I'm damn relieved you found them. I'm going to ask the mayor to give you a medal or something."

Sonny fingered the Zia medallion he wore around his neck.

"Thanks, Chief, but having them back is all the thanks I need."

"Yeah, sure," the chief went on. "Look, I had my men at Raven's place all night. Howard cleaned the place, but no luck so far. Lots of junk but no trace of drugs, money, nothing. Oh, yeah, Howard said to tell you there's a trace of lilac perfume in the air. You know what that means?"

"Maybe one of Raven's women," Sonny answered. Lilac was the perfume they had put in the water when they pumped Gloria Dominic's blood from her body.

"Look, Sonny, we need a statement from you. Just need to know what happened up there."

"Any word on Raven?" Sonny asked.

"No. That sonofabitch knows how to disappear! Look, I need you to come in," the chief implored. "The press won't let me rest. The press is hounding me for a story. Even José Armas called."

"Sounds serious," Sonny replied, still looking at don Eliseo across the street.

"Damn right it's serious. Don't you read the paper? You're splashed all over the front page. The paper likes you, Sonny. I don't know why, but they like you. Look, I know you're tired.

God knows Rita and the girl suffered. Come in tomorrow. First thing in the morning. Okay?"

Garcia hung up, and Sonny, too, cradled the phone. He had been fingering the medallion, feeling the dent caused by the bullet.

"Mira," Sonny said to Diego, pointing at the indentation the bullet had made. "I don't know where Lorenza learned to shoot, but she hit him dead center. The medallion saved Raven's life."

"Chingao," Diego exclaimed.

"You can't kill Raven," Sonny said, remembering Tamara's warning. Raven does not die, his spirit always returns. "I better move," he said, setting down his coffee cup and slipping on a light windbreaker.

They stepped outside into the bright, cool morning. The wide, blue sky was already dotted with balloons.

"Where to?" Diego asked.

"Go see Madge," Sonny replied.

"Why?"

Yeah, Sonny wondered, why not drop it? Return to normal life. Hang around Rita at the restaurant and learn to make tacos and enchiladas. Plan the wedding for just before Christmas. He knew now how badly he wanted to marry Rita, settle down, enjoy life as he once had.

"The dope," he answered.

"You think it's still in town?" Diego asked.

"It's got to be. Mira, with that much stuff going out, one of the gofers was bound to make a mistake, party too much, talk too much, start sharing some of the stuff with friends, and wind up busted."

"But not a single person's been arrested—except the one guy they wanted you to find." Diego nodded. "So it's still here, still intact."

"Yes," Sonny replied.

But finding the dope was Garcia's business, not his. Let Garcia follow the tracks. That was his job. He got paid for it.

Me, I should get back to a simple life.

Ah, he could never lead a simple life again. Raven was still out there. The score last night had been settled only for the moment, but Raven would return to haunt Sonny. As don Eliseo said, it had always been so, good against evil.

Lorenza had been fighting the sorcerers all along, and so had don Eliseo in his own way. Now Lorenza and don Eliseo needed help. Coyote spirit help.

Sonny called to the old man. "Buenos días le de Dios, don Eliseo!"

Don Eliseo looked up from his work. "Sonny, gracias a Dios you found Rita." He ambled across the road and embraced Sonny in an abrazo. "Gracias a Dios they are safe. Diego told me last night. I prayed, Sonny. Dios mío, I prayed. My wife—que descanse en paz—she really believed in the santos. She knew every santo in the book, and she knew how to pray to them. I learned many prayers from her, and I figured if anybody could help, my wife can. Pues, now she's a saint. That woman never harmed a living thing in her life. So I kept saying, take care of Rita, vieja. Tell your diosito and your santos to take care of Rita. It worked, Sonny," the old man said, and wiped his eyes.

"It worked," Sonny agreed.

"Y tú?" he asked.

"I stopped Raven, but you know he doesn't die," Sonny replied.

The old man's eyes glistened. "Sí. Now you know. The war is not won in one night," don Eliseo said. He sniffed the air. "Even now he is out there, planning the next movida. He will find a way to make more trouble. More evil things will come. Now you know." He put his hand on Sonny's shoulder.

"Yes." Sonny understood. The old man was blessing him for the struggle yet to come.

"Life is this struggle, back and forth, the force of evil and the force of good," don Eliseo said. "All through the centuries, man creates the gods and the demons, and they fight, back and forth. And where does the fight take place? In the heart. El corazón is the battleground. There is clarity for the soul if a person pays attention. If you don't pay attention, evil fills the soul. One has to pay attention, every day, every minute."

Sonny nodded. Some winter evening when there was time to sit in front of the fireplace and talk and eat piñon, he would tell the old man about last night. Don Eliseo would explain more of the movement of the soul, how it traveled, how it could fly, how to enter the world of spirits through the many paths.

"Cuídate, Sonny. Those evil people are never done." He looked at the Zia medallion.

"Lorenza said to keep it."

"Yes. So we let it be. Bueno, you're back, Rita's safe. Mira," he pointed at the tree. "Did you ever think it would look so good. The leaves are turning to gold. This is the only gold we need, the leaves, corn, pumpkins. Qué no?"

Sonny and Diego nodded in agreement.

"Bueno, cuídate. Come and have some red chile enchiladas this afternoon. Toto and Concha are coming, and you know Concha's enchiladas are the best. Bring Rita, all your friends. Let's celebrate!"

"Por qué no?" Sonny agreed.

The old man gave Sonny an abrazo, then ambled across the road, back to raking leaves. Sonny and Diego watched.

"Quite a man," Diego said.

"I still have a lot to learn from him," Sonny replied. "In the meantime, I've got a date." He turned toward the truck.

"You want me to go with you?" Diego asked.

"No, you stay. Your family needs you."

"Pues, be careful, bro."

"I'll be okay. Now it's just me and Madge. You stay with your wife and daughter. Lorenza might need you. All I'm going to do is twist Madge's arm until she talks. Keep track of me on the phone," he said.

"Okay," Diego reluctantly agreed, "but I don't like it. Every time you go near that woman you get in trouble."

Sonny got into his truck. "Es mi destino," Sonny said, and drove away.

He dialed his mother's number.

"Sonny!" she cried. "Malcriado! Why didn't you call me? Rita called me this morning. I was surprised, and so happy. So relieved. Gracias a Dios, she's safe! Where are you?"

"I'm here."

"I know you're here, but where? And why is your voice so gruff? You sound like a coyote with a hangover."

Sonny laughed. She hit the nail on the head. So she knew. A lot of people knew; they just didn't talk about it. Yes, he felt like a coyote with a hangover.

"How did you find her? It doesn't matter, she's alive. Is she all right?"

"Yes, she's fine."

"And the girl?"

"They're both fine."

"I'm so proud of you. Your father would be proud of you. And your bisabuelo, all proud of you. Was it dangerous?"

"Not really. . . ." He lied.

"Not dangerous. I bet it was. You have to tell me the whole story."

"I will, when I have time."

"Time. You're always so busy. But I'm glad you found them. It's like the movies! You rescued your sweetheart. Qué mas quieres, hijo? Marry her. Settle down."

"I think I will."

"Good! When?"

"I said I'll think about it." He teased.

"Ay, malcriado. She's a good woman. So beautiful, and she has her own business. You need to settle down, you need children."

"And you want nietos." Sonny teased her.

"Of course I do. Look, this heart attack I had taught me one thing. Life is short. I want grandchildren, and Armando is *never* going to get married. He's too busy running around with those flashy women. Ay, Dios, I don't know where he finds them."

"At used-car conventions," Sonny said.

"Ay, pobrecitas. Don't they know Armando will promise the world but then . . . He can't help it, that's just the way he is.

Anyway, bring Rita over as soon as you can. You don't know how much I've prayed. All day long, everyday, I was even talking to your papá."

"Talking to Dad?"

"Talking to his spirit. 'Keep Rita safe, keep Sonny safe.' I told him, and he did. Will you come over? With Rita?"

"I will. She's resting."

"Yes, she needs to rest. Gracias a Dios. Now I can rest."

"I'll call you."

"You say you'll call, but when? I worry, Elfego. Bring her as soon as you can. I want to see both of you."

"I promise."

"Promises, promises. A mother is a woman who gets promises."

"I really promise."

"Stay out of trouble. Marry her."

"I might. Adiós."

"Que'l angel de la guardia te cuide."

A blessing that the guardian spirits, the saints, take care of him, watch over him, deliver him from evil.

"Gracias," he said, and clicked the off button on the phone.

He drove toward the balloon field. El angel de la guardia, his guardian angel. Who was his guardian angel? Once it had been St. Christopher. Patron saint of travelers. Did the angels of the church have anything in common with the coyote spirit? Was the coyote spirit like the guardian angel spirit? Like the saints who could be called to watch over things? But the church would call anything that smacked of Lorenza's knowledge witchcraft.

Two worlds so far apart, and yet both were worlds of the spirits. His mother had prayed to her saints and to his dead father, asking for help. Don Eliseo had asked the spirit of his wife for help. The world was full of spirits. All those who had died were spirits in the wind that swept around the earth. Soul energy gathering on the mountaintops. Could they affect the life of one on earth? Could they return? Or did they speak only in dreams?

He had been filled with the coyote spirit, of that he was sure.

In the dark of night, he had met Raven on an equal footing. A transformation had occurred. Could it happen again?

Yes, both don Eliseo and Lorenza had hinted there were many ways to enter the world of spirits. He had only scratched the surface.

"What's the next step?" he asked Lorenza.

"Dreams," she replied. "To enter your dreams."

Dreams, he thought. The most common element. His dreams had always been rich with images, complex stories, prophecy. And so dreams were the next path into the world of spirits.

Traffic was thick and slow. The West Mesa was burgeoning, growing like mad, houses sprouted like tumbleweeds after a rain, and the new Cottonwood shopping center already attracted thousands. People traveled back and forth, from the east side of the river to the west, and vice versa, and today the usual rush was slow as people gawked at the balloons.

Hundreds of balloons hung over the valley like colorful Chinese lanterns. In an hour most of them would be down.

The balloon field was nearly empty. The chase trucks had moved out to follow the flights; the crowds that had come early to attend the ascension milled around the grounds, buying souvenirs at the midway tents. Buses full of tourists from the downtown hotels roared away, leaving clouds of dark diesel smoke in their wake.

Madge's red Vette was parked outside the Fiesta Control building. He had half-expected a Mercedes to be parked alongside her car. As he got down, he glanced at his face in the side mirror. The image startled him. He saw a different person.

Something in him had changed, matured overnight. There were thin wrinkles around his eyes, something he had not noticed before. He seemed too serious. Why? Rita was safe—that was the important thing—but he wasn't smiling. The muscles of his face were set.

"Qué pasa?" he asked the reflection in the mirror.

The image in the truck mirror stared back at him. The eyes were slightly different. Like Lorenza's eyes! One was the eye of Sonny Baca, the other was the eye of Coyote!

What did it mean? Was he on the road to becoming a curandero? Like Lorenza, a shaman, a good brujo?

He shook his head and started toward the building. It was strange how a bright fall day could have hanging over it an impending sense of danger. Fall was the most beautiful season along the Río Grande, but he couldn't shake the ominous feeling.

Rita's safe, he thought, and tonight you'll propose to her, set the date. So why did he need to bother with Madge? Maybe he should just tell Garcia what he knew and let him handle it.

She couldn't lead him to Stone. Stone was an untouchable, his operation was making millions from the dope traffic, but hell, it was going to take federal prosecutors with a lot of guts and information to ever do anything. And what if someone, somewhere, finally pointed the finger at Stone? It didn't matter, because the present William Stone would be replaced by a clone, someone like him with a lot of power who would step right in and take over.

Just like when the cops took one pusher off the street corner and then found two replacing him. As long as those like William Stone fed the need, the dope poured in.

But it didn't have to be like that, maybe that's why he had to shake the truth out of Madge. The drugs, he was convinced, had not left town. The bulk of the shipment was still here. They were too smart to have tried distributing it when the shit hit the fan. They were sitting on it, and that meant it was being stored somewhere in town.

The front door was open; he walked in. The lobby was deserted. No assistants running around, no zebras. The door to Madge's office was ajar, he could hear her talking on the phone. He walked to the door and pushed it open softly. A startled Madge Swenson looked up.

"I've got to go. I'll call you later," she said into the phone, then, "Sonny!" She got up quickly, came around the desk. "I heard the news! Thank God Rita's safe. But how are you?"

"I'm okay," Sonny said coldly. She drew back and looked at him.

"It's over, then. Can I pour you a drink?"

"No."

"Once the balloons go up, I pay myself with a brandy in my coffee," she said, opening a desk drawer and drawing out a bottle. "You sure?"

"I'm sure."

She poured a double shot into the steaming coffee cup on her desk. "I can't tell you how relieved I am Rita's safe," she said, and sipped. "What happened?"

"It's a long story," Sonny replied. "But that's not why I came."

She was wearing a dark turtleneck sweater and dark pants. Her bright eyes stared intently at Sonny. She brushed back her short blond hair.

"So, what's on your mind?"

"You. And dope."

Madge frowned. "You're still thinking the dope deal? It's done, Sonny, and there's not a damn thing we can do about it. Rita's safe, that's what matters."

"People are dead."

"So what am I supposed to do? Feel guilty? I wasn't involved!"

"You were with Gilroy the night he was killed!"

"So what! He had me over a barrel! I told you that!"

"You lied to me! There was somebody else with you!"

Sonny reached out and grabbed her wrist, spilling the coffee cup on the desk.

"You're crazy!"

"Stammer was there!" Sonny shouted, drawing her close, looking into her bright blue eyes, which radiated anger.

"You're out of your mind!" she protested.

"Stammer was there! It was his deal all along! Wasn't it?"

Sonny twisted her arm, and she groaned in pain. Tears filled her eyes. "You sonofabitch," she cursed.

"Stammer killed Gilroy!"

Madge cried out, then suddenly relaxed. Sonny let go of her wrist. She fell back into the chair.

"You figured it out," she whispered.

Sonny nodded.

"I didn't know what was going on, I swear I didn't. Jerry told me Gilroy wanted to see me. I had no choice."

"Stammer put the squeeze on you?"

"Yes." She held her wrist, then tossed back her hair. "He's crazy, you know. He put his money in the baboon lab, convinced himself that he could put baboon hearts into people. He went broke setting it up. Then when everything fell apart, he started—" Her voice broke. "He met Gilroy, learned I used to buy dope from him. It was Jerry who threatened me if I didn't play ball with them. But he was trying to double-cross us both, and when Gilroy pushed back, he killed him."

Yeah, Sonny thought, Stammer had been in it all along. With the dope coming up the Río Grande, he saw it as a way out of his problems.

"I didn't want any part of their deal! You've got to believe me!"

"Let's find out," Sonny replied.

Madge shook her head. "You won't believe it until he tells you to your face."

Sonny nodded.

Madge smiled and stood. She straightened her sweater and ran her hands down the front of her pants.

"I figure the dope's still in the city," Sonny replied.

Madge arched an eyebrow. "You said yourself the balloon fiesta was being used as a cover. You found a tankful of the stuff, but the rest must be long gone."

"Then why haven't the cops in a four-state area intercepted a single gofer? A shipment cut that many times is going to draw a few discontents, bad blood. Someplace or other a cop's going to run into a piece of the action. But no, it's been quiet, nobody's said a word. Nobody's made a mistake. The dope must still be here."

"And you think Stammer has it?"

"Juan Libertad has it," Sonny whispered.

"Who?"

"I have a photograph of a man standing in front of a cartel

building in Bogotá. Some people thought it was John Gilroy. For a while I thought it was William Stone. But, no, now I see the man is Jerry Stammer."

"Jerry in Bogotá? I don't know what you're talking about."

"Yeah," Sonny said. "Your boss played compañero with the Colombian cartels. And with the CIA. I read through old files at the library. It started out as a heart surgeon going on a mission of mercy. Then the American doctor began to teach at the Bogotá med school. He needed a reason to go there, and he found the perfect alibi. But he left a paper trail, and a very quiet but wonderful librarian found it."

"We knew he was going to Bogotá," Madge said. "It had to do with a medical exchange. I never thought—"

"That Dr. Stammer would be involved with the drug cartels? Yeah, he's the man in the photograph. At first he just brought in enough coke for himself, enough to share with friends. Then Juan Libertad learned about him, and they figured he was the perfect man for this big shipment."

"Juan Libertad?" Madge asked.

"CIA. Why should they use their men and the normal supply route? Now they had a 'respected' doctor they could use. Jerry Stammer was in Bogotá the day the photo was taken. I checked the dates. My friend, a journalist, was confused. But why not, she didn't know Jerry Stammer. Strange how Gilroy, Stone, and Stammer bear a resemblance to each other. Same build, same features. . . ."

He reached into his jacket pocket for the faded photo Alisandra Bustamante-Smith had given him and tossed it on the desk.

"You tell me? Is that Stammer?"

Madge looked at the photo. "It could be, but the photo's too faded. It could be anybody!"

He picked up the photo and looked at it. For him the faded face of the man looking at him was Stammer, but she was right. It could be anybody. When you wanted something bad enough, you saw it. He wanted to nail Stammer, so he began to see him in Alisandra's photo. Alisandra had wanted to finger Stone, so that's whom she saw.

"Yes, it could be anybody."

"You've concocted a wild story, Sonny."

"Why don't we show the photo to the doctor?"

"You want me to take you to him—"

"I wouldn't have it any other way," Sonny replied.

"And it's the only way I'm going to clear my name," Madge said.

"Call him," Sonny said, and handed her the phone. She hesitated. "Go on, call him! Tell him you need to see him!"

She dialed, lit a cigarette as she waited, then spoke. "Jerry. No, things are fine. No, the liftoff was smooth. I need to see you. Yes. Right away. No, I'll come there. No, it'll be safer. I'll come there." She hung up the phone quickly.

"Let's go!" Sonny said, took her arm, and hurried her to his truck. He swung out of the parking lot and sped up the road toward the freeway.

So he was going to get to Stammer, but where in the hell was Raven? Had he withdrawn for the day and left the field to Sonny? Had he already gotten his cut and flown? Had Lorenza's bullet hurt him? But no, Sonny knew he would meet Raven again.

"How well do you know Stammer?"

"I wish I'd never met the bastard," Madge replied, and lit a cigarette. "He was supposed to be a genius, a whiz kid of the heart. He and a very young team were working on a mechanical heart, but it wasn't working out. Members of the team moved on to other research, Jerry grew bitter. He moved out here and worked with the group here. This city has some of the most talented heart surgeons in the country. Jerry tied into the hospital and promised to put Albuquerque on the map as a heart transplant center."

"But he wasn't satisfied with transplanting human hearts."

"He always wanted more. He wanted to be a hero, make a name for himself. He knew the transplant industry couldn't depend on donated organs, so he turned to baboons. He got obsessed with the whole thing, tried to force a baboon heart transplant on a patient, but the Human Research Committee at the hospital stopped him. By that time the doctors really had doubts about him. Then his wife left him."

"He needed money," Sonny said, as he brought his rattling truck from seventy down to sixty to exit on Martin Luther King Avenue. The giant heart complex Jerry Stammer had built sat on a hill overlooking the city, right above the old Dog Town barrio.

Sonny drove into the deserted parking lot. Near the south entrance stood the only car in the lot, a black Mercedes.

"He'll be waiting for me," Madge said.

"Yeah, but not for me. Let's surprise him," Sonny replied, and drove around the building to the back lot. "Come on." He pulled her out of the truck and to the back door of the building. It was best to go in unexpected. Somewhere in the lab warehouse, he was sure, sat the drugs.

On the delivery dock a large sign warned the public: STAY OUT DANGEROUS ANIMALS. Sonny tried the door.

"The baboon lab," Madge said. "You can't go in there."

"Watch me," Sonny replied, and jiggled the door again. Inside, a loud squealing and rattling sound responded to his presence at the door.

So this was the famed baboon laboratory, Sonny thought as he took out his jimmy set and tried the lock. Here Jerry Stammer was breeding and raising baboons for the heart transplants of the future. From here he planned to revolutionize the heart transplant business of the country. Next it would be baboon livers, then kidneys, then . . . ? Where would it end? No wonder the Alburquerque médicos had turned away from Stammer. He was crazy.

Sonny's pick turned the pins, and he turned the knob. He opened the door and turned to look at Madge. Her face went pale from the putrid animal smell that came through the open door.

"No," she said, cringing.

"Afraid of baboons?"

"I can't." She squirmed. "I can't stand those animals!"

Maybe she would only make noise, warn Stammer. It was best to go in alone.

"Stay put," Sonny commanded.

She nodded and Sonny entered the large warehouse. He was assaulted by the strong smell. "Yuck," he whispered, and shut the door behind him.

The huge warehouse was brightly lighted. He hadn't expected the number of cages that filled the building, rows upon rows stacked three high. In each small four-by-four wire cage sat a dark creature. All turned to look at Sonny, their piercing eyes dark and ominous. A human in the building meant food, and so they rattled their cages and cried shrilly.

The smell of excrement and urine was overwhelming. The warehouse hadn't been cleaned recently, nor the animals fed. Stammer was too busy with the deal, Sonny reasoned. Or just didn't care. The animals were thin, nervous. They cried out, pounded on their cages, reached out through the bars to grab at him. The farther he walked the more animals joined in the screaming, until the entire building was one screeching, pounding zoo.

So much for the element of surprise, Sonny thought.

He was near the door marked OFFICE when the lights went out. The fluorescent ceiling lights and white walls had given off a harsh glare, now the dark was intense. There were no windows or skylights in the building, just a broken-down ventilation system. The baboons quieted down.

Somewhere Sonny heard a door open and shut. He had wanted to find the dope before meeting Stammer, but now he had been found.

"Stammer," Sonny called in the pitch dark.

He waited, but there was no response. Maybe not, he

thought, glancing back at the door he had entered. Maybe Madge had decided to come in.

He moved forward, feeling the cages for direction. At the end of the aisle, he felt someone grab his arm and he jerked away. He realized too late that it was a baboon that had grabbed him, and when Sonny pulled away, he brought the cage down on top of himself.

"Pinche chango," he cursed as he pushed the cage away, its occupant shrieking. Because of the screeching baboons, he couldn't sense the presence behind him until it was too late.

As he was getting up, something hard and heavy crashed into the back of his skull, and he went down.

Shooting stars went off like an explosion, then a curtain of darkness descended. He saw images of baboons, not the starving crazed creatures of the cages, but well-fed, powerful animals roaming the floor of the sunlit jungle. As Coyote, he sat on the perimeter and watched. For a long time there were only the images of the beautiful creatures moving softly along the grassy floor of the jungle, pausing to pick berries, sitting in the brilliant sunlight and grooming each other. Coyote sat watching over the family.

When the light of consciousness filtered through the cobwebs, he blinked his eyes. His head pounded. A bright light glowed directly over him, making his head throb when he opened his eyes.

He tried to move his arms and found he was strapped tightly to a table. An operating table. The bright light overhead was the kind used in operating rooms! A chill coursed through him. He had been stripped bare and strapped to the table.

A scintillating glaze of gold swung in the light. Sonny blinked, tried to clear the cobwebs, then recognized the Zia medallion. Whoever had strapped him to the table had hung the Zia medallion from the operating lamp. Now it swung softly back and forth, the gold shining in the bright light.

He looked sideways, blinking to adjust to the darkness around the table. Madge sat in a chair by a desk. She stared blankly at Sonny, then at the broad-shouldered man at the desk. Sonny watched the man lean over the desk; he recognized the sound of someone snorting a line of coke. The man coughed, then snorted the second line.

When a smiling, glazed-eyed Jerry Stammer turned around, Sonny knew he had been right. Somewhere in the warehouse sat the cocaine and the heroin. Stammer was sitting on the sugar that fed his own addiction. He was so desperate he'd taken his biggest risk and brought it right into his lab.

Stammer looked at Madge, then rose slowly and went to Sonny's side.

"Well, Mr. Sonny Baca, looks like you're ready for surgery. Time to prep you. I hear you have a heart problem," he chuckled, and turned to wink at Madge. "Doesn't he have heart problems?"

Madge shrugged. "Nothing wrong with his heart," she said coldly, and lit a cigarette.

Stammer frowned. "Oh, but he does have a serious heart problem! It runs in the family! His mother just had a bypass. And today I have to operate on the son."

He put the stethoscope to Sonny's heart. "Just as I thought, it's barely beating. He needs a new heart. A baboon heart." He laughed.

Sonny spotted a bottle of scotch on the desk. On top of the coke, the man had been drinking. He was really wired.

"Fix me like you fixed Gilroy?" Sonny responded.

"Ah, there's a little life left in the patient," Stammer said. "Yes, like I fixed Gilroy. So," he turned to Madge, "our home-grown detective figured it out."

"He's not dumb," Madge mumbled.

"No, he's not dumb at all. That's why he finds himself strapped to my table!" he shouted. "Tell me, Sherlock, how *did* you figure it out?"

"It had to be a big man to take Gilroy," Sonny replied.

"Very good." Stammer grinned. "I like that. Next?"

"The cut was surgical," Sonny said.

Stammer burst out in a fit of laughter. "The cut was surgical! I love it!" He chortled crazily.

Then as quickly as the paroxysm of laughter overtook him, he grew somber. His face grew livid; red veins mottled the pasty skin; his light blue eyes shone with hate.

"My cuts have always been precise," he whispered, and lifted his hands. "The best hands in the industry. And my colleagues dare to insinuate that I've lost the touch! I haven't lost the touch! Look!"

He held his trembling hands in front of Sonny's face. "I haven't lost the touch," he muttered, and moved to the corner of the room, to the cage in which sat a large male baboon.

"Meet your heart donor," Stammer said, swinging open the cage door.

The large baboon was instantly out, baring its fangs as if for attack. It rushed around the operating table, its hair bristling. The big animal stopped to pound its chest and let out a shrill scream.

Stammer laughed. "Ah, a strong heart, a real macho! Nothing but the best for Mr. Sonny Baca."

"Jerry!" Madge screamed. "Don't!"

She clutched at the arms of her chair, and the baboon, smelling her fear, raced at her, fangs bared, screeching a challenge.

"Oh, God!" She cringed in terror.

But the baboon didn't attack her; it turned and jumped on the operating table. The gold medallion had caught its eye. It reached up and struck the medal, making it swing back and forth; then it looked down on Sonny and bared its teeth. For a moment Sonny thought it was going to slash at him, but the animal had satisfied its curiosity. It hopped off the table and headed back to its cage.

"What a show!" Stammer shouted. "He's inquisitive, but he knows when to pull back. Unlike you, Baca," Stammer said, and again drew close to the table. "You should have stopped when you found your girl."

"I wanted to see how much dope buys a soul," Sonny said, looking at Madge.

"You knew all along," she whispered.

"Yes," Stammer interjected, "our precious cargo is here. So what? Note the UPS boxes lining the room. There's enough money in here to set me up in Aruba. Yes, there, there are research laboratories that respect my genius. With a few million a man can set up a state-of-the-art lab. You see, I still plan to perfect baboon heart transplants. I am dedicated to my work."

"You're a murderer," Sonny replied.

"People got in my way," Stammer said coldly. "And when people get in the way, they have to be axed, as my friend Billy would say."

"Stone."

"Yes, Stone. I heard you two had a run-in. He, too, will retire to Aruba. I to do my transplants, he to do his political thing. Latin America is a perfect laboratory for both of us. Governments ruled by cartels are so much easier to control. That's Mr. Stone's goal, a nice little banana republic to call his own."

He laughed and leaned over to lift something from the machine beside the table. Two round paddles attached to thick electrical wires. A defibrillator.

Sonny strained at the straps holding him on the table, but it was useless.

"But why kill Mario Secco?" he asked, trying to buy time.

"He was in the way," Stammer replied as he threw a switch on the machine. Buttons glowed red. "But I thought you knew everything?"

"Will I still know when I have a baboon heart in me?" Sonny replied.

Stammer laughed. "He's got a sense of humor," he said to Madge. "That's part of my research, Sonny boy. Will you dream Sonny Baca dreams? Or jungle dreams? This is a first. A medical first."

"You're crazy," Madge interrupted, but Stammer paid no attention.

"What about Raven?" Sonny asked.

Stammer paused. "Raven? Now there's a dangerous man. He's capable of anything."

"This is part of his plan?"

Stammer frowned. "We made a deal. Raven says you like animal spirits. He hired me to fix you up with a baboon heart."

"If you do it, he leaves you alone?"

"Raven's an evil creature. I don't want him as my enemy." Stammer shuddered.

"Where is he now?"

"Headed for the Ukraine. Said he was going to buy one of those nuclear bombs the Russians are dismantling. You know what? I believe him."

Buy a bomb, Sonny thought. Play with fire, the radioactivity of a nuclear core? So that was Raven's next move. Raven would return to plague the earth, as he had returned throughout the millennia. He would not rest until he found a way to utter chaos.

"Raven is evil. You have to believe him," Sonny said. "He'll destroy a lot of people."

"Tough." Stammer shrugged. "I won't be here when he returns."

Sonny looked around the room. His head was clear now, but he couldn't move. He tried to rock the operating table, but it was solid. He was completely immobile.

"Madge and I will be long gone," Stammer said. "She in her hot-air balloons floating above the Caribbean, high as a kite, and me perfecting the transplant that will make medical history. I vowed that long ago. I will be somebody!"

"Then get it over with," Madge whispered.

Stammer laughed. "Looks like you have no friends in high places, Mr. Baca. Too bad. You just never knew how big the shipment was, did you?"

"Enough to pay Stone."

Stammer nodded. "Everybody gets paid. That's the beauty of a shipment this big, there's enough for everyone."

"And Garcia?" Sonny asked, hating himself for asking.

"Garcia can't be bought," Stammer replied. "We tried. You'd think a small-town chief of police would be the first to get in line for a little fast money, but he wouldn't deal. Which is all right, because he knows nothing."

"Just get on with it!" Madge shouted.

"Sonny boy, it's the women in your life that are going to kill you." Stammer clicked his tongue and then turned to address Madge. "Do you know what'll happen when eight thousand volts hit his brain? It'll be fried. There will be no trace of a murder weapon, only a very dead Sonny Baca."

The brain, Sonny thought. He's not going to cut me open and put a baboon heart in me. He's going to put the paddles to my head and electrocute me!

"Just get it over with!" she shouted back, and started for the door.

"Where are you going?" Stammer exclaimed.

Madge opened the door then turned.

"I'm not going to do it alone!"

"Are you afraid?" Madge arched an eyebrow, then smiling she walked halfway toward the table. "The great doctor Jerry Stammer is afraid."

"No, not afraid, but we're in it together, my dear. Why should I deny you the pleasure."

He put the two paddles to Sonny's head. "Besides, I need you to push the button."

For a moment Madge hesitated. She looked at Sonny. His chest heaved as he struggled.

"We'll do this together." Stammer grinned. Beads of perspiration dripped from his forehead. The rush of coke was wearing off; his hands trembled as they held the paddles tight against Sonny's temples.

Sonny looked at Madge and saw the hatred in her eyes.

"Go on, push the red button," Stammer said. "We're only hours away from collecting on the dope and flying out of the country! Mr. Baca's standing in our way. He's the only one who knows. Millions, dear, millions, enough dope to buy Venezuela! Do it!"

"What a waste," Madge said softly, looking down at Sonny's naked body.

"He knows! He's the *only* one who knows! Push the button!"

Madge nodded, reached out, and pushed the red button on the heart stimulator.

"Good-bye, Sonny," she whispered, turning her head away as the burst of electricity became a muffled explosion in the room.

Sonny screamed, and the baboon returned the tortured scream, responding to the cry of pain he heard from Sonny.

Stammer was jolted backward when the explosion came, and the same surge sent Sonny into convulsions as the electricity passed through his brain. His eyes rolled back, his jaw clenched, his teeth gritted.

"God," Madge muttered, and stumbled to the desk. She lifted the bottle of scotch and drank quickly.

Stammer held the plates to Sonny's head again. "Hit him again!" he shouted. "He's not dead! Hit him again!"

But Madge turned away from the writhing mass on the table and didn't respond.

"Push the damn button!" Stammer shouted. "He's still alive!"

Stammer turned to the machine. He placed one paddle under Sonny's head and held the other on the forehead. "Damn you!" he cursed. "I'll do it myself!"

As he struggled with the machine, a figure entered the room and appeared behind him.

"Tamara!" Madge cried from the desk.

Stammer turned, but it was too late.

"Murderers!" she cried, raised her arm, and struck. The sharp stiletto entered the side of Stammer's neck.

"Bitch!" he cried, and stumbled backward, clutching at the dagger implanted in his throat, entangled in the paddles' wires. Blood spurted from the severed carotid.

"Help me," he said, and reached for Madge, stumbling over the machine and pressing the red button as he fell. The electricity that exploded from the paddles lifted Stammer off the floor. The machine exploded again, then went dead as a circuit breaker cut off the current. The office went dark.

Tamara turned to Sonny. He lay quivering on the table, the convulsions sporadic. She stepped forward and placed her ear to his chest. There was a faint heartbeat.

"Sonny," she whispered and touched his cheek.

He tried to open his eyes, but his eyelids fluttered wildly.

"Sonny!" Tamara cried, and shook him. "Damn them!" she cursed. "Damn them!"

Tears filled her eyes. Slowly she reached up and took the Zia medallion from where it hung on the light.

"Raven should have killed you," she said softly. "You are too much the warrior to die like this. Raven would have freed your soul, and it would have returned to me. Better to die at the hands of a warrior of the sun," she whispered. "Oh, God, it's better for you to die, Sonny. . . ."

She looked at Madge. The woman stood frozen, her complexion ashen. Her gaze was glued on Stammer. His body had grown still, the blood still draining from the wound.

Tamara reached down for the bloodied dagger she had used on Stammer and turned to Sonny. "Do you understand? It's better to die."

Sonny's head jerked spasmodically. He tried to mumble an answer, but his tongue was thick in his mouth. He commanded his hand to reach up to touch Tamara, but there was no response.

Tamara placed the dagger to Sonny's throat. "I have always loved you, Sonny, even if you didn't believe in me. You could have been the new Raven, the new sun king. And I your queen. But the vision grew dark and clouded. I saw you a prisoner of these two, and I came. I knew the danger you were in. Oh, Sonny, I came too late. It pains me to do this. But death will be kinder than what they have done to you. I will free your soul. . . ."

She was about to push the dagger into his jugular when a noise startled her. In the warehouse the loud banging and screeching of the baboons had exploded, responding to a police siren in the parking lot outside, doors crashing open, loud shouts.

She looked at Sonny and bent to kiss his lips. "I'm sorry. I have to go. Perhaps it's not time for you to die," she whispered. She placed the Zia medallion on his chest, then turned quickly and disappeared out the door.

Sonny's eyes fluttered open, and he looked at the blurred shape in front of him. Death was in the room; he could feel it. Not the death of the old penitentes of New Mexico, not la Muerte, the friendly doña Sebastiana, the skeleton in the cart who came with her bow and arrow to claim her victims, but a cold, detached death. Cold space, cold air, the kind of death one might expect in a laboratory. Disembodied, without mercy, without feelings.

A cold death. He felt cold. He was shivering. Death was the presence the baboon felt as it huddled in its cage, whimpering.

Sonny tried to turn his head, but his neck muscles were stiff, locked in place.

"Agh—ah—" he called. Help.

The baboon responded with a guttural cry.

Sonny closed his eyes and allowed a cold, sleet-driven wind

to envelop him. He was too weak to resist. He could hardly breathe; the cold seemed to freeze his tongue. Whatever blood was left in his veins had turned to ice. His body was a mass of trembling convulsions.

A glowing light drew his attention, a luminous ball of light rising over his body. He smiled when he recognized his soul rising from his body. His body was growing cold and dying, but the warm ball of light rising above the body was alive. It could look down and see the body it was leaving behind. He was no longer in the mass of quivering flesh, he was rising above the world of the flesh, into the whisper of the wind.

"Better to die," Tamara whispered, her voice a flutter in the wind. Yes, better to die, he agreed. The release of the soul was so pleasant.

He looked down and saw a spring of fresh water by the river, green with watercress, the tunnel into the world of spirits, there where his guardian spirits waited. So dying was a dream, a return to childhood, a return to the world of nature he had known along the river as a child.

He saw Lorenza. She was waiting for him, her arms open to receive him. "The medicine," she whispered, "use the medicine of the guardian animal. Fly with Coyote."

"Trust her," Rita said.

"Trust us," he heard his mother's voice.

Ah, they were telling him to take hold of the guardian spirit, the coyotes that had helped him defeat Raven. There was help in the world of spirits, guides waiting to take his hand.

Pozo, he thought. The hole into the underworld was also his grave. Better to die.

Let me die, he screamed, but only a growling sound came from his lips.

Something that he thought was his heart opened like a red flower, a pomegranate, red-seeded and juicy, bleeding. From the wound his soul was rising into the air.

"Brujos can fly," don Eliseo said.

I am a brujo, Sonny thought. For my spirit to fly is nothing new. I fly in dreams, I fly in love, I fly in the morning when the light of the Señores y Señoras de la Luz fills my soul with clarity. I fly in beauty, the beauty of the land I love, the people, the sounds, sights, and smell of all that I am. I am beginning to find my power.

He had found it when he faced Raven; he could find it again.

"The medicine," Lorenza called again.

He reached for his leather pouch that contained the coyote hairs, and for the Zia medallion. His medicine was intact, it was with him.

He looked down and saw the medics working over his frozen, naked body. Garcia. Diego. Someone was leading Madge out of the room. Head bowed. He smiled in relief. Garcia had come in time, just like a good cop should. Like old Elfego Baca had always done.

Sonny's soul was in the room, looking down at his body from this distance, with a clarity of light he knew don Eliseo would appreciate.

No more worries, only the transcendent bubble of light he had become. He was watching his death and he was smiling. Images. Good thoughts. A buoyant feeling, like a bright yellow hot-air balloon, a sunflower caught in the breeze of October, a bright marigold, everything suddenly not separated but together. Thank you, don Eliseo, for bringing me along this path of light. Thank you, Lorenza, for leading me into the world of my guardian spirits, the world alive with talking trees, river murmurs, mountain advice, butterfly souls, bluebird songs of wisdom, seeds of grass, words of the poet, cry of child, sound of door banging. . . . He had become a ghost, and the ghost was overcome by the beauty of colors and sounds all around him. Death, if that's what had crawled into his body, was not fearful. Death was a light that released the soul, death was a wind mourning around the corners of the earth, singing around the four cosmic corners of the universe. Far beyond the sun the wind blew and carried the souls. Somewhere in the soft breeze he saw the image of his father. He wanted to reach out and embrace his father, but the spirit of the man drew back.

Sonny's soul rose like a gold balloon into the light of the

sun. . . . And there, coming toward him, also smiling, was Rita. She was dressed in white, the flowing silk of a bridal gown, the lace on her head flowing in the wind as she ran to meet him. She was shining bright, her lips as red as the succulent prickly pears of the New Mexican cactus. Her eyes full of light, honey light, her hair dark as a summer night, glistening with moonlight, the drone of cicadas her music. He opened his arms to greet her. Yes, it was time to marry her, time to settle down. He had come home. She stood in front of him, smiling, asking how she looked, looking at him shyly, and he told her she looked beautiful as a summer morning in the Jemez Mountains, and the wedding party laughed, called him a poet, needling him. Sonny Baca, the great all-time bachelor, lover of the North Valley women, he who had lived hard, loved hard, and danced hard, was finally getting married. Even his ex-girlfriends were there, standing like good losers in the background, for after all, they respected Rita. She had won, fair and square, or maybe not so square because they suspected she had used some of Lorenza's love potions to land him. But they stood quietly, remembering perhaps a long-ago night they had shared with Sonny.

"You look beautiful, too," Rita said, and Sonny looked down at his pants, his tuxedo jacket, the white silk shirt, his favorite turquoise bolo tie, the tie his father had given him long ago.

"I should be wearing my black hat," he joked.

"I brought your hat," she said.

"You think of everything," he answered her, putting on his hat.

"Now you look like one of those cowboys in the movies," she teased.

"The only dogie I want to rope is you," he teased back. Lordy, Lordy, he was happy.

He looked from her to the people. Everybody was there. Everybody he knew and loved. Howard and Marie and their daughter. Diego and his family, the chief, all the old compañeros, even los vatos locos from the South Valley, the old veteranos who had taught him that life was to be lived hard.

Now the party turned solemn. Don Eliseo, dressed in a dark suit, stepped forward, cleared his throat, uttered, "We are gathered to join Elfego Francisco Baca and Rita López." He paused. "If there is anyone present who thinks these souls should not be joined, let such a pendejo step forward," don Eliseo intoned.

"His soul belongs to me," la Muerte said. Don Eliseo and the wedding party turned to see the figure of Death, radiant in white, far more luminous than Rita. She held out her hand for Sonny to take. "We will walk this path." She smiled, a smile so lovely that any man would have gladly followed. She was the spirit who launched a thousand ships, souls sailing the universal waters.

She pointed at the path of souls.

Better to die, Sonny remembered Tamara's words, and reached for la Muerte.

"No!" Rita shouted. "I won't let you have him! He's mine! I worked hard for him! You have no claim to him! He belongs to me! I want to marry him, to grow old with him, to have his children! He will get well! I promise God and all the saints. His is the path of the sun, not the path of death!"

She pulled, and don Eliseo pulled, and Lorenza, and his mother, and Diego and his family, and old friends, all pulled, all formed a wall of protection around Sonny until la Muerte backed away and laughed. "You win! You win!" she cried. "It's not his time to die!"

And Death turned and disappeared down the path of souls.

"Don't die! Don't die!" Rita cried. "I won't let you die," she whispered in his ear, her tears wetting his face, her arms cradling him. "Wake up, Sonny! Open your eyes! Don't die!"

"Sonny! Return to this place you know!" don Eliseo commanded.

"The coyote spirits can help," Lorenza whispered in his ear.

They were pointing the way. It was time to gather his soul and return to earth, this place, this love, this spirit living in the flesh.

In the dark whirlwind the coyotes appeared, dancing around his body, filling his soul with the energy it needed to return to the world. No, it was not time for him to die. Sonny entered the tunnel, returning from the underworld like a shower of golden light.

His eyelids fluttered.

"He's opening his eyes!"

"Gracias a Dios."

"Call the doctor!"

"Sonny?"

Sonny smiled. The icy cold in his muscles was gone, and in its place a fever. The coyotes cried in the distance.

He could hear Rita.

His eyes twitched again, blinked open. The tunnel was behind him; he was returning to the world he knew, the world of people. He was falling back to earth, back into his body.

"Sonny, oh, Sonny." Rita soothed his forehead.

For a moment there was no pain, then the pain returned, like fragments of broken glass, glittering spears deep in his head. A headache. His eyelids fluttered, shut, desiring to turn off the exploding pain. The glare of light was intense. Returning to the body on the bed was to return to the world of pain. Even the light was painful.

"Better to die," Tamara whispered.

"I won't let you die," Rita replied.

Not time to die, he tried to say, moving his lips. She touched a wet cloth to them. Dry, cracked, stiff, immobile like the rest of his body. He sucked, she touched a plastic straw to his lips. He gulped. Air and water. He was back on earth. His toes twitched, then his fingers.

"Oh, thank God, thank God!"

He couldn't stop his eyelids from fluttering, blinking. The glass cut through his eyes.

"Ri—"

"Yes."

"Wah—"

She gave him more water, and he sucked deep, emptying the large plastic cup, spilling it down his chin onto his chest. Cool.

He gasped for air, farted, felt pee wetting the bed. God, I peed, he thought, smiling.

"Oh, Sonny, you're back, you're back," she cried, and pressed her lips to his, warming him, wetting him with warm tears.

Earth could be so good. Painful, but good.

Figures appeared behind her. Ah, yes, the wedding party. Did we get married, he tried to ask, but no words came.

The doctor who entered the room pulled Sonny's eyelids back one at a time and shone a light in.

Hijo de tu chingada! Sonny tried screaming—but it came out a growl. He struck out with his right arm; instead, he felt the toe in his left foot wiggle. He cursed again and heard only a grunt. Damn! Nothing was connected! Nothing!

The doctor put a cold stethoscope to his chest, felt his pulse, poked. "Squeeze my finger."

"Nagggh—"

"He spoke!" someone cried.

"He said something!"

"What?"

"Good sign, good sign." The doctor patted him. "Now remember"—he was speaking to Rita and the others—"it's going to take time. We don't know what he can coordinate. His brain received a hell of a shock. It's like a power surge hitting your computer, everything gets jumbled up. Understand? I'm not making any predictions, but with therapy and time . . ." He shook his head and walked out.

That's where he was. In a hospital room. Alive. An image of Stammer applying the paddles to his head flashed through his mind. Madge. The baboon. Images flashed, jumbled, but a memory nevertheless. Tamara had saved him.

"Sonny," don Eliseo whispered, "you're alive, hijo. No te tocaba." The old man kissed his forehead.

His mother was at his side, crying, leaning over him to touch him, to be close. "Gracias a Dios. . . ."

Lorenza, the curandera who had been his guide into the world of the guardian spirits, stood by Rita.

"Who-ooooo," he said.

"He's trying to talk!"

I am talking, he tried to answer. His eyelids had quit their trembling, but the rest of his body was alive with twitches, hot pin pricks that made his nerves spasm, muscles jump.

"Sonny, can you hear me?"

"Yaaa."

Don Eliseo looked from Rita to Lorenza and bent close to Sonny's ear. "What's your name?" he asked.

"Agggh," Sonny replied, the sound wrapped around his thick, dry tongue. But there was another sound, a clearer, more distinct sound. In his heart. In his soul. He had to reach for that. He had to try hard, concentrate all his energy, reach to join the sound in his soul with the stiff flesh of tongue, lips, throat.

"Saw—" he said with all his might. "Saw-ny."

"Yes!"

"He said it!"

"Where do you live?" don Eliseo asked.

Sonny smiled. God, that was so easy. Everybody knew he lived in the North Valley, in Alburquerque, in New Mexico. Oh, the old man was playing games, testing him. Don Eliseo, after all, was a trickster. Okay. I'll tell him where I live. He gathered the sounds in his thoughts and forced them to his tongue.

"Novo Mexic," he said, and they cheered and kissed and hugged him.

"Yes!" Rita cried. "Novo Mexic! You live in Novo Mexic!"

He was returning to them.